Talismen

Birthstones

Φ   Φ   Φ

Metoka Publications
3418 Clear Water Park Drive
Katy, Texas 77450 USA

Robinson, Elizabeth C., 1998 –

ISBN-10: 0988197995 Carrie\Robinson, United States (Paperback)
ISBN-13: 978-0-9881979-9-2 Carrie\Robinson, United States (Paperback)

Printed in the United States of America

To my mother, my father, and my most supportive English teacher
Thanks for not giving up on me

Table of Contents

Prologue

Moonlight spilled onto the scarlet and green, mosaic-tiled floor. A man sat in a leather chair, head resting on his fists. The bluish-white beams turned his loose black hair silver, and his pale skin paler.

He sighed, lifting his brown eyes as a young boy, around eleven, with short, black hair and blazing orange eyes walked into the marble room, glancing nervously to the pillars surrounding the other seats.

"Mr. Garretson," the child fretted, "You know that the time has come." He hesitated. "You know that they will be on the move, and that we need the one from your dream."

"Oh, Richie," the man's voice was hoarse from exhaustion, "what are you doing in here? I guess you're right though," he answered himself. "They may be planning something, and we don't have enough new recruits."

His eyes wandered to the clear glass ceiling to watch the slowly drifting clouds make their way across the crescent moon. "But I don't think that we should bring him before he is ready."

"You must *not* underestimate his abilities," Richie insisted.

Mr. Garretson turned back to him, sorrow in his eyes. "Do you really believe that?" He stood up, walking toward the door Richie had come in through. He stopped next to the boy. "You are right, but we still have to be delicate with our word choice. If he goes to the wrong side..."

He led the way out of the room, Richie right behind him. Richie turned around, narrowing his eyes at the same spot in the sky as Mr. Garretson had watched, before following out with a defeated look on his face.

But Mr. Garretson couldn't leave completely, and the

chants whispered in his ear once again, clear but blurred, loud but silent, heated but cold.

> *All can change the future*
> *Few can change the present*
> *None can change the past*
>
> *But one is like the few*
> *Though varies drastically*
> *And claims them as his own*
>
> *Now he must be one of them*
> *Now he must discover his powers*
>
> *Later will he change the world*

Mr. Garretson clasped his hands over his ears, though he knew that it was useless.

"All right, I'll try!"

And as he spoke the words, the sunlight broke through.

1. Investigators

Thump, Roman's wad of quiz paper hit the bottom of the trash can.

"Ha!" Roman laughed, turning to Hal, who looked stunned. "Alright, that'll be five bucks."

"You hassled me." Hal crossed his arms. "Don't make me tell Mrs. Anderson that you're gambling in school."

"I could easily argue with the fact that you stole some of her index cards," Roman hissed, smiling.

"What?" Hal turned around, trying to see if anyone else in first period math had heard, but Reece and Colby were busy with their homework, and the remainder of the class had either been talking or playing their own trasketball games. "How did you know about that?"

"You're the only one in the class with a paper cut," Roman retorted, holding out his hand to collect his money.

"How did you know about *that*? I've got a band-aid over it! I was alone in the room! *How did you know?*"

Roman searched for an answer, as he always had when something like this happened. He could find none, instead deciding to torture Hal. "I have *ways*. Now, unless you want some more super-natural stunts from me, you'll cough up the five dollars."

"I don't have it today, I'll get it to you tomorrow."

"Tomorrow's Saturday. And yes, you do have it. That one new kid, what's his name? Clover? I saw him give you ten dollars today during line-up. Stop trying to weasel outta it."

Hal brought out his lanyard and gave Roman the five dollars. Roman counted and checked to make sure that they were each worth their name. The room was brightly lit, though the only window was built into the hallway door. Mrs. Anderson's desk was off to Roman's right, lavishly decorated with the ungraded quizzes and exotically shaped erasers. There were two computer monitors behind Roman at the back of the classroom. The desks were in rows, twelve across and four back. Reece and Colby were the only two, besides Roman and Hal, that remained in their desks. The rest of the class was crowded around the second waste basket in the far corner. The beige walls and spotted ceiling had marks from pencils being flung at them. Posters along the walls had statements about believing in your dreams, how math was important, and how you should turn your homework in on time. The over-head projector had been pushed into the closet because some of the other kids had been vandalizing it. The chalkboard had that day's homework listed underneath the announcement of the quiz that they had just taken. Roman glanced at the plain, black and white clock with his deep blue eyes. They had over ten minutes left in class.

"Speakin' of which, why'd that guy pay you ten dollars?" he asked Hal.

"His name's Cole, blondie. Believe it or not, he actually gave me the money to get you to walk home from school today. But you walk home every day, right? Easy money."

"Yeah…" Roman stopped counting. "Hope he won't be waiting for me then? I might just stay late after school just to tick him off."

"Yeah, but it's weird. I mean, these guys showed up at the same time as you did." Hal rubbed his chin. Thinking seemed like a very rare thing for him.

"Really? Then why do you guys call them the new kids? I've been here for two years, in case you don't remember," Roman snorted.

"I remember. But I didn't know his name until just today. They're always really quiet, and they're in academic *everything*. Not in any extracurricular stuff."

"Isn't there a girl that he hangs out with?"

"Yeah, there's like, four of them."

"That Cole kid's in my Spanish class, now that I think about it. The only time he talks is when Mr. Sapling calls on him.

[4]

And, of course, during the presentations," he added. "But who are the girls that he hangs with? I remember a ginger and some other."

"Dunno. I think that the redhead sits with the other girls at the window seats during lunch, but Cole sits by himself." Hal paused. "I know!"

"What?" Roman inquired.

"I figured out why they're all sullen an' stuff! They're all from the same orphanage place."

"I've never seen them at St. Jefferson's before. You mean a foster home?"

"No, they got sorta adopted or something." Roman gave him an incredulous look. "We should ask them sometime. Well, *you should*," Hal defended himself as Roman stared daggers at him.

"You know, some people don't like it when you ask them how their parents died," Roman growled at him, narrowing his eyes.

"Uh…yeah…so did you hear that Mr. Ferris got re-married?"

"If I did, I didn't care." Roman took out his binder, pointedly slammed it on his desk, and took out his homework. He refused to look at Hal for the rest of the class.

It was snowing outside. Roman knew this because he'd done nothing but stare out of the window since fourth period gym class was let out. Glittering flakes dazzled his eyes, taunting him.

Why can't they just have one day as a bad weather day? he thought miserably. He had just sat through the longest science class that he remembered, along with an assembly during reading class on the book that they were annotating. He felt like sleeping, but if they were let out, he would go straight to the park for a snowball fight. This was the first snow the town of Katy had seen in almost three years, unless you would count the hail or roads freezing over-night, although those were more inconvenient than fun.

"Oh, come on, Roman! Stop pouting!" came his friend, Caleb Haldrige's cracking twelve-year-old voice. "There's no way they can keep *us* locked in!" he boasted, as if able to read Roman's mind. "Remember that they can't control us completely. What are they gonna do?"

Roman turned his gaze down towards the end of the hallway to see Caleb walking towards him, only veering slightly away from the rest of the crowd heading to lunch. Caleb had short, mouse-brown hair and brown eyes. He wore a red t-shirt with horizontal white stripes along with jeans. He had a buoyant look at first glance, with a round face and eyebrows that were always raised matter-of-factly. They were raised now as he swaggered over to Roman.

"It's not *if* they'll let us out that I'm worried about," Roman replied. "It's *when* they'll let us out. I've got a vocabulary test for seventh period. Plus, the snow might not even last that long." He sighed, imagining himself running out of the school only to find wet streets and mud.

"Well, think about the elementary kids. They must be crying from the fact that they get let out an hour after us," Caleb pointed out. "Now let's get to lunch before the snack lines fill up. Tj won't hold off setting the blackjack cards for long."

"TJ's absent today."

"Darn! Did you bring any cards?"

"No. Do you honestly think that I'd even own a deck?" Roman bit back a sarcastic remark. "Where would I get one?"

He followed Caleb into the high-ceilinged lunchroom. As usual, just like any other average day, it was already packed with people when the bell had only just rang. The only difference today was that through the windows behind the stage he could see the snow accumulating on the ground. He could barely see the white floor tiles through all of the other sixth graders sprinting around. The seven rows of mahogany tables were a quarter full, twice going for the snack lines.

"Times like this, I'm glad that I brought my own lunch." He patted Caleb on the shoulder and smiled. "Good luck, buddy."

Caleb narrowed his eyes at him, eyebrows still somehow

raised, then raced to the rapidly filling lunch lines. Roman made his way over to their usual table, next to the stage, which was decorated for that weekend's "St. Patrick's performance of Guys and Dolls".

Once he sat down in his round, scarlet, creaking seat, he noticed Alan walking his way. With his shoulder-length black hair waving side to side, his brown eyes beaming, and his gray jacket zippers swinging, he pushed easily through the stampede of kids.

"Hey, Roman!" he called once in ear shot. "What's up?"

"Nothin' much," Roman answered. "You've probably noticed the snow. But Tj's absent today, so we need to find something to do today instead of blackjack."

"And do you have any suggestions, as usual?"

"We could always wait until Chrith and her friends get here, and then try to count how many times they say *'like'* or *'um'*."

"We're eating lunch today, not daring the impossible," Alan sneered sardonically.

"All too true, but unless you have another idea we get stuck with *talking* all of lunch. Oh, and nice new pants." He noticed that Alan normally wore sweat pants in winter, but now he was wearing shorts that were so short, they looked barely allowed by dress code.

"My mom made me wear them; she doesn't think it can get cold in Texas," he moaned. "And typically, she chose the day it snowed."

"Your gym shorts would be better than those."

"Your lunchbox would be better than these," Alan said, sitting down next from Roman. "Anything new packed?"

"Nope. Just another cold cheese-sandwich with a bag of grapes. I'm just worried that Ms. Smith will never decide that buying lunch is cheaper than packing it. It's like she doesn't trust me. And she's known me for two years!"

"That's *why* she doesn't trust you." Caleb was walking toward the table with one of the school's small, foam plates in his hands. It was full with an ice-cream bar, mozzarella cheese-sticks, milk, a loaf of corn-bread, and an apple. He sat down in his normal seat across from Roman.

"Can I have your corn-bread?" Roman begged.

"No," Caleb dismissed passively. Then he suddenly put down his mozzarella stick and pointed.

"Look! Everyone's watching the snow fall outside!" he said in awe.

Roman turned to the windows behind him, on the far side of the room. Sure enough, the windows were overrun with excited sixth graders.

"Big deal," Roman yawned. "It's not like looking at it will make it blast through the roof and fall in. Do you really expect anything else?" Roman wasn't in the mood for Caleb's optimistic attitude.

As he kept on watching some boys try to sneak out onto the patio-deck, Roman noticed Chrith along with her best friend, Victoria, walking up to the counselor.

Victoria was tall and had long, black hair and plain dark eyes. Both she and Chrith, who had curly ginger hair, were wearing sparkling silver jackets. Chrith wore pink Bermuda shorts, while Victoria had on the same kind, but a color that matched the jacket. They both held their *Coach* purses at their right hips, looking like they were in a badly-coordinated fashion show.

Roman watched the narcissists curiously, wondering what they could possibly want with an authority figure. They said something, but the counselor, obviously not taking whatever they had said seriously, turned away.

Victoria and Chrith sulked over to their table right behind Roman's to sit with Arnold and Sadie. They talked in hushed voices, their eyes gleaming maliciously.

"That can't end well," Caleb guessed.

"All the more fun."

Before Roman could wonder what they intended, Arnold stood up and yelled, "FOOD FIGHT!"

A brilliant plan...

Arnold threw his stuffed potato-slices at the counselor,

who was now talking to the school principal, Mr. Spided. The slices splattered as they hit an empty section of the table in front of them. Once a few words were shared among the window-watchers, the cafeteria fell completely silent. All eyes were on Arnold.

Arnold crawled down and hid underneath the table.

Mr. Spided strode over to the platform next to the windows, picked the microphone up off its stand and summoned Arnold to the stage. Arnold crawled in Roman, Allan, and Caleb's direction. Allan kicked him under the table. The previously silent cafeteria started calling out insults to Arnold, forcing him out. He walked regretfully over to the principal.

When he was standing before the principal, Mr. Spided motioned with his finger to the people who had been sitting with him to follow.

He marched with them out of the cafeteria, the other sixth graders still calling out at them.

"Well at least something entertaining came along!" Caleb beamed.

"Hey, guys!"

They turned their heads to see someone that Roman didn't recognize. It was a girl with long, curly brown hair and deep-hazel eyes that hid behind thin glasses. She wore a brown shirt with a design of a dancing monkey, along with a gray *GAP* jacket. She also had speckled gray and white shorts. The girl smiled at them as if they were old friends.

Roman looked from Alan to Caleb, who both shook their heads and turned back to the girl, each with a questioning look in their eyes.

"Hi! I'm Rachel. New here," she explained. "I just wanted to know where the teacher's lounge is. I can't find the teacher I was supposed to get a tour from and I lost my map in the mob." She indicated to the crowd of their classmates, who were still trying to force their way outside.

"Uh, sure," Roman replied uncertainly. "You know, the counselor's in charge of schedules, and he's right over there." He indicated towards the stage.

[9]

"Okay, thanks!" She grinned more broadly, then disappeared in the crowd again.

"Wow," Caleb said. He was trying to stare after her through the crowd. Then he turned to Roman, "Do you think saying "you have a *GAP* in your jacket" is a good joke?" he demanded.

"What? Someone's got a *GAP* in his brain," Roman answered, thinking that Caleb was in over his head.

Caleb hunched back and crossed his arms and muttered, barely audible, "You're not funny you know."

As Roman left the frenzy that now enveloped the school, light snow fell from a heavy gray sky.

The school board had agreed that the kids should be sent home around mid-seventh period before the roads froze over, granting them their long-desired snow day. Roman was walking down the street that led to Caleb's house, feeling satisfied about missing his vocabulary test. Caleb was trekking alongside him to his right. His hair was soaked from the snow that had melted on top of it, and his eyes were vibrating from the cold. The trees around them were stripped of leaves and replaced by snowy flecks. The streets were damp and wet and had a cold slur to them, like the smoky fumes that could be seen from the passing cars. The boys' breath showed clearly in front of them, even when they breathed through their noses. Caleb's cheeks and nose were red, and both sniffled every few seconds. Judging from how cold his nose was compared to the rest of his face, Roman guessed that his was red, as well. Caleb had gotten his thick, green jacket before leaving school. He had zipped it, so there was no sign of his red-stripped shirt. Roman had kept on his red coat throughout the day, but had zipped it when leaving. Caleb had left his backpack at school, as they had no homework that they hadn't already finished. The cold wind whipped Roman's eyes and hair. He narrowed his eyes.

"You know, I thought snow wasn't supposed to melt until it warmed up. My mom's going to kill me if I get any mud on my new shoes!" Caleb complained.

[10]

"Well maybe the mud wants your shoes too. Or if you stopped using your hot dragon breath to complain it might cool down."

"You know you're not funny," Caleb snorted theatrically.

The crossing guard smiled half-heartedly as they passed by on the crosswalk.

They reached the bayou, the half-forest, half-swamp part of town, which was adjacent to the school.

"So, how's Kayla?" Roman wondered, "Is she out of school, too?"

"Not as of this morning, so there's still hope that she won't be home."

"But has she told your mom about the Nerf gun thing? I mean, unless you're doing something for her..."

"Oh, I gave her bragging rights for having better grades," Caleb dismissed. "Mom'll never find out, and if she does, then I tell her about Kayla's makeup stash," he purred.

"As if she'd believe you. I mean, she's only eight. She may be the most evil sibling ever, but Spencer has kept her on top."

"Oh yeah, and I found out Spencer's address," Caleb whispered as they were heading past down the road through the bayou. Caleb's mom didn't enjoy them using this way, because a lot of highschoolers were rumored to smoke just a couple dozen yards within the forest. But Roman and Caleb wanted to make sure that they hid the Nerf gun in just the right place at the park before reaching Caleb's house, and Mrs. Haldrige would wonder where they were if they were late. This way was quicker, since it ran right by the fence to the park, and one jump over would get them settling the secret weapon safely out of sight and home on time.

"Ah, but did you snag the eggs?"

"Yup."

"How did you keep your mom from noticing?" Roman inquired curiously, thinking that he smelled cigarettes.

"Oh, I redid the expiration label, kindly pointed it out to her—"

[11]

"You mean complained like a toddler."

"—and they were in the trash on the second. At least ten are crack-free."

"Sweet, one for every window," Roman commented. "Let's not forget the tennis shoes, though."

"Uncle Greg will never notice they're missing," Caleb boasted.

"Your uncle's visiting?" Roman groaned.

"Oh, he—" Caleb stopped as he noticed the shadow on the gravel pathway.

Silently, two figures emerged from the thick trees. Roman had no idea how they could've concealed themselves, and how they could've been soundless on the gravel, but they were, and a pang of fear pierced him.

Half of his fear turned to confusion. These weren't the types who would be underage smoking, although they were definitely underage. The first was a highschool-aged boy; tall, with spiky, ruffled brown hair. He had a sort of swagger to his steps, sending a clear message that he didn't want trouble, and would make sure that he got none. He had on a black t-shirt with no design and black jeans. The jeans were long, but despite the cold, he had no jacket. His short sleeves revealed prominent biceps. Roman was struck by his unnaturally purple eyes; deep-set, rimmed with black, and electric. He had a half-bored expression to his face, but he raised his eyebrows when he saw Roman and Caleb. His eyes seemed to linger on Roman for a moment, before he signaled for the second figure to come out of its hiding place.

The second was even younger than Roman, and much shorter. He was paler than the first, with a black, zipped jacket and deep-blue jeans. He had no smoothness to his step, and seemed to actually fidget. He stayed behind the first boy, his frozen breath lingering only up to his chest. He looked much like a smaller version of the him, but with lighter hair and skin, and darker eyes. His eyes had no ring around the iris, and were more of an indigo color. His hair was a mouse brown in some parts, but as dark as the first kid's hair around the areas where the snow had fallen, and it was smoothed over instead of spiked. His pale cheeks were turned red by the cold, and he sniffled once. He looked Roman over, just as the first boy had. Neither said anything. Roman and Caleb were still frozen, both literally and with shock. As quickly and silently as they had come, they burst back into the tree-cover, and were gone within five seconds.

Without needing to speak to one another, Caleb and Roman broke into a run. When they jumped the fence, they headed straight for Caleb's house, the whole time cold air was stinging their throats.

"What's the matter with you two?" Mrs. Haldrige demanded at the front door of Caleb's white-bricked house, while fussing over them and inviting Roman in as a guest. Her lime colored, silk dress dragged on the floor. She had unruly, streaming black hair and smooth, tan skin. She had Oriental eyes, and resembled her kids in almost no way. Her lip gloss covered only half of her mouth and there was glitter splattered on her forehead, flashing against her green eyes. Roman guessed that she had been getting ready for the day when they had been dismissed. She probably would've been ready for them if Roman and Caleb hadn't taken the short-cut and ran half of the way. Roman and Caleb were panting uncontrollably, mouths dry and cold. Roman was aware that the back of his hand had red splotches.

"Oh, Roman, you look horrible! What happened? Are you hurt? Have you been in the water? You're shivering, you have to sit down. Caleb! You have mud on your new cleats! If your father were home, what would he think?"

"He'd ask you to buy a door mat," Caleb muttered.

"WHAT WAS THAT, MISTER?"

"That I should pay for new ones and be more careful next time," Caleb groaned robotically.

"Good. Now I'll get you two some blankets."

"And some water, please," Roman said in his politest voice, the one he always used around Mrs. Haldrige.

"Do you want some ice with it?"

"Erm, no thanks. I'm cold enough."

"Alright. Caleb! What are you doing just standing there? Show Roman to the couch!" She disappeared from sight.

Roman knew where to go without his friend's help. In the living room, the only thing that had changed since his previous visit yesterday, was that the Christmas decorations weren't up anymore. The shelf above the stone fireplace was still cluttered with small figures of buffalos in different outfits. One that had a space helmet was being ridden by a cowboy in overalls, and another one was wearing a blue-green tuxedo, performing a waltz with a black and white bovine wearing a red dress.

The rest of the walls were decorated with paintings of landscapes and pictures of the Haldrige family. One was of Caleb's father, a man that had been in the military for six years. The picture was in black and white, so it was nearly impossible to tell what color his hair and eyes were, though Caleb had mentioned that he had blue-dyed hair and unnaturally bright eyes. It was easy to tell that he was Kayla and Caleb's father. His eyes were compelling, as if they followed Roman around the room. The thought made Roman feel awkward as Caleb led him to the purple couch.

The floor was covered with a beige rug which clashed against the green wall paint. The sofa was set facing a snack table and a old-fashioned *Sony* television. A leather armchair stood near the couch. The remainder of the room seemed vacant without any holiday decorations up. Roman was sure that the Groundhog Day decorations would be up a week in advance, followed by the Valentine dressings. Caleb sat down beside him, making himself comfortable, propping his feet on the small table. Caleb turned on Nickelodeon. A minute later, Mrs. Haldrige came in with the last slice of Caleb's leftover birthday cake and Roman's water on a plastic tray.

"Caleb, get your feet off of the table! I raised you better than that! Where did you put your shoes?"

"By the door," Caleb moaned as he was letting down his feet. This was obviously the wrong thing to say.

"And put you them on paper towels, yes?" Mrs. Haldrige

narrowed her eyes suspiciously, setting down the tray. Before Caleb could answer, she looked back at the mahogany door. The entrance hall had Japanese decorations covering the walls, and the marble floor had one Japanese-styled rug. The black and white shoes lay next to the door, a few mud tracks leading up to where they sat.

Roman covered his ears, but it didn't help much. Mrs. Haldrige started out with, "If you had a girlfriend," and "If your father were here,", but afterwards he had no idea what she was saying. Caleb's red face turned green as he obviously understood. His mother stopped yelling when the doorbell rang.

Kayla, Caleb's little eight year-old sister, could be seen from behind the glass. She wore a pink jacket over a purple shirt with a picture of a yellow flower on it. She had black hair, startling blue eyes and an attitude that could take the Godfather down a notch. Mrs. Haldrige opened the door and started fretting over Kayla's cheeks, which had turned a purplish-red. Like Caleb, she resembled her father more than her mother. She started talking excitedly about making flower pots in art class as Mrs. Haldrige lost all hint of ever having fumed at Caleb in her life. Mrs. Haldrige looked at the clock and seemed to decide that she was running late for something. She disappeared up the stairs to get ready, leaving Roman, Caleb, and Kayla alone in the room.

"Saved by the bell," Roman commented.

"Good thing Uncle Greg's gone," Caleb mumbled.

"*Very* good thing."

"If I saved your butt, then Caleb owes me an Icee at the movies tomorrow," Kayla decided in her squeaky third-grade voice, losing all excitement over flower pots. She sat down in the armchair. "That reminds me, Roman, are you coming with us? We're going to see Exploding Cows: The Next Generation."

"What do you want?" Roman cut her schmoozing short.

"Spanish tutoring. Mom wants me focusing on my current schoolwork, but I'll give you an Icee and a hotdog and a movie ticket tomorrow if you give me lessons," she said in a business-like way, with one leg folded over the other, hands in her lap.

"Two things. Not worth it. Especially not worth *that*

movie. Also, you don't want *me* to try to teach you. You really don't. And why do you want to learn *Spanish*? You already know Japanese."

"That was three things," Kayla sneered. "And three languages are better than two. Plus, the kids in my grade are going to start Spanish eventually. And some kids already make jokes in different languages! I want to know what they're saying."

"There's a thing called *Google Translator*," Caleb said smugly.

"Caleb, if you're going to stick with English, at least say something intelligent in it."

"At least I don't make mom dominate my life," Caleb hissed. "'Oh, look at me! I'm in the advanced class! I'm going to be a doctor before I get out of highschool! I'm a total kiss-up!'" Why don't you go get some friends, Kayla?"

Roman groaned, knowing what would happen next.

"Mommy!" Kayla sobbed, fake tears beginning to swell her eyes. "Caleb said that I don't have any friends!" She wailed for some time after that, until Mrs. Haldrige had taken away Caleb's allowance for a month. Mrs. Haldrige led Kayla upstairs. Kayla turned her head halfway to the landing and smiled viciously. Caleb wrinkled his nose at her.

"Don't worry sweetie, he's going to buy everyone a hotdog tomorrow," Mrs. Haldrige promised.

"How am I supposed to pay for her hotdog without any allowance?" Caleb growled once they were out of earshot.

"Well..." Roman started, as if he was about to tell Caleb something secret. Caleb immediately took the bait.

"Well what?"

"Well...good luck, buddy." Roman patted Caleb on the back. "Next time don't spend all of your money on arcade games."

"Hey, you took the second gun."

"If it weren't for me, you wouldn't have made it to level four."

"Just shut up."

[16]

Roman laughed and changed the TV to the Cinema channel. He decided to forget entirely about the two boys that had walked out in their path.

But that wasn't an option.

2. Pickup

The day afterwards, Roman and the Haldriges went to see Exploding cows: The Next Generation. Mrs. Haldrige had insisted that Roman come with them. As Caleb would be going with his family, Roman had nothing better to do.

The sun was at its highest point when they pulled up into the movie theater parking lot in Mrs. Haldrige's brown Sudan 48. The Cinemark loomed over them. It was made from plain, beige bricks with a stripe of maroon stretching around the building. Movie posters were lined up in two neat rows on each side of the ticket booths. There were three posters of Exploding Cows: The Next Generation. They each had a brown, animated cow looking seriously off into the sky while a huge explosion took place behind him. They walked up to one of the ticket booths, their frozen breath billowing out before them.

"Can I help you?" asked the teenage attendant running the booth. He wore the black Cinemark uniform, and had ruffled back hair that reminded Roman uncomfortably of the older boy that had walked in front of their path. He shook his head to clear his mind.

"Two adult and two kids tickets, please." Roman crossed his arms indignantly as Caleb smiled smugly. Caleb's birthday had been a few days ago, and he had been rubbing the fact that he was now technically a year older than Roman in at every given opportunity.

As they walked through the doors, the ticket taker greeted them with a forced smile. It was relatively crowded, though it was only noon. The Icee machine noisily turned the rainbow flavors, and the popcorn makers let off an irresistible aroma. There were two pillars that were most likely just for decoration between them and the concession stands. There were two hallways, one left and one right, that led off to the theaters from the entrance. The new Toyota Sipranno car that was to be won in a drawing sat in the center of the theater and was being touched by envying fans, mostly toddlers, the same going for the cardboard cutouts of movie characters. The arcade was alive with kids playing the basketball-shooting, pinball, and crane machines, and Time Crisis 4, Caleb's favorite game at the theater. The lines weren't too long, about five to a line in six lines. The hotdog, nacho, cotton candy, and punch machines behind the concession stands were busily going, adding to the noise. The chandelier above head was shinning brightly, lacking a single dim bulb. The walls had a carpeted look and feel to them, and were a ruddy maroon color. The floors had creamy brown tiles. One person was sweeping the areas where people had spilled their popcorn.

As they reached the front of the line for their food, Kayla started begging Mrs. Haldrige for four different types of candy on display at the counter. The televisions showed commercials for banks and various plays and movies from *Fathom Events*. Roman stopped Caleb from walking over to the arcade.

Mrs. Haldrige ordered their two pizzas, Roman's hot dog, a soda for Caleb, Kayla and Roman's Icees, and a large popcorn.

"What?" Mrs. Haldrige complained, "The last time we came here you had free refills on the large popcorns! I want to speak to the manager!"

"I'm sorry m'am," apologized the woman running the counter, "But our manager isn't here right now. He's on leave in—"

"I'm not leaving until I see a manager!" Mrs. Haldrige crossed her arms.

"M'am, you're holding up the line…"

"I said that I'm not leaving until I get my free refills!"

Poor employee, Roman thought.

"*NO! Not Pokey! Every cow for himself! Retreat!*"

In the movie, there was a battle between two villages of cows, and Roman couldn't think of it as anything above an anticlimax. The theater, not surprisingly, held only them and a family made up of three kindergarden triplets and the two parents. They were sitting in the highest row of seats in the theater, and the other family was at the very lowest, right up in front of the screen. Mrs. Haldrige had been threatened banishment from the theater by the security guard, so she had warned the kids that they weren't buying any more popcorn once it was gone.

Roman had his head resting in one hand. He had finished his portion of pizza, his Icee, his hotdog, and was sick of popcorn. Roman was waiting long enough to say that he was going to look for Caleb. Caleb had "gone to the bathroom" and had never come back. His mother had tears in her eyes from the loss of Pokey the cow. She had her arm around Kayla, keeping her from leaving the forlorn theater. Kayla's eyes were wide and she was desperately trying to remove her mother's arm without being violent. Roman kept rocking his feet back and forth in his red, velvet chair.

Okay, it's been long enough, he decided.

"I'm going to go look for Caleb," he announced silently, as not to disturb the family far below them.

"Yeah," Kayla agreed. "I think that I'll go with you." She tried to stand up, but her mother pulled her back down. Mrs. Haldrige turned to Roman, "Go ahead Roman. Kayla was just trying to help her big brother, and for that she gets to see this movie again next weekend. What a treat, huh, Kayla?"

Kayla gave Roman a desperate look. Roman waved goodbye cheerfully, beaming tauntingly. He didn't know how Kayla would get her revenge on him, but he believed that this moment of fun might be worth it, since the movie was such bad entertainment. When he was outside of the theater, he went to the main hall where they had ordered their snacks. It wasn't as crowded as before, since most of the other movies had already started. He found Caleb in less than a minute at the arcade, looking underneath a Flintstones car ride.

"I thought I might find you here," Roman mused.

Caleb jumped and hit his head on Dino the dinosaur's tail.

"Ouch!" he complained. "Oh, it's you, Roman. You won't believe this! There's no loose change! How inconsiderate is that?"

"Oh, you poor thing."

"Hey, cut me some slack; I'm used to having money."

"No, you're used to *spending* money. But, seeing that we have none, I'm going outside," Roman told Caleb.

"But what if my mom gets worried?"

"Sure, *now* you worry about other peoples' feelings. If we go back into that theater, she'll keep us in there. So are you coming? I'm not going to wait around for Kayla to get her revenge for not taking her with me."

"I'll just stay here. According to my mom, you can do no wrong. And I'm already in enough trouble."

Roman shook his head and smiled. He left casually, making sure that he had his ticket stub in his pocket. Roman loved the feel of the cool winter wind when he still had the sun, high and burning at its prime, to warm his skin. It was beautiful outside, even though he was in the middle of a concrete parking lot. He started jumping from parking bump to parking bump, practicing his balance, which was relatively good. At first, he kept looking over his shoulder to see if Caleb had followed him out or not, but Caleb never showed.

One kid that was limping slightly caught his eye. Roman was halfway across the parking lot from the little boy, but he could still tell that he was limping. It happened again; Roman knew that the boy had a sprain. He didn't know how he knew, because the boy was dressed in long pants and a jacket like every other sensible person. Roman guessed that if anyone else was ten feet away from the boy, then they wouldn't even notice the limp, it was so slight. But Roman could see it very clearly. Further away, a girl, not old enough to talk, and just barely old enough to walk, fell on the pavement. Roman knew where she was cut, and that she wasn't bleeding. He knew the specific number of layers of skin broken through by pure instinct. Roman didn't know how many layers of skin a person had, but he knew how many that girl had broken.

[21]

Roman tried to ignore the odd feeling that always followed these sorts of incidents, but it was, as usual, very difficult. He tried to think of something else. He had never been behind the Cinemark before, so he decided to go around and check it out. Then, if there was nobody else back there, he could do whatever he wanted. And if Caleb was hiding from him in an attempt to scare him, he would hear him from a mile away. Roman glanced around when he was at the very corner, listening to see if anyone was talking. Then he peered around. He still couldn't get the two boys out of his mind, and was being cautious so as not to find a gang of smokers.

He could see no one. There were three overflowing dumpsters, and trash day was half a week away. There were puddles of melted snow here and there, along with plastic bags and other trash. There was a back door with rusty hinges, and some of the bricks had either half-finished or half-removed graffiti. Roman read what was on the dumpster, and decided that it wasn't written by anyone very young. He started to wonder what he would do back here. He could watch the passing cars without anyone else watching him, but that was all. He started walking towards the field that separated the parking lot from the highway. A trench filled with melted snow-water cut straight through the field. A metal rail was built around the edges, continuing underneath the street. It had some litter in it, and one duck floating contently. Roman watched the duck, at the same time looking around for a rock to throw at it.

"Cute little things, aren't they?" said a voice.

Roman spun around in the blink of an eye. He saw a girl, his height, with fluffy, curled red hair, beaming green eyes, and glasses with the sun reflecting off of them, grinning at him enthusiastically. She had long blue jeans and a black jacket. Roman thought that he'd seen her somewhere before, but couldn't quite put his finger on it. She kept smiling at him, and came to stand beside him.

"You don't know who I am, do you?" she said nonchalantly.

"Erm, no. Not really."

[22]

"I go to your school." With these words, Roman immediately knew who this girl was. He felt even more uncomfortable, remembering what Hal had talked to him about. He tried to look calm, but he was honestly scared by this girl. He had the odd feeling that she could read his mind. Normally, with fear, he would use logic to make things seem less intimidating than they really were. In this case, even his logic had the impression that she could understand every thought.

"You're one of those foster kids," Roman said, not knowing what else to say.

"I wouldn't say 'foster'. It's more like adoption, but we get to keep our last names. But you don't know my name?"

Roman shook his head. She laughed a little.

"Sarah Veihne. Your name's Roman, right?"

"Uh, yeah," he answered stupidly. His discomfort was not going away. "Um, I should—" He was interrupted by an ear-shattering sound. The duck flew out of the stream and started waddling across the field in a rush. Roman's eyes immediately caught sight of smoke rising from the Cinemark. This explosion had sounded nothing like any on television. Roman thought that he had felt the vibrations from all of the way across the field. He was shocked to see smoke rising from the building. It wasn't much of an explosion, since the whole building was still intact and he couldn't see any flames. But his discomfort vanished and fear took its place. Caleb, Kayla, Mrs. Haldrige, and a hundred other people were still in that theater. He heard screaming, but it was faint. If he ran, he might make it there in slightly less than a minute. He momentarily felt panicked, not knowing what to do, until he noticed Sarah shaking her head, eyes closed. She looked more annoyed than panicked, and Roman felt his apprehension beginning to rise again.

"Didn't you hear that?" he demanded heatedly. "Don't you see the smoke?"

"Yeah, but that's smoke, not fire. Ugh, he is such an *idiot*! It looks like I'm going to have to make this much less subtle. Follow me." She straightened up from where she was leaning against the rail.

[23]

"What?"

"Come on. Just trust me."

"I hardly know your name! An explosion just went off and you're not even surprised! Did- did you know that was going to happen?"

"Well, I *told* Danny to make a distraction, but apparently he's too stupid to figure out that he's going to be in big trouble for that. And relax, it's not an explosion. It's all smoke and mirrors. Or smoke and vibrations in this case. So, are you coming?"

"Wait, what? You mean everyone's all right?" Roman inquired, confused.

"Of course. And it's good to know you've got *some* thoughts towards others. Come with me, and I promise you, everything'll be fine."

Roman stared at her. She looked completely serious. She was speaking to him like a scared puppy. "My friend and his family will be worried about me," he said blandly.

"I told you, it'll be fine. As long as you're all right, they'll stop worrying once they see you. Coming?"

Roman swallowed. She seemed to know more than he did. Much more. And, according to Hal, this had been going on since at least yesterday. If these new kids were determined to follow him for three days, and he went to the same school as them, then he'd have to face them eventually. He nodded and followed Sarah across the field, his fear once again being replaced by nervousness. Sarah was marching across the part of the field that led behind the Cinemark. Roman looked back. The smoke was steadily curling off of the roof. No sooner did he look than something fell off the roof and landed noiselessly on top of the farthest dumpster. Roman jumped back when it started towards them, but Sarah crossed her arms and glared at whatever had fallen. It turned out to be none other than one of the boys from Roman's school. Roman didn't recall seeing him in any classes, but remembered him being at the lunch table in front of the one that Cole sat at. He looked older than the other sixth graders, but he was definitely in Roman's grade. He was relatively thin, with slightly-tan skin, smooth brown hair that reached past his ears and covered one eye, and deep brown eyes. Catlike, without any noise, he reached them.

"Oh, he was outside?" Danny asked, noticing Roman. His voice was also deeper than most other sixth-graders.

"When I said 'distraction', a fake explosion was *not* what I had in mind! This is the first *real* mission we've ever been on and you've ruined it! Do you *choose* to be such a dunder-head?"

Roman had no idea what they were talking about, but figured that *he* was whatever mission that they had been sent on.

"Well, *sorry*. If you didn't want an explosion then you should've just said so. Anyways, Jace won't mind. The odds are slim to nothing that Mr. Kyle'll ever find out."

"Not when *you're* on the mission. The odds are slim to nothing of Mr. Kyle not strapping a baby-monitor to your pants. Let's just get going." She sighed.

"Lead the way, princess." Danny waved his arm out for her. Sarah shook her head and indicated for Roman to follow her past the edge of the building. As they went by, before Danny came into step behind Roman, Sarah whispered to him. Roman didn't think that he was meant to hear, but hear it he did.

"At least *try* to control your power when you're not the one leading. It'll do you a big favor in life. If you don't learn to get along with people, then you'll be going to the Island alone."

"Got it, sweet-cheeks," Danny said more loudly, "I'll try to remember that during my next social hour meeting." He rolled his eyes and started walking behind Roman, with Sarah in the lead.

I just heard the words power, Island, *and* mission. *I really should get back to Caleb...* Then Roman thought that, if these two meant trouble, then it was too little, too late. Danny was behind him, and judging that he and Sarah could sneak up on him, be silent when jumping from a building, and be utterly soundless when walking in the first place, that if he tried to run, he wouldn't get very far. He'd had the odd impression that Sarah could read his mind back when they were leaning against the rail above the stream. If she could, then he wouldn't get anywhere at

[25]

all.

They walked past the road on the other side of the field, past the *Chucky Cheese*, and over a bridge that spanned the wider sewage river that the other stream branched off into. It was all slow-going, since they were just walking. Roman looked back, and could barely see the smoke anymore. Roman wondered where they were going, along with how Caleb's family would be reacting. Roman felt idiotic. He had immediately trusted a total stranger and left behind who he was safe with. He had been raised in Houston, which was much tougher going than Katy. He had broken rule number one of safety policies that every toddler knew.

Roman could hear police sirens in the distance. They were coming to inspect the cause of the vibrations and smoke. He couldn't see the flashing lights, though. All screaming had stopped.

Roman tried to see over the small hill ahead of them, but he couldn't see anything but blue sky at the hill's crest. The grass was meant to survive in Texas, from the hottest summers, to the coldest winters that Katy experienced. The grass had turned pale, giving the hill a sort of dead feeling. The cars on the highway, which wasn't far away from this spot, couldn't be heard. Even the police sirens passed out of hearing range. The wind, whistling through Roman's hair and banging against his eardrums, was the only sound as they silently marched towards the crest of the hill. There were now a few clouds in the bright blue sky, occasionally casting deep shadows over them. The rest of the time, the sun blazed against the hill, making a sort of glowing quality. The sun was behind them now, since it was past noon. At least it wasn't in Roman's eyes, and he was thankful for being able to keep an eye on Danny's shadow at the same time as watching Sarah's back.

Roman expected more bayou on the other side of the hill. It seemed appropriate that they might take him into the forest. This thought, once again, reminded Roman of the two boys that had stepped in front of his and Caleb's path the previous day. He had a hunch that these two at least knew of those two.

But over the crest of the hill, the first thing that met

[26]

Roman's eyes was something huge and black, with the sun burning brightly off of the polished metal, temporarily blinding him.

A helicopter, black with a green stripe across the middle, sat dormant and gleaming in the afternoon sunlight. Its runners were planted on the yellow grass, with its propeller blades turned off. The sides were designed much like a car's; It had black windows across one section, which also appeared to have a handle to open sideways. Roman couldn't see through the windows, which led him to believe that they were bullet proof. Its tail was pure black, even where Roman would expect an insignia to be. He also guessed that this was not one of the helicopters from the nearby military training center. The helicopter even appeared to have headlights, though they were switched off. Roman stared at it, open mouthed, for a moment. He had never seen a helicopter up close before, and never one that looked as polished as this on television.

"It's not going to do any tricks, no matter how long you stare at it," Sarah told Roman after a few seconds of his fixed gazing.

Roman shook his head to clear it. He was less focused on how he was at their total mercy, at least. Sarah and Danny walked right up to the copter, and once they were a few feet away from it, the door slowly slid open by itself. Roman was expecting to see someone behind it, someone that had opened it, but no one appeared. It had slid at an exact pace, like most automatic doors at supermarkets and in cars. Roman didn't think that this would be very abnormal, since the particular helicopter already reminded him of a flying car.

Sarah and Danny seemed to want him to follow them to the copter, but Roman stayed put. He didn't seem to be able to move his legs, even if he had wanted to. Sarah, sensing this, turned around. She might have seen his reflection in the helicopter metal, but Roman was almost convinced now that she could read his mind.

"He doesn't want to come," she said to Danny as he was clambering inside.

[27]

"Oh. Maybe we should explain before going. After all, he might get a little uncomfortable."

"A little uncomfortable? Don't you remember how Ellenore reacted? Hey, Jace! Mind comin' out here for a minute?"

"Or twenty," Danny corrected.

"I would," came a gruff voice from inside the helicopter. Roman, being a good dozen yards from it, could barely make it out. He wouldn't have if the helicopter hadn't been blocking the wind. "But I'm guessing you'll make me come anyway."

"Correct," Sarah chimed.

A moment later, a man climbed out of the helicopter. He had buzz-cut, black hair and gray whiskers on a tan chin. The man wore sunglasses with red lenses, a camouflage vest with a lime green layering-tee underneath, black leather pants, and a silver neck chain with a tar-colored shark's tooth on the end. Roman had more trouble believing that it wasn't a military helicopter once Jace had shown himself. He dropped to the grass as silently as Sarah and Danny had, straightened up, and crossed his arms.

Jace seemed to watch Roman for a minute, Danny and Sarah waiting for his thoughts. After a moment, Jace sighed.

"This'll take a while," he said in a mumbled tone.

3. Motives

"You may want to sit down for this one," Danny commented, waving towards the grass. Roman looked skeptically at the ground.

"I'd rather stand, thanks."

"Whatever you say," Danny shrugged. Roman couldn't help but want to strangle Danny. Roman had a short temper, but his temper was at its high-point whenever Danny spoke.

"All right," Sarah started, clasping her hands together, "You know those two guys that you and your friend saw yesterday on your way home from school?"

"What?" Roman started, "so you all *do* know each other. I mean-Hal told me that that boy that you hang out with wanted me to walk home, and then those two showed up and-"

"You mean Cole? Yeah, he was tired of the subtle method. But you were walking home, anyway, right?" Roman nodded. "That means I have bragging rights. Anyway, you know those two? Their names are Jacob and Millo. And they live with us at...well, they live with us."

"You were about to say something," Roman said accusingly. "What was it?" Danny chuckled as Sarah bit her lip.

"Come on, princess, you might as well tell him if he's joining."

"Joining what?" Roman demanded.

"Getting to that," Sarah dismissed. "As for your first question; at the mansion. Yes, didn't expect things to go about like Annie and have orphans adopted by a rich person, did you?"

"Who's Annie?"

"Never mind, then. Anyways, we sent them to check you out. They're both brothers. Jacob was the older one."

"Why would they need to 'check me out'? What for?"

"To see if you were a Genedeaue," Jace grunted, leaning

[29]

against the side of the helicopter.

"Am I the *only* one that likes the subtle method?" Sarah sighed theatrically.

"Gen-a-doo?"

"Gened*eaue*," Danny corrected. "Its spelled like it's French, but we never pronounce it that way. Really gets on Millo's nerves. "

"Yeah, and Millo was the small one," Sarah told Roman. "Jacob can tell whether people are Genedeaues or not, and Millo can tell what *kind* of Genedeaue they are."

"You lost me at 'Genedeaue', just saying." Roman crossed his arms, irritated.

"You know, you're not very good at the non-subtle method," Danny sneered at Sarah. "You should leave that to us, next time."

"I should also leave the job of human shield to you, but we don't always get what we want," Sarah replied coldly.

"Ooooh, burn." Danny laughed and licked his lips.

"Oh yeah, and Dan*ielle* here has a *really* rare power like me and Sarah," Jace grunted sarcastically.

"*Power?*"

"Yeah, any help, Jace?" Sarah pleaded.

"Subtle or non-subtle?"

"Oh, come on!"

"Okay, all right already. Roman, Genedeaues have powers. Each power is different. You've got a power. We all have powers."

"Exactly how much popcorn butter did you three drink before coming here?" Roman asked, alarmed at the thought of being alone in a field with mad people.

"We've got proof," Danny argued smugly.

"Um, I'm not sure if I want to see anything of that sort right—"

Before Roman could continue, Jace lifted up his shark's tooth, placed his thumbs on either side of it and pressed down. There was a popping noise and the top fell off of the tooth and landed with a *thud* in the grass. Roman's eyes grew wide.

[30]

Danny chuckled, "Dude, it's a fake."

Inside the half that Jace held, there was a caramel-colored, misshapen rock with a glowing light that beaconed on and off. Jace reached in and took the stone out. Roman wondered if it was some kind of drug, or how it had been made to glow otherwise.

"What is that thing?"

"We call it a Bermuda gem."

"Bermuda? You mean like the Bermuda triangle or like Bermuda shorts?"

Sarah smiled. "We mean *exactly* like the Bermuda Triangle. You see, there's one section, near the south of the area, that can never be picked up by satellite, and that's the area that no one's ever come out of. That section has an island. We just call it 'the Island'. Anyone who's ever tried to come up with a name disappeared."

"Disappeared?"

"Out o' thin air," Danny concluded.

"So we thought it was best not to try and name it. No one's ever made it out of that area or off of that Island, if they make it that far. The typical story, electricity goes berserk and dies, nothing that floats stays afloat, et cetera, et cetera. And that's why no one's ever come back out of that particular area. No one except Genedeaues."

"And…what does that rock have to do with this? If you're going to hurt or kidnap or kill me, at least don't waste my time with pointless anecdotes."

"First," Jace grumbled. "We're not going to hurt you. Second, Danielle, get an empty coke can."

"Why do *I* have to get it?"

"Because I don't like you. Now go."

"What if there aren't any empty ones?"

"Then pour one out. And don't waste time drinking it, Kyle'll get worried."

Danny disappeared inside the helicopter and reappeared a moment later. He opened a bright-red coke can and poured its contents out onto the grass. The soda vanished from sight a moment later as it sunk into the soil. Danny presented the can with mock importance, getting down on one knee and holding it out with both hands.

Jace ignored Danny's joke, holding up the caramel-colored Bermuda stone. He looked straight at the can. Then, instantaneously an equally caramel-colored ray shot out of his gem and hurled into the can.

Roman gasped. When the gem stopped producing the ray only a moment later, the can had rusted over. Danny straightened up and crushed it with the slightest reflex of his hand, turning it into a thin, ruddy powder.

"Well, as you can see, Jace's power is being able to rust things," Danny explained. "Which might actually come in handy if robots ever try to take over. Until then, it's pointless."

"How 'bout I rust a support beam's hinges while you're under it?"

"Someone sounds bitter."

"HOW THE HELL DID YOU JUST DO THAT?" Roman nearly screamed.

"Oh calm down," Sarah sighed. "No need to curse. Jace's first power is being good with machinery, by the way. It's sort of rude not to ask. Anyway, that was Jace's rusting power. He can do *that* because he has his Bermuda gem. He can do his first little thingy because he's a Genedeaue. Genedeaues can go to the Island and get their gems, which are only *found* on that island. Non-Genedeaues don't have any powers or gems. When Jace dies, then his gem will crumble into nothing visible or tangible. It's pretty much impossible to destroy gems any other way."

Roman took this in without interruption. He felt like saying something or challenging her somehow, but couldn't think of any way to. If he tried to open his mouth, he would start to stutter. The stone had obviously not been a drug, but that didn't mean that *everything* that they were saying was true.

"So if I'm a...Genedeaue? Yeah, if I'm that, then what do you want?"

"Well...what do you guys think? Subtle or non-subtle?"

"Well," Jace said, placing the top back on his fake shark's

[32]

tooth and hiding the gem from sight, "Considering what we just showed him, we should probably get on with the point before he gets scared again and runs off."

"Fine." Sarah shrugged, though she looked slightly exasperated. "Bottom line; there are good Genedeaues and bad ones. The bad ones think that they're better than regular people and want to take over and blah blah blah. Since this is a genetic kind of thing, that would actually work if they wanted to wipe out all other humans and just have their own species. But lately we've spent too much time trying to kill each other for them to get very far. And then *we* have to try to stop them. *Them*, are who we call the Strayers. We call them that because they're always crossing lines—"

"All right, that's a little too fast, Sarah," Jace interrupted. "How about we give him some time to ask questions?"

"Hey, she's doing a better job than I could," Danny said sincerely. "So I must be atrocious."

"Oh, shut up."

"Whoa," Roman interrupted them. "Save the world? Isn't that a little too cliché to believe?"

"You'd get used to it. Basically, we want you to join us. We can answer any other question you've got on the way to the mansion..."

"I haven't decided whether you're all crazy or not, let alone commited to anything," Roman snapped, "and you want me to go with you three, all total strangers, in your *helicopter*, to your house?"

"That's the plan. It's perfectly fine, there's about twenty of us living there...Mr. Kyle's pretty much the leader, and Jace is second in command. Danny and I are just students. Unfortunately, we're stuck with the same mentor. There's been a shortage of trainees lately. Our base in Katy is just the main training center in North America. There's other places all over the world..."

"Yeah, again, why should I join you guys, if all of this is true?" Roman demanded, raising his eyebrows challengingly, half hoping that they would give him a reason to believe that this was true. He wasn't sure if he wanted to do something with his life, or if he only wanted to know that he hadn't been a fool for following Sarah this far.

"Because, idiot," Danny straightened up from where he had been leaning against the helicopter, walking toward Roman until their faces were inches apart, "anyone that wants to stay alive will join either the Strayers or us or already have their gems. Anyone that's on their own or trying to live normal lives or become bank robbers or whatever *need* to have their gems because the Strayers see them as threats if they're not part of their cause. You need your gem to defend yourself if you want to live on your own. To *get* your gem, you need to get to the Island. To get to the *Island*, you need a plane or a boat. Do you think that you can get an adult, who would die anyway, to fly or navigate you into the middle of the Pacific—"

"Atlantic," Sarah corrected.

"—Ocean for no reason? And you're a little too young to fly a plane or drive a boat, don't you think? We learn how to fly the planes that we get from who-knows-where, and you'd get automatic protection from the Strayers. You don't have to stick around after you get your gem, you know. And it's not like the training costs anything. Some kids stay with their parents while they go through their training and if they live nearby. But, considering you live at an orphanage, our mansion might be a step up for you, *don't you think*?"

Roman was about to punch him when what Danny was saying sank in. If everything was true, then it might be a good idea to listen to them. They might be telling the truth, or they could be crazy, or they could be lying. It would be possible to set something like this up, since Roman had no idea how long they had been here. There might have been something else that rusted the can, or maybe that 'Bermuda gem' had some sort of technology inside of it. He had to get more proof. If he had to choose between his pride and his life, then he would have chosen his life.

"You said that you two have magic powers, also," Roman started. "And that I have a power from being a Genedeaue. So

[34]

show me your powers."

"It's not magic," Jace grunted.

"That's a matter of opinion, Jace," Sarah argued. "We've got no scientific explanation."

"If it were magic, then where are all of the pixies and unicorns?" Danny questioned snidely. He backed up to lean against the helicopter again, leaving Sarah to glare at him.

"Mine can't really be shown." Danny held up his arms like he was surrendering. "But Sarah's is slightly more prominent."

"At least tell me what your power is," Roman growled.

"He knows how to annoy people," Sarah replied.

"No," Danny shot dagger-eyes at Sarah. "I can just tell this…it's like a field, sorta. Like a field of irritation. I know what makes them tick."

"Well, that still doesn't mean that you have to use your power on everyone," Jace sighed. "Roman, here, probably already considers you a pest."

"Not like it's a surprise," Sarah crossed her arms.

"That, I can believe," Roman agreed, getting slightly anxious. "So, Sarah, what's your power?" he asked, turning to her.

"I can read peoples' eyes," Sarah answered tonelessly, looking him directly in his eyes. "I can tell if they're lying, happy, anxious, scared, sad, sincere, or anything else."

Roman automatically knew that *she* was being sincere. It would explain why he had the feeling that she could read his mind. He could've questioned her to see if she knew if he was lying or not, but didn't need to. Either way, she could've used some sort of psychological trick on him if this were fake. Coming from this, he knew that they were likely to be telling the truth about everything. For once, curiosity burned deep inside Roman and left him too permanently scared to refuse.

"The bad Genedeaues are called the Strayers, so what's your side's name?"

"We like to think of our gems as lucky charms," Sarah told him, losing the intensity in her eyes. "They keep us and

[35]

every other Genedeaue safe, from random things like guns and liquid nytrogen as well as the Strayers. And the mentors always talk about this rush that they get when using their powers. So we're proud to have the names of Genedeaues and Talismen."

Roman only remembered Caleb, Kayla, and Mrs. Haldrige when they were out of sight of the field where the helicopter had been parked. He silently cursed himself for this, but was otherwise preoccupied by the thousands of questions bouncing around in his mind. When Sarah had mentioned Genedeaues being resistant to guns and freezing from liquid nitrogen, she had been serious. Most of the way things worked, like how no one could name the Island anything besides the Island, was a mystery to the Talismen. And when people came back from the Island, they could hardly remember anything after they had passed into or out of its boundaries. Jace couldn't recall anything besides what he had seen from his nightmares. He said that the 'gremlins' were the most commonly recalled things from his trip.

From the inside, the helicopter seemed larger than on the outside. There was a door in the back of the compartment, the one that they had used to climb in, and the one opposite that. It didn't look like any helicopter Roman had seen on TV. There was carpet, which was salt-and-pepper style shades of pale blue and gray with a leather-looking baseboard. There were eight regular car seats, two rows, four columns, each with cup holders and armrests. The seats were even the same turquoise color that was used in Mrs. Haldrige's car. The controls were at Roman's far left, near the end of the compartment. There were the usual drivers' and shot-gun seats at the controls. Jace sat down in the drivers' and Danny took the one next to it. Sarah said that she liked sitting next to the window because the sights were amazing. The trip, overall, would be luxurious. This was the only Talisman helicopter, according to Sarah, and the back room was for storage. Next to the door that led to the back there was a trashcan, and a cooler was on the other side. The cooler was where the coke had come from, and the first place Danny had gone before taking off. The doors were automatic, and there was air-conditioning. Roman only remembered that they were on a helicopter when he looked out the window and saw the afternoon traffic far below them. The hum of a car engine and the flickering of the propellors didn't sound much different to Roman when he was considering how this could either have been amazing or stupid.

"How long have Genedeaues been around?" he wondered.

"As long as humans have been," Sarah answered.

"If guns don't work on Genedeaues, do knives?"

"Yes. The trainees and Talismen without comabitc powers use knives, arrows, swords, mechanical spiders—"

"Mechanical what?"

"I'll show you later."

"And did you say swords and arrows?"

"Yeah, it's pretty hard to get harpoons. And swords are just long knives. We mainly just use them for practicing and when people go the Island and stuff like that."

"That…doesn't make sense."

"Just wait. You'll be wondering why you ever questioned it," Sarah assured him.

"And what's with all of the secrecy?"

"Well, of course the Strayers work in secret. They may be powerful, but no match for the whole world knowing about them. They're taking it the easy way. And the world doesn't have a good history with dealing with people that are different, now do they?"

"Um, I guess not."

"You guess?" Danny sighed exasperatedly. "Here's an idea; yes or no answers, in the future. Guessing isn't part of the equation." he admonished.

"Whatever. So that part's all about fear, I guess. But you guys own a mansion?"

"Yup."

"Are you rich?"

"Mr. Kyle was some sort of special heart surgeon, so he used some of his own money to upgrade the base, but it was

[37]

already pretty huge. He still gets called off sometimes. But it's like, *only* hearts. Regular doctors sometimes have trouble when babies have heart problems 'cause they're too small. So they call in the professionals. It's pretty impressive, actually, since he graduated with all of his degrees at twenty-something. Right now he's about thirty-four."

"He had his doctoral degree at *twenty*?"

"Somewhere around there," Jace called back. "Just ask him, and he'll reminisce until your ears fall off."

"So he must have been in some pretty darn advanced middle-school classes," Roman commented, honestly impressed.

"Yeah, it's a little rare for Talismen to be that good in school, let alone *try* that hard in school," Sarah answered after glancing momentarily out of the window.

"Why's it so rare?"

"A few reasons," Sarah started. "First of all, it's hard to keep up with schoolwork *and* training. Second, have you ever had trouble concentrating? Like just you couldn't stay on topic?"

"Sarah, you should know by now that you don't need to ask," Danny ridiculed.

"Sometimes," Roman growled. He was very much disliking Danny.

"Yeah, well, traditionally Genedeaues have trouble staying on topic."

"Any examples?" Roman inquired, not being entirely sure what she was talking about.

"Like one time Renaldo went from talking about how he thought that orange lady-bugs were poisonous to how we should have a second training base in Cuba. I can't remember how, I just remember that one time because there was this dare in kindergarden. For that story you'd need to know that Danny actually wasn't the worse kid in my class. It was this one boy named Jared who was always breaking kids' crayons and replacing them with—"

"Did you do that on purpose?"

"Do what on purpose? Oh, yeah. Like I said; off topic." Sarah smiled. "And our theory on why guns don't affect the kids with their gems comes from that. Guns are very direct, and Genedeaues are very indirect."

"What about this whole Bermuda Triangle business?"

"What about it?"

"Would you care to elaborate, please?"

"Well, hundred or maybe thousands of years ago it's believed that the original island was spontaneously enveloped by destruction when a volcano exploded, somehow releasing enough energy to collapse the entire structure in on itself and produce a place out of space and time itself, because time on the Island is different than time everywhere else in the world, and the few descriptions of the Island from people who have been there vary drastically, leading us to think that it changes every time. Or at least that's our theory. Is that elaborating enough?"

"Sure, why not?"

With that finished statement, Sarah then reached underneath her seat. She pulled out a book, opened it, and began to read. When it was apparent that she was lost in the world of the book, Roman looked at the back of Jace's and Danny's heads. After a minute of waiting for someone to do something, he glanced out of the window.

They were currently flying over the Katy countryside. That meant that the bayou and every side-stream was visible, from the natural to the man-made. Occasionally they passed a small lake, some with logs, snakes, or even alligators visible. Roman wondered how far away they were from the highway. They went to his school, Roman knew, and to be enrolled, they would have to live relatively close by. Then again, every kid that rode the buses said that the Talismen kids arrived and left every day in their own bus. Roman wasn't too familiar with Katy, as he had only been there the two years and in that time he had a very early curfew from St. Jefferson's, which kept him from going to too many places. There was next to no grass visible, and all of the trees' leaves were vividly green in the bitter winter; all of the trees that grew naturally around Katy had leaves year-round. He couldn't see any people, houses, trash, or cars, but that didn't mean that they were very far away from all of that.

[39]

Then, a small road appeared at the very edge of his vision. It was very old, with cracks visible from up in the air, gravel along the edges, and it was white from being worn out over the years. The trees spread along the sides of the road, which meant that there were no other paths leading away.

"Almost there," Jace called back.

"Good, Treaver's probably been playing on the x-box for over three hours," Danny remarked.

"We haven't been gone for three hours," Sarah argued, putting her book back underneath the chair, "and he probably hasn't gotten the remote control away from Elliyo and Gabriel. And if he did that, he'd have to get through Ashley."

"I don't know who these people are, so can you not talk about them?" Roman requested irritably. He found that between fear, curiosity, and the overall fact that he had been stupid, whether this was real or not, to trust them in the first place, he was beginning to get angry.

"No need to have such poison," Danny teased. "I don't need to have Sarah's power to know that you're just *scared*."

"I am not!"

"Eleven-year-olds are so easy," Danny sighed, slinking back in his chair, head resting on top of his crossed-arms.

Roman decided that he didn't enjoy Danny's company as much as the others'.

He peered out of the window again. The closest side of the road now had a small, white-bricked wall that bordered the gravel. It disappeared as they flew over large, black, iron gates. They must have been ten feet tall, but they were out of sight before Roman could study them anymore. The road had gone through the gates, turning into gravel completely, and disappeared when they were flying directly over it.

Then, as they turned at an angle, Roman spotted what this had been leading up to. There was a small, pale-grassed meadow surrounding a massive, green-watered lake. From this new angle, there was, to the right of the mud-green lake, on top of a short hill, a true mansion. The mansion had a black-gray tiled roof, a red-bricked outside, and about seventeen white painted garages

[40]

off to its right side, making up a dirt-and-gravel parking lot. Roman could see a tall mahogany door at the front entrance to the gigantic house. The mansion was about five stories high and six long, also with another worn dirt-and-gravel path leading into the trees past the parking area. In back of the colossal building there was a courtyard with a fountain, smaller iron fences than the first, and trimmed hedges. There were a few lights on in the house, and a couple of rooms Roman was able to see into.

One on the second floor, he could see beige curtains and a hotel-room-like air-conditioner. But another on the third story, he saw that there was motion inside, plus a few bar bells and treadmills. Most others were closed by different shaded drapes.

They flew over to the garages and landed in a sort of cleared area in the center.

A bus sat in the shade of a green tarp that hung off the edge of one garage. It was too large to fit inside of any of the garages, which explained the tarp. The bus was white with a green stripe across the middle. Several numbers on the side told that it was registered and licensed. The sun was starting to edge its way down west. It was always dark by six o'clock in the winter, and they had probably left around one or two o'clock. Roman wondered how long it had taken them to arrive here.

"What now?" Roman asked warily.

"Well," Jace answered, "Kyle's always formal about things. He'll probably want to give you a tour himself, but you also might get stuck with Danielle. Speakin' of who, Danny, go tell Kyle that Roman decided to come."

The automatic doors slid slowly open and Danny was off down the worn path in an instant. Sarah was the next out, followed by Roman, and then Jace. Jace took out what looked suspiciously like car-keys out from his pocket and clicked a red button. The headlights of the helicopter blinked.

"Hey, where'd you get that helicopter, anyway?"

"Ugh," Sarah moaned, "Here we go…"

"I made it myself," Jace proclaimed proudly, straightening his back and speaking for the first time in more than a barely-audible mumble. "And it took me less than a year.

[41]

That's hard to come by when you work full time training kids like Danielle, back there…"

Jace spoke to Roman about things he had never heard of and how they were important in making that helicopter until they were outside of the mansion front doors. They were about eight feet high and looked mostly like larger versions of most of the entrances to houses in Katy.

Jace didn't even need keys to open the doors.

There was a sort of high-ceilinged entrance hall, with a grand, red-rugged staircase directly ahead. It split in two at the first landing beneath a picture of someone who matched Sarah's previous depiction of Mr. Kyle. There were two side coridors below each side of the stairs, with the same cherry-colored rug as the rest of the hall. Leading up to the steps was a neat line of four doors around the perimeter of the hall, all different shades and colors of white and brown. The farthest one on the right was open and heading into what Roman guessed was the kitchen, considering the peach, spotted tile floor, granite counter against the far wall, long table, and refrigerator. There was noise coming from the nearest door on the left, and nothing from the nearest on the right or the farthest to the left. A vast chandelier lit the hallway and its walls. Vases, tables, and sketches of life-sized animals with claws and sharp teeth such as lions, bears, wolves, and many other things dotted the white walls here and there throughout the hall. The instant they opened the doors, the younger boy that Roman and Caleb had encountered just yesterday, wearing a shirt with the picture of a new video game and plain black pants, started crossing the hallway towards the kitchen. Walking with him was something that Roman wouldn't have expected to be there, or anywhere for that matter. Roman could have sworn that he was seeing a life sized papier-mâché Labrador carrying a book in its mouth. It had outlines of its sleek, furry-looking body drawn onto the wrinkled, golden, word-strewn paper it was made out of. This wasn't the part that surprised Roman; it was the part where it was walking. But the boy spotted Roman, and looked moderately frightened, pausing and staring at him with huge, indigo eyes.

"Hey, Millo," Sarah greeted him. "Is that a new shirt?"

Millo nodded. The paper Labrador cocked its head as it stood silently next to him.

"*Hot Topic*?" Sarah inquired.

Again, Millo nodded.

"Good to know Jacob's taking you out in public without life-preservers. You've met Roman." Sarah's smile was slightly forced.

"Yes." His voice had the slightest jump on the vowel.

"Did Danny go straight into the lounge or did he actually follow orders this time?"

"He is not in the lounge." Roman caught the slightest bit of accent in Millo's voice, which would explain the jumping vowels.

"Where *is* Jacob, anyways?"

"He was with Ellenore the last time that I saw him."

"Typical." Sarah rolled her eyes. "Well, see ya." Millo scurried back in the direction of the kitchen and disappeared inside. The Labrador trotted happily behind him.

"Did I just imagine a paper dog?" Roman asked in a strangely calm voice.

"No. Mary Beth, one of the senior mentors, can turn her art to life. That's why we have all of these paintings and sketches around the hall." Sarah waved to the clawed and fanged, fearsome creatures. "They serve as a line of defense when Mary Beth's around."

"Ok then. Is Millo always that jumpy?" Roman wondered.

"More or less," Jace replied. "We'd better get you up to Kyle's office before anyone else finds out you're here."

"Why—" Roman began.

"Hey! New kid! What's your power?" As if on cue, another tall, brunet boy appeared from the door Millo had left through. He had baby-brown eyes to match his hair and smooth, pale cheeks. "Oh, where are my manners? I'm Chris. You?"

"Just a way to remember him, his full name is actually *Christopher Robinson*!" An even newer voice called, this time

[43]

from the stairs, with a strange accent. A boy even shorter than Millo with curly black hair, brown eyes, and dark brown skin came through the kitchen door. He wore a red soccer jersey and blue sweatpants. "Can you believe it? I think his parents liked Winnie the Pooh! So what's your name?" he asked, ignoring Chris's growl.

"Roman, this is Renaldo," Sarah sighed, leaning against the wall. As Jace followed her example, Roman wondered how long it normally took for everyone to finish meeting the new people.

"Roman," Roman replied irritably. "And I haven't decided to stay, yet."

Renaldo just shrugged and then walked out the main entrance.

"Don't worry, he doesn't live here. He just comes by for training and meals," Chris assured him.

"Good."

"What's up?" A soft voice came from the kitchen. A pretty girl, older than Roman, with long, mouse-brown hair, green eyes, a blue dolphin necklace, pink tank top, and blue shorts came into view from the kitchen. She had creamy-tan skin and stood in the doorway looking nervous. "There's a new smell out here." she stated, sniffing.

"Oh!" she exclaimed when she saw Roman. "Hello, are you new here?"

"I haven't decided to stay," Roman repeated, wondering why she could smell him.

"Stacy's first power is an overly-developed sense of smell," Sarah explained, reading his eyes again. "But if Roman decides to stay, you won't be the newbie, anymore, Stacy."

"Oh, well, I think I'll manage without Ringo treating me like a toddler." Stacy let out an unconvincing sigh.

"Anyway," Chris went on. "What *is* your power, Roman? *I* can see what color gray and shadows really are. But I don't have my second-rate power, yet," he added quickly, "It'll probably be more useful."

"You're fourteen, so you should be due to get your gem

[44]

soon," Sarah commented. "But I'm getting mine either before or at the same time as you."

"You've obviously never seen me train," Chris challenged.

"Renaldo," she continued as if she hadn't heard Chris, "can jinx."

"As a small example," Christopher interrupted, "I have tried on multiple occasions to ask him what country he's from. Each time some sort of random thing happens, keeping him from answering the question. Take a fire alarm for instance. Normally he's alright with controlling his power, but that's always a sensitive subject. So, Roman, *what's your power?*" he demanded impatiently.

"I don't know my power, okay?" Roman said crossly.

"You should see Jacob's little brother about that," Stacy suggested. "He's really quiet, though. Wait, didn't you already meet him when he and Jacob—"

"Yeah, he did," Sarah answered. "And just now, as he was crossing the hallway with Hamlet."

Their papier-mâché Labrador is named Hamlet? Roman thought. *Not I can guess where they got all of that paper from. Mary Beth must not like Shakespeare.*

"Oh, *that's* why Chris and Renaldo started off when Millo said something to them." Stacy smiled welcomingly. "Hope you decide to stay." She disappeared back inside of the kitchen doors.

"That's a good point she's got, though," Chris commented. "If you're not sure whether you want to stay or not, it's probably because you don't believe us about the whole Genedeaue thing, right?"

"Well, *duh*." Roman rolled his eyes.

"Millo's told Mr. Kyle your power, but not us," Chris said. "But powers are normally abnormal, if that makes sense. So that'd be all the proof you need, since its coming from you instead of us."

"That's actually *intelligent*, Chris," Sarah said, sounding surprised, "I'm so proud of you."

"You're *very* lucky you're a cute girl, you know that?"

[45]

"Come on." Sarah indicated to Roman. "Danny's either gotten to Mr. Kyle by now or he's not going to. Let's get you going before some of the more enthusiastic people show up."

4. The First Movement

The second floor looked similar to downstairs, save that the rug was the same color as Roman's school's. This floor had the same rows of doors, but further apart. There were fewer vases, peepholes on the doors, and had a more cozy feel to it. Beside Roman and Sarah was the next flight of stairs.

"His office is on the fifth floor," Sarah explained, starting to climb. Jace had gone somewhere down the left hallway while Sarah took Roman up to Mr. Kyle.

The mansion seemed bigger inside than outside. Each floor was much like the next, except the basic structures were different in various ways. Some had an extra bathroom or side hallway. The stairs after the third floor had black carpets, didn't creak, and looked somehow newer. Sarah didn't seem to notice anything out of order. On the way up, Roman had decided that all of the doors must lead into bedrooms, because from one he heard punk-rock music, and from others he heard either shuffling or televisions. That, the bathrooms, and they way things were decorated reminded Roman of a hotel, even though he'd only been in one once on vacation.

Roman was content with climbing the stairs, except, after the third floor, it started to get tedious.

"How long is each flight of stairs?" Roman asked.

"I dunno. If you'd mentioned that you might get tired earlier—"

"I'm not tired, just bored."

"—then we could've taken the elevator," Sarah finished.

"You have an elevator?"

"If we have a mansion then why is it so shocking? The stairs are better exercise, and the elevator's slower. It's mainly for Treaver. He…can't really climb stairs."

Roman didn't ask why Treaver couldn't climb stairs. He could see for himself later. One thing that Roman had learned in the past few years was to never underestimate the emotional levels of people, that anyone with a sensitive topic would deal with their emotions in different ways. But no matter how they dealt with them, it was never pleasant.

They turned the last corner of the last row of stairs to the fifth floor. This hall looked very different from the others. There were multi-colored squares instead of dots or black for the carpet. And there were things such as a glass door reading *Laundry*, potted ferns all along the way instead of flower-filled vases, and at the very end of the hall, there was a large, wall-length entrance with a glass covering. Scotch-tape letters on the door read:

Main Office
Please knock before entering
Currently residence of Dr. Kyle V. Garretson

"It's polite to knock, like the sign says, but you never need to," Sarah told him, seeing him read the sign.

"You're not coming?"

"I've got more important things to do with the fifteen seconds it'll take for Mr. Kyle to dismiss me, and they're ticking away as I say this. See'ya 'round." She bounded back down the stairs much faster than when she had been escorting Roman up.

He walked cautiously up to the office door. He felt compelled to make an impression upon this Mr. Kyle, or, as the sign had told, *Dr. Garretson*, because he was the leader and for another reason Roman couldn't decipher. As he was about to knock, he heard a voice that stopped him.

"Come in," it called.

Roman slowly turned the thin door handle. The clicking noise it made seemed to echo through the halls and over and over again in Roman's mind. He was definitely nervous. Roman slowly slid the door open, body slightly against its frame as he stepped forward.

It was a small room with simple filing cabinets to Roman's right as well as in the back right corner. A pile of chairs stood from the nearest set of filing cabinets to the door Roman had come through. The desk of the office was mahogany, and had papers scattered here and there, along with a few knickknacks that Roman would expect to find in a teachers' quarters. A side door led off somewhere in between those two sections of metal cabinets. The yellowish-beige wallpaper, like everything else in the hallway, looked brand new, along with the white carpet. At the desk sat the man from the painting in the hall, with his feet on top of the desk, pen to his chin, and a computer coned in his lap. He had ruffled black hair, and eyes only slightly lighter. His skin had a tan only slightly noticeable, like many people in Katy during the winter. He wore plain, black long-pants, black socks, and a black t-shirt.

When he saw Roman enter, he put down his pen. Mr. Garretson sat up in his seat, put his laptop on the desk, and cleared his throat.

"Hello, Roman." His voice was as his looks were: young and slightly elegant.

"Hello, sir," Roman replied.

Mr. Garretson smiled at Roman encouragingly, "So I'm assuming that you know who I am?"

"Your sign said 'Mr. Garretson', but everyone seems to call you 'Mr. Kyle'."

"Normally the new students call me by my last-name, but that stops once they get used to me. Of course, Richie still calls me Mr. Garretson, and he's been here for over two years. You'll understand why once you meet him. Have you talked to Millo about your power, yet?"

"Um, no. But I've met him twice."

"Well, Millo can be a little shy. I'm sure that if Gabriel had Millo's abilities then everyone would know their powers before they knew their own names. So, since I have just found that you've arrived, I know nothing about your trip here. Did Jace, Sarah, and Danny do a good job of explaining everything to

[49]

you?"

"Yeah…I mean, they say that it'll be less confusing as I go along…"

"So you don't have any questions?" Mr. Garretson inquired.

"Well, I'm still not sure that all of this is real in the first place…"

"Ah, say no more."

Mr. Garretson picked up a small, uncolored statuette of a fish with a dog's head off of the edge of his desk. Then he reached for his sock and pulled it down, showing an anklet held together by a black band with the same kind of gem that Jace had had, except it was deep purple instead of light brown, and symmetrical.

Roman took a step back as a burst of curiosity flashed through him.

Mr. Garretson untied the band and unattached the stone. He held it steady and positioned the figurine at an angle to it.

As suddenly as the last time, a bright purple beam erupted from the stone and hit the statuette. Right before his very eyes, Roman watched as the pure-stone statue morphed from a dog-fish into a kitten wearing a tutu.

"Um, yeah…" Roman said after a silence, "Jace showed me his, too. But it *could* all be staged."

"Then we really *should* find Millo, shouldn't we?"

Mr. Garretson could hear anyone coming from at least a floor away, and was able to keep Roman out of sight until they reached the kitchen. Roman wondered mildly why everyone was so worried about the other students harassing him. As they lingered momentarily in the doorway, Roman saw that the kitchen had more than just the peach-spotted tile, the wallpaper, and the one long, wooden table in the center as he had seen upon arriving. There were also two stoves and eight burners, a second gigantic refrigerator, a few windows looking upon the meadow that reached as far as the garages and behind them to the trees, a back door, an oven, a pantry off to the left corner, a large freezer,

[50]

another door leading into a bathroom to their right, and six microwaves.

I don't remember Sarah saying there were any more than twenty people here, why do they need so much stuff?

The long table had about thirty seats. Jace was there, drinking coffee and reading *The Houston Chronicle*, and Chris was having cereal, toast, bacon, and eggs in a seat close-by. There was a boy sitting next to Jace, looking between Roman and Millo's ages with hair even blacker than Mr. Garretson's, and much more unruly. He had a red shirt without any design on the back, and short jeans on. Roman couldn't see his face, since the boy and Jace were facing away from them. Sitting a few seats down from him was a tall girl with short, salt-and-pepper brown hair, dark brown eyes, and creamy tan skin like Stacy's. She wasn't eating, but she had a map of what looked like the whole mansion in front of her. She was holding the map down with one hand, but stroking the head of a purple, papier-mâché cat with her other. Millo sat alone at the end of the table to the left. He was having a pastry that Roman had never seen before, and the same book that Hamlet had been carrying was open a few inches away from his plate.

There he is. Finally, answers...

"Oh, you remember, I mentioned Richie," Mr. Garretson indicated to the boy with the black hair. Upon hearing his name, Richie turned around to look in their direction.

The only thing that seemed prominent to Roman was the boy's blazing orange eyes. Roman had missed the day in science class when they were supposed to be learning about how a person could have one orange eye, but hadn't bothered to look it up because they weren't going to be tested on it. But this boy had two orange eyes, which Roman didn't think possible.

"My name is Richie Calliber Newton," the boy said, walking up to them. He had a catlike calmness to the way he walked, and a both determined and a relaxed aura.

"Richie here's first-rate power is being able to find his way around almost any riddle," Mr. Garretson explained. "And he has a *unique* way of speaking."

"I personally would not emphasize the term *unique*," Richie stated, not losing his indifferent expression. "I *would* assume that you may be Roman." He directed this as a question raising his eyebrows.

"Yes," Roman said tonelessly, not knowing how to respond.

"Oh, are you the new student?" asked the girl with the map, glancing up to look in their direction.

"I haven't committed to anything," Roman reminded them sternly.

"Taking him to see Millo?" the girl questioned.

"Yes. And why am I doing this?" Mr. Garretson responded.

"So that he'll believe from his own personal experience that all of this is real, I'm guessing."

"That's better than a guess. Good job. Keep it up and one day maybe you'll replace Jace as second in command."

"Not likely!" Jace shouted over from his paper. Roman hadn't known that he had been listening.

"So…Millo?" Roman inquired impatiently.

"Yes, of course." Mr. Garretson clasped his hands together. As soon as they set foot on the tile floor, Roman's feet making ten times more noise than anyone else's, Millo and Chris' heads turned in their direction. Millo got a sort of pressured look on his face, while Chris grinned at Roman enthusiastically.

Millo's appearance of dread increased as they started in his direction. He folded his book and turned in his seat to face them. When they stopped in front of him he said nothing.

"Millo, would you mind telling Roman his first-rate power? We're having a slight problem with him believing that all of this is real."

"Your power would make you a great doctor," Millo began immediately, almost as if on cue. "You can figure out what would be able to cure nearly anything. Is that enough of an answer?"

"Can you give me an example?" Roman asked. It sounded illogically familiar in a sense. Roman stomach flipped from the possibility of continuing to doubt that this was real. What if he didn't believe Millo? But now, there was no way that he could walk away without hearing this with his own ears.

"If someone were to break their leg, you would know the precise area they would need a cast for. If someone had a cold, then you would know what they needed. Orange juice," he picked up his drink, "medicine, or possibly something else. You can also know if someone is sick or not and things like that," he finished. Millo's accent had been very subtle when he was explaining Roman's power, but every other word was flowing with unfamiliar vowels. He also had seemed uncharacteristically calm when using his own power, Roman noticed.

Hal's cut flashed through Roman's mind, along with the kids at the Cinemark. Every time that Caleb had said that he had been out sick, Roman had known ahead of time that he was faking. Roman himself never seemed to take ill, but this was very, very, *very* familiar. He knew that Millo was telling the truth, and that he meant it. Roman's mind ached as it adjusted to the facts that everything in the past few hours, which had felt like at least three days, had been completely real.

"T-thanks," Roman breathed, not hearing his own words. He snapped himself out of his small trance. "Can you tell what my future power will be?"

"No," Millo said plainly.

"If only," Mr. Garretson sighed. "But Millo doesn't have his second power, yet, so there's still hope." Millo let out a small laugh, and Roman saw his shy smile for the first time.

"So, what do you think, Roman?" the girl inquired. Roman hadn't realized that she and Richie had followed them over.

"I—my head hurts."

"Mary Beth was referring to your belief in Talismen, Strayers, Rouges, and all general Genedeaues," Richie corrected.

"Yeah, it's definitely real..." Roman breathed again.

"I think that maybe he should lie down before going on the tour," Mr. Garretson declared. "Roman, our first stop will be your new room. But only if you want to," he added.

[53]

"Yeah, sure..." Roman felt like the world was spinning somehow. After learning about his power, he had felt fully ecstatic for only an instant as he realized that he was familiar with it, but now he felt dizzy. The small part of the idea of lying down that he could grasp sounded very satisfying.

The third floor had a storage closet and a fire-exit right by Roman's new room, if he chose to stay. He subconsciously knew that he would have to wait until his brain was working to decide about his possible new life, because the idea of choosing a new life made his head ache even worse.

He didn't even pay attention to the details when Mr. Garretson opened the door to his room, or when he had to lead Roman over to the bed. Roman was already more than half-asleep before his head had touched the pillow. All he had time to take in was how comfortable the sheets were compared to his normal bed before he fell asleep.

Normally, in the morning, Roman would consider what to do first. If he should take one of St. Jefferson's limited water-level baths, eat a cold breakfast, or watch action shows on TV, since he had the television all to himself that early in the day, until he was fully awake. He didn't know if it was morning or not, but when he woke up, the first thing he was forced to do was remember where he was.

At first he jumped out of bed in a panic, not knowing why he wasn't in his usual room, until he remembered. The room was a very good reminder that it hadn't all just been a dream.

The whole place was probably seven times larger than his usual sleeping quarters. That, and it didn't look like he would have to be sharing it with anyone. There was a door that appeared to lead to a bathroom with his own tub, tile floor, sink, clothing-hamper, and toilet. The door was in the center of the wall to Roman's left.

The carpet was beige, same with the walls. The baseboard at the bottom of the wall was a plain, brown-colored wood. A half-covered window above the bed was looking onto the lawn in the direction of the road, with drapes that had an orange- and tan

[54]

diamond pattern.

Overhead, there was a ceiling fan with a beaded-chain hanging off of it. To Roman's left, next to the door, was a mahogany file desk with a thin mat resting on top.

The twin-sized bed had white sheets and a white pillow. Roman had fallen asleep in his shoes, but at least the mud from the rain had cleared up. The bed was at the nearest corner of the left wall, right next to an old television with a VCR and a DVD player built in. There was a bed-side table with drawers and an alarm clock that told it was nine twenty-four in the evening. Roman liked this room very much compared to the one he had been living in at St. Jefferson's for the past two years. It looked like he could actually take a shower at leisure, not have to fight for control over the television, and even fall asleep while it was going.

Roman didn't have any fresh clothes to change into, but at least the bed hadn't been used by others. When he opened the door, the lights hit his eyes like bullets. The lights in his room had been off, the only light coming from through the window drapes, and that was only moonlight. While he was blinking, he knew that somebody else was in the hallway.

"You must be the new kid," said a voice not completely unfamiliar. It reminded him of school. Roman was certain that he'd heard this voice before. When his eyes cleared, he couldn't believe that he hadn't recognized him before.

A boy, who *did* go to St. Patrick's, was sitting in the hallway slightly off to the left. He was in the same chair that he used to get around the school, with the pure black wheels and back-rest. He had hair that looked almost gray in the areas where the light wasn't touching, and the parts that were touched reflected the yellow glow. His skin was pale, even for most people this late in the winter time, and he had striking turquoise eyes. He was wearing a gray *Quiksilver* t-shirt and loose, gray and black shorts. Roman remembered seeing him in the hallways from time to time, mostly holding someone's books in his lap while they wheeled him. Roman couldn't produce a name from memory, but remembered Sarah mentioning how a boy named

Treaver couldn't climb the stairs at the mansion.

"Um, more or less," Roman answered. "I haven't decided to stay, yet."

"Even though you were sleeping in one of the rooms." Treaver raised his eyebrows. "Ah well, not the newest concept; sleeping after your life gets chewed up. My name's Treaver. It's Treav*er*, also, not Trev*or*. You?"

"Roman. Um, do you know where Mr. Garretson is?"

"Oh, he's helping Tyler cook spaghetti while Jace is fixing the *Wii*. Gabriel, Elliyo, and Ashley were at it again, and this isn't the first time they've broken something. If you want, I'll take you to 'im."

"Sure, thanks," Roman responded. As Treaver led the way down the hallway, Roman was trying to think of something to say. He felt uncomfortable when Treaver pushed the button for the elevator. He thought that Treaver, like everyone else that lived here, would be able to tell that he was uncomfortable, and him knowing would only add to it.

"You go to my school," Roman said while they were waiting for the elevator.

"Yeah. I'd be in the seventh grade, but I've got a summer birthday and the Texas school system does things at different times compared to Florida."

"So you're twelve?"

"Yup. And you're eleven?"

"Yeah." The metal doors to the elevator shaft opened. The floor inside of the elevator was carpet, the same pattern of multi-colored spots as the hallway they were in. Treaver wheeled inside right away, and Roman followed.

"So when's your birthday, Roman?" Treaver asked as he pushed the close-doors button.

"January twenty-fourth. But, do me a favor and don't tell anyone else."

"Okay, for one thing, Mr. Kyle probably already knows what it is. Second, why?"

"It's just...I don't want that many presents." It was partially true, and Treaver didn't press him. The slow ride down felt steadier than most elevators, but just as slow. Once the talking had stopped, Roman felt awkward, so he tried to move onto a different subject that had seemed to interest everyone at the mansion he had met so far.

"So, what's your power?"

"I don't have my second rate, yet, 'cause I've only been here for about a year. But my first rate's language-translations."

"Mind going a little more into detail?"

"Oh, understanding other languages, understanding babies, understanding animals…"

"Whoa, animals?"

"Yeah. Body-language isn't much different than verbal language. And I can communicate with any of the above," Treaver boasted. "But it's not as easy as understanding it. The body language is pretty much the only way I *can* understand any of that stuff. Like, if a robot were speaking in Portuguese, I'd be lost."

"Well, that makes two of us."

Treaver chuckled. "Keep up the jokes, just in case you get a grudging mentor."

"A what?"

"Your mentor. If it's someone like Tyler, then you might have some trouble keeping up. Tyler's my mentor, and he's *such* a jerk. And whenever he's not showing off to Stacy by lifting weights, then he's looking at himself in a mirror."

The doors opened into the left side hallway of the entrance hall. There was a door at the end of the hall with a sign on it. Roman couldn't make out what it said.

"That's Jace's office. Since he's SIC he gets his own little place."

"SIC?"

"Second-in-command. Pretty easy to remember the acronyms, but if you don't, once again, you'll have a tough time in training. HHC is hand-to-hand combat, RAA is random animal attack, PCG is physical characteristics of gemstones, and that class is just as boring as it sounds. A *lot* like math class. WUC is weapon-use class, TUC is tool-use class, SRP is second rate

[57]

power, FRP is first rate power, and of course, a lot like boy-scouts is MUC, medical use class."

"Someone's going to have to make me a list of all of that, because you lost me at 'acronyms'," Roman muttered as they started into the kitchen. The halls were brightly lit, like the third-floor, with the chandelier in full-blossom. Roman didn't hear much noise, and a lot of whoever lived here were probably already getting ready for bed.

"Do you guys have a curfew?"

"Oh, not for sleeping. It's your job to get yourself outta bed in the morning and get ready and everything. You can stay up as long as you want, as long as you're inside of the mansion and don't wake up anybody. But for the 'being-inside-of-the-mansion' curfew, it gets later with your age. Curfew for eleven-year-olds is ridiculously early; five-thirty. Anyone underneath eleven isn't allowed to leave the mansion without someone else in the first place. For twelve-year-olds it's six thirty, for thirteen-year-olds it's seven-thirty, and so on. You're allowed to get special permission to stay out later or go with someone older, of course. Otherwise it'd just be stupid."

"What if you've got extra-curricular stuff?" They were just outside of the kitchen doors, and Roman was just planning on finishing his questions. He would ask Mr. Garretson about his "mentor".

"That would be special permission. Well, hopefully I'll see you around." Treaver started off towards the room across the hall.

"Yeah. Hopefully," Roman called back.

Mr. Garretson was standing beside someone else, instructing him on how to work a stove. The other boy was tall, probably in high school. He was black with black hair, and Roman couldn't see his eyes. He was wearing a green t-shirt with a picture of *Chuck Norris* on the back and brown shorts. Roman remembered Treaver telling him that Mr. Garretson was teaching a boy named "Tyler", who was also Treaver's mentor, how to cook spaghetti. Perhaps all of the talk of other people that Roman didn't know wasn't completely useless.

[58]

As soon as Roman's shoe made contact with the tile floor, Mr. Garretson and Tyler's heads turned in his direction.

"Who's he?" Tyler asked Mr. Garretson. Roman now saw that Tyler had hazel-colored eyes, and a round face, though he had prominent cheek-bones.

"Tyler, this is Roman. Roman, this is Tyler," Mr. Garretson introduced them. "Please excuse me, Tyler. I'm going to take Roman on a tour of the mansion before he decides whether he wants to stay or not."

"But what do I do if a fire starts?"

"You play with swords, hundred pound weights, and arrows every day and you're worried about a kitchen fire? There's an extinguisher in the cabinet over there. As a matter of fact, there's three. And, since you're already on dish-duty, I would suggest that you don't punish yourself again, because you'd have to clean all of the damage done by any fire that you start."

"Me? Trouble? Why, it's like you don't even know me." Tyler pouted innocently.

"That's the trouble; I *do* know you."

As Mr. Garretson turned his back to lead Roman out of the kitchen, Roman noticed that Tyler had started hovering a few inches off of the ground while cooking.

"So, Roman, if you were to choose right now if you were staying or not, which would you choose?" Mr. Garretson asked him, bringing Roman's attention back to the hallway.

"I'd probably choose to stay, at least to try it out," he said slowly. "But Treaver mentioned something about mentors. What do the mentors *do*?" They paused just outside of the kitchen.

"Ah, so you've met Tyler's student. Well, since there's only me and Jace in charge, and the fact that we still have to work to sustain our bills, we need people who can more personally improve the students and steer them in the right direction. Your mentor normally chooses when you have classes and which classes they should be, so it's a good idea to get on their good side.

"Right now, we have a dearth of mentors, so each mentor

[59]

has at least one student, but most have two or three. It's a bit of a paradox, because if the mentors can't give the students as much attention, then the students will learn slower, and that will mean that they don't go to the Island as quickly, which keeps them from becoming mentors themselves. But, not too long from now, we'll get enough mentors to get things running smoothly again. As for the tour, let's start with the lounge."

Mr. Garretson led Roman directly across the hall. One of the oversized doors was partially ajar. There was red carpet that was half covered by sofas, chairs, and circular, glass tables. There was a big-screen TV in the center of the room, with a couple of video game systems attached, *Nintendo Wii*, *Game Cube*, and *PS'* one, two, and three included. There were also *Sony* DVD, Blue-ray, and old VCR players. There was an open section to the room with the tables and lounge chairs behind the TV, covering about half of the room. Another door led into a room so dimly lit it was blue, and which had a couple of computers with head-sets hooked up. The third, and last, room looked like some sort of formal party room with the same beige wallpaper and red carpet, also including restaurant-like tables, complete with special linen cloths.

Right now there were three kids fighting over the a remote in front of the wide-screen. Two of them look relatively the same, with dark-brown hair, tan skin, and brown eyes. Those two both looked about Millo's age. They were even wearing similar clothes. The third was a girl that looked about Richie's age with long blond hair, sparkling blue eyes, and was wearing pink everything. In the dark room was a tall boy whose blue eyes blazed in the light. His hair looked purple where the blue touched it, and scarlet-orange on the other side. Stacy was talking to Treaver in the corner, at one of the circular tables. Roman recognized Cole from his Spanish class. He was conversing with Danny at one of the round tables set up in the party room. Everyone, save the boy at the computer, looked up when Roman and Mr. Garretson entered.

"Hey, I knew you'd get here, eventually," Cole said when he spotted Roman. "Well, *buenas noches, amigo.*"

"*Donde esta su cerebro?*" Roman sneered at him.

Treaver chuckled, reminding Roman that no matter which language he spoke in, Treaver would understand it.

The blond girl rolled her eyes, snatching the remote when the two identical boys ran over to Roman and Mr. Garretson. Stacy and Treaver smiled encouragingly, and Cole and Danny went back to their conversation.

"Hey, what's your name?" one boy demanded.

"What's your power?" said the other.

"How long have you been here without anybody knowing?"

"*Our* record is two and a half weeks."

"Yeah! Try to top that!"

"Okay, um; Roman Rolfe Rowland, since about four, and no thank you," Roman answered. They both high-fived each other and went over to the blond girl to demand for the remote again.

"Roman, they're Elliyo and Gabriel. I see you already know Cole and Stacy. The girl in the pink's name is Ashley, and the handsome young man about to go off to college is Jill."

"Isn't Jill a gi—"

"He prefers to be called Jay," Mr. Garretson interrupted him.

"And...for Elliyo and Gabriel...which one's which?"

"Gabriel has slightly darker hair and eyes."

"Right...Are they twins?"

"Yes. Also, Elliyo's power is being good at impersonations, and he's the younger twin. So if you want to talk to them about something, ask Gabriel. Anyways, this is the lounge. You can watch whatever you want, and can record something as long as it's not on somebody else's recording device. Over there is the ballroom," he waved his hand over to the room with the round tables. "Inside it has the only door to the lab and an extra door into Jace's office. And that's an extra computer station." He waved in the direction of the blue room ahead of them. "We have more computers up in the library, but they're not as fast. And you can't get sound on those unless you

[61]

have your own headphones. So, we use headphones down here so that no one's bothered by the sound."

"All right. What do you do in the lab?" Roman asked as Mr. Garretson led him out of the room and back towards the stairs.

"Experiment with things, certain powers, technology, et cetera. That also leads off to the area where we keep prisoners. Currently, we have none. And—"

"Wait, prisoners?"

"It *is* a war, between us and the Strayers. They've gotten a reputation of killing instead of holding captives, which is another reason that most Genedeaues tend to trust us a bit more than them. As I was saying: there's also our main-computer down there, and it controls all of the other computers in the mansion and we can contact other Talismen sectors with it. It also controls the alarms, most of the electronics...Oh! And did Jace, Sarah, and Danny tell you about the barrier?"

"The what?"

"By definition, it isn't an actual barrier, but it gets slightly complicated for some of the younger members to grasp concepts like that...The best way to describe it would be the word 'fore-field', but it's not what most people would define as one. If we didn't have that surrounding the mansion grounds, then the Strayers could simply do away with us with bombs or any stealthy assault. Having one may sound a little cliché, but so is saving the world."

They turned into the right hallway beneath the stairs, pausing at the beginning. There were two doors, one at the end of the hall, and one in the middle. Also, it had three Laundromat-styled plastic bins across from it. Aside from that, it was an empty hallway.

"That door, along with the one in the main hallway that you haven't been in yet, is a storage closet. And over there," he indicated to the plastic bins, "is the lost and found. It comes in handy a lot when someone buys new clothes, since we have so many people living in one place. Everyone normally puts their names on the tags or collars or wherever on their clothes so that

[62]

we know who to give them to, but sometimes they forget."

As they left the hallway and headed back towards the stairs, Mr. Garretson continued. "One of the punishments we have for disobeying rules is laundry duty. Tyler was sent to cook as a punishment, as you may have guessed. Normally, the students get their own food, but occasionally it's convenient to have someone to make it for you. Mostly kids like Chris toy with whoever's on cook-duty by complaining that they asked for something different and making them work harder. It comes in handy, actually, because otherwise it'd be the easiest punishment that we've got.

"The mentors, on top of training and et cetera, do the chores when no one's been behaving badly. Normally Danny and Cole, occasionally Elliyo or Gabriel, and on most days, Tyler, and various others take care of the majority of chores. Dish duty, cleanup, cooking, and laundry duty are the regular ones. Mary Beth's little pets can help with small things, but paper is only so strong."

They started up the main stairs, this time veering to the right instead of the left. When they rounded the bend, there was a plain hallway stretching out in front of them. The carpet was the same color as the second floor on the left side. The walls were a plain white. There was a single door in the right section of the wall. A bend at the end of the hallway hinted that there was more to see than the room to their right.

"That door leads into the library," Mr. Garretson told Roman. "We don't have anyone as a librarian, but we have a list of books, and if a book is missing, then we check around for it. All that's in there are the computers and book shelves, so unless you want to see it, we can move on."

"We can just move on."

They crossed the corridor in the direction of the side hallway to find more stairs. The third floor's design very much differed from the second floor. The hallway part stopped almost immediately. The wall where the hall stopped at was curved slightly outward. The walls were the same white as on the previous floor, only changed by the wooden door. The door was planted in the curved wall. There was no other way to go, aside from the stairs to their side as well as in back. Mr. Garretson strode straight towards the door.

A smell like chlorine came to Roman, along with the sound of air conditioning and the sight of now hard-looking grey walls. A silver rack with white towels stood a few feet away from them, and in front of them were all sorts of different machines that could've been found in St. Patrick's weight room. Treadmills, ellipticals, presses, and other things that Roman could not name were lined up in rows, filling the whole room. Roman glanced to his right to spot the window that he had looked through earlier.

"As you may have guessed, this is our little gym."

"Little?"

"What did you expect? We live in a mansion," Mr. Garretson pointed out.

No other doors led out, so Roman and Mr. Garretson left the way that they had come, climbing the stairs that Roman had already seen before. As last time, the carpet turned black as soon as they crossed the line to the fourth floor. This floor had the same design as the previous level, except the wall to their left wasn't curved.

"Through there is the basketball court and the ball closet that we use to keep sports items and weapons in. Shall we continue? I'm sure that you know what a basketball court looks like."

"I might have some idea." Roman was beginning to think of this mansion less as a hotel and more as a resort. They climbed the stairs that loomed before them, and the carpet stayed black. The hallway was more like a huge room in itself, with another room at the end. The open space before them was where the fire exit was for this floor. To their right was a second door. Through the door was another section of room, except now with eight other doors in front of them. Next to each door was a screen of glass that could be looked through. Each had a simple desk with a chair inside. At least seven different types of papier-mâché animals, most with sharp claws, rested outside of the smaller

[64]

rooms.

"These are rooms for private studying. I'm not sure why some students don't just study in their rooms or in the library, but they complain about not having anywhere to study. And on top of it, they never use this place. We're thinking about replacing it with something useful."

"Like an indoor movie theater?" Roman suggested.

Mr. Garretson chuckled. "The paper pets tend to come here when they're tired or when no one needs them. The only reason anyone comes up here is when they need one of them for something. Well, that's the end of the inside tour, unless you want to see the laundry room, conference room, infirmary…"

"Um, no thanks. I think I'll just break in my room."

"Is that a yes to staying?" Mr. Garretson inquired, raising his eyebrows.

"Yeah, it is."

5. Roman's Mentor

Roman didn't remember falling asleep after testing out the interesting additions to his room, but woke up at eight the next morning, none the less. Today was the day that Mr. Garretson would have his adoption forms in, when Roman would be assigned his mentor, and when he would meet the rest of the Talismen. An uncomfortable mixture of uncertainty and excitement stirred inside of him.

He nervously got out of bed to find that all of his possessions from St. Jefferson's had already been brought over. His trunk was lying beneath the stand where the television was, and his computer was on the desk, plugged in, with an added mouse pad. His computer was the highest money value item that he still owned, although it was old and slow. Its screen was flipped open, and looked like it had been wiped clean. The paint stains on his trunk had been wiped off, revealing wood, which Roman didn't remember being there. Opening it, he saw all of his old pictures and projects that he had kept from school. Roman figured that he would've had to go with Mr. Garretson to be adopted, and he had missed curfew yesterday, which didn't occur to him until now. Not only would the Haldrige's be worried about him, but Ms. Callous would've been angry as well. She would not have been worried, but Roman would have been in deep trouble if he had showed up at eleven o'clock, several hours after he was due back. Roman was very grateful to Mr. Garretson and the other Talismen not only for taking him in, but also making it much easier than he expected it to be.

Roman checked his wardrobe, and all of his clothes were there. All of them took up not even a fourth of the space available on the first shelf. He grabbed his best set of clothing, a red *Aéropostale* shirt and grey shorts, then took a shower. Hair still wet and dripping onto his collar, he slid his door open, half expecting someone to be waiting outside of his door like Treaver had been.

With no one in the hallway, Roman started to head towards Mr. Garretson's office, him being the only one he knew where to find. When he had climbed the last stair to the fourth floor, a door opened at the end of the hall. Roman had the instinct to hide, but knew that anyone that lived here would still find him very easily.

He breathed a sigh of relief at the sight of Sarah. She was wearing a purple shirt with white outlines of flowers and blue jeans. Her hair was already washed and dry. She spotted him right away.

"Hey, new kid. Have a good night's sleep?" she called out to him, obviously not concerned with anybody else hearing.

"Yeah." Roman said more quietly, "I was just going up to Mr. Garretson's office…"

"What for? He said that he already took care of your adoption and all this morning." She moved past him, pausing to look back at the stairs down.

"I was hoping that he could sort of walk me through the day," Roman explained lamely.

Sarah shook her head, giggling. "He already spent a good portion of his time getting you adopted while you were missing. Do you really think that when he's running a mansion slash training center that he's got time to take an off day for the new kid when everyone else is available? C'mon, I'll show ya around."

Roman, half wanting to make a retort, followed her when she started down the stairs. She wasn't going at the same pace that she had gone the last time Roman had seen her, and Roman had trouble keeping up. By the time that they were in the entrance hallway, Roman was panting.

"For future reference, you're going to get into very good shape with all of the training. Most of the junior high and high school kids here are in the athletics gym period. That's including me."

[67]

"Sounds fun," Roman commented sardonically.

"It will be eventually," Sarah concluded.

I was being rhetorical, Roman thought, holding his tongue.

Sarah headed towards the lounge. Inside were more people than last night; Elliyo, Gabriel, Tyler, Stacy, Cole, Mary Beth, Richie, and a boy that Roman hadn't met before. The boy had dark skin, black hair, a red *Rockets* t-shirt, and long jeans. He looked around high school age.

Elliyo and Gabriel were playing *Mario Cart* on the *Wii*, Tyler was floating in midair next to Stacy at one of the tables while she was reading a magazine, Cole was talking to Mary Beth, who was petting the paper cat again, on the couch, Richie was on one of the computers, and the boy that Roman didn't recognize was working on something with a textbook at a table next to Stacy and Tyler's. His head was resting in his right palm. When he was reading a passage from the textbook, his free hand twirled a long, sharp blade that kept changing design and size. He turned around at Roman and Sarah's entrance, revealing deep brown eyes.

"Hey, are you—" The boy started to ask.

"The new kid? Yeah, that's me," Roman cut him off before he could finish.

"Roman, this is Ringo. Ringo, Roman," Sarah introduced them.

"Nice to meet you, Roman," Ringo smiled. He stood up and went over to shake hands with Roman. By the time he reached him, the blade was gone.

"Yeah, Ringo's got more manners than most teenagers," Sarah told Roman, "but everybody knows that he's only a kiss-up."

"Curses, foiled again," Ringo chuckled before going back to his homework.

"So, new kid, are you ready for your new mentor?" Tyler wondered, dropping back to the ground again.

"One thing first," Roman stopped him. "Stacy, how much longer are people going to be calling me the new kid?"

"They stopped calling me the new kid once you got here."

Roman moaned. "Fine then, any of you know who my mentor is?"

"I do," Tyler replied.

"Oh yeah? Well don't be shy, who is it?"

Tyler smiled and winked at him. Roman had to keep back another moan when he remembered Treaver's words from the previous day, *If it's someone like Tyler, then you might have some trouble keeping up. Tyler's my mentor, and he's such a jerk. And whenever he's not showing off to Stacy by lifting weights, then he's looking at himself in a mirror.*

"You?" Roman inquired politely.

"Uh-huh. So, Pixie, it would be *my* job to get him into the zone."

Did he just call me a pixie?

"And you're actually going to do your job for once?" Sarah responded.

Oh, so she's Pixie.

Tyler laughed. "I've decided to be more responsible."

Everyone in the room except for Richie burst out laughing, but Richie was using the headphones. When Elliyo started laughing, Gabriel took the time to throw a banana peel in his way in the game.

"Really, Tylacker, you're too much," Mary Beth shook her head.

"But that's the most fun you've had in the past four years. You're welcome."

Mary Beth creased her lip and sneered, obligating Tyler to laugh even more.

"So where's Treaver?" Roman asked Sarah.

Once again, nearly everyone in the room laughed.

"It's not even nine o'clock, and it's a Sunday. It would be a miracle if he even woke up today. Speaking of Sundays, it should be nice outside. I'll show you the fields."

Sarah led the way outside. There was a cool breeze blowing in from the east, since the mansion was facing due north, there were clouds in the sky, and it was still winter time.

[69]

"Can we go back inside and get jackets?" Roman begged.

"Why?"

"Because it's freezing out here!"

"Boy, you don't know the meaning of the word *freezing*, but since you're new, I'll go easy on you. Tough luck getting Tyler as a mentor in the middle of winter, you're gonna die."

Roman hoped that she wasn't being literal.

After Roman retrieved his yellow hoody and Sarah had demanded what had taken him so long, they headed back outside in time to see Renaldo arriving.

"Hey there, Renalda. Here for more free-loading?"

"You know it, Saro." He replied. Renaldo was wearing a much thicker jacket than Roman. Roman could just barely make out a green minivan at the gates.

"So where do you want to go first, new kid?" Sarah asked him. "The lake, the fields, or the courtyard?"

"Um, which one's the shortest?"

"The lake it is." Turning right, Sarah took Roman to the lake that he had seen yesterday from the helicopter. This lake was like every other natural lake that Roman had ever seen, opaque with soot.

"Are there fish in there?"

"Are there birds in the sky?"

Then, going around the back of mansion clockwise again, they headed towards what Sarah called 'the courtyard'. They passed by another door in the side of the mansion.

Directly in front of the back entrance to the mansion was the black gate surrounding the courtyard that had hinges and a slide-lock. It was open, casting an uneven shadow that clawed at the ground Roman and Sarah walked on. Roman put his hands in his pockets as he saw his own breath flowering ghostlike in front of his face.

The tall, black gate was circling around two rows of healthy green-colored hedge-growth. Each hedge was about five feet tall, three meters long, and a meter wide. There were sections in between the hedges on the outer layer roughly two feet wide.

Roman could see walkways in-between the inner and

outer layers of hedge. He could see one that had what looked like an empty flower bed along one side and a birdbath on the other. He could see that there were birds in the birdbaths, but no flowers in the flower beds, just piles of chocolate-colored dirt held in place by small marble bricks. A puddle of rainwater had collected in the middle of one.

"No birds in the sky," Roman commented. "Looks like they're all down here."

They strolled in-between two rows of bush parallel to each other.

There was a block of stone that formed a kind of bench with a design of different strange animals etched into the side. One animal looked like a griffin with tusks and a club tail. Another looked like a tapir with angelic wings. Some Roman could more or less recognize as normal, like a deer or a ferret, but not many.

There was a fountain in the center of the inner hedge row. On top of its platform was a sort of gigantic, stone-carved crystal. Many little spikes jutted out of the sides of what seemed like nothing more than a mass of needles. Water poured from the ends of various bristles and into the clear pool of the fountain. Some of the water turned into vapor and floated through the air from the cold. There were a few leaves floating in the fountain's water, and Roman was disappointed to find that no one had thrown in any coins. Four wooden benches with green, metal railings surrounded the fountain on all sides.

"Wow, I wish St. Patrick had something like that," Roman said as he was gazing at the spraying jets.

"It'd be broken within the week."

Roman told his consent and decided that he liked the courtyard more than the lake. They left the courtyard and headed clockwise around the mansion again, this time to the fields. Roman wondered why it would be so important to see fields of grass, but didn't protest. When they rounded the corner, Roman saw the pathway to the parking lot. The gravel slid under his feet as Roman shuffled across the parking lot, but Sarah made no audible sound. They walked down the path that led into the bayou, which didn't remind Roman of fields of grass at all.

Entering the forest, the path was nicely worn, almost as well-worn as a hiking trail. It wound its way clearly through the trees. When they rounded a bend, Roman was surprised the see a clearing large enough to fit five football fields directly in front of them. It seemed like it had popped out of nowhere, but since it could've held five football fields, it was obvious that the Talismen had taken that into consideration.

Roman saw a white goal post a hundred feet away, a soccer goal standing underneath. To the left of that was a baseball diamond, full size, with a backstop made of chain-link.

"The soccer field and the football fields are mixed together to save space," Sarah told him.

"As if you need it. Seriously, how big can this place get?"

"You still haven't seen the lab. Plus, we've got quite a few acres of bayou before the point where the boundary is."

"And how is it that the military isn't concerned about you guys throwing swords around at each other out in the open?"

"They don't know about it."

"All they'd have to do is look down through this 'barrier', aren't you worried about that?"

"You're cute, but don't ask questions that stupid around anybody else if you want them to stop calling you the new kid. If the Strayers could just *look through* that force field then we'd be dog food. The military's no exception."

"Right…So if I *don't* want a sarcastic answer I shouldn't ask you?"

"Ah, see? That's the type of quick thinking that'll get you far in life. If you're so cold, then let's go back inside. There's nothing else to see."

"Alright, listen up, maggots," Tyler ordered. "We've got a dead weight with us today, so let's try to pick up the slack in the RAA."

RAA, that's Random Animal Attack, Roman told himself.

"With all due respect, tall, dark, and loathsome," Treaver interrupted Tyler's speech. "There's only me and the 'dead-weight' here."

Tyler had pulled aside his two students to the far end of the kitchen before that night's training session. Roman felt like he was going to be sick, which the smell of freshly chopped onions did not help with. It was five in the afternoon, and they were going to go back outside for today's RAA. Before, Tyler and Treaver had shown him the basics of the available weapons; arrows, mechanical spiders, blankers (which were much like guns but with air instead of bullets), swords, knives, and some first-level fighting techniques.

"Actually, maggot," Tyler poked Treaver in the chest, "we're going to be practicing with Jay's students today, so there's more than one of you."

"But right—"

"Shh! Don't question your commander," Tyler said, smiling. "Now why don't you show me some respect?"

Treaver, gritting his teeth and recited what Roman took as another form of torture Tyler had concocted for them. "Because, due to the unpredictability of the Island, and all of the useless bones in my body..." Treaver paused, as if hoping for Tyler to take pity on him.

But Tyler was no such person. "There's an effect for every cause. Continue, *please*."

"Mister T, the holy reincarnation of all that is magnificent in this cruel world, has taken mercy on my hopeless form in an attempt to make me something worth looking upon in valor."

Tyler clapped his hands approvingly. "Roman, you'll learn that pledge soon enough. Except, it's getting kind of old, don't you think, Serapher?"

"I couldn't agree more," Treaver growled, curling his fists.

"Yeah...we should add onto it. I'm thinking...how does 'messiah of the worthless' and some motions added, like bowing. Oh! Or groveling."

"You know, the more classic things have the most sentimental value," Roman said quietly.

"Isn't he cute?" Tyler turned to Treaver, "He'll be

[73]

begging for a new pledge after this one session, if I've got any say in it. Which I do."

Jill's students were Jacob, Millo, Chris, and Renaldo. Each day, there were two mixed sessions, where two mentors and their students had one big practice together. Jace was in charge of the mixed sessions, so they trudged out to the parking lot to meet up with Jace, Jill, Jacob, Millo, Renaldo, and Chris.

Jace was leaning against the helicopter with Jill, while Jacob, Roman only recognizing him from Friday, Millo, Renaldo, and Chris standing in front of them while they were explaining something.

"Well, look who finally decided to show up," Jace called out as Tyler came within earshot. "We were starting to worry about you."

"Sorry to worry you," Tyler apologized. "But we *do* have a new kid to look after, and I wanted to make sure that he was clear on everything."

"Is that so?" Jace turned to Roman, making him feel uncomfortable. "Well then, Roman, what do we do to simulate the wild animals in this scenario?"

"Umm, our imagination?" Roman guessed lamely. Roman blushed when chuckles escaped from Jill's students, aside from Millo.

"Nice excuse, Tyler. All right, let's get started," Jace said.

"Wait. What *do* you use for the animals?"

"The mentors," Treaver whispered gravely, "and that includes Tyler."

"What about the paper animals?" Roman wondered.

"The ones we have are too cute, and if we made more dangerous ones they'd be too dangerous, at least for new trainees like yourself."

"Today, we're having a race," Jace explained. "This is for when you are unable to fight off wild animals and need to get to safety quickly. We're going to split you into two teams, and you'll race each other to a destination point while being run down by the 'animals' chasing you."

[74]

"Which animals are they going to be?" Chris asked.

"Well, since Roman's new today, we're going to let you all pick your own animals."

"Yes!" Treaver, Chris, and Renaldo cried at once, while Tyler did not look happy in the slightest bit.

"Each team will have a different animal. The first team is Renaldo along with Tyler's students. And team number two is the rest of Jill's students. Now, decide your animals with each other. There's no limit to what kind of animals you can have except that they must be dangerous."

Renaldo stalked over to Treaver and Roman, and Tyler went over to Jace and Jill.

"As if we need to race," Renaldo muttered. "We all know that our team's going to lose."

"Why?" Roman wondered.

Renaldo raised his eyebrows and gave Roman a look of contempt. "You honestly can't guess, new kid?"

"Is it because we have a dwarf with an attitude on our team?" Treaver replied. "Or just because you're insecure?"

"Shut up Serapher, or I'll see to it that you go down along with the fresh-meat."

"Are we going to decide on our creature or not?" Treaver sighed.

"How about a dragon?" Roman suggested.

Treaver covered Roman's mouth, glancing over at Jace. Renaldo shushed Roman after giving himself a palm-slap.

"What?" Roman demanded as soon as Treaver let go of his mouth and took the left wheel of his chair off of his foot.

"What are you thinking?" Renaldo sneered. "We can't take down a you-know-what-fire-breathing-thing with a new kid! Even Treaver and I'd have difficulty with that."

"Roman, it's hard enough for me to get around outside, in a muddy bayou with logs and rocks and streams, but I don't need to worry about a you-know-what-fire-breathing-thing."

"Right, sorry." Roman felt very uncomfortable. "How about pixies?"

"That's more like it," Renaldo congratulated him, turning

[75]

to Jace. "Jace! We're ready!"

"I heard," Jace responded, making Roman gulp, wondering which animal he had heard.

"So," Jace raised his voice so that everyone could hear. "We have pixies for Jacob's team and chimeras for Treaver's team!"

"What?" Treaver and Renaldo burst out, "We're the pixies!"

"You got that right," Tyler said. "But *I* suggested that ya'll switch creatures to make things a little more interesting."

"*Now* do you want to go with dragons?" Roman asked Renaldo.

"Shut up, newbie. We don't need your sarcasm."

"Actually it's more like irony than sarcasm," Treaver corrected.

"All right," Jace announced. "Everyone, back inside and pick your weapons! Be back quickly because it'll be dark soon, and we'd be wasting precious moonlight!"

"Wouldn't it be better if it were light outside for a training session?" Roman wondered.

Jace grinned. "Inside!"

Treaver and Roman were at the ball closet in the basketball court while Renaldo was scavenging through the supply closet downstairs. The walls of the court had blue padding, and the floor was well waxed, but not immediately slick. Along with the regular two baskets and backboards, there were four more in between and along the sides.

The ball closet itself could've fit two Romans and two Treavers along with their chairs at the same time, except for all of the shelves inside. The interior was made of the same teal metal as the outside, and on the very bottom shelf was a collection of four swords, two mechanical spiders, a bow with seven arrows, and three blankers. Roman couldn't count how many knives were in the drawer right above that shelf, partly because the light reflecting off of them made it hard to see very clearly. The upper shelves held regular things like baseballs, helmets, and air-pumps. The basketballs were on a rack at the entrance to the court.

"Knives won't be good in this situation, because you'd either have to get up close or be able to throw them. And you're not good at arrows…" Treaver muttered.

Roman had failed to get his arrows more than a foot forward, had been too nervous to hold his knife steady, was blown backwards when he tried to fire the blanker, and had mediocre, toddler swinging a light-saber, sword skills. He could fling the mechanical spiders well enough, much better than he could've done with a knife. But he had to switch the electricity off to keep from shocking himself, since he didn't know the proper way to hold it, and couldn't aim it straight enough to make the arms snag onto anything.

"Maybe traveling light would work," Roman suggested.

"No, you'd be too slow." Treaver said passively, thinking hard.

"Hey, I get six-fifty on the mile at school."

"Full or Leprechaun-mile?"

"Leprechaun," Roman grunted reluctantly.

"That's not fast enough. But at least it's not raining."

"Don't jinx it."

"That's Renaldo's job. Anyways, I normally *might* be able to talk to a chimera, but this is supposed to be when we can't beat it any other way. I'll be the one looking out for you, so we're reliant on Renaldo's jinxing to get us out of this."

"You think that I'm going to lose this for you guys, don't you?"

"I never said that. But yes. Either way, we need to find you something now. We can't just skip a session because we might lose a game."

"Whatever. Just give me a sword."

"Are you sure?"

"If I was sure on any of these, don't you think I'd chose that one?"

"Fair enough. At least I can give you tips on how to use it during the race, 'cause I'm taking one, too, along with a spider."

[77]

"How come?"

"Because those each only need one hand, once you're good enough at it. I'll also take a knife." Treaver reached in to grab a random sword from the closet. Out of the four, he chose one with black wrappings on the handle, and the blade was longer on one side than the other. Roman looked at it skeptically. Earlier he'd chosen one with an odd orange blade, and hadn't liked it. He didn't like the look of this one either.

Roman glanced back at the shelf that held the swords. A glint of gold caught his eye. He pulled out a sword that was relatively light, with brass-colored wrappings and an even blade. There was a design on the notch that reminded Roman of dragons, they didn't have wings. He wondered what they were and why they were on there, but he only wondered very vaguely. He liked this sword better than the one that Treaver was offering to him.

"This way I won't have to flip it to keep balance."

"Suddenly an expert, huh? Whatever." The final touch to their collection was three pen-sized, white flashlights for the dark winter night. Treaver, using his lap to carry their supplies, led the way out of the basketball court.

"It's funny that you chose that one, actually," Treaver said once they were inside of the elevator.

"Why's that?"

"That one's from Mr. Garretson's trip to the Island. It's one of the oldest that we have," he said.

"Mr. Garretson can't be more than forty, how's this one of your oldest swords?"

"Well, no one really likes to talk about it very much, since it can give you some pretty awful nightmares."

"Nightmares? I don't get scared."

"Is that so? Then you'll fit in just fine. But anyone that's gone to the Island always has nightmares on most nights, so this story's a walk in the park for most mentors."

"Bring it on," Roman challenged.

"Well, at least the race will get your mind off of it once you know it," Treaver sighed. "The shield that we have is run by the main computer down in the lab. You'll know that when you see it. So you might wonder why we don't just use that shield to our advantage, advance it, and somehow use it to protect people or hide ourselves most thoroughly."

"Um, I actually wasn't. But I'll bite. Why don't you?"

"Because it's too easily breached. Right now the only adults at this center are Mr. Kyle and Jace, who were in training together."

"What happened to the ones who trained them?"

"Exactly. Normally we have about as many students as we've got right now, but twice as many mentors. Mr. Kyle and Jace were students when they had too many mentors to have each one training a student. Some even shared mentoring. That was a good thing because it meant more Talismen. But Mr. Kyle's younger brother changed all that."

"He has a brother?"

"Yeah, but we don't know where he is. The Strayers got to him. He hacked the computer—No, he didn't need to hack it, he had full access. He shut down the shield long enough for the Strayers to get information on where the mansion was. He also deleted or burned any files that we had on the Strayers, which is why we know pretty much squat about them right now. Things like known areas for attacks, weapons, strategies, and even some people were identified. We couldn't memorize all of it. So, before anyone realized what was going on, one by one, when people left the mansion without proper protection, they never came back. Once everyone caught on to Mr. Kyle's brother, he left, and they did a lock-down. No students were allowed to leave the mansion, and mentors couldn't leave without heavy guard. Then the story gets really fuzzy. Mr. Kyle *hates* talking about this part in particular."

The elevator doors slid open and Treaver's voice dropped to a whisper. "Mr. Kyle went out to find his brother. He says that he's the new leader of the Strayers. Something happened between them, and the attacks stopped. At first we were edgy, but there's hardly been any attacks lately. And there's been more students. As soon as a lot of us go to the Island, then we'll have as many

[79]

mentors as before. That's what Jace says. I've only been here for a year, and I already know how often Genedeaues are found."

They paused in the hallway. It was the hallway that went right out of the entrance hall, next to the main stairs. The lost and found bins were behind them, with the supply closet across the hall.

"How do you know that you can trust Mr. Garretson," Roman asked, "if he didn't tell you what went on between him and his brother?"

"We've tested him countless times. Lying tests, scans for probing...and he's as clean as we keep the kitchen. No doubt about it."

"Now I know why you were worried about me getting nightmares," Roman said, head throbbing slightly.

"Yup. It's not that the story's scary-well, not in that low amount of detail, anyways. It's that we aren't positive if the Strayers are going to come for us again or not."

6. Second Movement, First Dream

"For chimeras, we'll have Jay with rocks for the poison, and a short pole that we'll pretend'll cut you like claws or teeth," Jace explained, speaking abnormally loudly. "As for the pixies, we'll have Tyler with a blanker to shoot...whatever pixies shoot."

Roman, Treaver, and Renaldo, who had brought two metallic spiders and a knife, were standing to the right side of the football and soccer field. They had named their team the Racers. The other team, with Chris, Jacob, and Millo, were the Napoleons. They were called the Racers because of Treaver's chair. Renaldo had had to hold some sort of secret against Treaver to get him to agree to that name.

"It's better than the 'Mr. T's'. Although name *does* start with a T," Renaldo had compensated. Roman vaguely wondered what Renaldo could've been blackmailing Treaver with to make him agree to that.

The other team was the Napoleons because Millo and Jacob were French, and had suggested it. At least they'd done that of their own free will.

"All right!" Jace announced, "The finish line is the smaller lake in that direction!" Jace indicated over his shoulder. "All of your team must reach the lake to win. If one team is partially there and the other team arrives with all of its members, then the second team to arrive will be awarded first place. Try not to hurt yourselves. The Racers will be going into *that* side of the bayou," he gestured behind Roman, Treaver, and Renaldo, "And the Napoleons to the other side. You are *not* to cross to the other team's side, or your team will be disqualified. Any questions?"

No one raised their hands or spoke out.

"Okay, then. The teams will have a two minute head start

before I send in the wild animals, also known as the teenagers. Once they find you, you can be killed. Metaphorically, of course, Roman. If one of the Napoleons are knocked off their feet by a blanker, they're out! If one of the Racers are hit by a stone, or hit with the pole, then they're out! On your mark…get set… GO!"

Treaver immediately sped off into the forest with Renaldo helping him along. Roman had to run at full speed, gripping his sword tightly, to catch up. By the time he had caught up to them, they were a good way inside the bayou. Roman was panting already. There wasn't much water around them, only a few ponds. That much was genial for Treaver. Roman looked over his shoulder. He couldn't see the clearing through all of the ferns and trees that steadily twisted in all directions. There was a smell like freshly cut grass that hung near the water, so mixed with sediment and dirt that it was a brownish color. The ground was an unorganized mesh of grass, dirt, mud, tree roots, and fallen leaves. Roman looked up. He could see the sky beyond the trees, dull and grey still. It was so late that small patches of orange stained the clouds and cast shadows as vibrant as the sun itself would have. Ahead of him, Renaldo and Treaver came to a halt.

"What's the plan?" he asked Treaver, who's gray-blond hair looked nearly black in the shadows of the deep foliage.

"Well, we don't know where the finish is exactly, but it's in that direction." Treaver pointed off to his left. "So I'd suggest going that way."

"And quickly," Renaldo added, starting Treaver off. "Because every second counts."

"I sure wish that Tyler used that sort of attitude every once in a while," Treaver sighed. "The only time he uses it is when he's with Stacy."

"Hey, less talking. Now Roman," he said as they started off at a trot, "don't swallow. You can make the motion, but don't actually swallow. Breathe only through your nose, and keep your head up when you run. Watch where you're going *while* looking out for everything else. Got it?"

"How's all of that supposed to help?"

"You're not properly trained. Just do it, and it'll help. Oh, and stay on flat ground if you can. All right, let's go!" He and Treaver broke out into a much faster pace. Roman tried to keep up, but inadvertently maintained a steady three yards behind them. There was no wind that could breach this thick area of plants, but Roman heard the air whistling past his ears as he ran as fast as his legs would carry him. He tried to keep his eyes on the ground while keeping his head level and concentrating on his surroundings while focusing on not swallowing and staying on the dry patches of ground. Since it had recently snowed, there were more mud patches deeper in the forest than usual, even though they weren't as bad as they could've gotten. Roman could hear Treaver's chair brushing against the leaves and occasionally cracking a twig or the collection of weapons bouncing in Treaver's lap very slightly over the wind that froze his ears. The ends of his jacket flailed behind him, sometimes snapping back and hitting him. The zipper made an annoying clicking sound.

This is more high maintenance than math class, Roman thought.

And things went wrong almost immediately.

Roman took the risk of slowing down to zip his jacket shut. But this not only slowed him down, but without concentrating on staying on the dry parts of the ground, his foot sunk into the mud next to a brown-colored puddle.

He tripped and his hands sunk into the mud on the bank, and his sword skidded away, stopping by a tree. He had to first haul his hands, then his foot out of the mud that had sucked in his ankle. He jumped to his feet and grabbed his sword. His foot, clumsy in his desperation not to be left behind, caught in a rabbit hole. Roman lost his balance and hit his head on the tree that had stopped his sword.

Roman had to handle his foot delicately so as not to twist his ankle. He could no longer hear the sound of Treaver and Renaldo crashing through the forest. He glanced in the direction they had gone, with no sign of them. The shadows that now made up the majority of the forest deluded Roman's sight starting not too far away, helped by the trees and ferns. Roman dared not to use his flashlight, lest Jill be nearby. Roman checked that his

[83]

zipper was done up and that his shoe was on straight before running after Treaver and Renaldo.

Treaver had said that Roman would be too slow, even traveling light, leaving Roman to only hope that they would realize he was missing and come back for him. He had ruined their chances of winning, and it wasn't even five minutes into the game.

Roman's breath was starting to show in front of him in the dim light. He was beginning to have to slow to keep track of where to step. Roman had lived in Katy for two years now, and knew well enough that with no moonlight or sunlight in the bayou that he would need his flashlight, but he also knew that he would continue being slow, since he couldn't process what he was seeing very quickly.

Roman dug his arm into his jacket pocket to take out his flashlight, which would be easier to use in the fading light because it was colored snow-white. But the flashlight was not in his pocket. He searched his other pocket and checked vainly whether his pants had pockets or not.

It must've rolled out when I tripped! Way to go. I hope that the zipped jacket was worth it. Roman could do nothing but scold himself as things continued to grow darker and the shadows fused together.

Roman started to grope around for protruding tree branches, managing to feel several that would have otherwise caused him to trip again or even hit himself on the head. He was also trying his best not to make any noise, though he had much less experience in doing so than the other Talismen. He was just thinking about how things couldn't have been worse when he heard it.

A few feet back, a small branch blowing in the wind, bouncing and receding, had caught him in the hair. But this time, he heard a twig snap.

Knowing that simply looking would do him no good, Roman immediately jumped, catlike in posture, out of the way and up to a nearby fallen log that smelled suspiciously like skunk. A rock about half the size of his fist hit the spot where he had

[84]

been a moment before. Roman didn't need a flashlight to see the shadow looming through the trees to his left.

Al lright, it's like Marco-Polo, Roman thought, *Jill won't have a flashlight because he's an animal.*

Almost as soon as Roman thought this, a small white light appeared, flickering over where the rock had just hit.

Oh, right, lions are cats. They can see in the dark. Roman would've groaned out loud and smacked himself on the forehead if he wasn't trying to be silent. Roman was certain that Jill could hear his heart beating, it was pounding so hard. The hairs stood on Roman's arms when he heard a scuffling behind him. Roman stole a glance, knowing perfectly well that Jill could easily get him in the split-second it took him to divert his attention.

It was not completely dark, and though Roman could hardly see the shadows of the trees, he recognized a small reflection of white amongst the black and deep grey. Judging from the pattern of its steps, and the increase of a smell that made him want to gag, it was a skunk.

At the same moment it appeared that the skunk was coming towards him, the flashlight found its way to Roman's leg. When Roman jumped out of the way, the wind from the rock blowing against his ear, he heard a sort of squealing sound on contact of wherever the rock hit. As Roman was running away, not rarely stumbling, he heard Jill holler.

Roman imagined that he could smell the spray of the skunk from wherever he was. He thought that Jill had found him when another flashlight came from his front at first, until he spotted a second one nearby.

"Guys!"

"Shh!" Roman recognized Treaver's voice.

"Don't worry about Jill, he's not coming back for a while."

"What?" Renaldo demanded skeptically. "What could *you* have done to him?"

"Not me. That skunk, Flower, from Bambi."

Treaver laughed so hard Roman thought that Jill would be able to hear him. "Let's hurry, we made it past the boulders

[85]

before we realized that you weren't following."

Roman saw their shadows turn around and set out at a slightly slower pace than before. Roman followed their shaodws and their shadows' movements. Occasionally Treaver would call out, not afraid for Jill to hear, something about where a rock was or where a tree branch was hanging off to the side. They were probably moving faster than Roman had been on his own, though still not as fast as when it was light.

"Why do we even *have* night—"

"Shh! I said no talking!" Renaldo scolded Roman.

It wasn't long before Roman heard a splash up ahead.

"We made it!" Treaver cheered before, "Aww man! My legs are wet!"

Roman felt the ankle-deep water sink into his shoes a they crossed the thin part that branched off of the lake, signaling that they had made it to the finish line.

"And we have our winners!" Jace shouted from somewhere up ahead. A set of lights were suddenly turned on, illuminating the clearing where the streaming branch of lake spread through. Jace was sitting in a blue-striped beach chair with a pitcher of iced-water, a small plate of cinnamon cookies, and a few magazines on a small, plastic table next to the chair. The lights were underneath the table and Jace's chair. Jace was applauding them.

Roman was bewildered. Surely he was faking their victory and then the other team would surprise them from the trees. But after a moment, longer than Roman would have been able to keep from bragging, a small flutter of hope started quavering in his stomach.

"Did-did we win?" Roman asked, knowing that he would just be called a new kid again if the question was stupid.

"No, I'm just clapping because it's a new hand-exercise." Jace must've been rolling his eyes, even though he was still wearing sunglasses, despite the darkness. "*Yes you won.* And impressive, too, with a new person on your team."

"We won?" Treaver choked disbelievingly. "But I hardly *ever* win RAA's!"

[86]

"Yes, good for you," Jace congratulated them, standing up, "And guess w—"

Jace was cut short from the mad-scrambling through the bushes off to Roman's left. Jacob, Millo, Chris, and Tyler stepped out of the darkness, squinting.

"Guess who I caught!" Tyler boasted, holding up his blanker.

"It's not fair!" Chris complained. "We never practice dodging blankers!"

"Actually, you did just now," Jace argued. "You just didn't succeed in getting here in one piece before they did."

"Wait, they *all* got here before us?" Chris repeated disbelievingly. "No offense, of course, to Roman." he added apologetically.

"Yup," Renaldo boasted proudly, straightening his back and holding his head high. "It's called *teamwork.* No newbie left behind." *Right, this coming from Renaldo,* Roman thought irritably. "We've been here quite a while and Jay hasn't even shown his face yet."

"You haven't been here *that* long," Jace mumbled, back to his usual reserved tone. "Where is Jay, anyways? You didn't meet him along the way?"

"I did," Roman said tentatively.

"And you didn't get out?" Chris challenged.

"Jay hit a skunk by mistake," Roman could now hardly suppress a laugh. Neither could most of the other people in the clearing.

"Well, that counts as being distracted and not technically defeating it," Jace concluded. "So the victory is legal."

"Congratulations," Jacob congratulated the Racers. Jacob's voice, which Roman had expected to be strong, was deep, but suppressed. He seemed almost as shy as Millo when he talked.

"It must have been quick dodging," Millo added bashfully to Roman.

"Not really," Roman said. "But thanks, anyways."

"But there might not be skunks on the Island!" Chris

[87]

complained.

"Yeah, there might be something that would eat the chimera, instead of just spraying it." Jace smiled.

"Don't mind him," Jacob told Roman. "Chris can be a bit of a sore loser."

"Looks like our newest member has some special talents." Mr. Garretson came out of the shadows behind Jace. "That quick thinking of yours could prove useful. All of you to the infirmary to get checked by Jace and Roman. And congratulations, Roman," he added, "you've won your first training session for your team."

Roman helped Jace check all of the minor cuts and scrapes. He couldn't believe how easily all of it came to him. He knew exactly what brand of creamy lotion to put on each injury, even though he didn't know the names of most. He knew exactly what angle to put a band aid on, and would correct every one that Jace, still wearing his sunglasses, put on. After a while, Jace just sat back and watched Roman work.

When everyone else was sent off, Jace stood up and walked over to Roman. "What was your power again?"

Roman sneered, trying not to smile. "Can't remember."

"One thing I actually *do* want to know is how you, a new kid on his first training session, managed to win it for your team. *Most* new kids fail miserably on their first go, whether they have a skunk or not. They would've been hit by that first rock."

"Dunno," Roman answered. "But how come we have training sessions at night, anyways?"

"We can't guarantee that it'll be constant light on the Island," Jace chuckled, as if this was completely obvious. When Roman realized that normally there wasn't even constant light, he also realized that it *was* obvious.

That night Roman had one of his strangest dreams. It was a rare dream where he was aware that he was dreaming. He was standing outside the mansion, but it looked different. There were only three garages in the parking area, and without the helicopter in the center. And the air of everything was different. Roman's dreams normally came to him in flashes, but here he could've studied every minuscule line on the grass. He couldn't smell anything, like he did in most dreams that involved something like food or the mall, and without having smell while his eyesight was so vivid, it felt almost like he was deaf.

"Heads up!" someone yelled, which meant that he wasn't deaf. Roman jumped when he saw a football about to hit him in the face. It went right through his neck, and hit the ground behind him with a thud. Then a small child ran right through him to pick it up and throw it back towards a few others as if he was nothing more than an apparition.

Roman didn't recognize any of the children that were suddenly there, playing in the field, even though the boy who had retrieved the ball looked strangely familiar. *Very* familiar. He was wearing a shirt with red and white stripes, similar to the one Caleb sometimes wore, ragged blue pants, and he looked about eight. He had beaming blue eyes, brown hair, and very pale skin. Roman had a sort of feeling that he couldn't place. He knew that the feeling was of where he had seen the face before, but he still couldn't place it.

As he ran towards the other kids, Roman heard a wisp of a familiar voice, but couldn't make out whose it was. "Trent, don't go that way!" It sounded almost like it was strained; like somehow it was being strained by something.

Roman scanned the scene to find where the voice was coming from. He spotted what looked like wind in the shape of a person running in slow motion toward the kids. It was just the background of grass and brick swirling together, though it had an outline. Roman looked away when he heard the kids screaming. They all ran straight past and through him and the wind figure. Everything froze for a moment, even the swirling thing. Another child that Roman thought he should recognize was about to run into him. It was a boy with sun-tanned skin, slightly older than the first kid. He had shaggy black hair and startlingly purple eyes.

"I don't know this kid, but he looks *so* familiar. Maybe as much as the first one," Roman muttered to himself in confusion.

Roman glanced back to the strange whirlwind figure. It

[89]

was facing towards the ferns surrounding the perimeter of the mansion.

Roman saw the first child cowering before something in the bushes. A man with eyes like sapphires and jet-black hair was emerging in front of him, looking intently at the boy.

"Leave him alone!" Roman yelled and ran toward them, figuring that they probably couldn't hear him. Roman passed right through the man when he tried to tackle him, falling harmlessly into a patch of bramble bushes. Then the dream unfroze.

Roman lifted his head to listen to what the man was now telling the child.

"Bad times are coming, kid." His voice was no more than a whispered growl. "Your entire home, your family, and the world as you know it will be *ours*." The man removed a knife from his pocket and put it to the boy's neck. Roman's heart skipped a beat. "But *you* can avoid it. You are going to be very powerful indeed, little one. I know that you've seen it. You will help us, or everything, including the thing closest to you, will be destroyed completely."

A tear dripped down the kid's cheek. The man with sapphire eyes chuckled, "You *have* seen what you will do. My scout was right, eh? You can see into the future, but not change it. It's the only way to avoid the worst. Think on that."

When the man disappeared back into the forest, Roman started breathing again.

He looked to where the man made of air was. It was still running at them, but wasn't making much progress. Then, everything started to slowly melt away, almost like paint dripping.

Roman heard the wind-man scream, "No, not now! *Trent*!" The last word was slowly dragged from wherever the figure's mouth was.

Roman was in his room, only recognizable through the wall, floor coloring, and structure. But it wasn't how he'd left it. His computer was replaced by a pile of board games with ribbons tied in bows attached to them. Another trunk was nearly empty,

[90]

and what was in it was spilled out onto the floor.

He was still dreaming.

Another boy, about Treaver's age, was sitting on the bed. He had smooth brown hair and dark blue eyes. Roman realized with a jolt that he was the first boy he had seen before. The calendar on the wall read:

September, 1990

He was dreaming about something that happened in the past, an entire generation ago. Roman searched for the wind-shaped person that he had seen before, but there was no sign of it.

Someone knocked on the door, "Trent! Quit skulking and get your lazy butt in gear for a HHC!" *That'd be…hand-to-hand combat. Yes, that's it.*

The boy, Trent, glanced up from his feet.

"Be right there, Jaycee," he answered gloomily.

Jaycee? Roman went through it in his head as Trent started mulling around in his spilt-over trunk for something. This was almost twenty years ago, before Mr. Garretson's brother had destroyed most of the old Talismen.

Could Jaycee..? No, it couldn't be.

Mr. Garretson was thirty-four in the present, where Roman lay, sleeping. Around this time, he would be fourteen. Jace was thirty-five, and would be fifteen.

Trent was leaving with a sort of brick in his hand, so Roman followed him out of the room. The boy that had been knocking on the door was gone. Many things were different in the hallway, the carpet brown instead of the dotted blue and greens, the tables gone, and the extra storage closet that marked the third floor instead had the same one-way glass on Mr. Garretson's door, except it had someone else's name;

Rico Martinez

Another thing that Roman noticed as they made their way out was that the stairs leading up to the fourth story were gone completely.

[91]

He followed Trent down the stairs to the first floor. The red rug he was used to was black, and the walls were colored a nasty brown instead of white, missing the sketches of predatory animals. The part of the kitchen that he could see had the same floor and wall, but there were more chairs that were smaller, and only one stove that had a burner underneath it.

Trent walked over to the storage closet and grabbed two swords, something that looked like an electric cattle prod, and a blanker-gun that had a bag full of something suspiciously similar to paintballs strapped to its side. He didn't look at all happy to be out in the open, frowning with bleary, narrowed eyes, like he was half asleep.

He dragged the swords along the floor, making a tear here and there, and through the entrance. Roman crept out behind him, seeing that the front yard looked just like the previous dream.

"Hey, don't drag them on the carpet," A girl with curly blond hair in a ponytail, short, pretorn-jeans, a tie-die shirt, and green eyes came up to him, "Martinez'll probably have your head if he has to pay *another* fifty dollars for *another* floor change."

"And you should *probably* stop wearing jeans that look like they were shredded by a dog," he sneered. "It'll never catch on."

"Just you wait and see, grumpy pants." She raised her eyebrows in a matter of fact way. "You should've had a vision of it by now, they'll be as popular as the Beatles."

"First of all, my visions come at random times, and are normally about *important* things. Second, the Beatles ended up with one kicked out, and one dead, Rita." He shoved past Rita, and she had to side-step to keep from being cut by the trailing blade.

Okay, Roman thought, *So...sweet little kid to very anxiety-depressed teenager. What the hell happened to him?*

Roman's question wasn't answered, because before he could follow Trent to the training clearing, the dream changed again.

This time, he was in Mr. Garretson's room, which

[92]

branched off of his office. Roman had never been in here before, the only thing that gave it away were the papers stacked on the desk and plaques for heart surgeon degrees, along with the fact that Mr. Garretson was in the bed. The room looked very similar to Roman's room, except without a bathroom leading off to the side and the window at a separate end of the room.

Before Roman could do anything, the Talisman leader sighed and sat up in his bed. He saw Roman.

"Did you have the same dream I just had?" he asked warily, "I thought I saw you."

"Um, we're still asleep...I think." Roman knitted his eyebrows. "But *why* are we having the same dream?"

If he really was with me...He must've been the wind thing!

"There's no way to tell. There was one part of the vision where you were at one side of the lawn, but then all of the sudden you were at the other. What happened to you?"

"I'm not sure what happened. Time just sort of...froze. And I walked over to the man talking to Trent."

"You knew that was Trent?"

"Um, I just heard his name in the second dream. Wait, who was Trent anyway?"

"What second dream?" Mr. Garretson either didn't hear or didn't care about the separate question.

"There was a second dream where he was sitting in his room, moping, and then he went out for a training session."

"Hmm." Mr. Garretson rubbed his chin. "Apparently you've been seeing some of my past dreams. The one that we were in together I've had for several nights in a row, now."

"Why?" was the only way Roman could ask the ever-growing list of questions in one word.

"I can only think of one explanation. And if I'm right, then there's one more dream that I want to show you."

"What? But how can you control which dreams you have?"

"I'm consciously awake, aren't I? All I have to do is think it."

[93]

"What if it's *my* dream and not yours?"

"It's obviously *both* of our dreams."

"Umm, okay," Roman sighed. "Whatever."

Once again, the dream shimmered and melted to liquid, and repainted itself into another. This one wasn't at the mansion, though.

Roman had no idea whatsoever where they were. They were both floating in mid-air like the gravity only existed in the middle of the sky, except there was no sky. In all directions were the colors from dark purple to black and every shade in between swirling together, besides the small, spherical, transparent open space where they were hovering.

"Dreams are supposed to be suppressed memories. And I don't exactly remember coming here. Exactly where are we?" Roman asked Mr. Garretson, trying not to sound panicked by the fact that he couldn't do much more than talk and move his limbs.

"Not all dreams are memories," Mr. Garretson said, not showing any sign of fear.

"What the hell does that mean?" Roman demanded, losing his cool.

"You might just find out one day. In the meantime, just watch."

"What's there to watch?"

Mr. Garretson flicked his head. Roman looked to where he was indicating. Part of the space in front of them was shimmering more than the rest. The purple part started to brighten into different shades and colors, and the black parts started to blend into shadows.

Mr. Garretson seemed to be waiting for him to react, but Roman still couldn't make out what the outlines were forming. Every time they came close to almost taking shape, it deformed again.

"What exactly is supposed to happen?" Roman asked, still trying to control his terror.

"You can't see it?" That was the first time Roman had ever seen Mr. Garretson look surprised and confused.

"Um, see what?"

[94]

"The pictures."

"Uh, I see swirling purple and black. But the purple keeps changing color…A little."

"Hmm," Mr. Garretson didn't look too disappointed, "I guess only *I* can see it."

"See *what*?" Roman repeated.

"You might not be meant to see it," Mr. Garretson continued. "I thought you were, since you appeared in my dream. I guess not."

"So, you *aren't* going to tell me what you saw?"

"Maybe they'll show you some day, but not now."

"*They?*" Roman felt his voice rising a few octaves.

"Oh, well. It's probably almost dawn. I'll just wake up about now."

"You can control when you wake up?" Roman thought that if he could get that out of him, then he might tell him more. Roman didn't want to be left alone, wherever they were, floating in midair, waiting to wake up himself.

"Only when I have weird dreams like this," he said calmly.

"You have these dreams often?"

"Millo claims that it's my first power. Having dreams with meaning, otherwise called visions."

Roman wanted to ask him another question besides the ones that he wouldn't answer, but the questions of where they were overwhelmed his mind. Mr. Garretson took that as an end to the conversation, because he started to shimmer like sunrise on a lake. Slowly, his body turned back into the swirling air, blending into its background, and then disappeared entirely.

Roman was about to scream but he felt like his eyes and mouth were closed, and his warm sheets were around him. He opened his eyes. They felt as if they'd never been open in the first place.

He was in his bed, facing his window. Relief almost chocked him, and felt almost as bad as the fear. Roman knew he should've felt as if he, his teacher, or both, were crazy. But he knew that if he wasn't insane, and he did have the dream, then

Millo must've been right about Mr. Garretson's power.

Once he stopped the uncontrollable shaking, he glanced at his alarm clock. It said *8:36*. Roman pushed the confusing thoughts to the back of his mind until he could think clearly. He shouldn't be in bed; it was a Monday. The immediate confusion disappeared when Roman remembered that they had this Monday off from school. He felt like going back to sleep, but was afraid of what other dreams lay in store for him.

7. Preceding the Third Movement

Φ   Φ   Φ

At first, he didn't know what to do after getting ready for the day. He couldn't think of anything already scheduled, so he climbed out of bed. Once he'd showered and slipped on a plain black t-shirt with a brown, unzipped hoody, and some ruffled gray pants, he started heading for Mr. Garretson's office.

Before he'd even left the hall, Treaver called his name. He was coming towards him, looking ready to go out on the cold winter day with his *Florida* sweater.

"You doing anything important, right now?" he asked.

"Um, no. Not really," Roman lied.

"Great! Chris agreed to take us to Starbucks next weekend, so do something important today!" he smiled.

"I'll probably be free anyway. Think he's still sore about last night?"

"Probably. But today Tyler's doing a WUC with us, so he won't be in our shadow for *too* long."

"Right, have you seen Sarah anywhere?" Roman wondered, wanting an excuse to get away from Treaver and see Mr. Garretson.

"Oh, she's probably in the lounge or her room. It's raining again, so she wouldn't be outside." He raised his eyebrows. "Why do you need to see her?"

"She, um, wanted to know about the timed-essays we're doing in English class."

Treaver narrowed his eyes and his smile grew wider. "What are you two up to? Knowing Sarah, she's up to *something* if someone has to make up an excuse for her."

"We're not up to *anything*," Roman insisted.

"You're such a horrible liar," Treaver chuckled. "Come on, I want in."

[97]

"There's nothing to get in on," Roman said.

Treaver scratched his chin. "You weren't lying that time. Well, like I said; she's probably in the lounge. So, since there's nothing to get in on, I guess I'll go with you."

Roman felt a prominent influence to do a face-palm.

"Sure, come on."

Sarah was sitting on the couch, watching Ashley arguing with Tyler, Renaldo, Elliyo, and Gabriel all at once.

"Never gets old, does it?" Sarah commented to Roman and Treaver when she spotted them.

"Better than cable," Treaver agreed, "except we've got satellite." He leaned forward, "so Roman tells me that he wants to ask your help on the timed-writing papers for English class."

At first Sarah frowned at him and glanced at Roman. Repeatedly, Roman cut his hands silently across his throat and shook his head.

Sarah took the hint. "Yes. I'm having trouble with the charts, and my teacher said that he was one of the best in the grade for the Pre-AP classes."

"The *best in the grade*, huh?" Treaver grinned. "So what are you two up to?"

Sarah glanced around to make sure that no one was listening. The others were still arguing, and were the only ones in the room aside from them.

"Follow me," Sarah whispered, standing up and heading out of the room with Roman and Treaver on her heels.

They stopped when they were in the courtyard, sitting on the edge of the fountain. Outside, it was as cold as the previous morning. The clouds were gone, and the sun was beginning to peak over the treetops, bathing everything in warm sunshine. No one was outside. They had complete privacy to talk.

"All right, what's up?" Sarah demanded as soon as they were settled.

"I've got no idea," Treaver said. "Roman here just made up an excuse when I saw him. And a bad excuse, at that. So, since it was that he wanted to see you, I figured that you'd know."

"So then what's with the secrecy?" Sarah asked Roman.

Roman remembered that she could read eyes. If Treaver could tell that he was lying as easily as before, then he didn't want to know what Sarah would be able to tell.

"Look, I'm really not sure myself," Roman told them.

"You're nervous," Sarah said. "Which tells me that you've got *some* idea of what's going on."

"I don't."

"Well, even *I* know that that's a lie," Treaver speculated. "Roman, if you don't tell us, then we're going to get it out of you *somehow*."

Roman bit his lip, knowing that he was completely giving away that he was hiding something.

"We promise not to tell," Sarah coaxed. "*Please* tell us. What's bothering you?"

Roman was shocked by how sincere she sounded. He wished that he could read eyes, to know if she was really that concerned.

He sighed. "Fine. But don't tell *anyone*. Once a secret's out, then it's for all to hear." Roman had forgotten where he had heard that from, but he'd kept it close for a long time, for many reasons.

Roman tapped on the door to Mr. Garretson's office, which was new for him, considering that Mr. Garretson normally saw him coming before he had gotten within a foot.

"One minute!" came Mr. Garretson's hoarse response.

Roman stood there for a moment, trying to find something interesting to focus on. He could faintly hear Gabriel shouting from somewhere below. For some reason, the smells of bacon and pancakes in the morning never wafted to the fifth floor. The fifth, and occasionally the fourth, always smelled like paint and laundry detergent. The fifth level always gave an aura of a business office that made Roman feel uncomfortable. He shifted his feet.

When the door opened, Mr. Garretson seemed slightly

different. He had on a bit of aftershave. Also, he had bags under his deep brown eyes.

"Uh, hi," Roman greeted him awkwardly.

"Come in. There's something we need to talk about." He slipped his head back inside.

Mr. Garretson sat down in his swivel chair and propped his feet on the desk. His laptop was closed at the edge of the counter, with the statuette now something that looked like a mix between a Cheshire cat and a rattle snake. There weren't any papers on the desk, leaving it with an eerie sort of reflection.

As beat-down as he looked, Mr. Garretson's eyes were bright as he watched Roman.

"I need to tell you something about the dream last night," he said clasping his hands together and leaning forward, like it was some sort of business talk.

"So you *do* remember?"

"Oh, yes. And I assure you, all of the questions you asked will be answered. Eventually."

"That's comforting."

"But for right now, there's only one thing you should know about what I saw. You are destined to do something *very* important. Something that no one else here would be able to do."

"What?" was the only word Roman could choke out.

"You're special, Roman," Mr. Garretson responded. "I don't know why, and I don't know how, but you could see into my dreams, and I'm still convinced that there's a reason why you could."

"Wait," Roman interrupted, "how could there be a reason for you and I having the same dream? It's not like someone can just, like, decide these things and just push us towards something, right?" He'd meant it as a joke.

There was silence when Mr. Garretson didn't reply.

"Right?" Roman repeated, his voice rising.

"I know somehow that that question will be answered along with, *who are* they?"

Roman sighed, "Just continue before I flip out or something."

"You've already started having the nightmares." Mr. Garretson smiled a tired smile. "But Roman, I won't tell you exactly what I saw, but I will tell you the sum. You're going to be some kind of hero."

"*Some kind of hero?*" Roman echoed. Then something occurred to him, "You said *going to*. You saw the future!" he guessed.

Mr. Garretson nodded grimly. "That was one thing that I always hated about my first power; the visions. It may seem like a rare gift, but it's a curse. My brother knew that more than even I did…"

"Your brother?" The first vision came back into his mind. The child cowering at the feet of the man. The person had said he knew that Trent had *seen* something, that he was going to be powerful. "Mr. Garretson, when did your first dream take place?"

"When my brother and I were kids at the mansion. The same thing has happened every time. The vision freezes, and I never know what happened when the other kids ran. I wasn't there at the time."

"Trent was your brother?" Roman breathed, astonished. "Treaver told me about…" He let his voice trail off.

"Yes, the sweet little kid playing rugby turned into the leader of the Strayers. I'm convinced that the dream is about *why* he joined in the first place, but I've never managed to see or hear it for myself."

"And Trent could see into the future?"

"Many powers among families are similar. I had dreams, he had day-dreams. The powers have certain significances to them. Sometimes when someone dies, another completely different person gets the same power. Sometimes family members have totally different powers. They just are that way." He stood up. "That's all I wanted to say. Just remember to train hard, Roman."

Then he shuffled Roman out of his office.

"You're serious?" Treaver whispered.

Treaver and Sarah sat across from him at one of the tables

in the center of the library.

"Why would I make something like that up?" Roman demanded. "And then he just shoved me out of his room."

"Hmm." Sarah was being less skeptical than Treaver. "Apparently you're destined to be the big hero that stops the Strayers. Forever, if we're lucky. You should be proud."

"You're not honestly buying this, are you?" Treaver whispered to her. "Mr. Kyle's never talked about his brother to anyone! Why would he tell Roman, who hasn't even been here two days?"

"Didn't you hear the part about being *the chosen one*?"

"He never said that!" Roman snapped, still keeping his voice down. "He said that I do something important, that's possible, right? His brother was probably the *me* of the Strayers, if you want an example."

"But I don't think he wanted to join the Strayers, by the sound of it," Sarah pointed out.

"What do you mean?"

"I meant what I said. The guy with blue eyes told the kid that he had no choice."

No one responded.

"Am I the only one who noticed that?"

"Well, the part that they had the same dream kind of drags your attention away from that," Treaver said.

"Roman, didn't Mr. Kyle say that he'd had dreams like that before?"

"Yes. Where are you going with this?"

"He also said that he didn't know why Trent joined the Strayers. You never told him what the man said."

Roman stared at her. She had a very good point. Why hadn't he told Mr. Garretson? "I didn't think about it."

"So let's go tell him." Treaver started to back up, but Sarah pulled him back.

"There's another thing you guys seem to be missing," she said.

"Huh?" Roman and Treaver wondered at the same time. Sarah sighed and rolled her eyes.

"You told us exactly what he said, right? Repeat his exact wording."

"Um," Roman wasn't famous for remembering things, but he could remember this time, "*Bad times are coming, kid.*" he started, feeling awkward, "*Your entire home, your family, and the world as you know it will be ours.*" he closed his eyes, concentrating, "*But you can avoid it. You're going to be very powerful. I know that you've seen it. You will help us or everything, even the thing closest to you, will be destroyed.*"

"So he joined them to protect something?" Roman had started to see what Sarah meant when he was repeating the final line. "He had to join, didn't he?"

"As far as I can guess." Sarah shrugged.

"How does this keep us from telling Kyle?" Treaver questioned.

"Because we don't know exactly what happened, or what he was protecting. If we tell Mr. Kyle, then he'll go berserk. If we can't give him all the answers, then who knows how that'll affect his brain? From the way you described the way he looked…One dream did that, Roman."

"So we're not going to tell him at all?" Roman spat.

"Not unless we find that last answer first."

The rest of the day flew by. Roman felt refreshed by the three-day weekend, though he still wanted more time off from school. The fact that Sarah and Treaver expected him to have another odd dream was not helping with his anxiety. Tyler's weapons-use class had not been fun, but Roman had learned to keep the end of his hoody out of the nose of blankers.

Roman collapsed in his bed, wondering what would happen in school tomorrow, and immediately fell asleep.

Great, pop quiz. Roman muttered to himself.

He was in eighth period Spanish class.

His teacher, Mr. Sapling, passed out the sheets. This was definitely going to be hard. They were covering the body parts right now, the one subject Roman wasn't grasping.

Roman stared in horror when he saw that the "quiz"

somehow had forty questions. He felt like his head would burst when he saw that the class only had twenty minutes left before the bell.

Roman looked at question number one:

1.) Eyes _____

Simple enough. *Ojos.*
Question five:

Translate:
5.) Cabeza _____

Darn it!

It went on like that for some time. Mr. Sapling decided to pass out the English papers, which was very unlike him. First, he was the Spanish teacher. Second, why during a test?

Roman got back his timed-writing paper. He'd gotten a sixty-eight! He hadn't even finished half of his paper!

Wait, he thought, *We aren't supposed to have our final grade until Friday.*

Roman lifted up his hand and moved his fingers. He couldn't feel them.

Not Friday. Next *Friday. I'm dreaming.*

Roman glanced to his right. Danny was in Cole's seat. Roman smiled, getting up out of his seat. Danny glanced up as he approached. Roman grabbed his arm and pulled him out of his seat. Danny looked confused for a moment. But the confusion disappeared when Roman kicked Danny as hard as possible in the shin.

Then the room started waving like a funhouse mirror. All around Roman were the same purple and black swirls he had seen when he was with Mr. Garretson.

Worth it.

Then, slowly the swirls receded. He was standing at a construction site he'd seen on his way to the Cinemark. It was a long and wide section between two roads. A man dressed like a green-blue Statue of Liberty held up a sign for a carwash.

All around Roman were piles of sand, dirt, and puddles of collected rainwater. There weren't any bulldozers. Most people thought that the construction site was abandoned. It had been so still for years that, every day at sunset, birds would rest on the dunes of gravel and sand. He looked up at the sun. It was high-noon.

Next, the sounds came to him.

All of the mid-day traffic was suddenly whizzing behind and twenty meters ahead of him. It was warm, but there was a cool breeze that indicated it was still winter. There was barely a cloud in the sky.

He wrinkled his nose when the smell erupted from his conscious dream. Now he smelled gasoline, dirty rainwater, smoke, and various exhausts from passing trucks.

When the smell melted down to Roman's upper-mouth he spat out the taste.

It was gravel. And for his conscious dream, tasting the smell would've been the same as the real thing.

This dream was just like the ones that he'd had last night, just as strongly detailed, and just as unnerving.

At first, the only movement in the intersection was the dazzlingly shiny ripples in the puddles that reflected the sunlight. Then Roman's eye caught a flash of gold.

He glanced over at a half-finished building structure made of metal support beams. He spotted the movement again. Just a slight shadow slipping through a pipe tunnel built under the nearest dirt pile. He followed, instinctively being quiet. The tunnel was dark and damp. The gravel taste faded away when the smell of dirty rainwater strengthened.

At the end of the pipe was a seven foot drop into a little ditch. Roman stuck his head out to look down into the ditch. The light hit his blue eyes like a speeding truck.

His head should have made a shadow easily noticeable. But he wasn't really there.

What he saw didn't make much sense to him. The flash of gold was curly, honey hair, shimmering in the brilliant light. The

[105]

hair belonged to a girl. She was wearing a peach uniform that almost blended into the sand, and she held binoculars up to her eyes while she peered over the side of the ditch.

Someone else was crouching next to her. It was a boy a few years younger than Roman, possibly Renaldo's age, wearing the same peach uniform. He had brown, almost auburn, hair. Roman couldn't see his eyes.

Darn, I'm stupid. Why am I hiding?

Roman climbed out of the pipe and dropped onto the gravel. He instinctively tucked in his head, expecting to get scrapes from sliding along the coarse ground. But he was just a ghost, looking in on the memory of someone unknown. The girl said something. Roman didn't quite catch it.

He slunk closer. He found it hard to walk casually toward two strange kids that were obviously spying on something. He glanced at where the girl was pointing her binoculars.

The Cinemark was on the other side of the street that rested a matter of feet away from them. A Sudan 48 was pulling into one of the empty parking squares near the building. Roman recognized that car.

It belonged to Mrs. Haldrige.

Roman, Caleb, Kayla, and Mrs. Haldrige had pulled up at the exact same time, with the exact same car, into the exact same parking space. Roman was watching the day he had met the Talismen.

"Let me see!" the boy complained. His voice was slightly high-pitched. He grappled for the binoculars.

"Quit it, butt-munch!" the girl snapped.

Roman froze. He *knew* that voice. And he knew exactly who it belonged to.

He stepped carefully in front of the pair, who were still wrestling over the binoculars. He looked at each of their faces.

The boy's eyes were pale brown, but they looked dull. They stared at nothing and were unfocused. He had freckles on pale skin. Roman thought he looked oddly familiar, but not as familiar as the girl. He immediately recognized the hazel eyes he'd seen more than he would've liked to.

Chrith Vladimir. The same Chrith from his school.

Roman tried to calm himself down. He hadn't realized that he'd stopped breathing. But now, he was breathing very quickly.

I haven't seen them at the mansion, so what are they doing spying on me?

He saw a dark figure like a shadow, almost pitch-black, even in the intense light. It was making its way on top of the roof of the Cinemark. It disappeared over the side of the building.

Then the dream changed again. Roman was at the same spot where Sarah, Danny, and Jace had first explained everything to him, with the helicopter just landing. The thrust of the wind did not affect Roman, though the grass looked ready to rip itself out of the ground.

Sarah and Danny jumped out of the helicopter as soon as the door opened. They both looked at the Cinemark. Sarah's face was grim, while Danny resembled a kid in a candy store.

"Don't mess this up," Sarah growled to Danny. "Mr. Garretson said that the Strayers might be on the lookout for him."

"I am *not* blind!" This was definitely not Danny's voice.

"Are too." Roman was back at the construction site. He was beginning to get annoyed with flipping back and forth between visions.

"I can see colors," the boy insisted. He had been the one called blind by Chrith.

"Not the colors normals see. Besides, that's just your first power. If you were a normal then you'd just be *blind* and *helpless*," she taunted. "And colors don't count, you can't judge distances. No tripped-out glasses are going to fix that."

"Some people who *can* see can't judge distances," the boy countered.

Chrith ignored him. "We'd better get him out of there soon, or we'll have to explain to Emote. He'll have his head."

The dream began to fade.

Roman awoke in his room, with the red light from the computer charger blinking in his eyes. He felt like he was still dreaming, like nothing he saw was real. He didn't feel tired in the slightest bit. His alarm clock said it was around three-thirty in the morning. His alarm would be ringing to wake him up for school in about two and a half hours. And then he would get ready, there at the mansion, where he was safe with his friends. He would arrive at school on the Talismen's special bus. And he would be at school. With one of his newly-adopted mortal enemies.

Chrith. A Strayer.

Roman didn't feel like going back to sleep, and probably couldn't have if he'd tried. Instead he decided to talk to Mr. Garretson about his most recent dream.

He was halfway down the hallway in his pajamas when he remembered that they weren't supposed to tell Mr. Garretson or Jace about their little investigation. So he crept back and knocked on Treaver's door, right next to his. *Tap, tap, tap.*

No response.

He tried again, knocking harder.

Nothing.

Roman climbed the stairs to the fourth floor and made his way down the hallway to the second to last room. He knocked timidly on the door.

There was no answer. He tapped, this time hard enough to make an audible sound.

At first, there was no reply. Then he heard footsteps. He looked straight at the peephole.

"Roman, what are you doing here at three in the morning?" came Sarah's groggy voice.

"I had another dream. It's big."

Silence.

"Okay, give me a second, then you can come in."

A minute later Sarah opened the door. She had on some light blue, fuzzy pajamas. Her red hair was tossed up and frizzled in some places. She had her glasses on. Her skin was paler than usual.

Roman hadn't been in very many rooms in the mansion, including Sarah's. Her room had a few pictures on the wall of friends, parties, other special events, and some of random times at the mall or at school. Some other pictures were of wolves and tigers. One was a *One Republic* poster. She had a calendar with a bear for the January photo. Her walls were a royal-blue color. The ceiling was the same white as Roman's and every other room that Roman had seen. The curtains covering the window were colored rainbow to turn the morning sunlight different colors. There was a *Dell* computer on top of her desk. The desk had sketches all over it, not only drawn on papers, but etched into the beige wood. There was a radio on a small table in the corner, next to a cage. The cage was too big for a hamster or a mouse. There was a small, plastic, green castle in the middle.

Sarah's bed had fuzzy, purple sheets, as did her pillow and blanket. The carpet was thinner in this room than in the hall in and Roman's room. There was a swivel chair at her desk and another revolving one next to the TV, which looked similar to Roman's television.

The door to the bathroom was closed. There was a wooden wardrobe next to the entrance. A short bookshelf to Roman's right had a clear, plastic, pink piggy-bank on top. The shelves underneath it had different kinds of knickknacks and books.

"What's in the cage?" Roman asked.

"A chinchilla. His name's Alejandro."

Alejandro the chinchilla stirred as his name was spoken, poking his head out of the castle. He had dark gray fur and small paws, and was roughly the size of a fat squirrel.

"Go back to sleep, Alejandro," Sarah said as she settled down in her revolving chair.

Alejandro's head disappeared back inside his little home.

"He understands you?"

"Of course. I had Treaver help me train him," Sarah admitted.

"Right. The animal-talk thing."

"All right," Sarah said, "enough small talk. I didn't get up at three-thirty-five just to talk. What was your dream about?"

"The Cinemark. Remember the day we met? Well, at the construction site I saw two people scouting out the scene, saying

[109]

that some guy named Emote wasn't going to be happy. Just in time, too. You and Danny were just getting off of the helicopter."

A look of shock slithered its way across Sarah's face.

"That's not all. The boy and the girl there watching another person sneaking into the theater. And the girl was Chrith."

"Who was the boy?" Sarah asked him after a silence. Like every other sixth grader, she knew perfectly well who Chrith was.

"I don't know. He was blind. Well, mostly. He said something about being able to see colors. Only colors. Not distance or anything like that."

"That's strange. Wave-lengths only, I guess."

"Right." Roman agreed, pretending to know what she meant. "According to Chrith, it's his first power. But who's Emote?"

"No idea. But this is *still* the best lead we have yet."

"Yeah, you were right about the dream."

She grinned. "I'm always right."

"Well, it doesn't look like there's much we can do, for now," Roman admitted grudgingly.

"We could hire a few eighth graders to dump Chrith in a garbage can," Sarah suggested half-heartedly.

"What about Victoria?"

"Who can say for sure that she's a Strayer? Just because she hangs out with Chrith? Arnold and Sadie sit with them at lunch, and we're not suspecting them."

"Because she copies Victoria in *every way*. She would probably notice if Chrith disappeared off the face of the earth to go training." Roman felt oddly powerful about his suspicion. It was as if he knew for certain that Victoria was up to something, Strayer or not.

"She could still be an "innocent bystander", as Mr. Kyle would call it. Danny's been talking to those two since he met them," Sarah pointed out. "Though that's probably because he's a weirdo. And *he's* a Talisman."

"Yeah, you're right." But at the same time, Roman felt an icy cold feeling creep up his spine. "Let's hope that we *don't* have a Strayer living with us, shall we?

"Of course that would explain all of the weird stuff that's been happening lately," Sarah said, not indicating any special significance in her words.

"Weird stuff? *Here?* Naw. We're talking about capturing a pretty little girl to question her about something that could be as pointless as a rubber duck to convince our secret society's leader's brother to stop being Darth Vader. Let's face it, our whole lives have gotten weird."

"Not funny this time, Roman. Lots of things in the lab have been going wrong with no explanation. And our funding is disappearing off the record."

"We have funding?" Roman asked.

"Wrong word for it, sorry. Mr. Kyle's savings from his days as a heart surgeon, along with the stuff he keeps from his appointments nowadays."

"Well, anyways…Mr. Garretson said that those dreams counted as visions because they had meaning. So that pretty much settles the fact that Chrith and that boy whoever he was that were sneaking into the building are—"

"Wait, sneaking into the building?" Sarah interrupted.

"Well, yeah. I think I already mentioned that."

"Damn it!" Sarah cursed. "A Strayer sneaking right out from under our noses."

"Oh, um. It probably won't happen again," Roman said lamely.

"If they didn't have their SRP's then it wasn't our fault. But this also means that the Strayers were after you before we found you, and that hasn't happened since Stacy."

"Then how do we keep them from killing me?" Roman demanded.

"They don't normally know the *exact* identities of Genedeaues, only their parents and how they were when they were babies. The fact that you've known Chrith for a long time and they haven't gotten to you yet helps. But if you want, like Stacy, you could have a bit of a makeover…"

"It sure worked for Stacy," Roman commented. "Treaver

[111]

and Tyler keep drooling over her. But if the Strayers knew Stacy's parents, then what happened to them? I mean, it's clear that *my* parents aren't in danger."

"They were killed," Sarah sighed sadly. "It happened with Jacob and Millo, too. But they don't like to talk about it. *No one* likes to talk about their parents dying. Stacy's parents were just about to be re-located to the mansion for safety, when the Strayers found them."

"What about Jacob and Millo?" Roman asked her.

"*That's* a really sad story. Their parents split up ten years back when Jacob was five and Millo was three months old. Millo had gone with his mother to France while Jacob stayed with his father in Ohio. Two years ago, Jacob's dad died of cancer and Jacob joined the Talismen. After another year, Millo came when his mother was killed in the crossfire when the Strayers had tried to recruit him back in France. We're lucky we got to him. He wouldn't join them and they'd almost killed him by the time we got there."

"No wonder they're so quiet," Roman commented breathlessly.

"Not once you get to know them. But we'll talk to Treaver about your dream in the morning." Sarah told him, "Get some sleep, we don't want you tired while you're going to school with Strayers. I'm starting to have doubts about not telling Mr. Garretson, though." She got up from her chair and opened the door for Roman. "*Hasta mañana.*"

"What?" he whispered in the doorway.

"I thought you were taking Spanish. It means either see you tomorrow or see you in the morning, I can't remember. Though, the morning ship has sailed."

"Oh. Okay. *Hasta mañana,*" he said before she closed the door behind him.

Roman somehow managed to fall asleep again that night, but had a nightmare about his "makeover", and woke up in a cold sweat to his alarm.

Time for school. I'll have to get Treaver in on this.

[112]

8. The Topic of Telling

Down the stairs, into the hallway, and finally entering the kitchen Roman saw that almost everyone was already up, except for the elementary-schoolers.

Roman spotted Treaver talking to Chris over about ten pancakes. Sarah didn't look very troubled by her lack of sleep or the fact of who they were about to go to school with. Danny and Cole were playing with something that Roman hoped was silly-putty. Jacob was sharing some sort of pastry with Ellenore, who was a tall, thin girl with curly brown hair and deep green eyes, not far away from the door. When Roman had been introduced to almost everyone by Chris, Treaver, and Sarah, on his second day at the mansion, he had been informed that Ellenore and Jacob had been dating for almost half of a year now. Mary Beth was discussing something with Jill not too far down the left side of the table. Tyler was sitting next to Stacy, Sarah, and Jasmine, who all looked slightly annoyed. Jasmine was supposedly Roman and Sarah's age, though they'd had to guess. Jasmine had been dropped off at the mansion gates as a baby with nothing but a basket and a name-tag. She was African American with dark brown eyes and long, thick black hair.

Rebecca and Ringo were not in the kitchen, and most likely not at the mansion. Most students, aside from Mary Beth, did not come to the mansion before school if they didn't live there, Roman had been told. Mary Beth was near graduating, anyways. The Talismen took their own bus to the schools. The same bus that Roman had seen in the parking lot on his first day there.

Roman walked over to Treaver and Chris.

"...better than *The Brave and the Bold*," he heard Chris say. "I mean, when I used to watch cartoons it was *Justice*

League this and *Justice League* that. I've honestly gotten tired of it all. Besides, they should've left Superman where he was. The rest of them just slow him down."

"You are *not* serious." Treaver did a fake punch on Chris's shoulder. "I mean, thanks to the *Justice League*, there were about ten cameos all at a time on Static Shock."

"No, Treaver," Roman interrupted, sitting down next to him, "*You* can't be serious, either of you. Arguing over whether the *Justice League* is better than *The Brave and the Bold*? We *all* know it's Batman."

"Ha! I *told* you!" Chris boasted.

"Treaver, can I talk to you for a second?" Roman asked.

"Go ahead," Chris answered for him, "I won't listen."

Roman stared at him for a moment.

"You really aren't good at the evil-eye, are you?" Chris guessed.

"Sure," Treaver said to Roman. "I'll be out in the statuary." With that, he left the room.

"What's all that about?" Chris asked.

"Nothing."

"Greatest excuse ever."

Roman ignored him and started walking over to Sarah, Jasmine, Tyler, and Stacy.

"Good-bye to you, too!" Chris called after him.

"Sarah," Roman whispered urgently. "Meeting in the courtyard. You know what it's about."

"Hey, maggot," Tyler greeted Roman. "Don't work your brain too hard in school, today. The greatest mentor in the world has arranged your first PCG! Now you might stop acting *completely* clueless."

Ignoring Tyler, Roman looked hard at Sarah. She frowned, and Roman slunk outside.

He decided to push breakfast aside until they decided what they were going to do with their new-found information. He wandered down the halls of cherry rugs and cream walls. He took a right down the side-corridor, and out the light-tan door at the end of the hallway.

The pre-dawn light was a gorgeous collection of gray and purple in cloud patterns focused around a bright-orange circle. Sparrows were fluttering from tree to tree and bush to bush. Even though it was winter, and Roman was shivering slightly, he liked it much better outside. It was no wonder why most of the other kids were in the kitchen, with the large windows, instead of in the lounge.

Roman found Treaver next to the fountain. Sarah joined them shortly afterwards. After much getting off of topic and mulling it around in their heads, they were forced back inside by Jace's call for getting ready.

Roman packed his backpack as quickly as he could, wanting to get to school to get his mind off of things. On the Talisman bus, there would be no privacy for talking. Out of all of the solutions that they had considered, the most obvious option was that they should speak to Mr. Garretson about it. The only argument against this was of Mr. Garretson's emotional status and a question; if the visions had meaning, and Mr. Garretson had had dreams like this for some time, then why hadn't the dream come to him? Surely he could've asked one of the students if they knew Chrith and the boy. If Roman and Mr. Garretson could have the same dreams, then why only Roman?

This might be easier if he had answered my stupid questions! Roman growled to himself, *then I'd know how we get the dreams in the first place.*

Inside the bus, the seats were black leather, and the black floor looked the same as any other bus Roman had seen, except much cleaner. The white ceiling wasn't curved outward like most school-busses, and instead lay flat. There were the usual emergency exits, along with a small compartment in the back of the bus, behind the last seats, where they kept a few knives. Roman didn't think that it was a good idea to bring knives to school, whether they were going inside or not, but they were never checked by anyone or anything.

Roman, being the new kid, and this being his first time, sat alone near the front. He had at first tried to sit in the back rows, but everyone knew each other and sat in the same seats every day. The eldest kids had the first choice of seats, as it was on the regular school buses. Roman wasn't at the very front of the bus, but he was closer than any other kid. Treaver and Chris sat together, Sarah and Jasmine, Ellenore and Jacob, Jill and Tyler, and without surprise, Danny and Cole. Stacy was lucky enough to be only thirteen and sitting in the very back with Tyler and Jill, since those seats were slightly larger. The other middle-schoolers tried their best to keep Roman in the conversation, but it was more difficult when he was a row in front of them.

They were mostly discussing things that Roman wished he understood ahead of time. Not only were they exchanging fighting-strategies, but they were also talking about creatures, people, and things that Roman had never heard of. Jasmine claimed that she'd figured out how to create a few batches of 'teleliquid' without Jace, Mr. Garretson, or any of younger teachers finding out. Treaver seemed convinced that some people called 'The Hochbringers' wanted to help him invent some sort of communicator to help on missions. And Sarah continually tried to share her theories on 'hytbeauxes' and 'fragmorphers' with the others, to no prevail. Anytime that one of the others students paid attention to Roman long enough for him to ask his questions on what they were saying, they were pulled back into their chatting when someone asked a more interesting question, having to do with the fact that they already knew what they were talking about.

Roman thought that he would be more relaxed when he arrived at school. But as it turned out, when Mr. Garretson said that everything would be cleared with the Haldriges, it was also evident that that included mentioning Roman's adoption and somehow connecting it with his disappearance. Since Caleb walked to school in the mornings, he was one of the first there that day. And since Caleb became excited very easily, he had mentioned Roman's adoption to quite a few other students. So, even though the Talismen bus arrived before any other bus, the majority of the sixth graders already waiting to be dismissed to their classes in the cafeteria knew about Roman leaving St. Jefferson's. Many kids congratulated him when they saw him, some of whom Roman didn't know. Roman, knowing of the Talismen kids' odd reputation, mixed with the fact that many others were interested in his new home, snuck away from the other mansion students as soon as he'd had the opportunity. It wasn't hard; all he had to do was say that he needed a book from the library for reading class.

"Roman! ROMAN!" Caleb called out when Roman entered the cafeteria. He was sitting at the closest table to the windows, where Roman was reluctant to sit because of the crowd that was sure to gather at the windows in hopes of another snowfall. Today Caleb was wearing a grey shirt and jeans. Rachel was already sitting next to him. She was wearing a fuzzy, purple jacket and shorts, which was an odd choice for winter time. She was wearing a necklace that read *Peace*, and a few bands with kittens on her arms.

"Roman! Why didn't you call me afterwards?" Caleb wondered.

"I was kind of busy getting settled in," Roman explained. "And it's a pretty big house. Lots to explore and easy to get lost."

"You'll have to invite me over sometime," Caleb said. "You owe me after the thousands of times that I've invited you over."

"I'd have to check with my new step-parents," Roman dodged. He was positive that he would not be allowed to let Caleb anywhere near the mansion, and Roman was afraid that Caleb might tell that he was living with the Talismen. Roman had no trouble with lying to Caleb, but found it slightly disturbing imagining Mr. Garretson as his 'new parent'.

Rachel seemed to enjoy hanging around Caleb. She would try to get his attention in the hallways and Caleb claimed that she volunteered to be his science partner, despite the other students' warnings of Caleb's bad grades. During first period math, they worked on adding positive and negative numbers, which was perhaps the most boring math lesson they had executed all year. Then, for their project partners in second period science class, Roman had been forced to pair up with Eric, who would not cease talking about *Crazy Boris* games online. By third period

[117]

reading class, Roman was very annoyed with his school day so far. Since the later classes were behind from school being dismissed early the previous Friday, his reading class had a day watching *The Rescuers*, although the majority of students had begged for *Pirates of the Caribbean*. Roman was glad to have time to nap from the long day he had had so far and from his lack of sleep the previous night.

Roman lay his head down, almost immediately drowning out the noise of the class talking through the movie. He had not been expecting to re-visit the conscious dreams any time soon after it had been revealed that Chrith was a Strayer. Roman was lying on something cushioned. It felt like an air-mattress. He tried to open his eyes, but all that they met was darkness. Roman tried to smell or hear something, anything. The only thing that he could smell was cool air. The air burned his nostrils slightly, it was so dry. He suddenly was very thirsty, and wished that he hadn't fallen asleep. He tried to move, but he could not. His face felt like it was still buried in the invisible air mattress, and his limbs felt frozen, like when he woke up in his bed from a nightmare where he had been running.

The only thing left to do was to focus on whatever noise there might be. His ears felt cold, but they should've been able to hear. At first, he thought that he was hearing things back in the classroom, and that perhaps he was waking up, but then the noises came into focus.

"What is it that you want?" came a booming, echoing voice. It belonged to a man, an adult by the sound of it. "You are not to enter here!"

"I can do whatever it is I want," came another hiss, except this one was fainter than the first.

"Get out before we make you get out!"

The second voice laughed. "You can't *force* me out! Not unless you find a better way to share your information without frightening your victims."

"My son is not a victim!" the first voice howled. Roman felt himself shake from the power that rebounded over to him. In his previous dreams, he couldn't feel anything. Roman felt the

[118]

hair on his neck raise when he realized that in his other dreams he couldn't feel the cold that he now felt. He tried desperately to move again in vain, wanting very much to wake up.

"Oh, isn't he? What about the other two? Not them, either?"

"You know that I changed my mind! I settled down with Kasumi and I meant everything that I told her!"

"Is that so? Then I guess that you won't care for this one. I wonder what would happen if he had a small…accident."

"YOU DARE TO THREATEN ME?"

"You're old. You've lost your edge," the second man laughed a high, cold, piercing laugh. "YOU'RE SO OLD, YOU'RE PRACTICALLY DEAD! Hahaha! You brought him here to tell him not to tell. Well, I *would* conduct my little experiment on him, if I didn't agree with what you were thinking. And so, once again, you'll have no choice but to give me what I want."

There was a pause in which Roman felt his hairs tingling with the static of the heated conversation.

"Very well. But if you want me to carry out what I want, then why come here in the first place?"

"You still don't get it, do you, old man?" the second voice taunted, "Tisk-tisk-tisk. And to think that you taught me everything I know. Well, almost everything. And I didn't learn everything that you tried to teach me. Well, I'm sure that your brother would be able to figure everything out. If anything, you should be thanking me for showing your son in the first place. Of course, you know that you nearly killed my cousin, so I almost killed your son. But I succeeded in killing your first love. Although you succeeded with my family, I didn't care for them, and you failed to kill me. I might actually thank you for ridding me of that burden. It makes things much easier. So until you think on that, as far as you know, I'm here to taunt you. It's quite fun actually. As you would say: treason and true are the one and the same."

There was a popping noise that hurt Roman's ears. A silence followed for a moment as Roman wished that he knew what the two men had been talking about, along with him hoping that someone would wake him up telling him that the bell was about to ring.

But when the silence ended, what Roman heard was not the other kids in the classroom talking. It was some of the words that the second man had said to the first, repeating over and over again, overlapping as if reflecting off of the walls.

Tell him not to tell, tell him not to tell, tell him not to tell, it continued. Each time that it sounded, Roman's head pounded. Roman tried desperately to think of something besides the words, his headache was so horrible.

The words finally stopped when he spontaneously remembered that the dreams he had were visions that so far had applied to important things that had or would happen. All of the conscious dreams meant something. When Roman realized that this had stopped the words from pounding into his head, and that he couldn't get that thought out of his head, he tried speaking, hoping that he wouldn't be heard back in reading class.

"I-I won't tell him," Roman gasped. The coldness started to lift, though Roman could tell that he wasn't waking up. He tried being slightly more convincing.

"I won't tell him," Roman said forcefully. Gulping, knowing what this meant, he finished the sentence. "I won't tell Mr. Garretson about my dream."

Good boy, something whispered back softly.

Roman woke up in a cold sweat.

"Are you all right?" asked Ms. Auster, whose desk just so happened to be next to the spot where Roman had fallen asleep.

"Y-yeah. Just a bad dream."

"Have you considered watching the movie?"

"Erm, I'll-I'll go do that." Roman got up and moved to the corner of the room where some kids had taken out a deck of cards to play with. It took a while for Roman's heart to stop thumping so hard that it hurt.

His newly found dream brought up an inevitable issue; Now it was clear that telling Mr. Garretson about the discovered Strayers, along with Roman's other dreams, was not an option.

[120]

Tyler called Roman aside after he'd set foot inside of the mansion, while the rest of the students were still finishing their conversations started on the bus.

"Hey there, larva."

"I thought that I was 'maggot'," Roman said irritably.

"Treaver's 'maggot'. Anyways, Mr. Garretson wants to know how you're settling in."

"Fine. Why can't he ask me himself?"

"He's been called off to Poland for some baby who's mom had some sort of heart disease. I don't know, but they want the kid looked at. So he'll be back in a few days, and Jace is going to call him later."

"How do you know all this?"

"It's called *breakfast*. Where were you this morning, anyways?"

"Outside," Roman replied vaguely.

"Whatever. The PCG's at six. It'll be boring, so eat something beforehand. It's torture having to sit through an actual *class* without any dinner."

Tyler disappeared into the lounge. Roman looked around. Sarah, Treaver, and everyone else that had walked in had successfully disappeared. Roman cursed under his breath. At least the elementary students wouldn't be back with Jace for another half-hour. Roman was lucky to find Sarah watching TV on the couch in the lounge, ignoring Tyler, Cole, and Chris playing hacky-sack next to her.

"Hey, Roman!" Chris called out when he saw Roman enter, "Wanna play?"

"Aw, come on," Cole complained. "He'll fail faster than Mary Beth would criticize me on my knife skills! It'll be boring."

"I'm busy, anyways," Roman said.

"With what?" Tyler chuckled. "You middle-school kids have it easy."

"None of your business," Roman retorted. "Sarah, can I talk to you for a minute?"

"Oh." Tyler, Cole, and Chris all smiled at once.

"Smooth as sandpaper, Roman," Sarah sighed.

[121]

"Yeah, we know Sarah better than to hear the words 'none of your business' and then talking in secrecy and not suspect anything of her," Chris explained.

"Well, you'll find out soon enough," Sarah promised them, which set Roman's stomach turning.

"Trying to get the new kid in trouble? You can count me in," Cole told her.

"Shouldn't you be kicking puppies with Danny right about now, Cole?" Sarah demanded.

"Couldn't find 'im," Cole smirked.

"Even after sitting with him on the bus?"

"I turned to say something to Mary Beth when she pulled into the driveway bus and then he was gone. He's probably planning something *big*," Cole boasted.

"A shame that he decided not to include you, don't you think?"

"He'll get me involved."

"Then you won't have much time for what *we're* doing, now will you?" Sarah sneered. "See you guys later," she said, turning to follow Roman out of the room. "Oh, and don't forget to save me a spot in the game for later."

"Don't be late, then."

"Uh-oh," was the last thing that Roman wanted to hear as a response when he told Sarah the message from his vision. "We've got to find Treaver."

They couldn't find Treaver until the elementary school kids arrived, when he, accompanied by Jacob, came out to greet Millo. Roman and Sarah quickly ran over to Treaver, pulling him aside.

"Treaver, we need to talk *right now*."

"Oh, hey guys. What's up?"

"It's about our little *project*," Sarah whispered.

"Oh yeah. Jacob knows, by the way."

"*What?*" Roman felt his stomach drop out.

"Well, he was wondering why we weren't at breakfast today and—"

[122]

"Roman, we need to get Treaver and Jacob somewhere private where we can talk about this. Treaver, we'll explain later, but don't tell anyone else about this, all right?"

"Erm, slight problem," Treaver whimpered.

"*What?*"

"Jacob and I came out here to tell Millo."

Roman turned around with his eyes closed, hardly daring to look for fear the memory of his dream would come back to him. When he opened them, Jacob was with Millo, who had a look of horror and fear across his face. Roman could easily guess that Jacob had just told Millo. Sarah, knowing this as well, quickly ran over and steered Millo in their direction, with Jacob following confusedly.

"Study rooms," Sarah ordered through gritted teeth. "*Now.*"

Sarah quickly shooed the paper pets off of the fifth floor and ushered the others inside of one of the farthest study rooms.

"Millo, do you have any homework?" Sarah asked once the door to their study-room was closed completely.

"Only math…" Millo whimpered.

"Get it out, please," Sarah requested softly. "That way if anybody comes here they'll think we've been helping you with that."

Millo obediently took out a sheet on simple area equations.

"What's the big idea?" Jacob demanded, frowning. "And what's this Treaver's telling me about a girl at your school being a Strayer?"

"Okay, look. Yeah, we have one identified Strayer and one that we might have the chance of seeing, but there's a bit more to it than that. But, Treaver, quick note; DON'T TELL ANYONE ELSE!"

"All right, all right," Treaver muttered. "I figured since no one could think of anything else we could use some help…"

Millo and Sarah sat down in two of the black, plastic chairs while Jacob and Roman stood. Roman rapidly explained in as little detail as possible his first three dreams, then, with

Treaver listening intently, he described in greater detail his most recent dream. Millo and Jacob were excellent listeners, and didn't ask any questions during Roman's elucidation. Millo seemed to grow more and more apprehensive as Roman continued, and Jacob seemed to be curious for as much as possible.

"So we're basing our every move on your dreams?" Jacob inquired when Roman was done clarifying their situation. He leaned against the wall of the room with his arms crossed.

"But they're so *real*! And even Mr. Garret—"

"I wasn't being skeptical," Jacob added swiftly. "Just checking."

"Well, yeah then," Sarah said.

"Then we shouldn't have to worry about what we do next," Jacob stated. "We just wait for Roman to have another dream."

Roman shuddered at the thought.

"All of this has happened in the past." Millo spoke very quietly. "Even the dream at the theater. Wouldn't the next dream be of something in the past, as well?"

"We can't be sure when the last dream took place," Treaver mumbled. But Millo had a point. What if they *did* rely on another dream to tell them something, and then nothing came? Roman didn't enjoy the prospect of having these dreams every night, especially if they were anything like his latest. But he also didn't enjoy the prospect of racking their brains again to try and figure out a solution. Roman imagined telling Mr. Garretson. A simple thought flashed through his mind with the force of a missile, though it was very brief. What if they told Mr. Garretson and it turned out that there was some unknown reason for not telling him? What if they were missing something, and then disobeyed the dreams? Whoever Mr. Garretson had implied was controlling the dreams, they seemed to know more than Mr. Garretson, who already knew more than all of the Talismen students combined on the matter. Mr. Garretson trusted the dreams, and the dreams had told Roman *not* to tell Mr. Garretson.

"It'd be disobeying Mr. Garretson if we told him. Whatever's going on, Mr. Garretson obviously doesn't know the whole of it. And I don't think he's supposed to." Roman was talking to himself, but mutters of concurrence came from the others, even Millo.

"How about we just wait for tonight before we stress over this?" Jacob and Sarah suggested at the same instant. They stared at each other for a moment before turning to Roman.

"Why are you looking at me?"

"*You're* the one having the dreams," Treaver snorted.

"Sounds reasonable," Roman concluded. "Not pleasant, but reasonable."

Millo looked very sullen. Roman wanted to comfort him, but had no idea of how. He hadn't known Millo for very long in the first place, and Jacob seemed to have much experience with him. When Jacob led Millo out of the room, Sarah stared after them. Once again, Roman wished that he had Sarah's power, wondering what she found in other people from their eyes.

He had only been at the mansion for a few days, and he was already more deeply involved than most of the students that had been there for years. But that did not keep his head from hurting by the end of his PCG class that afternoon. Treaver had fallen asleep before Jace and Tyler had joined them in the conference room on the fifth floor. Normally, the PCG classes would be held down in the lab, but there had been another malfunction, causing Jace and Tyler to be late. Jace had come back inside complaining to Tyler that they would have to make more, since the liquid nitrogen had turned back into gas.

The conference room was a room made of mainly a large, oval-shaped, wooden table with plush, blue chairs placed around its perimeter. In one corner was a potted plant and in another there was a picture of Mr. Garretson. To Roman, it resembled a room for corporate CEOs, but to Treaver all it meant was a nap.

"I've already covered all of these classes," Treaver told Roman with his head buried in his arms. "Let me know when it's over."

"Don't count on it."

To Roman's surprise, Tyler did help explain the lesson

almost as well as Jace. They covered how every single gem was unique, along with a few other things that had already been explained to Roman, and much of how trips to the Island worked. But with both of the teachers and the student being Genedeaues, nearly fifteen minutes was spent trying to stay on topic. At one point, Jace had gone from explaining how the Bermuda triangle corresponded with the ancient Greek myths to discussing with Tyler how the metric system worked. Another time, when Jace told Roman how they would all be plummeted into unconsciousness once they passed inside of the Island's barrier, Roman started daydreaming about bringing a large packet of *Cheese Ballz* in for lunch, now that he could get them, and using them as tokens in a game of slapjack. Roman had missed something about gremlins and stupidly asked something that Tyler and Jace had apparently spent three minutes explaining and debating.

Once the lesson was over, Roman woke Treaver. It felt as if someone had taken his brain and hit it with a mallet. The concepts were unusual, though not difficult to grasp. But Roman's attention span seemed to have gone on vacation without him.

Roman followed Treaver down into the kitchen. Even though Roman had had a bowl of Spaghetti-os before the lesson, he was famished. But when Roman headed into the pantry to get some rice, he forgot why he was in there, stepped out, remembered his rice, stepped back in, and then forgot again. After a few minutes of this, Roman decided to grab a few slices of cantaloupe from the refrigerator, and then nearly ate the crust.

"Dude, if you don't get in your bed then you're going to drop. And if you hit your head too hard, there'll be too much paperwork," Treaver told him.

"I'm not tired, just…lots to remember from that training session."

"I'd hardly call it training," Treaver snorted. "But you look ridiculous with that glazed look in your eye. Uh…your cantaloupe's dripping onto your shirt."

Roman looked down and quickly put the cantaloupe onto

the table. Roman then realized that he had neglected to get a plate. Roman rubbed his forehead.

"Roman, this is pathetic. 'Sides, we've got school tomorrow. The more sleep the merrier."

"Whatever. I'm going into the lounge."

"Didn't you hear a word I just said?" Treaver shouted as Roman was walking across the hall. It didn't occur to Roman that he had left his cantaloupe on top of the table until he was on the couch. Jacob, Stacy, and Chris were at a table in the corner, watching Ellenore levitating three textbooks at once with ease. Now that the elementary kids were in bed, no one was occupying the television. Roman noticed that the remote was on top of the TV. He thought vaguely of getting up and taking it, but couldn't manage to make his arms and legs move.

Roman didn't want to go to bed. The odds of him dreaming when he was asleep were more likely than him dreaming when he was awake. This did not seem to be working out for him, though. Roman could hardly keep his eyes open. His left eye kept going cross whenever he blinked. Roman started hearing vague voices, like he *was* already dreaming. He tried closing his eyes and taking deep breaths, though he stopped taking deep breaths almost immediately when he drifted off to sleep.

9. Emote, Airvo, and Aesthe

Φ   Φ   Φ

Roman wanted to curse himself awake when he was suddenly on top of the roof near the school's main entrance, feeling like he was really there. The tiles were the same brown color, and Roman couldn't help but notice that he wasn't slipping off the edge, even though it was very steep. It was cloudy outside, and Roman could smell that rain was coming soon. Turning around, he could see the school's track, football field, and tennis courts. The road was busy beyond the parking lot. There were several large, canary-yellow buses pulling into the parking lot. Roman couldn't see through their opaque windows. He wondered what time it was. Even though there was some light coming through the clouds, it could still be early springtime, when it was bright out when school started.

There were several wooden platforms set up on the rooftop behind him, near the library's sky light. Several workers, most in stained blue uniforms with yellow helmets, were walking amongst the platforms or kneeling down to work. They were replacing the roof tiles around that area. Roman remembered that around the beginning of the year, it had been rumored that someone had thrown a metal mallet onto the roof that had later been struck by lightning. There were several different versions of the rumor, all coming from the fact that the roof tiles near the sky light needed replacing. In the waking world, the project had been finished months before. Roman figured that the dream was taking place sometime in September.

Roman's question about when this took place was answered when he heard the echoing sound of the bell. Normally, the bell was enough just to get everyone's attention; while on the roof, near the speakers, Roman had to cover his throbbing ears until it was over. This was obviously a signal to the construction workers that their shift was over. Several began shouting to each-other and packing their things. A few pointed to the sky, most likely considering the rain clouds.

Then the sixth-graders started pouring out from the school entrances. The seventh and eighth graders wouldn't be let out for another five minutes, so it was easy for Roman to find what he was curious to see. Sure enough, coming out of the entrance were Caleb and Roman, exactly how they had been at the beginning of the school year. Caleb was carrying his old purple backpack, holding it very close to his shoulders. Roman had recently heard that having your backpack further down on your back was popular, and realized that he looked much like a small donkey with it up to his neck. The backpack would later be caught on his locker hook before being torn in half by attempts to remove it. Caleb was wearing the green jacket that he had worn every day throughout fall, until he had switched to a thicker one in the winter. His hair was waving down past his ears, since this was before his mother had forced him into getting a haircut.

It was strange for Roman to see himself and Caleb walking from up on top of the school roof, but it was also strange to be on top of the school roof in the first place. Remembering that Sarah, Treaver, Jacob, and Millo were counting on him to have a dream that would help them with their dilemma, Roman started looking out for the familiar golden hair that belonged to Chrith. All Roman had to go on was that she didn't ride the bus.

It wasn't Chrith's curly hair that caught Roman's eye, but the sparkle of Victoria's *Coach* purse. Roman turned his head to the right, near the tennis courts to see Victoria and Chrith talking with the younger Arnold and Fiona. Fiona was a short girl with mouse-brown hair and wore pink. Chrith and Victoria looked almost exactly like they did in the present, except shorter. Arnold looked odd without his buzz cut, but Roman had to suppress a laugh at how he was holding a *Tweetie* in his right hand. The *Tweeties* would later be banned, reminding Roman that Arnold was suspended for selling them to other students inside of the theater's Props Closet. Chrith motioned for Victoria to follow her before waving goodbye to Arnold and Fiona. Chrith was leading the way off into the bayou, with Victoria walking slightly behind. Roman was struck by curiosity. Victoria would have been walking beside Chrith if this had been the path they normally took after school.

Roman was faced with the challenge of following them when he gathered that they would be hidden from view once they entered the bayou. This issue was relevant for two seconds before the dream shifted in the same sudden manner as in his dream of the Cinemark. He was suddenly in a part of the bayou that he did not recognize. It was similar to the construction site from his last dream, but still varied. It was a man-made hollow of sand. The hollow was deep enough that he could not see over the edge, except for a few towering trees.

This must be very deep inside the bayou, Roman thought, *otherwise the trees wouldn't be that thick.*

Around the perimeter of the hollow there were crates, much like those used for moving zoo animals. They were different sorts of colors, with writing on the sides in various languages, none of which were in English. What caught Roman was that they were in a fashioned circle around the hollow. Roman wondered why they were positioned like this, since it would be easier to simply leave them in a part of the recess, and it would be harder to move them when their sides were touching in such a tight formation.

The sky indicated that it was either seven o'clock in the evening or six in the morning, assuming that it was still September. If it was the same day then most of the clouds had shifted, but a few still formed a captivating pattern of swirls and bumps. Although the hollow was dry, those clouds looked as if it had recently rained. The orange and purple shades reflecting off of the clouds made Roman squint, the sand under his feet shining as if it were fire.

It wasn't long before Roman heard shuffling from behind him. He turned around. A shadow passed over his head. Chrith jumped over the edge of the hollow, sliding smoothly down on the loose sand. Coming up panting behind her was Victoria. She clumsily tumbled down the side of the crater, coming to a stop

[130]

next to Chrith on top of a turquoise crate. She sat there, clutching her side, until Chrith helped her up, a stony expression covering her face. Roman saw next to no difference in Chrith's appearance, only that she seemed unnaturally serious. Victoria, however, was hardly recognizable. Her normally cool expression was severely daunted. She looked close to crying, with no sympathy coming from Chrith. Her clothes were tattered, and in some places, torn or wet. She seemed to have had a hard journey through the more wild parts of the bayou. Sweat was dripping down her forehead, causing her makeup to run. Roman guessed that she had been crying at one point, because her mascara was running down her cheeks, and her eyes were puffy. Her hair was matted and tangled, and she seemed almost dizzy. Roman wondered what they had gone through in the woods, why it had taken them four hours to get to wherever they were, and if this was even the same day.

When Victoria was on her feet, she swayed slightly. Chrith's expression was undeterred by her friend's condition. There was a certain light in her eyes that normally meant trouble was coming. Chrith leapt off of the crate with ease, leaving Victoria looking disconsolate at the fact that she had to get down as well. When she half-jumped, half-fell off of the crate, she was caught swiftly by Chrith, who now looked almost disgusted at her weakness.

Chrith stepped into the center of the hollow, right next to Roman. Roman self-consciously moved away from Chrith, not used to seeing her up close. Victoria whipped her head around, looking afraid and confused.

"Where are they?" she croaked, sounding several years younger than eleven.

"Shh!" Chrith snapped at her.

"Relax, Chrithesma," came a familiar hissing voice. The same hissing voice from his last dream. "We will teach her not to make such fool-hearted mistakes."

Victoria tried to hide behind Chrith.

Roman felt cold again, and felt his own weight on his feet. His dream was becoming more detailed like it had been earlier in reading class. Nightmarishly detailed.

Roman felt an almost animal-like instinct to get away from Chrith and Victoria, worried that they might notice him somehow. But they did not change expressions or even glance in his direction. Almost as soon as Roman felt himself relaxing, he noticed movement behind him.

It was apparently where the hissing voice had come from. Roman turned around. A shadow was there. Nothing was where the shadow led up to. It was a simple shadow, falling in the same direction as Chrith's and Victoria's. Neither Chrith nor Victoria seemed to notice that there didn't seem to be anybody there. Roman saw the shadow shifting as if someone really was there.

"Now, she doesn't look completely hopeless," came the hissing voice again. The voice came from where the shadow began, but Roman still saw nothing.

"She isn't physically," Chrith said matter-of-factly, "and *definitely* not mentally. She has the will."

Thinking that the owner of the shadow would answer, Roman walked a few feet past the shadow. He was right in assuming that the person would speak.

"So...tell me your name." The voice came from in front of Roman, from exactly where the shadow started.

Then the vision froze, just as it had when he was in Mr. Garretson's dream. Victoria looked like she was trapped in mid-breath, about to answer the man's question. After a few moments of nothing happening, Roman felt like he had to do something. He cautiously crept forward and stuck out his hand to where the shadow's person would stand. His hand felt nothing. He bent down, feeling the ground where the dark was. He could feel the rough texture of the sand, though it was odd when it didn't shift at his touch, as if each grain weighed three tons. Roman walked through where the shadow was, still feeling nothing. He looked over his shoulder and noticed something that made his stomach flip over.

He had a shadow.

But Roman wasn't really there. His shadow didn't belong there. He looked around wildly, feeling his eyes going round, heart racing. There was nothing else to make the shadow. He stumbled back, bumping into Chrith. She too, would not move even slightly. Her clothes were unruffled by all of Roman's weight. Again, Chrith was as hard and solid as ice. Roman could feel the pressure from the ground when he fell, which was something else that was new. He was sweating a cold sweat. He could feel himself thinking. But now, it was as if his eyes were straining, too. It was like he was completely awake and alert, wherever they were.

Then the dream unfroze. Chrith was shifting behind him. He scrambled to his feet, wondering if she had felt him, though she gave no such hint. As he pulled himself up, Victoria spoke.

"Vickie," She whimpered quietly. Her voice was shaking so much it was almost impossible to hear. She was staring, transfixed, at the spot where a person would have been standing if the shadow had had a tangible owner.

It's like I'm the only one that can't see it... Roman considered. This was his best theory so far, yet it didn't change the dream in any sort of way.

"Your full name, my dear," said the invisible man.

Victoria hesitated, swallowing and gasping. Roman expected tears to start falling at any moment.

Finally, she seemed to muster up what was left of her courage. "Victoria Genevieve Chuffinch." Her voice was still shaking, but it was more audible.

"Ah, a middle name," commented the man. "I'm not very fond of middle names. I much more appreciate nicknames. My preferred nickname is Emote."

The voice had been calm, but the name Emote hit Roman like a truck. That name had been mentioned in his dream about the day he had joined the Talismen. Chrith had said, *"We'd better get him out of there soon, or we'll have to explain to Emote"*. Emote seemed to be introducing himself to Victoria.

This is when Chrith told Victoria about the Strayers...

Roman's instinct had been correct. Victoria was a Strayer, along with Chrith.

"As for your friend here, her little nickname, I shall only

[133]

say once you've been…properly inducted. Pleased to meet you, Miss Chuffinch. I'm sure that you'll get along with us just fine. Why don't we have a little chat about your initiation?"

Victoria swallowed. The dream shifted before he offered any explanation.

The coldness had gone, and Roman was back to being nothing more than an apparition. It was very dark. Roman could hardly tell what was going on until light shifted across the wall behind him. It had come from a car's headlights shining through a window on the wall in front of Roman. He was in a room that was in the standard shape for bedrooms in Katy. He could hardly see anything else when the street went dark again. Roman couldn't understand why the streetlamps weren't turned on, but he heard the creaking of a door behind him. Roman could just make out a shadow against shadows. A small glint hit his eyes for a moment as something metal shifted.

Someone stepping lightly across a carpeted floor was all that Roman could hear. Then he heard a swishing, and a sickening thud that sent shivers up his spine. A shifting of sheets. A second sickening thud after a swish. The sound of small impacts hitting cloth. Roman waited with baited breath to see what was going on.

A flash of something horrible sent him screaming awake.

"Hey, my hair isn't *that* bad," scolded Sarah.

They were the only two in the lounge. The lights were not on in the computer room or ballroom. The main hallway was lit just enough for basic sight, but not for anybody whose eyes had been seeing light for many hours. The lounge lights, however, were on full blast and stung Roman's eyes. Rubbing them, Roman sat up. He was still on the couch. The cold sweat that had left him was back again, and his heart felt like it would burst from his chest at any given moment.

"W-what time is it?" Roman asked Sarah.

"It's about one in the morning. Something wrong with your bed?"

"What? No. I fell asleep on accident." Roman tried to

[134]

regain his breath, but it wouldn't come. He looked over his shoulder into the darkness of the other rooms, and suddenly felt thankful for the lights that were on.

"Have a nightmare?" Sarah whispered.

Roman wanted to say something along the lines of *no duh*, but instead he swallowed and nodded.

"Anything about you-know-what?"

"Yeah," Roman breathed.

"Well?"

"I think I might know where we can get a hint of whatever we're trying to find. And Victoria's a Strayer."

"Mind giving any more details?"

"Right now I would," Roman's throat felt dry, and his head was throbbing as if he had never gone to sleep in the first place.

"Why? I don't have all night."

"Because I just watched Victoria murder her parents. That's why."

Roman slept with the lights on that night. It wasn't hard to get to sleep; it was hard staying asleep. He did not dream any other tangible dreams, but had flashes of nightmares of knives and guns. When he woke up, he was conflicted between being happy to be going to school and the urge to milk his newly-found excuse to miss school. He would be happy to be going, so that he wouldn't have to attempt to sleep anymore, but he was also very tired. His experience told him that it was better to miss school when sick, then do the makeup work when feeling better. But this time, he could hardly stop pacing while waiting for the bus to arrive. His pacing was interrupted by Jacob, Millo, Sarah, and Treaver asking for details about his latest dream. This time, they met beside the lake. It wasn't obscured by anything, but they were out of hearing range. They would be able to see anyone else coming from a mile away.

Roman was shaking by the time he had finished telling them, this time in greater detail. Surprisingly, Millo was the least horrified. Even Jacob's mouth was open slightly, while Sarah

[135]

looked close to screaming. Treaver looked more like Roman had, horrified and unsure of how to react at the same time.

"How d'you know that they were her parents?" Jacob broke the silence.

"Well they looked exactly like her," Roman said, "but I also just sort of knew. It's like how I automatically assumed that Victoria was a Strayer in the first place."

"Well, I think we can all agree that that was her initiation," Treaver panted. "That's the Strayers for ya."

"But *why*?"

"Being a Genedeaue is genetic," Sarah spoke. "So one of her parents was probably a Genedeaue, or both. If they hadn't already joined the Strayers, then they were a threat. Or there could be some other reason. What *I'm* wondering is: if there was a murder here in Katy, then why haven't we heard about it before now? Don't you think that would have been on the news?"

"You've got a really good point there," Jacob agreed. "How come? I mean, sure, she pro'ly lives with the Strayers now, but there would've been some sort of adoption form or something."

"Yeah..." Treaver rubbed his chin. "But how are we supposed to find anything like that? I mean, if there was a case, then it might be online. But if there wasn't, then there isn't much of a lead."

"Yes, there is," Millo said quietly, catching everyone's attention, "Roman, do you remember what part of the bayou that Chrith and Victoria were about to enter before your dream changed?"

"A bit...but judging from how long they were walking, it could take us forever to find," Roman sighed.

"On foot," Jacob pointed out. "If it's a regular meeting place, then they'll have some sort of anti-radar like us. But do you remember what was written on those crates?"

"If I spoke French or Chinese then I might have."

"Well, you don't remember *any* of it?"

"I was a bit preoccupied."

"It probably said something about the company," Sarah

[136]

dismissed, "but it'd have to be a universal shipping company."

"They looked like those things in that movie *The Wild.*"

"The green box that Ryan snuck off into?"

"Yeah, like those."

"Well, they're adding onto the zoo, but they wouldn't just leave their crates lying around."

"I'm not sure if—"

"Shh!" Treaver silenced them. Roman glanced at where he was looking. Jill was running toward them.

"What are you doing?" he demanded. "The bus is about to leave and—Millo? What are you doing up so early?"

"We just wanted to talk before school," Jacob said coolly.

"Well, Millo, you'll need your sleep for today. I got you guys a combat session with Jace."

Jacob moaned. "Well, it's too late for 'im to go back to sleep, anyway. C'mon guys, let's go."

Millo went back inside the mansion. Sarah, Treaver, Roman, Jill, and Jacob rushed back to the bus. What hit Roman wasn't that they'd had another dead-end, but that the Talisman bus was late to the school. Every kid who was paying attention from any other bus saw that Roman had gotten off of the Talismen bus, and then the rumor that they were who he had been adopted by spread like wildfire throughout the school. Even seventh and eighth graders that did not know him seemed intrigued by this. Chris was in the eighth grade, and Stacy was in the seventh grade, which meant that they were already labeled as Treaver, Sarah, Danny, Cole, and Jasmine had been. This meant that most of the school was very curious and asked Roman questions about the mansion. Roman refused to answer them, and other rumors similar to the old ones sprang up, only this time they applied to Roman. No one knew anything about the mansion, and ever since someone wondered why none of the many students who lived at the mansion ever spoke about their home, there had been an aura of eccentricity around the mansion kids. Now that Roman was known as being a resident of the Talismen mansion, several kids that Roman had considered friends began avoiding him. Hal turned out to have given spark to many of the rumors, since he had mentioned to a few people that Cole had paid him to get Roman to walk home. There were thoughts as ridiculous as mind control and aliens and ones that were as suspicious as the witness-protection-program and kidnapping. There were a chosen few who either didn't care for the Talismen students, didn't know who they were, or thought that everyone was overreacting, but not many. This was some of the thickest gossip that everyone at St. Patrick's were so rarely able to enjoy.

Caleb, Allan, Tj, and Rachel seemed unaffected by the rumors, aside from asking many questions to which Roman did not answer. Tj, Rachel, and Allan had never heard any of the talk, and were very interested in what Roman had to say about them. Though Roman was careful not to contradict any of the rumors too closely, he still managed to rant for almost the whole lunch period. The rest of their time in the cafeteria was occupied by people walking up to them to ask for a chance to sit next to them. Caleb and Allan took this as a good thing, and that Roman was now very popular. But even Rachel seemed to know that this was not the favored kind of popularity. It struck Roman that he neglected to watch Victoria and Chrith's table during lunch. He spent all of English, Spanish, and Advisory fretting over the fact that Chrith and Victoria weren't thick enough not to put two and two together and realize that the Talismen were at their very school, and that Roman was one of them.

As soon as Roman stepped off of the bus when they arrived back at the mansion, he dashed back inside and up to Mr. Garretson's office. He was thankful that he sat so close to the front, otherwise Treaver, Sarah, or Jacob would have been able to cut him off.

It occurred to Roman that Mr. Garretson was off on a business trip when he knocked and there was no answer. Upon realizing this, Roman dashed back downstairs to wait for Jace to come inside. Sarah and Treaver were waiting in the hallway, though. They called Roman over.

"You look like the living dead," Treaver commented. "What's wrong?"

"What's to keep Chrith and Victoria from knowing who we are?" Roman demanded silently.

"Roman, do you honestly think that *that's* what we have to worry about?" Sarah scowled. "We've had that covered for years after Mr. Kyle had that episode with his brother. But it's a closely guarded secret for mentors only. Anyways, where'd you go?"

"I was looking for Mr. Kyle to ask him how we kept Strayers from keeping track of us *outside* of the mansion."

"Couldn't help but notice," Treaver interjected, "that you said Mr. *Kyle*."

"What? No, I didn't!"

"Roman, it's nothing to be ashamed of. You should be glad, you're catching on quickly."

"Probably because of how much he's going through with our little side mission," Treaver mused.

"*I didn't say Kyle.*"

"You did, newbie. Just face it. Oh," Sarah smiled, "here comes Jacob."

Jacob was emerging from the right side-hallway.

"Yep, he decided to show up once I left," Jacob commented.

"That's how you know when the food will arrive when you're at a restaurant," Treaver said factually. "When somebody leaves the table. Especially when Renaldo's one of the people at the table."

"Anyways, I was thinking—" Jacob started.

"How about we go out for a walk first?" Sarah asked, her eyes flicking to the kitchen. A second later, the door opened and Stacy came out, yawning and stretching her arms.

"Oh, hey guys. Have you seen Tyler around?"

"Nope, sorry," Treaver replied. "But knowing him, he's probably in the gym waiting for you. You're looking great today, by the way."

"Oh, thanks. Well, if you see Tyler, tell him that I'll be napping. We had *four* exams today. I hate French. No offense, Jacob," she added quickly.

[139]

"None taken. But I can tutor you any time you want."

"Right. Well, TTYL!" She sprinted up the left flight of stairs.

"Treaver, that was truly pathetic," Roman told him.

"Oh, shut up. I'd like to see you come up with anything when she's just walking out of the kitchen."

"You know, if you want a small chance with her, then you should tell her the truth," Sarah said nonchalantly. "I mean, she'll probably just feel awkward, but still...Tyler's kind of a butt-hole."

"Excuse me, but can we go for that walk now?" Jacob asked. "I mean, as interesting as Treaver's love life is, we've got slightly more pressing matters."

"Whatever," Treaver crossed his arms, "but where should we go? I don't think it's such a good idea talking about you-know-what outside of the mansion grounds."

"How about we just go to the courtyard?" Roman sighed.

"Well, it's obvious enough that you're still getting dreams," Treaver concluded after they had been talking for a few minutes.

"Unfortunately."

"So we keep doing nothing?" Sarah inquired.

"I didn't say that. We'll still have to keep an eye on them. We also *could* try to find that place. Or, what would be easier, follow them."

"What? Stalk them? What if they catch us?"

"Then we run back to the mansion. But unless Roman gets a new dream—"

"—which'll probably happen—"

"—then it's the best we've got. So yeah, we do nothing."

In the tool-use class, Roman learned that the reason that throwing knives took practice was because he had to use his fingers. This time, he managed to get inside of the second ring of the target Tyler had brought into the basketball court.

"Excellent!" Tyler commented. "Trev, he's giving you a run for your money. Who knows? Maybe *he* should be maggot

[140]

and *you* should be larva."

"Oh, I can't take the pain!" Treaver mocked theatrically. "How can I ever *possibly* go on?"

"So," Tyler said to Roman, ignoring Treaver, "why not give it about six more shots, then we'll move onto arrows. With arrows, by the way, you *don't* use as much finger-coordination. It's more just the muscles next to your index finger and your thumb. But try using all of your fingers, and the floor'll need some *serious* waxing. Same goes for…everything, pretty much."

Roman was beginning to wish that he'd had the knives back. On his second-to-last try with them, he would have gotten a bull's-eye if Treaver hadn't sneezed the moment that he had thrown it. It missed the center by a centimeter, and his confidence was gone on his last go. His largest accomplishment with arrows was managing to hit the target once, and hitting the center of the backboard, which then was taken down for repairing the crack. Tyler and Treaver introduced him to the different uses of pocketknives. These were harder to throw, and not worth throwing in the first place. There were several other things that Roman didn't think would ever come in handy. Afterwards, Tyler went off to instruct Treaver on some of the more advanced tools, some that required skills only useful at the mansion, and left Roman swinging a sword, feeling asinine.

Once the session was over and several scratches had been made in the padding along the walls, Roman, though not tired, went directly to his room. Something was nagging at him. It was something about his dream, though he couldn't put his finger on it.

Then a question that none of the others had asked occurred to him. In Mr. Garretson's dream, he had been frozen along with the dream for a moment. Roman hadn't froze in that dream, and the same when his latest dream had gone still. In the first vision, Mr. Garretson had not seen the man talking to his brother. This, Roman was sure of, was the reason that it had been frozen in the first place; so that Mr. Garretson would miss that particular part. So if the last dream had frozen for *that* reason, why had his latest dream frozen?

Roman tried to recall every detail of the hollow, but after a few minutes of lying in bed, his mind started wandering. He wished that his attention span was slightly longer. He focused on every detail of his dream, even trying to read the writing on the crates at one point. At the very end, all Roman had needed to see of the scene was the one last flash of murder that he had caught. But was the flash the *only* thing that he was supposed to see in the first place?

Roman tried to remember how he woke up. It had been a horrible nightmare, he had awakened in a cold sweat. But he'd had a cold sweat two other times in his tangible dream, so why had he awakened that time? Was it Sarah that had interrupted his dream, or had that been the time that he was meant to wake?

There was only one answer to that question, and the only way to find it was to see if the dream was continuous. This time, the only thing that would interrupt his sleep was his alarm clock. Though, when he turned off the lights, he was ashamed that he kept looking over his shoulder when tossing in his bed. He eventually gave in and turned on the television, letting the pictures substitute for the light that had let him sleep last night. With the sound, he need not hear every creaking floor-board or the footsteps of other students out in the hallway.

The answer was immediate once he was asleep. The flash had turned into a scene. Suddenly, he felt a spinning sensation, and knew that the dream was changing.

They were back in the hollow. Now, the crates had no writing on them. Roman cursed under his breath. It was mid-afternoon, most likely around four o'clock. Chrith was at the end of the hollow where she and Victoria had entered previously, leaning against a blue crate and checking something with her nails. Victoria was in the center of the hollow, walking in the direction opposite of Roman.

Then Victoria turned around, still appearing to pace, but walked through Roman. The cold sensation came back to Roman. Chrith and Victoria looked over at an orange crate to Roman's left. Roman felt his breathing going shallow as the shadow appeared to have landed on the ground next to the crate, scattering sand and dust.

Chrith came forward to stand slightly behind Victoria. Victoria stood still, almost like a statue, a gaunt expression on her face, but a fiery glint in her eyes. Roman noticed that her hair was in a pony-tail, and that she had no makeup on. She had planned on coming here this time.

"Good work. And on the first night." The snakelike voice did not fail to send shivers up Roman's spine, as if he were hearing it for the first time.

"From now on," the voice continued, "you may call Chrithesma by her usual name in school, but *otherwise* as Airvo. And of course, for you, you will be…Aesthe."

Victoria lost the glint of fire in her eyes, looking at where the shadow's owner would be standing.

"It's…an honor…"

"Oh, no need for speeches. They're a waste of time. As much as I'd like to give you time to…compose yourself, there's much work to do. You will be—"

The rest, Roman didn't hear. The dream faded, and Roman felt his eyes opening, feeling almost dizzy from lying down.

It *had* been a recurring dream. But the writing on the boxes was gone, which could've been a very useful lead.

The dreams have meanings… Roman concentrated. What were the meanings of the other dreams? The first, at the mansion, was that Trent had joined the Strayers to protect something. The second, years later, was how he had changed from that experience, that there were signs that he would join the Strayers. The third at the construction site, he had found out that Chrith was a Strayer and had heard the name Emote for the first time. For the one in reading class, Roman had been told not to tell Mr. Garretson about *any* of his recent dreams. Then, he had found out that Victoria was a Strayer, and about the hollow. But knowing about the hollow was useless unless they could find it. This time, the writing on the boxes had been erased completely, which meant that he wasn't supposed to be focusing on that.

[143]

This dream had been short, it should be easy to find the meaning. That Victoria had succeeded in becoming a Strayer? But if she hadn't, then she would be dead, or at least wouldn't be hanging around Chrith. What else had they done in the dream?

They got their nicknames, Roman suggested halfheartedly to himself. But soon he felt himself opening his eyes again. He didn't *have* to have heard the nicknames if they weren't relevant, did he?

They were Emote, Airvo, and Aesthe...

10. Answer and Lead

Φ   Φ   Φ

"So we're sticking with nothing," Treaver commented.

"Not exactly. Keep on the lookout for those names."

"But they're *weird*. I know *I'm* going to have trouble remembering them. Except Airvo. That one's kind of easy."

"And then there's Emote and…Asethe?" Sarah said.

"*Ae*sthe," Roman corrected.

Roman could hear Millo muttering the names under his breath.

There was hail outside, so Roman, Millo, Jacob, Sarah, and Treaver had been forced inside. Mary Beth, however, was in one of the study rooms measuring the walls and floor. Right then, they were in the storage closet of the right side-hallway. Roman was sitting on an upturned pail, Jacob and Millo next to him. Sarah was looking uncomfortable against the wall, since they had to make room for Treaver's chair.

"And the writing was completely gone, so this is what we've got left," Roman concluded.

"Don't you think it's convenient that every time we wish for something in one of your dreams, it comes true?" Jacob pointed out. "First, you get suspicious about Victoria, then when we wait for you to have another dream, one comes immediately with your answer on a silver platter. And then, once we try to get a clue out of the boxes, it gets really obvious that we're wrong."

"So?" Sarah said. "It's not like wondering about this will get us anywhere."

"Actually, it could," Jacob argued.

"How?" Asked Roman, Treaver, and Sarah at the same time.

"Well, that means that '*they*' obviously know what we're doing outside of Roman's dreams. So as long as we don't act rashly, we can't really go wrong, now can we?"

"That's a comforting thought!" Treaver responded enthusiastically.

"Yeah, so we just watch our steps," Roman summarized. "It's kind of annoying, though."

"The dreams are pretty bad, huh?" Sarah sympathized.

"Oh, yeah. They are. But I was thinking; if I have to look for a plot in the dreams, isn't that what they're teaching us about in reading class? Summarizing passages? I mean, I'm kind of pissed that the class isn't completely useless. That means I have less argument against it. Ms. Auster is *really* strict."

"Dude, school sucks in particular. But we can't do anything about it until high school," Treaver daubed.

"What can *we* do about it?" Jacob asked.

"Oh, it's just that you can drop out in high school."

"If we're done with our meeting," Sarah sighed. "Can we please get out of this closet? I think that whatever's behind me is going to tear my shirt any second."

Roman, now paying attention during lunch, kept turning his head to the table where Chrith, Victoria, Arnold, and Sadie sat. They seemed to be acting perfectly normal, if writing on Sadie's face with mascara counted as normal. After a dozen looks, Tj wondered why Roman kept looking over his shoulder.

"Hmm? I wasn't," Roman responded.

"Whatever. Are you going to try to slap back in or what?"

Tj was slightly taller than Roman, and older. His hair was often compared to fire due to its orange color, turning a deeper red the closer it was to his scalp, and almost mouse-brown down near his shoulders. He grew his hair long, and his bangs often covered the majority of his eyes. He had brown eyes and a disposition much like Jace's, normally quiet and he mumbled when he talked, though he was very observant. Today, he had on his denim jacket with jeans, covering most of his freckled skin, and his wristband from *Hot Topic*.

After Rachel, who everyone else was starting to warm up to, had taken her turn, Roman noticed that she had laid down two sixes in a row and slapped it to get back in the game. He collected his cards and nearly dropped them when Chrith yelled at the top of her lungs, *"That's what she said!"*

The rest of the cafeteria responded by calling out different colors. Mr. Spided had to calm the crowd by threatening detention.

"Hey, I said green *first!*" Allan growled at Caleb.

"*I* did!" Caleb argued.

Noticing the familiar twitch in Caleb's left eye, Roman knew that he was lying.

"*I* heard Caleb say it first," Rachel mused.

"*What?* You need to check your hearin', girl."

"Hey, she has a name," Caleb said heatedly.

"You're just saying that because she sided with you," Tj chuckled.

"No," Caleb defended calmly. Roman hadn't seen the twitch.

I must've blinked, Roman dismissed.

Roman was happy when Mr. Spided escorted Chrith out of the cafeteria, and felt his shoulders relax slightly. There was still Victoria, though. This kept him looking over his shoulder every time that one of the others made an impressive save in their game, while they were distracted. Victoria was acting perfectly normal by her standards. Roman had never had much interaction with her in elementary school, and since she had assumedly joined the Strayers at the beginning of the year, Roman had little to no memory of her and how she had acted before she had committed her first murder. Had she always been like that? Did she change when she met Chrith, or had Emote done something to her? How had her parents treated her? Had they neglected her? These mind-boggling questions caused Roman to lose almost as badly as he had the first time he had ever played the game at lunch.

Treaver had some sort of competition for orchestra, and had stayed after at school along with Jasmine. Sarah invited Roman to sit in her row on the bus. Chris enjoyed the elbow room in his seat across from theirs by lying back against the window and propping his feet up onto the edge of their seat.

"Ya know, it's not all that bad when Trev's got concerts," he commented.

"Just keep your shoes on, CR," Sarah told him, staring disapprovingly at his *Sketchers*. "We don't need your foot stink on our seat."

"Well, in that case," Chris immediately did the opposite of Sarah's request, using his ankles to kick off his shoes into the isle.

Sarah smiled. "Tisk-tisk-tisk, you aren't *that* gullible, are you?"

"What?" Before Chris could do more than narrow his eyes, Sarah grabbed his shoes off the floor and threw them to the back of the bus.

"Hey!"

"Yes?" Sarah asked innocently. "Oh, by the way, someone wrote gullible on your socks," she added.

Chris looked down at his socks before he realized Sarah had tricked him. He growled and shouted to Tyler, telling him to give him his shoes back. Sarah popped her head over the back of her seat and motioned to them not to oblige Chris. The others in the back made up their minds; they immediately started playing catch with Chris's shoes.

Chris stood up.

"Hey, Chris! Sit back down!" Jace called from the driver's seat.

"But they took my—"

"You think I don't know what happened? Don't let Sarah trick you next time."

Chris crossed his arms and sat down, glaring at Sarah.

"So did you hear anything?" Sarah asked Roman.

"Um...no."

"I still don't know why Mr. Kyle doesn't just punish you two right now, when you're so *very* obviously up to something." Chris muttered.

"Innocent until proven guilty," Sarah chimed. She turned

back to Roman. "Anyways, I haven't either. And neither has Treaver."

"How do you know that?"

"He's in my advisory. Are we just going to wait?"

"What do you want from me? Want me to take a nap when we get back to the mansion?" Roman demanded sarcastically.

"Yes. Yes, I do."

Roman's dreams weren't anything special. By the time he had awakened, it was time for his first medical-use class. His power being medical related, Roman had to use almost no concentration during the hour, leaving him plenty of time to run over the flashes of dreams that he had had, except when Treaver needed his help remembering what was poisonous and what would reduce swelling. Roman recalled having a dream about small dolls that opened up to have even smaller dolls inside of them, eventually ending in a Slinky. Then, he'd had a dream that he was a character in *Island of the Blue Dolphins*; they had been reviewing the last chapter in class. First, he was a wild dog watching the fight for dominance before the girl had arrived. Then, his dreams changed to something about kangaroos. Roman knew that since he hadn't experienced the same vividness in these dreams, or the coldness that he had started feeling very recently, that it was pointless to try and interpret these as visions. Roman also knew that he shouldn't have eaten *Coca Puffs* before he went to sleep, unless he wanted to have more dreams like those.

"Hey, Roman?" Treaver nudged him in the side.

"Yeah?"

"This cream starts with the word *di*, so that means that it isn't safe to eat, right?"

"No, *di* means two in Latin. And technically it's a prefix."

"That's stupid. Maybe *die* is like...your soul leaving your body, so now you've got two selves," Treaver wondered.

"Whatever helps you remember it."

The MUCs took place outside when the weather was

[149]

clear, and in the lab when the weather was bad. This was to prevent anything poisonous, or any dangerous chemicals, from accidentally being misplaced or getting anywhere that they could be touched or consumed. The lab supposedly had sinks at the exit. Roman wondered cynically why the tool-use classes were in the basketball court if they could be outside. Even if it wasn't ideal to have people with dangerous weapons moving around people with dangerous substances, they could have one class on either side of the mansion.

"Dude, if you're good enough with weapons, then you wouldn't *have* to worry about anything inside," Treaver explained like it was obvious. "Besides, why *should* we do it outside? I mean, inside it's air-conditioned and safer. You can get extra practice outside if you want, on top of the animal-attacks ones. And we have those outside when you're ready for cross-country, but you're a little early."

"Then why didn't *you* have your last one outside? Needed Tyler's help?"

"It's just...I like a smooth floor."

Roman immediately felt guilty. "Guess it's not worth complaining about, anyways," he mumbled in a subdued tone as Tyler walked towards them to examine Roman practicing leg-bandages.

For the remainder of the week, Roman still had no hint that he was going to have any more dreams. It was agreed that none of them were willing to try anything outside of the boundaries that they had established until each of them had given in. Millo suggested that they tell Mr. Kyle, which shocked Jacob, who knew Millo the best.

"That's deliberately going against what Roman was told. If we're trusting that the other dreams are real, why not that one?" Jacob inquired.

Millo shrugged and didn't answer, looking even more apprehensive than usual.

Roman's training was going well, since Treaver had taken time off of his spear-practice to show Roman how to hold a sword. Tyler was agitated when he put two and two together and had figured that Treaver had been going against him saying to practice with a spear. His punishment had been polishing the tips of the only two spears that the Talismen owned, except that Tyler would use one while Treaver was cleaning the other, leaving him the first to clean again. This went on for longer than the rest of the training session, and Roman had finished watching *The Last Airbender* before Treaver came in, complaining that chores were meant to be useful.

The PCG classes were becoming increasingly boring. Roman found it harder and harder to concentrate on the lessons, now that he was used to the feel of the room and had been settled in his chair. Jace and Tyler, more grudgingly, allowed Roman to bring a pencil and paper to class and draw while they were talking. This worked for about ten minutes, before Roman lost what they were saying and became absorbed in his badly drawn dogs and cats. But Roman remembered almost everything from his last time, which was more than most students could say for their PCGs, according to Sarah. Without as many chores as at St. Jefferson's, Roman had spare time even on the days that he had homework in three different subjects. He found himself trying to hang around his friends above anything else. Mr. Garretson returned from his trip Thursday afternoon, and called Roman into his office not long after.

"Come in," came the usual reply before Roman had gotten a chance to knock.

"Why does the sign say "please knock" if you're going to call people in beforehand?" Roman wondered as he slipped inside. There was a black briefcase opened on Mr. Garretson's desk. Unlike how Roman had ever seen him, Mr. Garretson's hair was smoothed over, by either a comb or gel or both. He was wearing a white suit, not different from how doctor's uniforms were. He had glasses on, but the lenses didn't seem to have any glare and were thinner than its rims. When Roman walked in he took the glasses off and set them down on his desk.

"Well, then the sign would have no meaning, would it? Everyone here knows that they need not knock, but they also all know that I am resident to this room, which is the entire purpose of the sign in the first place."

"Then why not take the sign down?"

"That particular sign will have been on the Talismen leaders' doors for two centuries starting in June. We simply find a way to wash off the name and replace it with the new name. Most adults nowadays would refer to it as being *sentimental*."

Roman cleared his throat apologetically. "So you wanted to see me?" he prompted. Roman could already guess that Mr. Garretson wanted to check and see how he was adjusting to mansion life. But Roman was slightly suspicious as far as he was concerned about the dreams he had been having lately, and hoped desperately that it didn't show in his eyes.

"I just wanted to see how you were getting along with the other students, dealing with schoolwork, et cetera. The first week's always the hardest as far as training goes, you know," he told Roman.

"Well, it's going fine. Except..." He was on the edge of possibly giving a hint to Mr. Garretson about his dreams. He swallowed, fretting the answer. "Well, uh, Tyler keeps calling me larva," he covered.

"Oh, Tyler. He's actually a very bright boy. Just a little thick sometimes. He knows what he's doing as far as you and Treaver are concerned, though. Just not very good social skills."

"Yeah, but he made Treaver polish the spears, and kept getting them rough and dirty again!" Roman took advantage of his words and added more passion to make it slightly more convincing. This wasn't hard, considering that he honestly thought that Tyler was being unreasonable.

"Well, I'm sure that Tyler had some sort of character trait in mind that he wanted to impose onto Treaver. Perhaps to follow rules, as all punishments are—"

"But then he could've given Treaver a punishment that benefited someone! Like washing dishes!"

"Ah, but Tyler hates washing the dishes, so why would he put Treaver through that? By singling Treaver out with a different sort of punishment than others get, added to the constant attention required if Tyler kept giving him more spears, that serves as a much more effective punishment than simply telling him to stand in a corner or teaching him a valuable cleaning skill."

From the way Mr. Garretson said it, Roman could find no possible way to argue.

"He stills calls me larva, though," Roman muttered.

"We all have our nicknames," Mr. Garretson said absent-mindedly, unpacking some dark-colored socks from the briefcase. Roman felt the hairs on his neck standing on end at the word *nickname*.

Mr. Garretson, not noticing anything, continued. "As a matter of fact, I strictly recall Jace referring to me as "goat" for almost all of my training because of how well I could climb rocks. I complained that it was technically incorrect and that rams were the mountain-goats, but he wouldn't listen. He was having too much fun. But old habits die hard. I remember hearing this morning, Jay calling Stacy a newbie by accident."

"So would it be all right if I called you "goat" from now on?" Roman inquired after breathing a sigh of relief.

"No," Mr. Garretson responded flatly.

"How about ram?"

"No."

"Mountain-goat?"

"No."

"Almighty destroyer of universes?"

"Creative, but no."

"Cheshire Cat?"

"*That*, I might settle for. Except most students manage to settle for 'Mr. Kyle'."

"Well, I'm not most students, am I?"

"You certainly aren't," he agreed quietly. Roman was struck by how gravely serious the Talismen leader sounded. Remembering his dream, and all of his other, more recent dreams, he wondered: Was this all because he was somehow singled out from the other students, as Treaver had been singled out by Tyler? Roman wasn't sure if he could very well stand being singled out amongst people as unique as Genedeaues.

"How come you always seem to make me think about life?" he asked Mr. Garretson.

"I like to call it a striking disposition," he answered cheerfully, closing the top of the briefcase, locking it, and throwing it onto the bed in his room through the open door.

That night, instead of being so exhausted that he could hardly keep his eyes open, Roman tossed and turned around in his bed, flipping the covers off, and hitting his pillow in frustration around one a.m., knowing that he had to wake up in less than five hours to get ready for school. He cursed the school's early schedule under his breath. That was why the next day at school went by very slowly, with Roman absorbing very little.

On Friday, after his next PCG class, Roman purposely forgot to wake Treaver and stumbled into bed. Roman fell asleep before he had managed to fully pull the covers over himself.

This was by far his oddest dream yet. Once again, he had the floating sensation that he had felt at the end of his first dreams with Mr. Garretson. All around him were not purple and black swirls, but blue, yellow, and red stripes. Once again, he tried to move, but failed miserably. All around him, the stripes stood petrified, making Roman feel strangely giddy if he stared at one point for too long. While trying to control his breath, which came in short gasps, and his heart, feeling like it would burst out of his chest at any moment, he willed the stripes to do something.

Instantly, taking his mind off of his fear, the stripes mixed with each other, forming every other color that he could think of. Soon, the colors had a certain pattern. Roman didn't know why, but he was forced to look in one direction. It wasn't that he couldn't move his head or eyes, it was more as if he was tired and spacing out. The top edge of his vision had warm colors, the bottom corner turned so cool that it was nearly black. Each layer of color was blending into the others as it sloped down. It might've been almost beautiful if Roman had control of his body, or at least had his legs on the ground.

From the darkest part of the green, a splotch was breaking off. It formed into a massive blob larger than the whole green

[154]

area, though it moved steadily right and it was as if nothing had ever been on the other side. The blotch rearranged itself, forming shapes. Roman recognized first the shape as an 'o'. Steadily, he recognized the shapes of the different letters, except for one shape near the bottom. But every time that Roman tried to focus on the last shape, it moved to the edge of his vision. He couldn't chase it around the place, since he couldn't move his head, and could hardly focus on different areas without moving his eyes. He noticed that the letters were next to each other, and there were many of them. He tried to see if they spelled out anything, but just as he couldn't focus on the last shape, he could only focus on one letter at a time.

It was like his brain was working three times slower. He could identify the letters, but he couldn't make them spell out anything. He was growing furious with himself. Then he couldn't even kick his legs, or move his arms. He tried once more to move his head, but as soon as he had so much as twitched his head to the right, everything went dark.

Roman could see only darkness because his eyes were shut tight. He couldn't move his legs because they were stiff from being in the same position while he slept, the same going for his arms. He was breathing through his nose, but his mouth was open. He felt a cold area stretching from his lips down his right cheek. Sitting up, he raised his arm to wipe the drool off of his face. Looking at the dim light coming from the hallway, his eyes hurt slightly. It had been a very deep sleep.

Glancing at his alarm clock, it was two a.m. He had been asleep for over six hours. Roman didn't feel tired in the least bit, now that his eyes were open. He tried to think of something else do, and a minute later found himself on the fifth floor checking inside of the conference room to see if Treaver had ever woken up. Since his seat was vacant, Roman assumed that he had.

Going back to the stairs, Roman felt the hairs rising on the back of his neck. He turned his head, and realized that he was looking right at the door to Mr. Garretson's office. Was he having a dream like Roman's? Was he in Roman's dream without Roman knowing about it? Was he the one sending the dreams in the first place?

Roman shook his head to clear it. He ran down the stairs and into the lounge, making sure that the lights were on in every direction he could see. He flopped down on the couch, but didn't feel like watching television. What would've been on, anyway, at two in the morning? He could do his social studies project on the Columbian Exchange, but his brain wasn't working fast enough to remember what century it had taken place in without straining himself. Roman felt his eyes wandering absently around the room. A folded up paper had been missed in the corner of the room, and someone's clear, plastic cup, half full of orange juice, was left next to one of the computers. It was no doubt Jill's, since he had been going online searching for colleges every day, and that orange juice had citric acid in it. Since Jill's second power involved being able to create acid, Jill normally took to things acidic, or at the very least, uncomfortable to most people's skin, settling for things that were warm if it came down to it. There was a notepad on the nearest table, moved around so that it was in sight of the TV. The top corner of the last sheet was still there, Roman guessed that whoever had scribbled something down on it had been in a rush.

Roman went to look and see if he could read what was written there. He could just make out a dollar sign before the tear in the page. It had definitely been scribbled down in a hurry, since it was only barely distinguishable. The pen it had been written with lay right next to the pad, cap off. It had definitely been thrown aside after the message had been written. Staring at the pen, Roman suddenly had an idea.

Grabbing the pen, he closed his eyes. The dream, he could remember as vividly as the back of his hand. The first letter, the one next to it, the ones below…

He wasn't even watching where he was writing, since his eyes were closed. His hand didn't go off the page. When he had reached the symbol at the bottom, it was almost distinguishable, and very familiar. Opening his eyes, Roman read the letters. They looked slightly different from in the dream, since they had been in green bubble letters, and were now in blue ink. But there was no misjudging what the letters spelled out.

St. Patrick's Art Committee is proud to present...

The St. Patrick Junior High School Art Club! Meetings every day during advisory. Advisory passes will be supplied by the 8th grade art teacher, Ms. Hue.

Below, in his dream, there had been lines with more letters on top of them. These were what was staring Roman in the eye, what were making his stomach lurch.

ASHLEY DOPPIO
Vicky Chuffinch
Chrith Vladmir

This wasn't even Roman's regular handwriting. Stomach turning, he looked further down the list:

Jack Sulivant
Rachel Rivera

Roman's stomach performed another back-flip as he read these names. The remainder of the lines Roman had left out, since they were only lines without names. He suddenly knew what the shape at the bottom of his vision was supposed to be; the official stamp of a leprechaun hat with a four-leaf clover in it. This was the official symbol of his school's front office, so that the teachers knew what was real and what was forged. Two known Strayers were part of this new 'Art Club'. Roman remembered vaguely that it had been mentioned on the morning

[157]

announcements the day before.

It couldn't be possible that Strayers had time to have after-school activities if they wanted their gems as soon as possible, could it? It was worse that Rachel was part of this club. Roman knew that spending too much time around Chrith and Victoria could be dangerous, and he felt suspicion creeping up his spine like a tick.

It was a slight hope that, if not enough students signed up for the club, that it would be cancelled. This, however seemed unlikely. A vast majority of seventh and eighth graders were in art. If Stamp Collecting could be sustained for more than a year, which it had, then this club could, too.

Roman knew that now, if he could sleep, he would not enjoy the dreams he would have. On the weekend he, Treaver, Sarah, Jacob, and Millo would have more time on their hands to deal with this.

11. Names and Numbers

The news shocked everyone. Treaver and Sarah seemed thoroughly convinced that the whole Art Club was a trap set by the Strayers, though for what, their guess was as good as Roman's. Jacob seemed to be considering every possibility there was. That perhaps the Art Club was a cover-up, to keep Talismen from identifying Strayers if they ever got nosy. And he also thought of the different reasons for setting traps. Millo simply sat looking devastated in the grass.

Gathering beside the lake was much better than in the broom-closet, but this did not help to raise their spirits.

"Well, I think it's a simple question," Sarah sighed after a moment's silence.

"Is that so?" Treaver grumbled. "Must be so simple that we're not even thinking about it, right?"

"Exactly," Sarah said, straightening her back. "We haven't heard the nicknames, yet, right?"

"Right." Roman tried to follow this. It only seemed odd, though he couldn't shake the feeling that he was forgetting something.

"Well, you said that it was a runoff dream, correct?"

"Recurring dream, technically. But yes."

"So, if each dream had a message, and the first part had a message, then wouldn't both, if they were the same dream, only at different times, only have one message?"

Roman gasped, amusing Jacob. Millo didn't react. But Treaver smiled.

"I know that must be really smart, because I couldn't follow. So what does it mean?" Treaver inquired.

"Well..." Roman faltered. "Wait, that just means that we know what *not* to do. This isn't exactly multiple choice."

"Nope, because your latest dream was about that Art Club. Do we really want to take the chance of letting them keep up whatever they're up to, even if we don't join ourselves? I mean, even if it *is* just a hobby of theirs, then we still don't want anyone else interacting with them. So..?"

"How are we supposed to stop them from going to meetings, if that's what you're suggesting?"

"We don't. We stop it at the source."

"Get the club shut down? They could just get it set up again." Roman crossed his arms, tilting his head to one side.

"And how would we stop it in the first place?" Treaver demanded. "It'd take a lot of people signing a petition to get a club shut down. And in case you didn't notice, a lot of kids at our school enjoy art."

"There'd have to be a different reason to stop it, without the class's approval," Sarah pressed, looking at them expectantly.

"Just spit it out, we haven't got all day." Treaver rolled his eyes, exasperated.

"What if there were a safety issue, or a lack of volunteers to run it?" Jacob answered as Sarah opened her mouth to snap back at Treaver.

She smiled. "Exactly along the lines I was thinking. A safety issue should be easy to create, but getting it to seem like it's the art concept is a different story. As for lack of volunteers, having a disruptive class would be good for that kind of thing. Unless they kick us out, of course."

"Or a combination," Jacob grinned, rubbing his hands together mischievously. "I'm liking where this is going. Not *only* do we finally get to do something, but we get to be *destructive. In school.*"

"What about not being reckless?" Millo wondered feebly. He seemed to have gone very pale.

"I think that the rest of us agree that this is a good plan," Treaver pronounced rather smugly. "'Sides, we've got all weekend for Roman to have another dream telling us not to do it."

The others muttered their assent. Millo bit his protest off, before quickly catching himself. Roman wondered for the first time why Millo was so skittish. He figured that anyone with someone as confident as Jacob for a sibling would at least try to act dignified. Millo obviously wasn't living in his brother's shadow, since he voluntarily hid behind him whenever worst came to worst. Roman's thoughts were interrupted by Treaver clearing his throat.

"Actually Jacob, you and Millo won't be in the Art Club. Pantano's got its own art program, same with Tarea Elementary. That's why the districts restricted this one to middle-schoolers only."

"What?" Jacob moaned. "Fine, then. But I want something to do. Maybe I could look up something about Victoria's parents…"

Roman had almost completely forgotten that searching for information on Victoria's parents was an option. What about Chrith's? Was the initiation the same for every Strayer? What about the Strayers that had no parents?

"I've got the perfect idea for exploding paint," Treaver mused dreamily. "Just add a little bit of—"

Roman zoned out as Treaver started listing ingredients that would produce sparks and burn your eyes, even when soaked in paint. Were they finally getting somewhere after…had it only been a week? It must have been longer than that since Roman had joined the Talismen, hadn't it? There was no possible way…

With no nightmares over Saturday or Sunday night, mixed with the relaxing fact that they had a strategy was enough to get Roman out of bed on Monday morning with no hesitation. Tyler also had officially knighted Roman 'maggot'. Roman was anxious to find the sign-up sheet for the art club, at least to see how many people had signed up. Rumors would also be a traditional asset for scandalizing the art club. Thinking of rumors was amusing, and Roman could hardly suppress his excitement at causing mischief that would have a productive outcome.

During breakfast, several times he choked on his grape juice from suddenly breaking out into fits of laughter. He would be very interested in seeing how quickly each rumor would spread. He decided to eat cottage cheese, which he couldn't choke on very easily, while he mapped out the personalities of each social group and how each would best affect them. Some, Roman decided, were uncalled for, such as the volunteers fraternizing with the counselors. Some of Roman's rumors were as meek as the school being so cheap as to fund this, when funding computers would save trees. Others were as horrid as the paint being toxic. Some were ridiculous, but a good topic for conversation; such as the particular room the club would be held in being haunted by the ghost of a construction worker. This was one of Roman's favorites, as he had taken several factors from other ghost stories he had heard about the school and other schools in the area.

Before boarding the bus, the others pulled Roman aside to clarify that they were proceeding with their plan. Jacob and Millo had had very little luck searching the internet for information on Victoria's parents, mostly due to the fact that they knew very little about Victoria and her parents.

"You wouldn't think that "Chuffinch" was a very common last name, would you?" Sarah sighed. "I'm sure they'll get somewhere."

"Yeah," Treaver said quickly. "'Cept Jacob's got homework, an' Millo's not exactly computer-expert Sam."

"If you'd rather do all of the work-" Roman started.

"Oh, look at the time. Got to get to the bus. Early for everything, you know," he called over his shoulder as he wheeled out. "Early to get on the bus and early to leave for class! *Adios!*" Treaver disappeared from the room in a comical fashion before Roman could get another word out of his mouth.

Roman shook his head, noticing that Treaver had three minutes before he would've normally left. At the least he had his own amusing thoughts to keep him occupied.

"Have you guys heard about that new Art Club thing?" Roman asked the others at lunch.

"I think I saw a poster of it," Tj recollected.

[162]

"Nope." Allan didn't give it another thought.

"Shouldn't we already have an Art Club?" Caleb wondered through a mouthful of chicken with some sort of slimy orange sauce.

"Ooh! I signed up the day it went up! Don't any of you listen to the morning announcements?" Rachel exclaimed enthusiastically.

"Nope," Allan replied again.

"Uh…oh yeah! It's being held in that room…which was it again?" Caleb covered, sipping some of his milk from the taste of the horrid looking chicken.

Their lunch table was unusually crowded. The front tables were folded up against the walls to make way for some mechanics. Evidently, someone, while making something for the play, had dropped a pickax from a height of twenty or so feet. This was convenient, Roman thought, since now he wouldn't look conspicuous spreading his rumors from table to table.

He could hardly suppress a chuckle at how pathetic Caleb was acting.

"Room one-fifty-six. Ms. Hue's classroom."

"Who's Ms. Hue?" Tj asked tediously.

"The art teacher! Don't you know anything that's going on at this school besides sports?" Rachel demanded. Since basketball season had started, the regular lunch conversations were over the games, and how it compared to the already over football season.

"Nope," Allan repeated, a smile tugging at the corners of his mouth.

"I thought *I* was supposed to be new here. I've only been here for a little more than a week—"

"Hey, we get it." Tj interrupted smoothly. "Tell you what, you keep your art thing and we'll keep our sport thing."

"Well, art is kinna interesting, isn't it?" Caleb suggested feebly.

Roman took this as an opportunity.

"Yeah, art may be," he started out, "except the school's only got so much money in their pockets. The state cut funding recently, and basketball isn't as popular—"

"Wait, *what*?" Allan took interest in the conversation for the first time, setting down his apple, eyes flashing. "You mean they'll cut the b-ball budget?"

"That's what Mr. Davis says," Roman nodded. "I mean, basketball season won't last forever," he yawned and pretended not to take interest in this, "and they don't make money off of snacks like they would at the football games *outdoors*. I mean, the co-ed sports just aren't as interesting as the boys' football or girls' volleyball. I swear, *golf* gets the school more cash."

"But-but-" Caleb stammered. Allan seemed to be thinking whatever Caleb couldn't put into words.

"But we're trying out next year! If the school cuts the funding, then that doesn't affect *this year*, it'll affect *next year*!"

Tj looked up. "Uh-oh," he gulped.

"What?"

"You said that sports get the school money, right? So do the tickets to the plays. The play so far isn't going too well, I've heard. And you can see for yourself," he gestured behind his back to the closed-off stage. "If *that* isn't good and doesn't make us as much money, then that's even *less* money for sports."

Allan considered this while Caleb started sipping his milk nervously. Roman pretended to have a curious look on his face. He noticed Geoff walking by their table.

"Hey, Geoff!" Roman summoned him. "How's the play coming along?"

Geoff didn't seem surprised by the question. His brown eyes darted to the stage and back to Roman. When Geoff spoke, it was in an undertone, since a few kids had turned their heads to hear what he had to say.

"Well, we're postponing it an extra week. That means that my crew, advertising, will have to do a lot of posters and bulletin boards all over again. The actors are getting kind of impatient, since they had all of Christmas break to learn their lines. They keep interrupting our work. And when that hammer fell—"

"I thought it was a pickax," Allan inquired.

"What would we use a pickax for? Anyways, the hammer

[164]

knocked the tower over, and it'll take a while to put it back together. I just hope that no one decided to look at the old poster dates and not the new ones." He sprinted off to the full-sized table closest to the windows, head down, paying no heed to other students that tried to call him over.

"You know, Ms. Hue *would* be the kind of person to get involved in that sort of scum-ridden-scam," Allan sneered, crossing his arms. "I'd help out the theater kids if it took people instead of time."

"Hey, Ms. Hue probably doesn't even know about any budget cuts!" Rachel cried indignantly, "Stop jumping to conclusions!"

"Well, personally," Caleb bit his lip, wondering which side to take as everyone turned their attention to him, "I-I agree with Rachel."

"What?" Tj demanded.

"I'm going to a different school if they cancel football," Allan scowled, his head held high.

This statement seemed to get the attention of the table in front of theirs, which happened to hold many students in the advanced classes.

"What's this about cancelling football?" asked one boy, "My brother goes to Katy High, and we pride ourselves in being football champions."

"I doubt that they'd cancel the high school football season just because of a middle-school art club," Rachel said, exasperated.

"Haven't you been listening to the news?" asked a girl at the other table, narrowing her eyes.

"No."

"Well, they're cutting the budget for every district in the state. Sports and electives go first, since they take money from the core-classes."

Roman guessed that this girl just wanted her friends to think that she was the first to hear about the budget cuts, even though Roman had completely made them up.

"If they cancel orchestra, then someone's going to be

[165]

sorry," commented another boy. "I've already learned cello, bass, viola, and violin. I'm not throwing away a whole period of practice a day."

"We make money off of the tickets to our recitals; they wouldn't cancel us if there's a money problem," the girl frowned.

"That money pays for *our* stuff," the first boy corrected, "not the school's stuff. And what happens if something goes wrong, like it has for the play? Then we wouldn't get any help from the school and—"

"Oh god!" moaned another girl from the other side of their table. "This has *got* to just be a rumor! Orchestra *is* an elective! Football's more popular than orchestra! Everyone in boy's athletics *has* to be on the football team to get into athletics in the first place, and that's a hundred per period!"

To Roman's immense pleasure, the first girl left to talk to some other girls over at the window seats. Sarah sat over there. If she caught wind of this, then she would reinforce it, not including the fact that the most reliable source of information in the advanced classes believed that their programs were in danger.

And I've got the Pre-AP classes covered, Roman thought, checking an invisible box inside of his head.

"Allan," Roman said. "Aren't the majority of academic students in theater and home-economics?"

"Yeah…And we've got two different home-ec classes. What if they fire Mrs. Peace? But that'd leave a bunch of eighth graders without a class…"

"Then they'd go into office-aid," Rachel dismissed indignantly. "No problem there," she added, as though this settled the matter.

"That doesn't solve it!" Caleb panicked. "If they put more eighth graders in places where they do teacher work, then it's more likely that they'll fire those people!"

"But my mom works at the front office!" A girl passing by had overheard their conversation.

"The only person who's job is safe is the principal," Roman claimed off-handedly.

"Not him! He gave my sister a suspension for dying her

hair blue!"

"If he touches Mrs. Effet then the whole spelling club'll trample him," growled the second girl from the other table.

"If there's a spelling club left," Roman pointed out.

"That was so much fun," Roman said to Sarah and Treaver on the bus ride before Jace had retrieved the high schoolers. They had also, of course, signed up for the Art Club, and meetings were starting next week.

"I know," Treaver smiled, his eyes blazing playfully.

"The Scatterbrains totally freaked out when I told them that the water they wash the paint-brushes with goes into the water-fountains." Sarah rolled her eyes. "As if they'd drink 'high-carb water' in the first place."

"Scatterbrains?" Treaver inquired.

"You know, Kelsey, Lindsey, Merion, Natalie…"

It was hard not to repeat the rumors to the high schoolers once they had been picked up, especially since if the other Talismen kids told the high schoolers the same thing, then their younger siblings would hear about it, too. But Sarah warned them to let the rumors simmer for a while, so that not all of the rumors seemed to be sprouting from them. Also, Jacob would not be happy if his opportunity to play elf was crushed.

But Jacob's fun was not crushed completely. That afternoon, after Roman's first ever HHC class, in which he had lasted four whole minutes with Tyler out on the baseball diamond, Sarah pulled Roman and Treaver aside, telling them to meet her in the library.

Ellenore was leaving, looking confused, when Roman and Treaver arrived, pushing the doors open. Jacob, Millo, and Sarah were at the computer closest to the entrance, leaning over something on the screen. Roman knew immediately from the expression on Millo's face that it had to do with their research on Victoria's parents.

"Why did you guys choose the computer the farthest in the open?" Roman demanded in a whisper.

"We're not supposed to be up to anything," Sarah told

him, "and there isn't a window in sight of here, so we'd see anyone coming from a mile away. But I think you'd better take a look at this."

Jacob moved his chair out of the way so that Roman could lean in, Treaver watching over his shoulder. The screen, surprisingly, featured some sort of hotel-resort. It had colorful pictures of tropical palm-trees in the corners along with little straw huts and a beach along an ocean. The title was in letters that kept changing colors.

Layway Vacations

"What's this about?"

Jacob scrolled down and clicked on a deep green colored tab that read "Residents: Contact Friends and Family at leisure!". It took them to a page filled with names, all listed in alphabetical order. Jacob scrolled down to the *C* section. Roman's jaw dropped. Listed as one of the first, were the names "Kesha Chuffinch" and "John Chuffinch".

Jacob clicked on Kesha's name as Roman felt Treaver stiffen beside him. It pulled up a small tab underneath the name. Jacob clicked on the third option, which read "Information".

This pulled up a whole new page.

Kesha Chuffinch

Age: 34

Resident for: 4 Months

Status: Out

Relationship Status: Married

Comments: *There are no Comments available right now. Please try again later.*

There was a picture of her a the top of the page. She had long hair the same color as Victoria's, and slightly darker skin. There was not one doubt in Roman's mind that this was Victoria's mother. She was smiling and wearing a loose shirt with a flower-print. In the photo, she was standing in front of a volleyball court where some people were playing, others resting on mats.

There was more information about recent activity, but Roman had recoiled away before he had given himself a chance to read it.

"What *is* this?" he repeated. "They're dead! Why would they—"

"Exactly," Sarah interrupted. "Same with Victoria's dad. Jacob says that their statuses have been changing regularly. But who would stay at a resort for four months without their child?"

"*And* this thing doesn't say where any of these places are," Jacob said. "I also wanted to see if Chrith's parents were on here. Sarah, can you hand me the yearbook?"

"Sure." Sarah picked up the fifth-grade addition of last year's Tarea Elementary yearbook and handed it to Jacob. It had sand as a background, with a horse galloping across the bottom of the page. He opened it for them all to see. Victoria's picture was in black-and-white in the second-to-last row of pictures. Sarah leaned over his shoulder as he started flipping through it.

"There!" Sarah pointed at an equally colorless photo of Chrith as she had been a year previously. Small print next to her photo listed her last name, "Vladmir".

Maybe now's a bad time to mention that she signed her last name on the sign-up sheet...

Jacob went back to the list of names and scrolled down to almost the very bottom of the page. There were another two names listed as "Vladmir". "Philip Vladmir" and "Feline Grace Vladmir". Jacob clicked on Philip's, and a picture popped up. He had striking blond hair and green eyes.

Philip Vladmir

The picture of Feline Vladmir showed that she had very pale skin, mouse-brown hair, and brown eyes. She looked much less like Chrith than her husband, but Roman still assumed comfortably that they were her parents.

"Three years? But then—"

"It's all fake," Treaver finished his sentence.

"So *everyone* on here's dead?" Roman breathed, noticing how small the scrollbar was.

"Possibly," Jacob said.

"Or some might be Strayers who want an excuse to drop off the face of the earth," Sarah agreed.

"But how does this help?" Roman wondered.

"It helps because now we can search for last names of other Strayers we might know. And we've even got pictures."

"In the meantime," Jacob interjected. "I've got an algebra test on Friday *and* a geography project due Thursday. So knock yourselves out searching for names." He stood up from his chair and stretched.

"But you've been with this website the longest," Treaver said.

"Exactly. All you have to do is flip through the yearbooks and find some last names, if there *are* any," Jacob told him.

Roman watched him push the door open and slide through and out of sight.

"You guys go ahead," Roman prompted. "I'll do this."

"Why?" Treaver and Sarah asked at the same time. Millo, however, hurried out of the library.

"I concentrate better on my own."

Sarah and Treaver didn't question this any further, and left obediently, Treaver more docile than Sarah. Sarah looked over her shoulder and kept a questioning look towards Roman, until he couldn't see her face anymore. Roman had a theory why; his explanation hadn't been entirely true. He had gotten an odd feeling about this website, even though it seemed obvious why he would seem slightly tense. But he felt almost self-conscious about it now. It was getting late, and he knew that he would have to come up with a good excuse for volunteering to check out the website again. As soon as Treaver and Sarah had left, and he was alone, the self-conscious feeling dissolved, being replaced by a feeling of intense curiosity.

He scrolled back to the top of the page. But after reading about thirty names, none of which rang a bell, he began to get impatient. He kept subconsciously glancing at the scrollbar, and imagining it moving down much more quickly. He glanced at the open yearbook and the middle school one next to it. It didn't help. He wanted it to close. The hairs on his arms were starting to stand on end.

Roman closed his eyes and took deep breaths, thinking that he was overreacting after he had tried to squeeze the mouse to a pulp. His hand was still on the mouse. He started tapping the surface. Then, without even thinking about it, he rubbed the scroll button twice, fast and hard. Roman opened his eyes, jumped back, and cursed himself for losing his place and the agonizing work. But when he grabbed a hold of the mouse, this time with his right hand instead of left, he saw something on the screen that froze him in time and space.

There it was, on the page taken up completely by people with last names that started with *R's*. At the top of the page, right underneath the search bar, was a person with the very last last name that he would've ever expected to be on a list of possible Strayers or Strayer murders.

Kelvin T. Rowland

12. Useful Lessons

"Welcome to the first official meeting of the St. Patrick Junior High Art Club!" Ms. Hue clasped her hands together enthusiastically. She was a stout woman. Her pink-dyed hair had small flecks of gray here and there, and she had streaks of blond hair at the tips that reached down to her shoulders. She was wearing a pastel-stained smock with a baggy, plain looking blue outfit underneath. Her rosy cheeks were freckled, and she had wrinkles around the edges of her eyes, as if she were accustomed to smiling often.

The art room had a calming aura to it, though it was annoying when Roman was trying to focus on how to cause outbursts. The smell greatly reminded him of the kitchen back at St. Jefferson's, which was infuriating to have to think of again. There were windows at the far end of the room that overlooked the main entrance of the school and where the buses picked everyone up each day. Roman sneezed, running the possibilities of what artistic tool caused it this time; pastels, chalk, paint, power, or the dust coming off along with the heat from the shrink-e-dink machine to his right.

The door was to his right and forward, in a small indent. The tiny wall separating the indent from the rest of the room was only three inches thick. On the other side of that wall were the turquoise cabinets, holding the different supplies, two sinks, and the shrink-e-dink machine. The tables normally used for art class had been moved to the right side of the room, leaving only a small space for people to walk out of the door. The overhead was behind Roman's black chair, unplugged. The floor was assumed to be tile, though different colors of paint that had been spilled over the years covered up any visible trace of such. The trash cans to Roman's back left were almost all completely full. The students were sitting in chairs that faced the right side of the room, side by side in three rows. Ms. Hue was standing before them all, directly in front of the tables.

Sarah and Treaver were on either side of him, in the very back row. Chrith, Rachel, and Victoria were in the very front row. There were two boys in the second row, along with a girl. From remembering the sign-in sheet, their rumors had apparently worked, and only one extra boy had joined. Roman assumed that the girl was Ashley Doppio, and one of the boys was Jack Sulivant.

Ashley was likely an eighth grade black girl that had striking amber-colored eyes. Her dreadlocked hair reached nearly a foot past her shoulders. She was tall, which was why Roman guessed that she was in eighth grade. From the way she kept shifting in her seat, she looked almost nervous. She was wearing a pink shirt with flower designs, much like the blue one that Sarah owned. She also had pre-ripped shorts that looked barely allowed by the dress-code, even though it was winter. The first boy was two seats down from her, and in front of Treaver. He had bowl-cut brown hair that reached almost to his ears. He was wearing a white jacket and had square, black glasses. Roman had never seen him in the sixth grade hallway or during sixth grade lunch, though he was as short as a sixth grader. He had walked in after Roman, so Roman didn't know what color his eyes were. He was wearing long pants, which seemed sensible compared to Ashley's outfit. The second boy, sitting in front of Roman and next to the first boy, was the type of person that Roman assumed had experience with art. His hair was dyed an unnatural ruddy-orange color, and gelled into a spiked Fauxhawk. Roman wondered why he hadn't been suspended from school for having a hairstyle like that. He was wearing a blue, denim jacket and black jeans. Roman had seen briefly that his eyes were hazel when he walked inside, before looking away when the boy had noticed him watching. His skin was slightly tanned, though hardly any patches were visible through the long clothes and black gloves. Roman had been wondering whether or not he had a tongue ring when Ms. Hue started speaking. Roman granted

[173]

that he was in either seventh or eighth grade, since he would probably have noticed someone with his complexion in the hallways from time to time.

Roman hadn't told Treaver, Sarah, Jacob, or Millo what he had found on the computer. He had pressed the emergency shutdown button as soon as he had come back to his senses, and gone straight to his room. He had gotten maybe three hours of sleep from staying up as long as possible, and then waking from nightmares. Roman had started wishing that he'd had more tangible dreams by the end of the night.

"Today, I think we'll just be introducing ourselves to the rest of the class," Ms. Hue continued. "For those of you who do not know me, or otherwise have not properly read the fliers for this club, I am the eighth grade art instructor. I'm sure that each of you know my name, Ms. Hue. But I'm seeing some new faces here today! Who would like to go first?"

Rachel and Chrith's hands both shot into the air. They glanced at each other, and to Roman's horror, giggled. They *had* been conversing when he, Sarah, and Treaver had arrived. He knew that things would become much more complicated if Rachel became friends with Strayers.

"Alright, how about we let someone else have a chance at a little attention for once, Chrithesma, sweetie?" Ms. Hue beckoned Rachel forward as Chrith put on a theatric pout.

"Hi, my name is Rachel Rivera," Rachel started, bouncing on the balls of her feet. "I'm in sixth grade, and I'm new here and honored to be in this club."

"Why don't you tell us a little bit about some of your interests, honey?" Ms. Hue inquired. "Anything outside of art? And what's your favorite kind of art? Drawing? Painting?"

"Oh! Well, I was in volleyball and tennis at my old school. And I like painting and pastels the best out of everything I've tried so far!"

"Excellent! Not very many students are fans of painting! Very good! Chrithesma, you wanted to go next?"

"Yes!" Chrith bounced out of her seat, hugging Rachel as they passed each other. Chrith and Victoria were very hard to think of as Strayers from the way that they acted in school, which was probably what they were going for. If they wanted something with Rachel, then Roman would have a hard time stopping them. Roman forced himself to clap along with everyone else as Rachel sat down.

"Hello, my name is Chrithesma, but all of my friends call me Chrith," Chrith started, her arms twined together in front of her. "I'm also in sixth grade, and I'm hoping that we're all going to be BFFs in no time!"

"I think we can all hope for that!" Ms. Hue encouraged her.

"And I like basketball and painting as well."

Roman clapped, thinking that Chrith enjoyed knives more than basketball by a long shot.

"Anyone else?" Ms. Hue asked.

Ashley raised a shaky hand, rather unsure of herself. Ms. Hue didn't get a chance to call her up, though; Victoria had already stood up and walked to stand next to Ms. Hue.

"Hey, I'm Victoria. I'm also known as Vicky, Sparkles, and Tooth Paste. And I like all types of art, and…not really much else."

"Then this class sounds perfect for you!" Ms. Hue grinned. Then the clapping started again.

This time, Ashley took her place at the front of the class.

"Hi, I'm Ashley," she started, looking very self conscious and moving some of her hair out of her eyes. "I'm trying to find something that really fits me, so I decided to join Art Club. So I'm probably not as good as anyone else here."

"Aw," Ms. Hue sympathized, "which grade are you in? I don't think I've ever seen you here before!"

"I'm in eighth grade," Ashley said, smiling nervously.

"All right. You can sit back down, now. Who's next?" She smiled as the rest of the club clapped.

"Anyone else?" Ms. Hue continued to grin, even though no one raised their hands.

Then, the boy in front of Roman stood up abruptly and pushed his way to the front of the room.

[175]

"Oh good! You want to introduce yourself, Jack?"

"Yeah," Jack mumbled. He faced the class, still frowning, though his eyes had some sort of curiosity in them. "I'm Jack, and I'm in seventh grade." His voice was slightly monotone. "Um, aside from this, I'm also in theater. But the winter play's almost done, so I wanted something to keep me occupied. I was actually in Props Crew, so we made some artistic stuff, which is what I'm looking forward to." He paused.

"Anything else you want to say, Jack?" Ms. Hue wondered.

"Nah," Jack shrugged, and then took his place in front of Roman again.

"How about you next, young man in the back?"

At first, Roman thought that Ms. Hue had been talking about him, until Treaver jumped in his seat. He dropped something like grey putty onto the floor. Victoria and Chrith were scowling at him from the front row.

"Er, sure." Treaver took an awkward minute to get his chair around everyone else's, his putty left forgotten on the already dirty floor.

"Hey, my name's Treaver Serapher, and I'm in sixth grade. I'm here because…um…I wanted to try something new, and sometimes orchestra can get kind of boring…" This got a few laughs out of Rachel, Ashley, Jack, and the boy next to Jack. Chrith and Victoria continued to glare.

"So yeah, I'm interested in orchestra and—"

"Which instrument do you play?" Ms. Hue wondered, grinning encouragingly.

"Oh, I play the violin."

"Oooh, how long have you been playing?" Ashley wanted to know.

"For a while now…after I got bored with piano and stuff. You can probably guess I'm not that into playing sports…" The boy next to Jack nodded his head. "So…yeah. I have absolutely no clue what part of art I like the most."

Roman clapped for real when Treaver did a half-bow and returned to his place next to Roman.

[176]

"Smooth-going, Treaver," Sarah congratulated him.

"Well, you three seem to know each other," Ms. Hue commented, noticing Sarah talking to Treaver. "Why don't we have you next, young lady?"

Sarah's cheeks turned a shade of pink. She got feebly to her feet and walked to the front.

"Hi, my name's Sarah Veihne, and I'm in sixth grade. I used to play softball, and I like sketching the most out of everything," she said quickly. "Bye, then."

"Whoa, whoa, why don't you tell us why you joined Art Club?" Ms. Hue held her, smiling sympathetically. Sarah glanced at the clock, and it was five minutes until advisory ended.

"I joined because I quit softball a while ago and wanted something to do. Plus, I don't really like Mr. Callaux's advisory."

Some of the kids chuckled again, this time Treaver and Roman joining in encouragingly. Victoria and Chrith were glaring again, and Rachel seemed to take their example by not saying anything.

"Well, thank you for that," Ms. Hue didn't seem to have as much kindness in her smile anymore. "How about you, in the back row?"

This time she was talking to Roman. Chrith and Victoria clapped exactly once as Sarah made her way back to the third row. Roman stood, but he was too tired to think much about being nervous. Standing before the club, he saw that none of them seemed to care much for him. With Sarah and Treaver, some kids had been glaring, and with Chrith, Victoria, and Rachel, they all had had support from each other. Sarah and Treaver had recently been introduced to Roman, and were not too interested in being introduced all over again. That, or the putty was stuck to the ground, and Sarah was trying to move it with her foot.

"Hello, I'm Roman Ro—" Roman stopped himself from saying his last name abruptly. Whether or not Sarah or Treaver had seen the screen or not, he still felt odd about seeing it on that page. "I'm Roman." He continued, much less monotone, now. He had caught a few people's attention with his sudden agitated

[177]

complexion. "I'm in the sixth grade. Besides this, I'm pretty much either studying for Spanish or on the computer…" Roman felt the stares of everyone boring into him. He swallowed, knowing that he couldn't stay frozen forever. "And I'm normally in Mr. Ferris' advisory. My favorite thing about art is…"

He had never given much thought to what he liked in art, because he had never very much taken to art. They had been forced to have art in elementary school, and many kids were grateful for not having to in middle school, too.

Hey, come to think of it, this is perfect timing, Roman realized.

"Papier-mâché!" He said enthusiastically. He quickly sprinted to the back of the class where his backpack was waiting for him. He was surprised that no one noticed that the backpack had been moving the whole time. Opening it quickly, he ducked back as Mary Beth's paper cat, Huck Fin, sprang out of Roman's pack with a silent screech.

Huck Fin didn't need to shriek, though. The rest of the class did it for him. As Huck sprang from head to head, the kids jumped out of their seats and shuffled to the back of the classroom. When Huck finally hurled himself at Ms. Hue, Roman sprang forward and caught the paper cat in his hands, stroking its head to calm it down.

"Sorry, the animatronics must have a little glitch," Roman apologized to Ms. Hue, who looked about ready to throw up. "I'll go sit back down now."

Roman gratefully took his seat, a sly smile spread across his face. The rest of the class followed back, the other boys looking exhilarated, and the girls except for Ashley looked disapproving. Chrith and Victoria glared at him, but Rachel simply gave him the cold shoulder.

Treaver leaned nearer to Roman, part of the putty stuck to his jeans.

"Nice show. Ya know, this might not be as bad as it could've been." He reached over to pet Huck, who had settled down in Roman's lap.

The boy in front of Treaver stood up and made his way to

[178]

the front of the classroom.

"Hi, my name's Edward. I'm in eighth grade. I joined because I was thoroughly bored. And I have no idea what my favorite kind of art is because I don't really like art."

Ms. Hue might've burst at this, but Edward had timed his speech perfectly. The bell rang the next moment, dismissing them. They each grabbed their backpacks and hurried out of the door.

Jacob and Sarah continued to comb out people from the yearbooks from the website in private. Millo was never very interested in their mission, and Roman and Treaver had more important things to do.

"Pass."

"Hit."

"Hit."

"Darn, over twenty-one!"

In the lounge, at one table behind the television, Roman and Treaver were playing blackjack with Chris, Cole, and Danny. Chris had just gotten a five, putting him over twenty-one by two.

"Looks like it's two-on-two, now," Danny grinned maliciously. "Told ya we could whip 'em, Cole."

"Hey, it's bad enough that you insist on putting us into teams," Treaver sighed, "but now you insist that we do something else that's never happened before: Let you win a game of cards."

"He beat Hector in a game before!" Cole growled.

"Never heard of him," Roman said absentmindedly.

"The eighth-grade champion," Danny said slyly, "figures you two aren't cool enough to know him."

"Didn't he get suspended for bringing in a Nerf gun?" Treaver asked, glancing up.

"Yup," Cole concluded.

"He wasn't using it," Danny snapped testily. "He was just showing it to his friends."

"Would that include you?"

"It looks exactly like it does on TV."

Treaver sighed and rolled his eyes.

"Can you four *please* talk about something else?" Chris

[179]

muttered, "I'm starting to get bored."

"How about how I've just gotten twenty-one?" Roman suggested, grinning.

"You did not!" Danny gasped, brow furrowing.

"Very correct. I'm actually three away. But I enjoyed your reaction."

"Pest," Danny mumbled, clearly audible.

"Maggot, larva!" Tyler entered the lounge. "Five minutes 'til today's training! Start getting ready!"

"But it's only four-thirty," Treaver complained, checking his watch.

"Well, today maggot's going to get his first look inside of the lab," Tyler leaned against the table, "so I want him to have time to look around before we start the PCG."

Roman groaned. There would be no possible chance of him being able to concentrate on his PCG with new surroundings.

"Oh yeah, I forgot," Danny sneered as Tyler walked away, "you're both still doing the baby classes. Wouldn't want to keep your mommy waiting, now will you? Run along, now."

"Danny," Treaver said coolly, "today, when you sneak off in the middle of the night to steal more of Elliyo and Gabriel's splat-balls, look up when you're exactly three inches away from the fridge."

Danny narrowed his eyes. As Roman and Treaver moved away, Roman whispered to Treaver.

"What's a splat-ball?"

"You'll know if you're ever on cleanup duty. Let's let *them* clean up our mess," he added. Roman wondered if he was referring to Danny and Cole having to pick up their cards, even though it wasn't much compensation.

They didn't need to walk far. The entrance to the lab was just through the ballroom and down a flight of stairs and ramp. Treaver had to struggle with not sliding too fast down the ramp. Roman wasn't having any more luck with the stairs, which were narrow, wooden, and felt like they would cave in at any given moment. The pathway was dim, light only coming from below, as the door behind them shut on its own.

[180]

"How come the elevator doesn't reach down this far?" Roman asked Treaver.

"Oh, from its position," Treaver said, his voice slightly forced from having to hold back his wheels, "if it just descended, then it'd crash right through the main hallway. And another elevator would cost a lot. And we don't like having non-Genedeaues here. Most of the most recent things, we've done ourselves."

"Even the last two levels of mansion since the Trent-thing?"

"Okay, something tells me that we probably brought in somebody else for that one," Treaver said satirically.

They were very close to the light now. Roman could see beyond the end of the small passageway they were in, but didn't catch much except for a very smooth marble floor. The smell of pure coldness reached Roman.

"Is that smell from the nitrogen?"

"Oh, the smell changes *really* often. Get used to it. And if you can't, bring some plugs," Treaver advised him. "Not for the soft-nosed."

The light was almost piercing, and Roman had to squint hard before they had even reached the lab. But it was much more than a lab, Roman saw once he had reached the bottom of the stairs. He was faced with the conflict of the light making him narrow his eyes and the vastness of it all making him want to open his eyes as wide as possible. He shaded his eyes with his hand. The marble floor was white, mostly. Some spaces had blotches, much like stains. Next to the entrance was a rack stacked with things that Roman would've expected to find in a high school lab: gloves, goggles, close-toed shoes, a sink and jumpsuits. The jumpsuits varied in color and size, and many had blotches just as the floor did.

The lights of the room were nearly blinding, each about five feet long and three inches wide. They were florescent-neon with glass over their bulbs. The room was as large as the lounge, with other hallways branching off to the sides. There was an emergency exit at the other end of the corridor, but otherwise the walls had nothing disturbing its plaster-smoothness. The walls were the same white as the floor, though it had fewer stains. There were three hallways leading off from the room; one to Roman's right, and two to his left. The room that they were in was dominated by what Roman could only assume was the main computer.

Roman had heard stories about computers being as large as a room back in their early days, with cords bigger than hose-pipes, but he had never expected those to look so new. It was mainly black, its surface looking much like that of a black car's, and clashing with the whiteness around them. It had several other computers attached to it by very tiny, multicolored wires which could've probably fit into his laptop. The colors made Roman's eyes hurt. Some of the computers just looked like regular monitor computers, and others were almost like spheres and engines. There was a socket in the screen of the main computer, around the size of a CD, but shaped like a hexagon. There was a soft humming around the computer, and Roman felt the hairs on his neck involuntarily standing on end. He glanced around the computer's edges, wondering how many outlets it would take to power this beast. But if Roman spotted a single outlet in the walls of the room, then he was going to kiss Chrith.

Treaver smiled at the gawking look on Roman's face. "I told you you'd know it when you saw it."

"Yeah…I guess I'm not *that* stupid."

"That's arguable, maggot." Tyler stepped out silently from behind a cylindrical-shaped machine.

"Hey, Tyloser," Treaver greeted him. "Didn't see you there."

"That part was intended. So, I've got a fun lesson in store for you two today. But don't get used to it."

"Gee, thanks," Roman muttered. He hadn't had Tyler as a mentor for very long, but whatever Tyler thought was fun, it probably involved injury.

"Show some more enthusiasm," Tyler criticized him. "It's no surprise. Today, it's not just textbooks, notes, and graphs. *Today* I'm demonstrating how indestructible gemstones are."

[182]

Treaver's eyes lightened. "Really? Am I coming?"

"You've already had your demonstration."

"Yeah, but I've had to come to all of the other PCG's! And I can show him some creative stuff that I got from last time!"

"All right, but only 'cause I'm in a good mood."

Roman was surprised to see Treaver miss this opportunity to diss Tyler, since his being happy normally involved getting a mediocre job done on one of his chores or something involving Stacy. From the expectant look on Treaver's face, this was going to be an interesting lesson.

"First thing's first. Jace is supervising another RAA, so we're on our own. I want as many people down here as possible during our session, and most people normally come down during lesson time. So, larva, let's play tour guide."

They started with the hallway leading off to Roman's right. It was long and narrow. The stains on the pure white tiles became more and more frequent as they went along. They turned once and found themselves in a room, larger than the last one, with what looked like a gas chamber off to the right again. Most of the spaces in the room had multicolored stains, some more blatant than others. The room was divided in two by a large, transparent wall, not quite glass. There was a camera in the corner of their half of the room. There were two doors leading into the other side of the room, where the walls and floor were currently consumed with a neon-purple color. There was an even larger rack of coats, gloves, jumpsuits, and more high-intensity goggles against the left wall of the area, about as tall as one would have been in a hardware store, and with about thirty of each item. There were two large buttons on either end of the side chamber's door. One was sky-blue, and on its right, closest to the doorway they were standing in. The other was blood-red, much like every cliché self-destruct button Roman had ever seen on television.

To the left of their doorway, there were about five chemical showers, each as large as a high school shower, and seven eye-washes. The ceiling was littered with sprinklers that

Roman knew would release water if there was a fire. Along with the concept of fire, a few devices that looked like smoke-detectors were also attached to the ceiling.

"This is where the majority of chemical experiments take place. Notice the protective tools," Tyler told him. "We haven't used this place for about a month. Notice the purple walls? I was lucky enough to have been on dish-duty. Ringo lost his eyebrows for a while..."

"What're the buttons for?"

"Emergency releases. The blue one's for the chamber, and the red one's for lifting the protective wall. Both also contact the main computer and send off an alarm when pressed. But remember, if you're not allowed to pull the fire-alarm in school, then, if you value your life, no false alarms on those."

"What's the chamber for?"

"Classified," Treaver rolled his eyes, crossing his arms. "We help people who turn out to be just regular rouges to get their gems. *That* is purely Talisman, so we don't tell you unless you're officially with us."

They went next through the hallway across the main room closest to the door on the left side. This passageway was much longer, though slightly wider than the last. It had at least four or five twists along the way. When they reached the end, there was a fork in their path. One led through a door, metal and bolted. The other led off into darkness, without having any lights.

"What's through that passageway?" Treaver asked Tyler.

"You don't know?" Roman wondered.

"No, he doesn't," Tyler sneered scathingly. "Curiosity killed the cat. You'd be in more trouble than pressing those emergency buttons by going down that hallway. There are cameras, so don't even think about it. And we've also got sensors. The computer senses any movement and sounds the alarm. And you need a pass code to turn the sensors off."

"Bet you don't even have the pass code," Treaver muttered.

"These are the oldest additions to the lab, which is the oldest addition to the mansion," Tyler explained to Roman.

"Before, without that shield of ours, we were underground. Today, it's much more pleasant.

"How long ago was this?"

"Sometime before the World Wars," Tyler dismissed. "Not important. The other passageways were added sometime after the fifties."

"You're telling me that the whole mansion was just these two passages?"

"Oh, some tunnels were removed. Too many deaths. This door is the storage closet for things that we wouldn't want most people to find. Pass code, again. Except, instead of it being a regular pass code, it's touch sensitive. You just need to know where to touch. And it's different for every person," he added to Treaver, who was already sulking.

"The last hallway," Tyler said as they made their way back into the room with the main computer. "Leads off to where you'll be having today's PCG, Roman. I'm going to get some things from that room you just saw, and then the fun begins."

The final hallway had several side rooms, much like offices, since they had plain wooden doors with windows that had wires branching through them. Tyler explained the use of almost every door as they passed. Others, he was not supposed to tell them. They finally came to a room at the end of the corridor before it turned a corner. Opening the door, the room was about as large as a classroom. It was very plain, the walls looking more like white metal than white marble. There was a single platform, about as high as Roman's waist, in the very center of the room. It reminded Roman of an interrogation room instead of a classroom.

Tyler soon left them to get the tools, coming back with a crate that rattled as he carried it along with some of the protective gear. Inside, it had several bags full of things that sloshed, banged, or squished, along with several power tools and a single textbook. Roman's stomach churned at the sight of the textbook, fearing that he would have to study it.

"All right, I'm supposed to lend you two my gem to practice on," Tyler told them sharply. "But just because it's unbreakable, doesn't mean that I trust you with it. And *don't* try

[185]

to hide it, larva. I'll know where it goes."

"Whatever. I've heard this speech before, remember?"

"A little extra instruction, since you've practically fallen behind."

Tyler took out his gem. It was in the shape of a five-sided star, bulging out in the center to make it three-dimensional. It reminded Roman greatly of a large model of a maroon star that was at the mall next to the store for Texas souvenir items, and of several key chains that could be found in that store. This one, however, was a mixture of bright orange, reddish orange, and pink near the bottom.

"Pink is definitely your color," Treaver mused.

"You want me to use those power tools on you?"

"No thanks."

"How about these?" he asked, indicating to the jars and bags.

"What do they do?"

"Don't you *ever* pay attention?"

"I will when I have more than just an egotistic tenth-grader to stare at."

"They're acids, courtesy of Jay, and explosives, courtesy of Rebecca. Those are why you'll be needing these," Treaver tossed Roman a suit and goggles.

"Don't I get any?" Treaver demanded.

"Say it."

Treaver bit his lip. Roman handed him the gear that Tyler had given to him. Tyler narrowed his eyes and tossed Roman another set.

"I'm *supposed* to supervise you two, but I'll be outside of the door. Holler if you need me, because if I stay in here I'll be tempted to start an explosives fight. And we could do with conserving as much as we can right now."

He held up a bag full of a fine, scarlet powder. "Mix this with that blue stuff," he pointed toward a jar full of blue liquid, "and you'll get a minor explosion. Just a little bitty puff of fire.

"Squish the liquid out of this, and it'll be enough to melt through a car," he indicated to what looked like a glob of green

[186]

gelatin, "And—"

"Wait, if it's strong enough to burn through a car, then won't it burn through these coats?" Roman asked tensely.

"You never stop underestimating us, do you?" Treaver rolled his eyes. He already had his goggles on, and he was zipping up his suit. He had an expectant look on his face, and, as Roman watched, he glanced at the scarlet powder at least twice. Roman looked away, and attempted to pull on his coat.

"Anyways, mix this white stuff with that purple stuff for another minor explosion, except this one will get ruined by water. But don't mix it with the stuff inside of the green thing."

"Why not?"

"Because then it'll start a chain reaction that'll make it grow rapidly and then suffocate us if we get caught in it," Treaver said knowingly.

"Oookay then. Should I ask how you know this?"

"Probably better not to."

"All right then."

"If you two are done," Tyler raised his eyebrows, "then will you listen? The last blue stuff just powers the tools, that way you don't have to plug them in. It won't do anything if it gets mixed with any of the others. Got it all down?"

"Yup, scarlet powder to blue acid, acid out of the green stuff, purple to white but not to green, and blue to the power power tools," Roman repeated.

"*See*?" Tyler inquired of Treaver. "*This* is why he's maggot and you're larva."

Roman soon found out why Treaver had been anticipating this lesson so much. The best way to demonstrate how very indestructible the Bermuda gems were was to use as much firepower as possible. Roman very much enjoyed the explosions, ignoring how uncomfortable the suit was. It was much like how some kids described snow days to him: that the coats are too big, but the snow is worth it. Roman used much of the white and purple, and all of the blue acid and scarlet powder was gone by the end of the session. The green stuff felt hot underneath his coat, so Roman tried his best to be more tempted by the power

[187]

tools. The jackhammer was a disappointment, as the gem kept sliding across the room. The same held true for the drill, until Treaver showed him how to fire nail-thick staples at the gem from across the room. This was perhaps the shortest lesson yet. Roman was missing exactly one eyebrow at the end of it, but he would've easily traded his other to have another class like that.

"Boys and their toys," Mary Beth muttered as they passed her working on the main computer, smirking at them.

"Like you wouldn't have done it," Tyler retorted.

"I would've if I didn't have to organize these files. It just doesn't make sense…there was the same amount of deposits, but something's just gone missing…"

"The bank again?" Tyler inquired, frowning.

"Yes. I had Danny check it earlier as a punishment, and he said that two thousand dollars just weren't on the chart. He was right."

"*Two thousand?*" Tyler's jaw dropped. He turned to Roman and Treaver, looking unnaturally serious, "You two get goin', I'm gonna stay back for a bit."

Treaver and Roman obliged, glancing over their shoulders to see Tyler leaning over Mary Beth's shoulder to take a look at a small, glowing screen on one of the smallest computers. They did not talk until they were back in the ballroom, as Treaver had a hard time pulling himself up the ramp and talking at the same time, refusing to accept Roman's help.

"What do you think Danny got in trouble for?" Roman asked him, shutting the door to the lower levels.

Treaver quickly smoothed his hair to hide a few beads of sweat. Then he smiled maliciously. "Oh, he got blue paint all over the kitchen floor."

"How do you know?" Roman wondered.

"He looked up when he was three inches away from the fridge last night."

13. Clubs and Missions

Roman sprang bolt upright in bed, wondering who had screamed. His heart was beating fast and hard, his hair was standing on end, and a cold layer of sweat had broken out. Head pounding, he strained his ears for another sound, wondering if he could distinguish the voice. He felt the icy sweat ebbing away. A cool spot remained on his cheek. He wiped it, realizing it was drool.

He tried to recall his dream. He could only make out flashes, but knew it had been another nightmare. Normally his mouth went dry when he slept, but this time he had drooled. He glanced at his alarm clock. It was exactly five minutes before it was scheduled to go off.

The fan was on, and Roman realized how breezy it was. He'd kicked his sheets off of the bed. Putting this together with his nightmare, Roman had been the one that had yelled. He had apparently been mumbling and kicking in his sleep. He was suddenly glad that he could get ready for school, because he didn't feel like taking another chance at sleeping.

Roman's mouth was dryer awake, in the shower, than asleep in bed. He was hardly paying attention to what he was doing, and nearly put his shirt on over his pants. He had remembered enough to know what he had dreamt about, and it was the same thing as the past few nights.

The others were still investigating the website, but he was certain that when he had said that he had found nothing immediately interesting, Sarah had known he had been lying. He'd tried to avoid eye contact, but that would've made even the others suspicious. He tried his best to shake the thought, reasoning that it was a common last name. But the more he told himself not to think about it, the more he thought about it.

Roman shook his head. He had his comb in his hand, but he had been running it up and down his jean leg. He quickly made his hair lie relatively flat and got out of the room as quickly as possible, though he was back a minute later to get his backpack.

"Where'd you *get* that?" Roman gaped, accidentally making a large peach line across his person's face with his brush.

"Where do you *think* I got it?" Treaver retorted sarcastically. "We just had that class yesterday, don't tell me you're *that* thick?"

Roman felt a smile creeping across his face, and lifted his hand subconsciously to his seared eyebrow. "Do you have the blue stuff, too?"

"Why else would I have the powder?" Treaver said, taking a small vile of the same blue acid out of his pocket and holding it next to his plastic bag full of the scarlet powder from yesterday's training session, shifting to his side to block it from view. They were partners together on their portrait project, working next to the cabinets. Sarah was paired up, reluctantly, with Rachel, along with Ashley. Jack and Edward were together, and Chrith and Victoria were paired up. Ms. Hue had insisted on keeping at least one good student paired with Edward, Roman, and Sarah. It had surprised Roman that she had perceived Treaver as a "good" student, but was thankful that he alone would probably be blamed for this planned disruption, if Treaver had not thought that particular part through.

"*That's* why we ran out so quickly."

"Don't pretend you noticed. Anyways, the paint should delude the fiery part of the explosion, like Tyler said."

"When did he say that?"

"Remember? 'This one is water-resistant, unlike the other one'? Or something like that. Anyways, there *should* be an impact if we time it right. Wouldn't be that way with regular explosions but..."

Five minutes later, just as Ms. Hue was passing, Treaver poured some of the blue acid into the orange-red powder. He didn't need to move quickly, as when the bubbles started, he had to drop the bag into the paint to keep from being burned. The reaction was instant. Roman had just shielded his eyes in time to avoid the paint splattering out at him. Ms. Hue was lucky to have had her back turned.

Roman made sure to comically fall to the floor as Treaver wheeled out of the way, clutching half of his putty from yesterday. Treaver had talked his plan over with Roman beforehand, and as Roman jumped to scramble away from the vat of still-frothing paint, color now changing, he made sure to purposely crash into the shrink-e-dink machine, striking the floor and sending up sparks. Roman was glad that he had yellow paint all down his front, otherwise his shirt might have very well caught on fire.

Everyone was yelling. Roman scrambled to the edge of the classroom, where he had expected everyone else to be. But he found that Chrith and Victoria were the only ones there. The rest of the class had actually come as close as the edge of where the paint had splattered, which was nearly halfway across the room. Ms. Hue was making a good show of sliding and tripping over the floor in her high-heels. Treaver was in the other corner of the room, doing a good job of looking shocked, scared, horrified, and enthusiastic all at the same time, like most of the class.

Victoria practically kicked Roman away when he was close enough to their corner, and Roman crept across the tables to join Treaver, tracking paint across those as well. The already paint-stained floor was now a quarter covered in a perfect rainbow of paint that bubbled in unexpected places. It took a few moments, even after the paint had settled, for everyone to grow quiet, as there was much shouting.

"All right, quiet down, now!" Ms. Hue ordered, pulling herself up by clutching the overhead projector. "Settle down! I SAID QUIET!"

The class fell silent. Chrith and Victoria came out of the shadows as Rachel beckoned to them. Jack's hair had gotten a bit of blue paint on the back, but he didn't seem to notice. The left half of Ashley's face had a splash of turquoise and purple. The rest of the class was virtually untouched aside from their shoes. Sarah looked amazed, as Treaver hadn't told her that he had brought the chemicals. But, upon catching their eyes from the back of the room, she came to join them, working hard to suppress a smile.

"Mr. Serapher, Mr. Rowland, Miss Veihne," Ms. Hue started quietly, mispronouncing Sarah's last name for the tenth time that day, "can you please come here, and join the rest of the class? Can anyone tell me what just happened?"

"I think the paint exploded," Jack said simply.

"Well, Mr. Sulivant, I believe that *that* is quite obvious." Ms. Hue had lost most of the sugar in her voice by this point, the lines around her eyes disturbingly visible through the multicolored paint that now covered most of her face. All of her painting smocks were dripping with the same stuff, especially on her back where the first blast had hit her.

"Um, Ms. Hue?" Treaver spoke up tentatively, twiddling his thumbs. He had covered his eyes, as well, which had left an odd hand-shaped mark. The rest of his body was, like Roman's, entirely covered in paint from being blasted and then falling and crawling.

"Yes, Mr. Serapher? This was your project, wasn't it?"

"Yes m'am."

"Well..?"

"Um, right before the paint exploded, it started bubbling—"

"So that's why you knew to cover your eyes," She interrupted, her eyes lingering on Roman, who tried his best to look back at her with an innocent expression. At least he had paint to cover most of his face. It was starting to itch, though.

"Yeah, and um-before that...I kind of...dropped some of my putty in the paint." Treaver said, holding the remaining half of his putty, now covered in paint, up with a shaking hand. Roman had to nudge Sarah in the ribs, since she looked like she was about to say something. He knew that the other half of Treaver's putty was stowed safely away in Treaver's pocket, and not melted somewhere in the paint. He wondered vaguely, looking over at the bucket that had tipped over, if the whole thing had splattered out, since it seemed like every ounce of it had jumped out of its container, as if trying to escape.

Ms. Hue's eyes were dangerously cold, but her voice was as sweet as ever when she spoke next. "And why were you playing with your putty?"

Roman's stomach dropped, since Treaver had not told Roman what would happen if Ms. Hue asked this. Treaver still looked nervous to Roman, but he felt Sarah relax beside him.

"I-I didn't like the plain grey color, so…I guess it kind of wasn't an accident."

Ms. Hue's smile disappeared. Her eyes were still cold, but she didn't burst at Treaver. Chrith, Rachel, and Victoria were glaring at Treaver heatedly. What surprised Roman was not that Ms. Hue was keeping her temper, it was that Ashley was glaring at Treaver, as well. Edward was trying not to look positively ecstatic, but Jack was keeping a straight face with no difficulty. Normally, knowing people like Jack, he would've tried to look bored, but he kept shooting glances back at Treaver, and they were not looks of admiration.

"Well, I'll go call a few custodians in here," said Ms. Hue, walking gingerly over to the door. "You all go wash up in the bathroom. We have some extra painting clothes if you need to take your clothes off. Then you can all go back to you regular advisories until the bell rings."

Roman and Treaver headed for the bathroom, while Sarah waited outside. They saw Ashley going into the girls' bathroom to wash her face, and Roman felt slightly guilty thinking of the judgmental stares she had given them. The rest of the class wiped their shoes on some of the towels in the room and left.

"At least if the security camera caught us dropping anything into the paint, then we'll have the putty excuse," Treaver told Roman in a whisper.

Treaver and Roman explained to Sarah what happened on the bus. At first, Sarah was very skeptical that Treaver had stolen explosive chemicals from the Talismen mansion, and told them that it was a very bad idea if they were thinking of doing it again.

Then she switched to talking about how cleaver it was that they could get it into the paint without having it burn out or killing themselves.

"It wasn't *that* strong," Treaver muttered, his arms crossed.

"Uh, yeah it was. Don't you remember what's in those?"

"I don't 'remember things'."

"Well, with a dose that big, it could've taken out the whole class."

"You're lying," Roman accused her, getting a sinking feeling that he could've gotten himself and several middle-schoolers and his teacher killed.

"No, I'm not. You use smaller doses in the training sessions, but that was half of the bag of powder and three quarters of the acid."

Roman and Treaver swallowed in synchronization.

"Well, you think Tyler would've been impressed?" Treaver raised his eyebrows hopefully.

"No, I don't think he would have."

The first thing that Sarah and Treaver asked Jacob and Millo on sight, once again, was how the research was going, reminding Roman of his most recent nightmare. He felt slightly thankful that it hadn't been a tangible dream, otherwise it would've been ten times worse. He thought of earlier, when Ms. Hue had called him by his last name, and glanced at the others, wondering if they had found his last name on the website, too.

It's a common last name… Roman told himself for the thousandth time.

But then how come the rest of the names are in pairs? How come you felt the urge to go down the page? If the tangible dreams have powers in the real world, then who's to say that it wasn't? asked another voice in rapid fire, before Roman could shut it off. Roman pondered over these questions all through his MUC, distracting himself, and managing to accidentally need to bandage his finger by the end of his class.

He didn't get much sleep the next night, but in school, there was a notice on the morning announcements that the Art

Club would not have a meeting that day. The rumors of exploding paint had spread quickly through the school, earning Roman back some of his old friends, which he did not welcome back as warmly as they expected him to.

Art Club was also cancelled next week, according to Friday's morning announcements. The regular art classes would take place out in the portable buildings, as well. This led many of the students to ask the teachers questions about radioactive poisoning and fatalities, to the response that even they did not know.

"You don't think that they're getting rid of the art classes?" Rachel fretted during lunch.

You don't think that the plan worked on the first try? Roman wondered to himself.

The answer was that it had, to everyone's astonishment. The morning announcements told that the art classes would now be held on a regular schedule, but the Art Club would no longer meet.

"Does this mean that we...we did it?" Treaver asked the others uncertainly that evening, before the training session, in the courtyard.

"Did what?" Roman picked up his question. "Yeah, we stopped the Art Club, but what did that do? I mean, Chrith and Victoria are still Strayers, aren't they? They're not going to get kicked out of the Strayers just because their plan or whatever failed, are they?"

"That's a very good question," Jacob agreed. "Looks like it's back to the dreams again." Roman wanted to protest that his dreams were bad enough, except that he didn't really have much of a choice in the matter.

Millo became more relaxed, while the others panicked. Roman woke up only to say that he had absolutely no dreams, except an irrelevant one about mutant waffles.

"What are we going to do now?" Treaver fretted.

"We've had this problem before," Sarah consoled, sounding uncertain herself.

"Yeah, now we're just getting worried because Millo isn't

[195]

at his crying point, anymore," Roman mumbled, not meaning for anyone else to hear, except Jacob did.

"Hey! Leave Millo out of this. Just try not to dream about waffles and actually help us out with something. In the meantime, we're going to keep looking at that website, but it's got a blockage and we *don't* want any of their tracking cookies getting into *our* computers."

Roman caught up with Caleb before proceeding to lunch after gym class.

"Hey, Caleb. I figured you'd be inside with your girlfriend by now."

"She's not my girlfriend," Caleb said rather nervously, "and I wasn't out here yesterday because she pulled me aside in the hallway, so I was late."

"You two weren't kissing, were you?"

"Dude, c'mon, you're not funny."

"What'd she want with you, anyways?"

"Oh, I invited her to come over to my house this weekend."

"She pulled you over in the hallway so that *you* could ask her out?" Roman inquired.

"I did *not* ask her out!" Caleb argued, his cheeks turning pink. "Okay, so *I* pulled her aside in the hall."

"And what did she say?" Roman wondered casually, stopping so that they could finish their conversation before Caleb got in line.

"Oh, she was busy with this club or something," Caleb replied, looking crestfallen.

"You know, the Art Club was cancelled," Roman told him sympathetically before walking off.

Roman yawned as he sat down, thinking that he would take a nap in social studies. Allan, Tj, and Rachel joined him shortly afterwards.

"Hey, Rachel, Caleb tells me that you're busy with a sort of club this weekend. What's up with that? I thought you were just in Art Club, otherwise you would've mentioned it when introducing yourself to the class. Not *avoiding* Caleb, are you?"

"I'm not," Rachel said coolly. She had not been on friendly terms with Roman ever since their first Art Club meeting. "I was going to talk to you about it today, actually."

"Really?" Roman pretended to sound interested, while he was almost completely convinced that she had not been planning to tell him about this 'club'.

"Yes, really!" Rachel repeated heatedly. "I'm trying to tell everyone that had previously been in the Art Club." She added something to herself that Roman was sure that she purposely kept him from hearing. "We're starting our own after-school club for anyone who wants to join. And we can do more than just art! I mean, we don't need the school to sponsor anything just to have fun, do we?"

"Gee, that sounds great, but, where would we get all of the supplies?"

"I guess we buy them. But just think! Our parents can bring us snacks, we could walk around town, we could have cool nicknames, *and* we could raise money for charity by auctioning our art…"

"Whoa, back up," Roman said suddenly, trying to hide choking on his milk. "By any chance, have Victoria and Chrith talked to you about this?"

Rachel's face lightened at Roman starting to take interest in their plans. "Oh yes! They were the ones who suggested it to me! They've had their own little bitty club for a while but haven't considered getting any new members, but now they've thought about it, and they said we could all join! It'd be a bit different though, with more people…But they've already raised money for charity and stuff, but there'd be even more if everyone joined! We could even get our own website!"

"They already have nicknames and stuff?" Roman demanded more sharply than he had intended to.

"Ooh!" A smirk spread across Allan's face, "I want to be "Ninja"! Or "Agent Double-0-Three". *Or* "Agent Double-0-Ninja"!"

Tj chuckled, "I'll be Bob."

[197]

"You'll be Timothy Jasper and like it," Roman told him.

"Stop it!" Rachel snapped. "If you're not going to take this seriously, then don't listen! But yes, they've already got their own nicknames! But we shouldn't call them by them in school, because then other people might steal them. But we can still call each other them during meetings! It'll be fun!"

"What are their names, then?" Tj asked innocently, finishing his garlic-bread and bending over to take his cards out of his lunchbox.

"Oh, well I just remember Vicky's because it's really cool! It sounds like something magical, you know what I mean?"

"Not if you don't tell me, I won't."

"Well I probably shouldn't...it's for meetings only..."

"I won't remember."

"Oh, all right then!" Her voice dropped to a whisper and she leaned forward across the table. Allan pretended to bend closer to eavesdrop, but Rachel slapped him, and he sat back with his arms crossed, muttering something.

"Chrith calls herself by something that also starts with an A, but Vicky's is Aesthe. Kind of hard to pronounce, but that's what make it so cool!"

"So *that's* why you haven't been having any dreams!" Treaver laughed. "I was starting to think that we were doing something wrong!"

"That's very good and very bad all at the same time," Sarah said grimly, with Jacob's consent murmured a moment later. Millo had gone back to looking more devastated than ever. Treaver seemed taken aback by the little enthusiasm that the rest of them were showing.

"What's wrong with you guys? *This* is what the Art Club was leading up to the whole time, wasn't it? I mean, this thing's almost over!"

"Assumably," Jacob agreed. "But this means that even without the Art Club, the Strayers really want these art students for something. And-or, their little 'club' that they've started? We all know what that club really is."

"But they're not Genedeaues, are they?" Roman inquired. "And they can't know that they're Genedeaues just from the fact that they signed up for some stupid art class, can they?"

"No way that we know of," Sarah answered.

"But it's almost over! How can you not be happy about that?"

"Because, in a video game, if you're close to the goal, then you still have to fight the boss," Roman told him. "We've had it awfully easy, so far, so who's to say that it'll stay that easy? And the Strayers want these guys for something, they're in danger, and so are we. Now do you get it?"

"Oh…" Treaver looked crestfallen, "But we could tell Mr. Kyle once we've found that one place from your dream, can't we?"

"It's possible," Roman considered this. He hoped that once again his dreams would tell him what to do. But he was getting sick of the dreams and sick of their mission, whatever it was. The other Talismen didn't go about their missions like this, so why did he have to?

"We'll have to wait and see," Sarah voiced his thoughts. "In the meantime, it looks like we're joining a club."

"Great," Roman's stomach lurched. "Hey, the Art Club was during school. We can't go to any other meetings after school without being noticed."

"We'll just tell Mr. Kyle that we're in a club, big deal," Treaver sighed. "Besides, now Jacob and Millo might be able to join."

Millo shook his head vigorously, but Jacob had a thoughtful expression.

"I'll go if I can. Are we trying to sabotage again?" he asked hopefully.

"I don't think that this is a good idea," Millo argued, his voice shaking slightly.

"Why's that?"

Millo opened his mouth to speak, but closed it again, looking very put out.

"It'll be okay, Millo," Jacob consoled patiently. "And you

don't have to do anything if you don't want to."

Millo let out a small sound. Roman couldn't decipher its meaning, but Jacob took that as a simple acknowledgement that he understood.

Roman hadn't known Millo for very long before they had discovered that Chrith and Victoria were Strayers, and even then Millo had seemed nervous and scared most of the time around him, but comfortable around other students. It could have simply been that he took a while to get used to new people. He would have to ask Stacy. Stacy hadn't appeared to even know his name when Roman had first arrived, so she couldn't have spent much time with him. But Millo seemed curiously nervous when it came to Roman. Roman wondered if it was just Millo, or just himself. Millo never seemed to like their side mission with Chrith and Victoria, while the others were perfectly willing to help in any way they could, especially if it meant getting to do the job that they were training for. Did Millo even want to be a Talisman? Or was he just waiting to get his gem and set off to become a Rouge? Roman made a mental note to ask Stacy later how Millo normally acted around her, and he had a hard time thinking about what he would do depending on her answer.

14. Happy Birthday

Φ   Φ   Φ

Roman stared hard at the piece of paper in his hand. It was blue, with nothing visibly special about it. He held it up to the light in the hallway. He could not see through it. Flipping it over, it seemed fine. Making sure that no one was looking, he sniffed it. It was perfectly normal to every extent that he could tell.

Perhaps too normal...

Oh, shut up, Roman told himself.

He pocketed the piece of paper that Rachel had just given him, bearing the address of where they were to meet for their club. The time was also scribbled neatly underneath the address. It was a business address, which told Roman that they weren't going to be meeting at anybody's house. At best, they would be meeting inside of some store or restaurant.

He glanced around. He was just outside of his locker, and, luckily, his class was only a few feet away; if it hadn't been, then he would've been late for Spanish class since Rachel had stopped him in the hallway, telling him everything on the paper, even though he could read it over anytime he wanted. It had been torn untidily off of a larger piece of paper, and scribbled in what might as well have been doctor's handwriting.

The meeting was at three o'clock on Saturday. Roman breathed a sign of relief as he straightened up, dialing his combination into his locker. He was glad when it turned out not to have been on Sunday. At least on Saturday he could still have training early, since Tyler wasn't likely to have homework or school. He wanted *nothing* of importance to happen on Sunday...

He had trouble in Spanish class, as they actually had a pop quiz with three questions from their last unit: the body parts. Roman sighed, remembering that part of one of his first ever tangible dream had been taking a pop quiz in Spanish class about the body parts. It was worse now, since he had decided to forget the majority of the body parts. Ironically, the three questions were the ones that he had hardly remembered in the first place. He could've sworn that they never *had* learned how to say 'finger' in Spanish, and it wasn't multiple choice.

During advisory, Roman asked Sergio if what he had answered correctly. He could not have been more wrong. Sighing, he turned to his math homework. At least in math, they were doing unit conversions, and had been given a chart with the amounts on it. He also had two pages of multiple-choice questions for science on the three types of rocks. Roman wondered if Tyler was going to explain to him what kind of rocks gemstones were. When was he going to get his gemstone, and what was it going to look like? What would it do? Would it have anything to do with his health-power? Or would it be something that inflicts pain? He had a short vision of himself breathing fire before he realized that he had been drawing something on his math paper absentmindedly.

He had never been a good artist, which would've been proven if he'd stayed in the Art Club much longer, but this sketch was far beyond his abilities. It looked a lot like one of the blankers that the Talismen used. It was a perfect model, with not a mark out of line. It looked much like one of the diagrams in their science textbooks, with perfect shading, angle, and proportion. He would've bet his left hand that Ms. Hue couldn't draw that.

The only difference between a blanker and this was that this had a small pod on top of the barrel instead of an aiming tube. Roman stared at the drawing for a moment, wondering how in the world he could've done it. He glanced at the clock. It was only five minutes into class, and he was certain that, if he could've ever drawn anything nearly as good, that he would've needed days, not minutes. He questioned if he had really been drawing it, and if it had been there the whole time. He had sharpened his pencil before leaving Spanish class, and hadn't started on his homework, yet the tip of his pencil was nearly depleted. Also, his wrist hurt, which, he realized, was why he had noticed the drawing in the first place.

Roman glanced around at the rest of the class. Mr. Ferris looked half asleep in his chair, the rest of the class immersed in work or a book. He quietly put away his math homework and took out his science questions and his pencil sharpener.

What about that other thing on the computer? he asked himself. It was almost like being possessed, if something was moving his hands for him. But when he had needed to scroll down on the website page, it had taken him to the name that had been haunting his dreams. Roman fretted to know what that meant. Did this have something to do with that? If not, what did it mean? Was he supposed to take its life replica to the meeting with him? But no, he had never seen this gun before. How could he use it if he didn't know what it was?

He noticed that once again, his hand, with the pencil, was moving slowly towards his paper without him thinking. He sprang his hand back. He could *not* be distracted again. He quickly put down his pencil and re-read chapter thirteen in his textbook, as he had nothing else to read, and Mr. Ferris would not be happy if he was just sitting there, trying to make sure that his hand didn't move on its own.

The rest of the week came and went in a haze. He had another RAA on Friday, which his team won once again. This time, though, he hadn't been on the same team as Treaver, and Roman was anxious for Treaver to be on his good side before their meeting tomorrow. He had no homework, and couldn't focus on his favorite computer game to save his life. And without Treaver to talk to, he couldn't stop pacing around his room. He wished that his Genedeaue symptoms would kick in. If his mind would wander, then maybe the knot in his stomach would go away. Would nothing happen at the meeting? Would he have to endure this a second time? Were the other three feeling the same way? Jacob had agreed to come, and Sarah and Treaver had already been in the Art Club, but Millo hadn't wanted to come. Roman had neglected to ask Stacy what she thought of Millo's

[203]

behavior.

That was what he needed to do. He would get his mind off of this by asking Stacy about Millo. That might even lead to some other thoughts. He quickly sprinted downstairs, going much faster than his first time descending them. He spotted Renaldo leaving the kitchen.

"Oh, it's you," Renaldo sighed when he saw Roman. "Is that the best that you can do? Most of the kids here can slide on the rails like skateboards."

"I would probably break my neck," Roman answered coolly.

Renaldo smiled. It wasn't his normal, malicious smile, but a genuine smile. Roman realized that he could tell the difference between a genuine and fake smile now.

"Try it sometime," Renaldo told him.

"Anytime? You don't want to watch and see me thoroughly embarrass myself?"

"You know, my jinxing power can apply whenever I want it to," Renaldo said slyly. "I was being very generous with that."

Roman took a moment to review the words they'd just shared. *Is that all you can do? Most kids here can slide on the rails like skateboards…*

"Did you jinx me so that I could do it?"

"*Now* he catches on," Renaldo snorted.

"How come you're being so "generous"?" Roman demanded.

"Truth be told, I'm testing out my power some more. Mr. Kyle said that I'm almost done with my training, and I want to keep it up."

"So I'm your guinea pig?"

"More like a regular pig, but yeah. In the meantime," Renaldo reached into his jeans pocket and removed a small, pink piece of paper, "Tyler asked me to give you this. It was his turn to get the mail, and this was for you, Sarah, Treaver, and Jacob. I didn't read it, but it's not exactly sealed…"

Roman rushed forward to retrieve the note. Renaldo looked slightly surprised at his enthusiasm, handing it to him hurriedly.

"It was addressed to you, but it's got all four of your names on it. But how come someone would just send you—"

"Thanks, Renaldo," Roman cut him off, knowing exactly the nature of why someone would send this, "but I've got to go. Have you seen Stacy around?"

"No," Renaldo sneered, unhappy at being interrupted, "probably with your slave-driver, Tyler. Or maybe she's trying to avoid your friend, Hot Wheels."

"Honestly, I don't know why people don't mistake you for a toilet, considering how much of a potty mouth you are," Roman growled, turning to go.

"I didn't say a single curse word, so you can't call me a potty mouth!" he called back, sounding much more like a regular eight-year-old than usual.

The first place Roman went was the gym, where Stacy could normally be found watching Tyler lift weights, reading the note as he went. It was in Victoria's handwriting. The note itself was brief. The only thing that made it longer than the original note was the mailing information. The pink of the note reminded Roman of someone being fired.

Meeting's cancelled. We'll tell you when the next one is during school.

The pink-slip now seemed like a very good analogy. There was no meeting...The knot in his stomach, instead of going away, tightened. He *would* have to go through all of that again. His dreams would continue until the next meeting. The meeting itself seemed like a sort of breaking point. Like Treaver had said: it was almost over. The dreams would end when they did what they were supposed to do, wouldn't they? Was that what he had been hoping for? It was good news and bad news. He could see the bad side, but even though he felt as if the meeting being postponed should be good news, he didn't know why.

Would there be no meeting, as there hadn't with the Art Club? And *why* was the meeting cancelled? A technicality? Someone sick? Roman was coming up with possible answers when the gym door was in front of him.

Opening it slowly, he saw that he had been correct about Stacy and Tyler, but Jill was also in the gym. He hoped that Tyler would let him talk in private with Stacy.

He asked Stacy his question carefully, ignoring Tyler's taunts.

"Oh, he'll warm up to you."

"Yeah, but when? It's been, like, three weeks."

"When he's ready. I'm not really the one to ask. I don't really hang around him very much. Maybe you notice it more because you're with him more often."

She left Roman with his mouth half open. That had been briefer than Roman had expected, and instead of feeling happy or upset, he was only agitated, which, at the thought, agitated him even more thoroughly.

It was past their training session, and he had nothing else to do. The earlier he woke, the earlier he could get at the television, where the early-bird always got the worm. He went to bed without another thought, forgetting completely about the pink note that had slipped from his hand in the gym.

For once, his sleep wasn't disturbed by nightmares, and by the time he woke, it was past noon. He felt so content, he would've stayed in bed even longer if his stomach hadn't put up such protests.

He dressed in some of his more casual clothes, taking his time with everything. It was the first night that he had gotten sleep in ages, and he was even more tired than when he had gotten about three hours of sleep...

He had just made some toast with raspberry jelly for breakfast before he was intercepted my Treaver and Sarah.

"Dude, where have you been?" Treaver demanded. "It's twelve-thirty!"

"What do you mean?" Roman wondered blearily.

"The meeting!" Sarah persisted. "How could you have

forgotten?"

"Oh, I-I didn't tell you guys?" Roman's confusion suddenly turned into a pang of apprehension. "Oh! I didn't! A note came for us from the others-meeting's been cancelled. Where did...what happened to the note?" He returned to being confused.

"Cancelled!" Treaver burst. "And I got up this early for nothing!"

Sarah was looking thoughtful. "Wonder what happened..."

"Who cares?" Treaver scowled. "At least we don't have to waste our Saturday afternoon. Who wants to go to La Centara?" Treaver beamed, looking around, before realizing that they were alone in the kitchen.

"We should tell Jacob," Sarah said with remorse. "He'll want to know. Have either of you seen him?"

"Ah, he'll come an' find us," Treaver dismissed irritably. "It's not like he'd leave without us."

Sarah shrugged, looking almost crestfallen. Apparently, she was taking this just as Roman had, confused, and thinking of it as bad. Roman followed Treaver into the lounge, where still no one wanted to go to La Centara. The only remaining Talismen were Millo, Elliyo, Gabriel, and Ringo, who would be leaving shortly. Everyone else had plans for the weekend already made. Treaver, observing that going with only two people was pointless, decided to do some extra sword practice.

Roman chose his favorite sword, and followed Treaver outside. This time Treaver lost to Roman at least twice in practice fights. Roman couldn't wipe the smirk off of his face even when they were going inside two hours later. Treaver had been at the mansion for a year, and Roman hadn't even been here for a month.

But Roman had to stop smirking when there was still no sign of Jacob around three o'clock. They started asking around to see if anyone knew where he was, and calling his cell phone. There was never any answer. And then, he was absent for his training session. Jill was furious and bewildered, since Jacob had hardly ever missed a lesson before, and never once on a weekend. Their tension rose along with everyone else's around eight o'clock, when there was still no sign of him.

"He's not answering!" Ellenore was exasperated as she called yet another of Jacob's friends to see if they knew anything of his whereabouts. Mr. Kyle and a few other Talismen were working with something down in the lab. Sarah was trying to comfort Millo, though she looked just as worried as he did. Missing curfew without any explanation or response was bad at St. Jefferson's, but it was ten times worse here. Roman took to pacing again, much to Treaver's distress.

"What's the worst that could happen?"

"You'd better hope that Renaldo didn't just jinx that."

Treaver tried to convince Roman to stop pacing, and even started following him around the kitchen during his pacing, but his arms got tired eventually.

"Look, if you insist on making a rut in the floor," Treaver sighed, "then at least eat something or say something or do something because you're really starting to depress me."

Roman sighed and stopped for a second. It felt slightly like he had just stopped walking on a treadmill, and he was tempted to continue. He considered eating, but he felt queasy. His mouth was dry, and he was sure if he opened his mouth he would tear his lips apart or get sick or both. He stood there for a second, closing his eyes, breathing too heavily. He could feel Treaver's eyes on him. Having his eyes closed was the only thing that could block out the rest of the world, and his head was pounding so much…

"I'm going to bed," he announced, leaving before Treaver could comment.

Everyone was up and about as he made his way across the hallway. Most of the kids were simply running around talking to each other, or else pacing like Roman had been. Sarah and Millo were still in the lounge. Most of the mentors were still down in the lab. Roman noticed Danny leaving through the entrance, which was the most prominent thing that anyone was doing then. Faces turned as Roman made his way across the hall. Renaldo,

Elliyo, and Gabriel ran up to him, asking if he knew anything that they didn't and listing what they knew. They let off about halfway up the first flight of stairs when he did not answer them.

Roman felt unusually tired, especially since it was a Saturday night. He wouldn't mind missing a good portion of tomorrow morning...normally. He wondered where Jacob was. He wished that he knew how to tell where he was and that there was nothing to worry about. He felt somehow that he was forgetting something, and strained to remember until it felt as if he would faint from it. He didn't remember entering his room, but he was there and pacing none the less when he stopped to breathe.

Mr. Kyle will take care of it... he told himself, *If anyone's going to be able to find him, it'll be the other Talismen, not you.*

With this thought hammering in his head, he fell face first onto his bed, still fully clothed. For a while he just lay there, praying that sleep would come, until it finally did.

The library was as quiet as usual, not because it was a library, but because hardly anyone spent time in there. It was the library at the mansion. It had the same shelves of books, the same carpeting and the same computers, but it had an odd feeling to the air. Roman wondered if he was dreaming or not. If he wasn't dreaming, he didn't remember waking up or coming here. He couldn't imagine why he *would* want to come here, since no one was with him.

But he recognized the odd air when the hairs on the back of his neck started standing on end. It was just like the one time in his dream about Victoria. He swallowed, suppressing a shiver that seemed almost uncontrollable. Then, someone ran past him, actually knocking him over. He rubbed his elbow, though he didn't have rug burn or anything that might normally appear when he was pushed over. It was once again like his Chrith and Victoria dream where he could touch things and practically be crushed by a speck of dust. He wondered if something would be missing from this one, like Emote had been from the other one.

Looking up, he saw that this time it had been Danny that

had knocked him over. He was heading toward the entrance, but then turned right a few yards away from it. Roman followed him, still having trouble remembering that no one could hear him, and being instinctively quiet.

Danny was heading towards the computers. Roman could see that one was occupied by Jacob. Roman recognized the screen, and saw that it was the Strayer website. Another open yearbook was on the table beside Jacob's computer. Roman wanted to call out to Jacob, but wasn't sure if he would end up warning him that Danny was about to see what was on his computer screen, or if he would demand to know where he was. Glancing at the windows, it was about noon. Roman wondered when exactly this was.

Jacob's head turned around just in time and he pretended to have his elbow fall on the keyboard as Danny approached. His screen flipped to the desktop with the internet minimized.

"Hey, Danny," Jacob greeted him, looking mildly curious, "what's up?"

"I just wanted to show you something outside. Not busy, are you?"

"Not very. I can do this later." Jacob pressed the power button on the computer, and it immediately shut off. He made sure to close the yearbook on the desk beside him before following Danny out of the room.

It was then that Roman noticed the swirling air behind him. It was the same figure from Roman's first dream that he immediately recognized as Mr. Kyle. He was thankful that he was there, and wondered if he knew that Roman was there again. He waved to him, but there was no response. Mr. Kyle wasn't running in slow motion, but was slowly making his way over to the computer, not pausing for an instant as he passed Roman.

Then the scene changed. Roman fell forward into a puddle of water, which, unexpectedly, held up his weight. He gingerly straightened up, not wanting the water to break. Not a ripple passed over it.

Jacob was following Danny. They were in the bayou, around the same time as before. Danny seemed to know where he

[210]

was going, but had evidently not told Jacob, as his expression had changed from mildly curious to almost anxious.

"Seriously, where are we going?"

"Relax, we're almost there."

"What out here could possibly be that important?"

"You'll see."

Roman glanced around, and spotted Mr. Kyle's air figure slowly moving towards Danny and Jacob. Roman was about to follow, since they were about to pass out of sight, but had not taken a single step before he leapt three backward from the shock of a high-pitched beeping noise.

"What was—" Jacob gasped. A second later, Jacob was bound and gagged, though it was as if time had lapsed. He was a few feet left of where he had been an instant before, and Danny was grinning maliciously down at him. What surprised Roman the most was that there were several other people standing over Jacob, all wearing pure black clothing and masks.

Roman stood frozen in his tracks as Danny started saying something to one of the people in black. Mr. Kyle appeared to have stopped in his tracks as well. What Danny was saying was muffled, and no sooner had Roman started to move forward, did the dream change, again.

It was the same hollow as in his other dreams, and this time the writing was back on some of the boxes, but only in characters instead of letters. It seemed close to sunset, and the gravel was stained blood red. Roman felt the shudders passing through him unstoppably now. The cold feeling was increasing. Roman was on a red box and Mr. Kyle, now fully visible, was on a green one. Roman heard scraping behind him. The people dressed in black were dragging Jacob over the rise. Mr. Kyle made a reflex, then paused again. Roman knew why. Suddenly, everything was moving in fast forward. Jacob was in the center of the clearing, struggling, then he wasn't moving, then he was strapped into a chair. The sky grew darker and darker all the while and the ground turned an even darker red to purple to deep blue. When it finally stopped, the stars were out, lighting the hollow in a silvery bath. Jacob was awake again and struggling.

He was still strapped into a plain black chair that somehow held firm while he wiggled. But now he wasn't gagged. He alternated between cursing and calling for help, both in French and in English, his violet eyes blazing dangerously in the darkness.

The people in black were standing in line between the boxes, apparently staring intently at the spot where Jacob was latched into the chair. Most looked like adults, but some were anywhere from teenagers to much, much smaller. One shadow was moving around in the clearing. Roman assumed it was Emote, as this was how he had appeared in his other dream. The shadow was circling Jacob like a hawk, the people dressed in black stiffening as he passed them.

Finally, Emote turned to stand either facing or facing away from Jacob, Roman couldn't entirely tell. Mr. Kyle jumped off of his crate and stopped a few feet away from Jacob and Emote. Roman jumped carefully down from his box, trying his best not to look at the silent figures behind him.

Emote spoke in the same hiss, sending even more chills through Roman. It was eerily quiet, a soft ringing aside from Emote's voice, which seemed to become magnified oddly, echoing off of the sides of the hollow and the crates.

"It's almost midnight. You're not going to change your mind, are you?"

"*Never you dégoûtant hybride!*" Jacob growled. Closer, Roman could see that Jacob was sweating. There were cuts, some still bleeding, all over his face, and one on his left eye. The eye was pink, red around the bottom, swollen, and watering with blood. Roman could tell that half of Jacob's struggles were from keeping himself from crying, though he couldn't help the steady trickle of blood. Roman's mouth was so dry that he nearly choked when he tried to swallow.

"I don't speak French, but I can guess what you're saying. Let's see, ah yes, one minute to midnight. Tick-tock. You *know* we'll do it."

"When in doubt, don't do anything," Jacob blurted out.

"A bad motto to live by. Fifty-five, fifty-four, fifty-three..."

Jacob started struggling more madly. Roman heard one of the people on the sides counting along with Emote before…

"SILENCE OR YOU'LL BE LIKE EXPEDITOUS IN ABOUT TEN SECONDS, RAGNROK!" Emote bellowed. He turned back to Jacob. "Forty-three, forty-two…Tell me, Makivik, what would you do if I sent Vang back for your little brother? Hmm? Couldn't do anything about that if…"

"You wouldn't," Jacob gasped. His eyes were now starting to cross out of focus, smearing the blood from his eye.

"Oh, wouldn't I? I tried it once before, didn't I?"

"I *know* you wouldn't. And he's not going to have much luck. They'll notice he's gone. And Sarah will know if he's lying!"

"She hasn't been able to tell up to now, has she? No, his power counters hers, doesn't it? Sometimes I marvel at my genius, he was the perfect match. He could make up some cock-and-bull story, but it's not like this is his first time skiving curfew, now is it, Vang?"

"It isn't," came a weak reply from Roman's right. Turning around, one of the smaller shapes was standing so stiffly that he was practically shaking. Roman recognized its eyes as Danny's. A surge of hate flooded Roman from head to toe. He felt an actual growl rising in his throat before Emote began talking again.

"See? Hmm, twenty seconds. Why don't you count with me, while Vang does the honor of bringing it out for me?" Danny shuffled out of sight. "Nineteen, eighteen, seventeen, sixteen, fifteen…"

Danny had returned with something wrapped in green cloth, bulging out oddly around the sides. Roman reached out, but drew his hand back. Emote had suddenly appeared as the black outline of a man instead of just a shadow, and was facing Danny. Danny held out the bundle to Emote, his hands steady, but the rest of his body shaking. Danny fell back as Emote roughly grabbed it from him and he scrambled back into line. Emote let the cloth drop.

Roman was suddenly on his knees, neither knowing nor

[213]

caring how long he had been like that. Emote was holding the same gun that Roman had drawn on his math homework, pointing it at Jacob's head. It seemed blacker than black, as the starlight didn't seem to touch it. Jacob was now still, not shaking at all as the blood flowed freely from his eye, dripping onto his shirt.

"What a brave boy. Aren't you going to be brave for your baby brother? You know, people used to say that, if you died in battle, getting shot or stabbed through the heart was a hero's death. What do you think?" He called out to the people standing around him, still holding the gun in a slightly crouched position. "Should we give the boy a hero's death?"

An indistinguishable murmur swept through the crowd, quieter near the area where the gun was generally being pointed.

"I said; *SHALL WE GIVE THE BOY A HERO'S DEATH?*"

A few people called out, slightly panicked, before several stronger voices called out 'no'. This seemed to satisfy Emote, which satisfied the audience.

"Six, five, four, three..." Jacob still seemed calm, staring Emote apparently directly in the face. He had successfully kept himself from shivering up to now.

"Two..."

A shot, a cry, and a laugh, and Roman was sitting up in bed, strangling the air in front of him. He was shaking, and he nearly flipped over to check his alarm clock:

12:01

Somewhere, in Roman's head, for the third time, rang the familiar three words.

Happy birthday, Roman.

15. Preliminary Conclusion

Φ   Φ   Φ

No one was awake, but Roman didn't have to be the one to wake them up. Mr. Kyle had seen the dream, too. He would be better to tell them…More than ever, Roman prayed that his dream wasn't real. He couldn't stop thinking that the tears running down his face were the blood that he had seen coming out of Jacob's cut eye. Hugging his pillow, Roman stared at the wall, his throat dry, shaking, head pounding, eyes watering, for hours. When the first light of dawn showed itself, he wished it would go away. He told himself not to waste his wishes on daylight, only to use them for Jacob…

Maybe it was just a nightmare. After all, he had been worried about Jacob before going to sleep.

Or maybe you're just trying to fool yourself.

Roman stayed there until Tyler knocked on his door. When he spoke, his voice was hollow.

"Hey kid, you awake?"

"Yes. And I already know." Roman's voice didn't even sound familiar. Tears had left his eyes hours ago, but he was still surprised that he could speak without his voice choking.

"You…already know?"

"Yes," Roman repeated. There was silence for a moment, then Roman heard Tyler's footsteps heading towards Treaver's room. He heard him knock on his door and ended up having to go into the room to wake Treaver up. It was odd, how much Roman could hear when he was being quiet, but he didn't dwell on the thought. He knew, somehow, that he couldn't fall asleep if he tried. On either account, he did not want another dream. He wished the world would go away…

Why are you getting so upset? The small voice that had tried to convince him that it had only been a dream before now appeared again, loud and clear, as if the speaker were actually there in the room with him. *You've only known him for a month.*

Because it's my fault again. *Because I'm the one who got him into this, and because it's too much like last time.*

The voice was silent from then on. Roman wasn't much aware of what he spent the day doing, except sometimes he found himself pacing, and sometimes lying in bed as if he had just awakened. Once, Sarah knocked on his door, but he did not let her in. He tried not to think about anything, for when he did his brain throbbed, as if it would explode from his skull. He spent most of the time blaming himself for what happened, thinking of what else he could have done, and what he did wrong. If there were only a way to make it up to Jacob, or at least to himself…but that sounded selfish. What could possibly make up for death?

One time, he glanced over at his alarm clock and saw that it was ten o'clock p.m. He hadn't eaten all day, but he felt too sick to eat, anyways. He didn't want to talk to anybody else, and that was sure to happen if he went outside.

He set his alarm clock for slightly earlier than usual and lay back in bed. He didn't know if he had time to think before falling asleep again.

When morning came, Roman knew that Jace wouldn't drive him to school on the bus since it was so early, and he didn't want to ask. Around five thirty, after sitting at the kitchen table, thinking about nothing in particular, and spooning at his cereal, he decided to try and walk there on foot.

Roman emptied his untouched bowl in the sink, then put it in the dishwasher. He wrote a note, saying that he'd be at St. Patrick's for the day. He slung his empty checkerboard-patterned, black and white backpack over his shoulder and marched into the hallway.

He stopped and gaped at Millo, standing in front of the door, watching him intently. No one was normally up this early, so why would *Millo* of all people be awake? Roman couldn't read his expression, and the more he tried, the more he thought about Jacob. Millo had the same purple lines under his eyes that

Roman had seen in his own that morning in the bathroom. His hair was unkempt, and he was wearing the same clothes as when Roman had last seen him. His indigo eyes were red in the whites, which Roman knew meant that he had been crying.

"What're you doing up?" Roman asked meekly. Once again, his voice sounded somehow different from normal.

Millo stared at him for a second through his hollow eyes. "I could ask you the same thing." His voice cracked, as if he hadn't spoken in a long while. Roman couldn't find any trace of his French accent, which worried him even more.

"I'm going to school," Roman answered flatly.

"Jacob's being buried today," Millo told him, not even blinking. "They found him outside the gate. You'd miss it. It's at noon."

"I don't want to go." Roman dropped his gaze, unable to meet Millo's eyes. Would he be mad? The more Roman thought about it, the more it felt like he was being confronted.

"It seems like a horrible thing," Millo's voice was still clear and unwavering, "but it's to honor him, and he deserves it. I'm going, but I'm not going to enjoy it. No one is."

Roman glanced up, his mouth feeling glued together.

"You don't have to go." Millo shrugged like he didn't care. He never shrugged like he didn't care.

"Are...are you feeling all right, Millo?" Roman regretted the words once they were out of his mouth.

Millo looked him hard in the eye, which he also never did.

"I should learn to stop eavz-eaves...eavesdropping," his accent showed a little. "Sorry, I haven't used that word in a while in English."

"What do you mean?" Roman wondered, ignoring Millo's apology.

"You're not the only one in the mansion that has dreams, Roman. I know a few others that have dreams much like ours, but they won't tell anybody. Some, not even Mr. Kyle. I had the same dream that you did last night, but I made sure that you couldn't see me."

[217]

"I'm not sure if that counts as eavesdropping," Roman said lamely.

Millo looked at him for a moment. Then, something that Roman didn't expect happened. The kitchen door was around six feet from the main entrance door. Millo was a foot in front of the main entrance, and Roman was about a foot out of the kitchen. Millo quickly sprinted the next four feet in a flash and hugged Roman, crying into his jacket.

Roman put his arm around Millo's shoulders. For a few moments they just stood there. Millo was already ten, not much younger than him, but his entire life changed when his parents were killed by the Strayers. And he was a very young ten. That wasn't too long ago. Roman remembered how reserved he always was, and how Millo seemed to be even afraid of him. Roman still didn't know why, and he wasn't about to ask.

"It's my fault," Millo whimpered, his accent showing again. "I knew something bad was going to happen as soon as Treaver told us about those girls. I had a dream about it. I should've done something about it."

Roman thought over what he said for a second.

"No, everyone's trying to blame themselves. I think it's my fault because I was the leader. But those dreams...I'm not sure if anyone could go against them. They're so real, and you can't escape them. If you were warned, then my dreams went against yours. But we were both warned, and we couldn't figure out what it meant. It's the fault of the Strayer who shot him, no matter what led up to it."

Roman didn't know how much time had passed when Millo let go of him and ran up the stairs to the left wing, not even looking back.

Roman knew now that there was a way to resolve his conflicts about Jacob.

Millo.

Roman walked to school. His brain felt numb the whole way. By the time he reached the school, the only ones who were arriving were the basketball players for practice and the teachers.

[218]

He had to wait outside until the school opened for the rest of the students. It wasn't too cold, but it was dark outside, and he didn't have anyone to talk to.

None of the other Talismen came, as expected. Roman didn't regret missing Jacob's funeral. He was sure that if he'd had to attend it that he would have to be sent home in a straitjacket.

To Roman's utter astonishment, people were giving him presents and wishing him a happy birthday as he walked into the school.

He got a set of green *Conectimals* from Tj, nothing from Alan, a chocolate bar from Caleb, and even a *Target* gift card from Rachel, along with a few other things from various different people.

Roman felt like yelling at anyone who said 'happy birthday' to him. There was absolutely *nothing* even remotely happy about spending his twelfth birthday crying in his room over his friend's death. But he tried to smile and say thank you to all of the gift-givers; they didn't know what had happened.

The day dragged on. Roman couldn't concentrate in any of his classes. His head hurt from everything that had happened over the weekend. Whenever he didn't think to avoid this, the teacher would call on him to ask him what they had just said, and Roman didn't know the answer.

Some people asked what was wrong with him. He just said that he hadn't had much sleep, and they believed it. He didn't eat around lunch time, and regretted it later when his stomach scorned him, since he hadn't eaten for over twenty-four hours. He didn't see Danny, Chrith, or Victoria the entire day, even though he kept a sharp eye out for them.

He dreaded what would happen when it was time to go home. He hoped that Mr. Kyle would understand why he didn't want to attend Jacob's funeral. But as he was leaving school, he saw the Talismen bus pull up.

Roman sheepishly approached the bus. Jace was in the leather driver's seat, as usual. Roman searched the windows as he passed them to see if anyone else was with him. He didn't spot anyone.

[219]

Jace opened the door, and watched Roman come on. Roman paused at the top of the steps.

"Look…"

"No need, Roman." Jace smiled. "We don't blame you. It's not your fault." For a moment Roman felt panicked. Had someone told him? But then Jace continued, "There was nothing to be done. But you missed his burial."

Roman nodded sadly.

"Well, get seated. It's gonna be a while before we get back to the mansion because Kyle asked me to pick up some more spray paint for the football field."

Roman sat in the very back. Normally the high schoolers got age rights over the middle schoolers, but this time Roman was the only kid on the bus. He turned on his Ipod. He had to turn down the volume; it was normally higher because of the other kids on the bus talking.

Roman got lost in the song and his own thoughts. He had slept a lot, but it didn't feel like it. He closed his eyes.

Sarah and Treaver were keeping Millo company in a corner of the biography section of the library. Millo was crouched, leaning back against a bookshelf. Sarah was hugging him. Treaver was watching awkwardly off to the side.

Treaver saw Roman approach and watched him with a look of curiosity. Sarah turned around. She smiled encouragingly. She stood up. Millo went to stand beside Treaver, which made Treaver regain his uncomfortable complexion.

Roman stood there, not knowing what to say, and wondering suddenly if anyone else was in the library to see them and overhear anything that he did say.

Before Roman could come up with something, Sarah hugged him. Roman held down a blush.

"Look, guys…" Roman started to say, but then Sarah stopped him.

"Oh, shut up. Don't embarrass yourself, newbie." She winked at him. Jace, Mr. Kyle, and all of the older Talismen were being strong for the younger students. This was the sort of thing that happened when they had to share a world with the Strayers, to many of the students. But when they thought no one was looking, they all mourned Jacob. Roman wanted to scream; none of this should've happened. The dreams that were sent to him had been entirely pointless. Not only had they lost a teammate, but gained nothing from it, except to get rid of Danny. Even though Roman couldn't read eyes like Sarah could, he could tell that it was hard for her to act strong like the adults. In his mind, she didn't have to pretend, but she did.

Roman frowned and shook his head sadly.

"We could use a change of scenery," Sarah whispered to him.

Roman nodded, giving in. If there was one thing that he owed to the others, it was to stay with them right now. It was him that had gotten them into this mess, and he was going to get them out of it. "Frappuccino?"

Treaver nodded. Millo looked doubtful, but Roman nudged him along down the stairs and up the other side. They split up to go to their separate rooms. Roman got on a deep green *GAP* jacket that was lying on his desk chair.

He met up with them in the entrance hall. Millo was the last to arrive, and Roman couldn't help worrying about him. Everything still felt like they were walking through some strange dream, his eyes searching for nothing in particular at most times, his feet adhering to thoughts that Roman barely processed, simply letting his mind wander wherever it desired.

"Hey, you four!" They turned around to see Ringo walking quickly towards them, which was unusual, considering that he wasn't normally at the mansion this long before the daily training session.

He came to a stop in front of them. "Where do you think you're going?" he demanded. He didn't normally demand things.

"*Starbucks*. Why?" Treaver replied.

"It's not safe to go outside," he told them. "If Danny *did* go to the Strayers, then he could tell them all of our identities."

Roman stared at him for a second. How did he know about Danny? Mr. Kyle must have told them. Also, Danny

[221]

wouldn't be at the mansion right now.

"But I walked to school this morning and nothing happened," Roman protested, recovering himself.

"Which you didn't have permission to do. Why do you think they sent Jace to pick you up?"

"You mean you aren't allowed to go home?" Sarah speculated.

Ringo shook his head. "The same goes for the others."

"But will I be allowed to go to school again?" Roman asked.

"No, even though it's very crowded, which is what Chris was thinking when he first found your note. We didn't even know where you were until he told us half an hour before you get off."

"Seriously?" Roman looked at the others.

Sarah nodded. "We thought you were in your room."

Roman sighed. "Well, there goes the Frappuccino."

Ringo nodded. He turned to leave, the added behind his back, "Those are *really* good, by the way." He vanished inside the kitchen.

Millo looked somewhat crestfallen. Roman found more sympathy than he would've thought possible well up inside him. He *had* to find a way to make Millo feel better.

"Hey, he said we weren't allowed to go anywhere outside Talismen territory, right?"

"Right," Sarah responded.

"Well, we can still hang out in the bayou."

"Why would we want to hang out in the bayou?" Treaver stipulated.

"We agreed on a change of scenery, it's the farthest place away from the mansion. Besides, it's not that bad, is it?"

Sarah shrugged, Millo copied her. Treaver finally sighed.

"Fine, as long as we pick a *dry* spot, city boy."

"That's what I thought, farm boy."

They spent the remainder of the time before the day's training in a not-too-far-off area in the more forest-like part of the bayou. They started out with small talk, until they were one by one pulled into conversations and were disappointed by the

[222]

setting sun that signaled that it was time to head inside. They were all laughing on the trudge back, even Millo. When Roman noticed, not long after Sarah and Treaver, he guessed, a grin tugged at the ends of his lips.

They had a RAA bout. Whenever Roman passed a familiar clearing, he broke down laughing, and eventually Tyler caught up to him and Richie, who had stopped to try to get Roman to start running again. Roman was fine with that, even though he lost to Sarah, who he knew would never let him live it down.

Tyler scolded him on how pathetic he was, and how he would never make it to the Island at this rate. Roman knew that he was just taking advantage of his mistake, since he didn't make them often. Everyone seemed to find it strange that he had lost the RAA session, though they assumed that Jacob's death had something to do with it. Roman realized that he had been exceeding expectations in all of his training sessions and was even at Sarah's level.

Which is exactly why what happened next came to be.

16. Islanders

Φ   Φ   Φ

It was April when Mr. Kyle announced who would be going to the Island next. Roman had kept his resolution to help Millo and had gone outside with him, Treaver, and Sarah every free opportunity that was given to him. Millo had grown happier and closer to them as the days went by. There weren't as many missions without Jacob to tell them when a potential Talisman or Strayer came along, aside from the usual sweeps of town. There was nothing but dead ends in the search for Danny. Roman, Sarah, Treaver, and Millo neglected to tell Mr. Kyle or Jace about Chrith and Victoria. At one point it was decided that it was too late to tell them, that they would not only be in serious trouble but that the trail would have gone cold by then. Roman spent much of his time in training sessions and sometimes attempting online classes in mathematics and engineering science in order to continue pursuing his desire to become a civil engineer, even though he had been pulled out of school and was now being home-schooled on slightly different topics.

The days in home-school didn't last quite as long as regular school days because of not having to rotate around or having as much free time as was offered. They didn't have study hall, considering that everything was technically homework, which took out an entire period, and they could continue working as soon as they were done with their lunch, and they could bring their backpacks with them instead of having to go to their lockers every period. Caleb had no way of communicating with Roman, but Roman had no idea how he and the rest of his friends would be reacting to him disappearing without a trace. Some would assume that he had moved, but normally if a student didn't tell all of their friends that they were moving, then they would tell one person and have them spread it around once they were gone.

Roman hadn't given any clue that he wouldn't be going to St. Patrick's anymore, let alone had he even known.

On April fourth, Mr. Kyle called Roman, Sarah, Richie, Renaldo, and Ashley into his office along with their mentors Tyler, Mary Beth, Rebecca, and Jill, who were all standing behind Mr. Kyle's desk when they arrived. Rebecca was a short, slightly-tanned sixteen-year-old with green eyes and black hair. Mr. Kyle had the students sit. Roman wondered why he would choose such a random assortment of students. They couldn't have been in trouble, since Roman had been behaving himself and wasn't very involved with Richie, Renaldo, or Ashley. And since they never hung around each other as one group or even had many training sessions together, Roman couldn't imagine what it had to do with all of them.

A nagging voice in the back of his mind kept insisting that Mr. Kyle had somehow found out about Roman and Sarah's little expedition; but if he had, he wouldn't have called the others in with them, and he wouldn't have left out Treaver and Millo. Roman hoped that he wanted to reward them in some way. But for what exactly?

Mr. Kyle sat behind his desk in a formal position, sitting up straight, which he rarely ever did. Jace stood next to the door at the back of the room, Roman not being able to tell through his sunglasses what he was looking at. But both he and Mr. Kyle seemed excited, and so did their mentors. At one point, Richie started shaking in his seat, his fiery eyes gleaming with anticipation. Roman figured that, like any other riddle, he had figured out why they were there, piece by piece. Roman felt jealous of him for a moment. It was like some huge secret that the others shared with each other, and Roman wanted to know what they were about to explain.

"Good afternoon, Roman, Richie, Renaldo, Sarah, Ashley, Rebecca, Jay, Tyler, and Mary Beth. Today is a very special day for the students sitting before us," he indicated to Roman, Ashley, Renaldo, Sarah, and Richie. Richie bounced with excitement at the formality in Mr. Kyle's tone.

"I have discussed your training with your mentors and

[225]

Jace. I have personally witnessed your training firsthand and have concluded that you each deserve a very important opportunity that countless before you have received." He paused for a moment, holding the tension. Ashley looked like she wanted to pry the words out of his mouth, Richie had closed his eyes as if cherishing the moment, Sarah seemed to gleam with happiness, Renaldo sneered at not being able to figure out what he was trying to tell them, and Roman felt like it should be obvious to him what Mr. Kyle was about to tell them. He glanced at Tyler, his mentor. Tyler winked at him, which was also unusual. Tyler was never very supportive. Roman started to think that this was some sort of late-executed April Fool's joke, and didn't rule out the possibility that the mentors were pretending to be proud and would end up giving each of them a mint and sending them out again.

"I, being the leader of this Talismen organization, currently, have decided that your training has come to an end," Mr. Kyle continued.

Wait…does he mean..?

"You are all about to receive your trip to the place most commonly known as the Bermuda Triangle, but, to us, it is the Island. From this day, you have the right to board one of our planes crossing the barrier into the Bermuda Triangle to collect your Bermuda stone and receive your second-rate power."

Roman stared at him in disbelief. He barely processed Richie letting out an excited squeal two seats down from him, Ashley tensing beside him, Renaldo coughing as if he had been drinking water on his other side, and Sarah seeming like she was trying to hold back tears of joy. Thoughts were jumbling around in his mind. He had only been there for less than half a year; he wasn't supposed to be ready for the island. Was this really the end of his training? Would he get a pupil of his own to be responsible for? What would his power be? What would his gem look like? Would he still stay at the mansion after he was safe enough to take care of himself? That one was immediately answered with a yes.

Mr. Kyle tried and failed to suppress a smile as he stared

[226]

at their shocked faces. Jace snickered from behind them. The mentors gazed proudly at their students. Tyler gave Rebecca a high-five. After a few minutes Roman remembered to breathe. A few extra moments and he started to wonder what would happen next. Everyone still seemed to be in shock. He had, for the most part, gotten his jumbled mind under control. One thought still nagged at him though.

I've only been here for four months, if even that.

Sarah and each of the others had been there for at least three years, Sarah's third year anniversary was in February.

Mr. Kyle eventually coughed and, being back to his old self, said to Jace, "I'm starting to think that they're as stone as my little milky friend here," he indicated to the stone figure that he kept on his desk, now a cow wearing a space helmet, molded partially after some of the figurines at Caleb's house that Roman had eventually told him about.

Roman shook himself to try to snap himself back to reality.

"Is this some sort of prank?" Renaldo asked disbelievingly.

"No, but I wonder if that wasn't hope that I detected?" Mr. Kyle smiled mischievously.

"No, no, sir!" Renaldo squeaked feebly.

Jill stifled a laugh, Tyler and Rebecca had less luck. Mary Beth smiled, but didn't laugh. Renaldo realized that they were chuckling at his expense and his dark skin turned ruddy as he blushed. Sarah still looked like she was trying not to cry. Richie was trying to look his normal expression; serious, but had as much luck as Tyler had holding back on giggling.

"Mr. Kyle," Roman spoke for the first time in what seemed like hours, "I've only been here for a few months. Why am I going to the island?"

Ashley whipped her head around, which made Richie jump out of his seat. He quickly sat back down and hung his head, hiding his blush while the mentors and Jace continued laughing. But Ashley was not laughing.

"Yeah, how come he gets to come with us?"

[227]

"Have you ever noticed that he beat you in every training session," Tyler inquired, "or am I delusional?"

"But he's...he hasn't been here long enough!"

"Ashley," Mr. Kyle said calmly, "he has succeeded in his training as well as you have. He has every right to go with you."

"But..." she stopped when no argument came to her lips.

Mr. Kyle nodded at Roman. Roman glanced at the others. Renaldo looked too happy to be anything less than indifferent. Sarah grinned at him, and Roman half expected her to hug him again. Ashley didn't look too happy. Richie was watching Roman curiously. There was something looming his eyes that Roman couldn't make out. Pride? Jealousy? Anticipation? Expectancy?

Mr. Kyle stood, pulling everyone out of the silence.

"Well, you all might want to start packing for your trip. I suggest that you don't bring any valuables, since the plane itself won't even make the journey. You know what you'll need. With all of your training, you're perfectly capable of handling things there without us, since we need as many people here as possible."

"Wait, we're leaving *now*?" Roman choked out the words.

"As soon as you all are ready. Remember, if it feels like you're forgetting something, *don't* leave until you find it."

Mr. Kyle dismissed them from the room to talk with the mentors and Jace alone. Outside of the office, the students all stared at each other.

"No more PCG classes!" Renaldo broke the silence excitedly.

"We will be the instructors of the PCG's," Richie said.

Sarah hugged Roman at that point.

"We're going to get our gemstones!"

"Yeah..." Roman kept staring blankly ahead, even as Sarah let go of him to hug Ashley.

"At least there's going to be *one* other girl on this mission with me," Ashley proclaimed as her voice started to choke with excitement like the rest.

"Feel lucky we're going at all!" Sarah laughed.

"We have a full squadron that will be arriving at the Island." Richie laughed as well. "We should feel lucky that we are going at all *and* that we will have a full team."

"More people to watch out for," Renaldo shrugged, then added, nearly yelling, "but who cares? We're going to the Island! We are outta here!"

Roman rushed down the stairs with the others. They all stopped at the bottom of the steps in the main hall, not knowing where to start.

"Well, we aren't going to keep this to ourselves, are we?" Renaldo asked.

"No, no we are not," Ashley agreed with him. It was the first time Roman could remember her agreeing with him.

Roman broke off in the direction of the lounge. It was noon, and everyone would be there while it rained outside. He found, after a moment, that the others were following him, since everyone that they wanted to tell would be in the lounge as well.

He slipped over something at the bottom of the stairs as the others rushed on ahead. He looked around to see what he'd slipped on. A crumpled old piece of paper, not unlike the paper that the paper pets were made out of, was jammed in the bottom stair. Roman pulled it out so that no one else would trip on it and looked it over, wondering how long it had been there.

It was something printed out here at the mansion, and dated *January 15, 2010*. All that was on the paper was the ending of some article that had been cut off at the bottom. Curiosity peaking, Roman looked it over. It was evident why it would've been here at the mansion; the article was mainly about an old legend of a gemstone granting peoples' wishes. Roman shook his head, smiling at the fact that this sort of thing really did exist, and tossed the paper out in the nearest storage closet trash bin.

In the lounge, Roman spotted Treaver talking to Stacy at one of the tables behind the wide-screen. Cole was sitting at one of the tables in a corner drawing something Anime alone, which he had done a lot ever since Danny had betrayed them. Cole had spent most of his time with Danny and not with many others or even his mentor, Mary Beth. Having been the one closest to Danny. Renaldo sometimes made fun of him, saying that he would be a traitor, too. Cole would always end up hitting

[229]

Renaldo with various things if he caught him before he managed to get into his room and lock the door. But everyone could tell that Cole was bothered by what Renaldo said to him.

Chris was watching TV while Elliyo and Gabriel were occupied with having mud-fights outside, taking advantage of the spring showers. Roman first went over to Chris, and began spreading the word.

"You're leaving *now*?" Treaver inquired. Stacy nodded, wondering the same thing.

"Yes, Mr. Kyle wants us to prepare immediately and depart as soon as the preparations are finished," Richie concluded. He'd joined Roman in the lounge along with the others almost immediately.

"Then what are you all sitting around for?" Stacy asked. "Let's get these guys going!"

She stood along with Treaver, Ashley, and Sarah. Chris shrugged and stood, too. Cole kept staring at them as Jasmine came into the room and had a group-hug with Sarah, Stacy, and Ashley.

"I can't believe you're getting your gemstone! It's so exciting!"

"You'd better believe it," Sarah answered.

"Congratulations," Cole said unexpectedly. All eyes were turned on him as he continued with his sketch. A silence descended upon the room and all of its inhabitants.

"Well, let's get packing!" Ashley lightened the mood and clapped her hands. They all rushed out of the room. Richie started giving out orders to everyone.

"Jasmine, would you be so kind as to retrieve some of the knapsacks from the storage closet down the hallway near Jace's office? The people who will be arriving at the Island should all pick out their choice of arsenal. Stacy, would you please ready some rations? The items that we will need are different varieties of vitamin C sources such as..." Roman stopped listening when he sped off up the stairs to pick out a sword and a mechanical spider out of the ball-closet.

He picked out his favorite sword, the one with designs of

dragon-like creatures at the bottom of the hilt. He got a mechanical spider out of the back compartment. He sprinted back down the stairs, nearly ramming into Mary Beth at one point around the third floor.

"Hey, congratulations, Roman!" she yelled as he ran past.

"Thanks!" Roman said over his shoulder, which made him nearly crash into the papier-mâché pony, dropping his mechanical spider in the process. He sighed and scooped it up in his arm again before continuing on.

Richie had gone off to get his set of arrows and other weapons, leaving Ashley and Renaldo fighting over who was in charge of the mission.

"I'm older and smarter than you!" Ashley was arguing.

"Smarter? Uh-uh. Not in a million years are you smarter than me, drama queen!"

"You're just a dumb boy! We've both been here the same amount of time so it should be the one who's older!"

"If that's so," Roman interrupted them, "then I'm in charge because I'm older than everyone else going on the mission."

Ashley considered this for a moment. As Sarah and Richie were coming back she motioned them over.

"Okay, we've got an eleven-year-old newbie—"

"Twelve."

"—an amazing ten-year-old," she indicated to herself, "an eleven-year-old brain boy," she gestured at Richie, who didn't look like he knew whether to take that as a compliment or not, "a twelve-year-old girl, that is *awesome*," she added towards Sarah, "and an eight-year-old bug that has a weird accent, is half bald, and honestly is not fit to be going to the Island in the first place, let alone lead the mission there. Who's it gonna be?"

"You referred to the all the boys in a negative tone." Richie raised an eyebrow, which looked at odds with his orange-pigmented eyes.

"There's a reason, Richie. There *is* a reason."

"Yeah, it's 'cause you're sexist," Renaldo muttered.

"Okay, we've pretty much ruled out Renaldo," Roman

confirmed, with a sneer from Renaldo. "And I don't really feel comfortable with Ashley as leader." he tried to sound as casual as possible to avoid getting his lip stretched over his head by her. "And I honestly don't want to be leader." He held up his hands as if surrendering.

"No one was going to pick you anyway," Ashley rolled her eyes.

Sarah gave Roman a pitying look.

"Aren't we supposed to be working together?" Roman asked skeptically.

"Well, we need someone to make the hard decisions," Renaldo said coolly, as if it weren't an actual question.

"That leaves Sarah and Richie," Ashley concluded.

"Rock, paper, scissors?" suggested Chris, who was passing by with a pile of specialized clothes.

Ashley smacked his arm as he passed, but he couldn't react with his arms full.

Roman chuckled and received a punch from Ashley as well. He tried not to show it, but it actually hurt.

"Well, we might not be able to understand the instructions coming from *Tolkien*-fan over there," Renaldo complained.

"Well, I'm not going to be the leader!" Sarah sounded appalled.

Ashley leaned over and whispered something inaudible to Sarah. Sarah gave her a dirty look and Ashley shrugged innocently.

Richie considered for a moment. "I do not wish to be the leader of our group, either."

"Oh, that's just great." Ashley sighed. "Why *don't* you, exactly? It's one of you three, since no one wants the *children* to make the big decisions," she added sardonically.

Richie motioned with a lopsided-shrug. He never shrugged much, since he normally found something to say.

After a moment, he added, "Sarah and Roman are both the same age. I am an entire year younger than them. If we are to be judged by our age, then it should not be me."

"And he's chicken," Renaldo put in.

Richie scowled at him.

"Neither of us want to be the leader," Roman dismissed the thought. "I still think that we should work together. We got the same training."

"Yeah, well some people do better in those training sessions." Sarah looked at him.

"Oh, no," Ashley contradicted, "I'm not putting my life in the hands of a newbie with three months of training."

"Three and three-quarters," Roman pressed.

Renaldo rolled his eyes.

"Vote? It's either that or agree to disagree, which won't get us anywhere until someone gives."

"Vote," they agreed.

"Who votes Richie?"

Richie seemed to shrink back, but only Roman raised his hand, since Sarah didn't want to lead.

"Oookay, Sarah?"

Ashley and Renaldo raised their hands.

"And Roman," Sarah said, lifting her hand. Richie did the same. Roman was surprised at Richie voting for him.

"It's a tie," Renaldo sighed and glared at Roman as if it were his fault that they did not agree.

"Well, it's simple," Sarah said. "We rule out Richie because he got the least amount of votes, and vote again."

"Fine," Ashley snorted.

"All is very well then," Richie stated simply. "Who has their vote set for Roman?"

Sarah and Richie raised their hands again. Roman knew where this was going and wondered why they went on from there with Sarah's vote. Only two out of five had voted for him, and he was going to vote for Sarah, which would make three with Ashley and Renaldo. But Roman thought that he saw movement in Richie's eyes. He could have sworn that he saw fire licking at his pupils.

"And who has their vote set for Sarah?" he said calmly, giving Roman even more doubts of what he thought he might have imagined.

Ashley and Roman's hands both shot up, but Renaldo's stayed at his side.

Roman noticed that Renaldo was staring transfixed at Richie. Richie was looking back with the same flame in his eyes that Roman couldn't be sure was real or an illusion created by their unnatural color.

"Renaldo," Richie continued calmly, not even blinking, "who does your vote state allegiance to?"

Renaldo blinked, then pressed his lips together. Slowly, but surely, he lifted his finger to point at Roman.

17. Airport Oddities

Richie made sure that Jasmine and Stacy had retrieved the right food for their trip. He asked Tyler, who at this point had had the most experience thanks to his frequent punishments how to cook in the kitchen, and Gabriel, who could tell how clean things were, to make sure that the food would last for a week at the very least.

Roman tried his best to organize most of what was going on. Sarah helped him along, but Ashley gave him a hard time, making him explain every simple request down to its roots, and complaining that he was only in charge of organizing the mission, and not the mission itself. Though every time Ashley suggested this, Sarah, Richie, and even Renaldo told her that it was unfair to suggest so and ended the discussion. Ashley still spent most of her time glaring at Roman while she pretended to do her assignment, which Roman ended up having to do personally.

It was all done in less than an hour, at around one thirty. Before they realized that they were done, they had spent time pacing back and forth, trying to see if they had forgotten anything. But they all ended up back at Roman's place by the stairs, then recognized the fact that they were finished with packing.

"So now we have to leave?" Renaldo asked timidly.

Roman shrugged, and then nodded, having made up his mind in the split-second difference.

Sarah swallowed theatrically. It then occurred to Roman how perilous the trip they were about to take really was. He wondered if they would survive the island, or when and where they would land on the island, or if time even existed there. According to what he had learned in his PCG classes, none of these questions could be accurately predicted.

He nervously suggested going up to see Mr. Kyle, breaking the silence that followed his response to Renaldo's question. Jasmine, Stacy, Chris, Treaver, and now Millo were all there, waiting off to one side of the entrance hall.

Roman sighed when no one moved. He started up the stairs and felt the gentle vibrations of the following unhurriedly. Everyone else slunk quietly back into the kitchen or the lounge.

Ashley pointedly ran ahead to lead the way, even though Roman knew that she was scared out of her mind. Ashley glanced back and raised her eyebrows. It was a direct challenge; she wanted to test him. She kept at a steady pace, a sort of casual walk, waiting for him to take back the lead. Roman started at a faster pace, passing Ashley by an inch. Ashley didn't try to run ahead of him again, but Roman glanced back and she nodded her head. Afterwards Roman tried to figure out what had just happened. Had she just accepted him as their leader? Or was she just playing with him?

Roman shook the thoughts off and focused on calming his growing fear of the island.

This is what we've been training for. Everyone here with their gems have gone there and come back in one piece.

But at the last thought, the part of his mind that so often argued with him and wormed around whispered so that Roman thought that the others were sure to hear it. *You don't know that. Maybe they came back in more than one piece but they've healed somehow. They couldn't tell you what to expect. You can't know how they came back and some others they were with didn't. After all, they never talk about it.*

Roman shot the quickest look over his shoulder to see the others following close behind him up the fourth flight of stairs, their expressions contorted with their own thoughts. Roman kept his eyes on the office door as they headed towards it, determined not to let the paranoia that they might hear his thoughts engulf him.

They were at the door with Mr. Kyle calling them inside before he could process another thought. The mentors were back inside. Mr. Kyle raised his eyebrows in a question of what they wanted.

"We're done packing," Renaldo said feebly.

Mr. Kyle nodded and smiled, apparently indifferent to their seen-a-ghost expressions.

"Well, shall we head to the airport, then?" he asked formally.

Roman glanced at the others, who nodded slowly, one at a time. Roman returned their nods to Mr. Kyle. He stood and beckoned the mentors over to him.

"Make sure that your students are seen off safely. The plane will be occupying gate thirteen. Mary Beth, I'm sure you remember our friend Chad Braisly from your first little expedition? It's your job to find him; he'll be expecting you. Being Sunday, some people will be flying off for weekly work-trips, so you should be well covered. Try not to look like you're guilty of something, especially for you five." He turned to Roman, Ashley, Richie, Sarah, and Renaldo, "Once you get there, don't look out of place, don't keep that frightened look on your faces. Remember, stay away from the regular security, and meet Chad outside the terminals. Try not to loiter around too long, or the security guards will come and check you. Stay away from the metal detectors." he emphasized. "We can't have them finding those swords and spiders of yours."

"Or the arrow heads," Sarah added helpfully.

"Also, we should account for the pocket knives," Richie concluded.

"We were supposed to have pocket knives?" Roman asked.

Renaldo and Richie nodded.

Mr. Kyle smiled. "You four are really good at hiding these kinds of things. Isn't that right, Sarah?"

Sarah blushed. "Needed to ease some of the tension."

Sarah pulled a small, metal object out of a drawer in his desk. Sarah tossed it to Roman. It was red with shiny silver-colored edges. Roman tested it out by flipping everything out at once. It had scissors, a knife, something to shave with, a needle, a sort of scoop, and something for opening jars.

"Aw, he got a red one!" Renaldo complained. "Want to trade? I have a purple one, but it has a chain-driver and something else that I don't know what it's for."

"No thanks, I don't think that I'll need this when I have a sword."

"You'd be surprised." Mr. Kyle winked at him. "You were trained to use that, weren't you?"

"Well, yeah in TUC's, but…I don't know, it just seems kind of small compared to the sword."

"I'm sure that you'll need it at one point or another," Mr. Kyle dismissed.

Yeah, if I have a sudden shaving-crisis.

"Well, Jace and I will see you all off as far as the front gate. Good luck. And if something seems dangerous and you can avoid it, just don't do it. You aren't running a race. You each only have one life, so don't risk it, if possible."

With that, Mr. Kyle led them out of the room. Roman remembered when Mr. Kyle had had the first dream with him and how it had affected him so negatively. He thought of how he had simply seemed to have forgotten the whole dilemma afterwards. Roman remembered what they had discovered about his brother, or had tried to discover. Roman found an odd comfort in that Treaver and Millo weren't coming with them, that they would still be safe at the mansion in case…

He didn't let himself finish the thought. He thought that he had been afraid for the others that were going with him on the mission, but now he knew that he was much more afraid for himself. He had only been there for less than four months, and it was astounding that he had received the honor of leaving for the island so early in his training, but he wasn't sure that he liked it.

The sooner the better, that was what his mom used to say when he didn't want to get a flu shot at the doctor's office. Remembering those words made him feel sad, but it was nice somehow to recall them so clearly; that he hadn't forgotten them, even though he never thought of them.

He snapped out of his thoughts when he tripped on the

carpet and stumbled trying to keep standing. No one had noticed, since he was at the back of the group. Sarah glanced back, but Roman was walking along as casually as he could by the time she did. She dropped back slightly to walk along beside him. Roman was thankful that she kept him from blanking out again.

"Have you noticed that every boy going to the island's names start with an R?" she asked him.

Roman raised his eyebrows. "I didn't. Sort of off topic, isn't it?"

"Nope, I'm talking about the mission. But only the funny parts. Like how the person who's taking us to our plane is called something as ordinary as Chad."

Roman smiled the best he could. "It's been years since I've been on a plane," he said as they descended the stairs.

"Yeah? When was your last time?"

"Five years ago when I visited my aunt Rosy in Nevada for Christmas."

"Was the airport crowded?"

"Oh, yeah."

Roman was staring at the steps that he was climbing down, but somehow he instinctively knew that Sarah would be smiling.

"What happened to your aunt?" she wondered quietly.

Roman was silent for a minute. "How'd you know that something happened to her?"

"You were in an orphanage for two years. Even if she wasn't fit to take care of you, she still would've been somewhere on your record."

"You looked through my files again?"

"Do you even have to ask? It's more addictive than you think."

Roman felt a strange surge of anger, which happened anytime someone asked him about his family. He didn't say anything else, but kept staring at where he was walking. There was a silence between them, broken only by the others ahead of them with their various conversations.

When they were almost at the last flight before the main

[239]

hall, Sarah decided to speak again.

"Do you want to play Chopsticks?"

"Nah, it's more of a girls' game."

Sarah and Ashley went at the game while they were waiting in the entrance hall for Jace and Mr. Kyle to check all of the preparations. They had been told to eat while they could. Ashley had a loaf of Hawaiian bread, Sarah a slice of cheese pizza, and Roman a corn dog. Sarah scolded Roman at one point that he shouldn't chew with his mouth open. She lost the game when she accidentally bopped Ashley's one-finger hand with a two-fingered hand. Ashley re-bopped the same hand, and that was the end of the game for Sarah. She said that there was a version of the game with things called 'bumps' where you could bring a hand back in by transferring one finger to another, but Ashley didn't like to play that version.

"That's just because she stinks when she can't keep someone's hand out," Sarah whispered to him.

Roman chuckled, and Ashley kicked him, obviously having heard what Sarah had said.

They squeezed into Jill's *Sudan* and Mary Beth's *Bug*. The *Bug* had been painted white with black dots, reminding Roman of a Dalmatian. Roman wondered why an eighteen-year-old girl wanted a *Bug* that probably had insurance for *Cruela De'ville* attacks.

Renaldo asked the same question out loud.

"It's more a camouflage kind of thing. We're trying not to draw attention to ourselves. If we brought a limo that would be slightly obvious."

Ashley snickered and shook her head. Roman knew exactly what she was thinking; there was no way that that car wasn't going to attract attention.

Mr. Kyle and Jace walked along with the slowly-cruising cars down to the front gate, where they drove until Mr. Kyle and Jace were out of site. Mary Beth's car took the lead. Roman noticed that Mary Beth was almost at Jace's level as far as students' involvement, even though she was younger than Jill and didn't live at the mansion like he did. But then again, Mary Beth

[240]

wanted to stay permanently, while Jill was now going to *Northwood University* to become a doctor at the nearby hospital.

Halfway through the suburbs, Mary Beth, seeing the hollow look on Roman's face, suggested that they sleep while they could. Sleeping sounded like a good idea to Roman, since he now hadn't had a tangible dream since Jacob's death.

He didn't think he could've fallen asleep in the very little time they had before reaching the airport, but moments after he closed his eyes and put his head against the windshield, he fell unconscious.

It seemed like only a second before Sarah was shaking him awake.

"Are we there yet?"

Mary Beth giggled at the obliged road-trip line while she got out of the *Bug* and opened the trunk.

"Yeah," Sarah responded in a small voice. "You've got a little drool there."

Roman quickly wiped it off before Ashley could make fun of him.

Roman sat up in his seat. They were in a dark parking garage that smelled of cigarettes. The walls and ground of the lot were plain grey anywhere that could be seen. Around the edges, sunlight was pouring into the structure. They were on the ground floor, five yards away from the spiraling track that the cars would climb to find the higher levels. The cars were all around them, dropping others off, being chauffeured for the airport's parking, being parked by their drivers, being stripped of their luggage, and some moving slowly up the spiral track.

Even the one floor was bigger than Roman remembered, or had possibly imagined. He couldn't see the end of the bend in front of them that led to the valet parking. The ground was black where cigarettes, gum, food wrappers, and other things that Roman tried not to step on had fallen or been placed. He climbed out of the *Bug*. Roman saw Jill's *Sudan* three spaces back from them. Ashley and Richie were already helping Mary Beth with getting their luggage out of the small trunk of the car. They had taken seven bags with them, none so large that they couldn't put up the handle and carry them as backpacks, but none so small that the weapons were showing through the sides. As soon as Roman climbed out, Sarah followed closely behind. Some car's fumes were billowing out into the enclosed space, others made as much sound as roaring motorcycles. The walls had more than just grey here and there; posters saying what parking sector you were about to enter, which way to the elevators and the entrance. The security guards in blue uniforms looked uncomfortably like police officers to Roman.

The cars parked around them were in more varieties than Roman had ever seen, some he had only seen in commercials or in old black- and white movies. There were a few airport buses taking people who had just arrived to their specified areas. Roman saw all sorts of different people: goths, business people wearing suits, people going on vacation with or without their children, people who seemed to have just come from a costume party, and of course the ones who worked at the airport. It would have been a good place for people-watching if not for the car fumes, pounding racket, and smokers.

Roman took a normal-sized brown suitcase. It didn't look any different from most of the luggage that he was seeing, but he knew that that particular bag held his weapons, pepper spray, a few rags, rope, and many food bags. Sarah grabbed the dark-green case that held her arsenal.

Mary Beth took one that looked like an oversized, royal-blue briefcase. The other mentors climbed out of the *Sudan*. Renaldo took the brown-leather case that held most of the clothing and his weapons. Richie had one that was a sort of scarlet, which Roman knew held his weapon of choice, a *Wilderness Survival* book, extra food-provisions in case something happened to the other suitcase, and other things he couldn't remember. Jill also took a case that looked like a duffel bag. That was all of their luggage, seven in all, which left Rebecca and Tyler with nothing to do.

"How about we park your cars while you're helping the minis out?" Tyler suggested.

Mary Beth raised her eyebrows skeptically. "You're only fifteen."

"But my birthday's the twentieth," he insisted.

"You don't have a license," Jill retorted.

"I have a learner's permit."

"Which requires an adult in the car." Jill rolled his eyes.

"But Rebecca would be driving the other car. And she's sixteen and *has* a license."

Rebecca looked up at the mention of her name. "Hmm?"

"She has to be *in* the car. We won't be gone that long."

"But what if the airport workers are Str—" Rebecca covered his mouth and hissed something into his ear.

When she retracted her arm, all Tyler had to say was, "Good luck minis."

"You really need to come up with a better nickname for us," Roman responded, grinning.

"You're my finest work yet, Rowland," Tyler told him, "Don't mess this up for me, 'kay?"

"I'm about to risk my life, and you want me to dedicate that to *you*?"

"Yup, good luck." Tyler and Rebecca waited next to the cars, trying not to look to the security guards.

Mary Beth and Jill led the way into the inside of the enormous structure that was the airport. They smiled at the officers as they passed through the automatic doors. White tile wrapped itself around all of the walls and floors. The ceiling was stone, as far as he could tell from squinting through the florescent lights that radiated on everything in sight. Roman blinked from the transition between the partially underground parking structure and the lively, buzzing, gigantic interior. All sorts of smells mixed with each other and produced new smells that Roman couldn't process. One smell that he could identify reminded him of the art room at St. Patrick's. He was surprised that he still recognized it after months of not going to school. It reminded him of Caleb, Tj, and Allan.

Around the edges were all different assortments of *McDonalds, Pizza Huts, Starbucks, Wendy's, Taco Bell, Subway,*

[243]

and dozens of others that had fancy names that probably sold fast food. Different popcorn, pretzel, ice-cream, cotton candy, and funnel-cake stands roved slowly around the perimeter, weaving through the crowds and occasionally stopping to sell something. Vending machines were occupying the corners. Bathroom signs held fast to the walls as teenagers slapped at them. Roman guessed that they were in the food court. Parents and children and crews of teenagers and single adults sat at benches and tables that made up the center of the room. Elevators with bronze doors were next to the bathrooms.

Roman wondered if all of Katy had come to meet at this one place, but he knew that more than just people native to Katy were here. It also occurred to him that they had driven into a place that was more Houston than Katy. The sounds that assaulted his ears were impenetrable. Here and there he could make out random conversations that included everything from business to dating. The aroma of food made Roman's stomach growl, even though they had eaten before leaving. A few other smells made him want to vomit.

"Terminals are this way." Jill and Mary Beth started forward; Roman and the others sprinted to follow in their wake before the floods of people could squeeze into the spaces they made. Roman could now see escalators at the opposite part of the hall, which turned out to have an ending. They avoided kids that were trying to run down the escalator in the wrong direction while keeping Renaldo from joining in. The rubber rails that they were supposed to hold onto were worn with scratch marks and tears. A few announcements regarding which flights were leaving were made. Roman tried not to bump into people who were riding and climbing the escalator at the same time in their rush.

Roman thought that the sharp end of the escalator would damage his cargo, so he tried to hold the bag while he passed over, not bothering to use his suitcase as a backpack. Sarah smiled at him.

"Every person makes that mistake their first time. But haven't you ever been to *Macy's*?"

"Where?"

[244]

"Never mind. There's this store at *Memorial City* Mall with escalators."

"We are about to arrive at the security portion of the airport," Richie announced.

An astonished expression crept across Sarah's face. She looked like she wanted to stop for a moment, but wouldn't want to get lost.

"Why is security *after* the food-court?"

"Maybe so that people can buy food here as a pit-stop," Roman suggested, not knowing what was so wrong about security being after the food-court.

Sarah shook her head.

"As long as we get on our plane, it doesn't matter," Ashley concluded optimistically.

Sarah didn't look too convinced, but shrugged as well as she could at the pace they were moving at.

Mary Beth and Jill had obviously spotted the security. They looked around and headed to the edge of the second floor where there was a metal- and glass rail overlooking the lower section. Roman, Renaldo, Richie, Ashley, and Sarah followed. Mary Beth, Jill, Richie, and Sarah peered over the edge. Roman wondered why Richie and Sarah were watching along with Mary Beth and Jill, since they had never met Chad.

"Sarah, what are you looking at?" Ashley asked.

"It's all still down there," Sarah murmured absently. "People would normally come around the closed off area over there." she looked in the direction of a hallway with yellow tape blocking it off from the rest of the bustling crowd. A sole guard stood watch.

"You mean the old security?"

"Yes, they used to go through there. The doors are new, this sector is just the second-checking. It's a backup. But the first part's closed off."

"Well, there's your answer." Roman replied, "The other part had maintenance or something, and this part's still open."

"But then why would they add another entrance, genius?" Ashley rolled her eyes. "There's more than one entrance to this place. The people could've just walked or taken those busses to another entrance."

Roman was taken aback. "I don't know."

"Exactly," Sarah murmured.

"There he is!" Jill sounded truly enthusiastic that they had found the person who was going to take the others to the plane that would fly them straight into an inevitable crash.

"Good, let's hurry. Security will be wondering why we aren't going through."

"Would they really care about seven random kids?" Roman whispered to Sarah as they started down the other elevator, this time avoiding kids that were going up in the wrong direction.

"Depends on how well dressed they are," Sarah assured him.

The answer didn't satisfy Roman. But he was partially disappointed that they had found their guide so early. He had been secretly hoping that they might even be able to turn back around, even though he knew that they wouldn't get their gems if they did. Roman had concluded that, as a Genedeaue, getting his gem was his current top priority. He couldn't live his life regularly, he couldn't have done that in the first place without a family, and he refused to go to a foster home, other than the one he was currently at. And it would be very difficult fighting Strayers without his most valuable weapon that even protected him from gunfire and any average criminal. He now knew the full extent of the choices that he had been given before he had joined the Talismen; pick a side, get your gem, or die. It wasn't a large variety of options.

They headed towards a place where its name had all sorts of accent marks on letters that Roman hadn't known there could be accent marks on. There were three people working there, and no customers except for one man in a classic, tan-brown undercover-detective coat. He had sunglasses and a hat that reminded Roman of *Indiana Jones*. His coat was tied around the center with a sort of built-in belt. He was flitting through the pages of a *Houston Chronicle* from last month.

"Chad, could you be any more obvious?" Mary Beth sighed.

Chad took off his sunglasses to reveal startling grey eyes. He winked at her and smiled, showing poorly brushed teeth.

"Ah, these must be the new recruits." he said, examining Roman, Renaldo, Ashley, Sarah, and Richie. His voice was high-pitched for someone who looked about in their mid-twenties, and he talked more quickly than Roman thought normal.

"They really *should* come up with a special name for us," Roman commented.

Chad smiled. "I like this one." He wrapped his right arm around Roman in a half-hug. Roman tried not to look awkward.

Once Chad let go of him, he stood and shook hands with Jill and kissed Mary Beth's hand.

"Charming," Sarah whispered to Ashley, who tried not to giggle.

"Well, let's get you a speedy trip to your plane, shall we? Secret passageway this way," he added with a mischievous smile. "Try to keep up."

"Oh, no you do—" Before Mary Beth had even finished her sentence, Chad had disappeared completely. A sharp breeze ruffled Roman's hair, and also blew Ashley's into his face.

"Ugh!" Mary Beth groaned. "Is he *trying* to get caught?"

"What was it that just occurred?" Richie voiced everyone else's thoughts in his own words.

"His second-rate power," Jill said coldly. "Super speed."

"What's the matter, you guys?" Chad's voice came from over Roman's shoulder. Renaldo nearly jumped out of his skin. Roman spun around, but no one was there. The laughing then came from the direction he had just been facing. Chad was standing where he had been before with his hands stretched out innocently.

"Chad, what the hell is wrong with you?" Jill demanded.

"Hey, no need to curse, Jelly." Chad sighed. "Oh, I forgot. You guys *can't* move at a hundred-and-fifty miles per hour!"

"If you'd been running that fast, you'd at least be out of breath," Mary Beth dismissed. "Can we get a move on?"

[247]

"Sure, the short cut's through there." He pointed to a door next to the restaurant that looked like it led to the food-locker.

"Yeah…" Jill hesitated, "Actually, Mary Beth and I need to get back to our cars before the security guards get suspicious and ask for a luggage check."

"Yeah, we'd love to stay and catch up, but we're strictly on business, here," Mary Beth agreed.

Roman was bewildered. They weren't in very much of a hurry, since their flight could be postponed for as long as necessary. Tyler and Rebecca shouldn't have any trouble unless Tyler suddenly had the desire to go for a joyride. The security guards let them past once, and wouldn't bother them, considering all of the other people that looked far more suspicious with their tattoos and randomly-exerted piercings.

The others, along with Roman, looked about ready to use the same argument out loud, but Mary Beth and Jill vanished into the crowd as fast as Chad could've gotten take-out from a store on the opposite side of the food-court.

Chad rolled his eyes. "Jay doesn't like it when I call him 'Jelly'. But if you think about it; Jilly, Jelly…" he laughed at his own joke, but his laugh was over in an instant. Before they knew it, he was pulling them along the corridor behind the metallic door and talking as fast as humanly possible about how things were going for the Talismen in Sugarland. Chad was only walking, but for him, walking was about six miles per hour, so Roman had to jog to keep from being dragged all the way to the plane. There were a few guards that only had to check their Talisman ID's. They were on the plane in about three minutes and off in the air in ten.

Their plane was a small one that was probably previously used to transport mail. It had the one hotel-room sized compartment, a regular bathroom for airplanes, a back room to which the door wouldn't open, and the cockpit. From the TUC's they had learned the specially-modified controls used for the Talismen helicopter that would also apply to this plane. One of them would have to fly, and it was immediately conceded that

Roman, who had the least amount of experience, shouldn't even count as a contender. Richie quietly volunteered, as Renaldo tried to get Sarah to, while Ashley defended her.

Roman had complete faith that Richie would fly the plane with ease, whether it was by his natural seriousness or from him wanting to brag once they got back. If they got back.

Ashley suggested piling all of their luggage in the back of the plane.

"No, we should keep it with us, so that if we lose something we don't lose everything else, Ashie," Sarah corrected gently.

Each time that Sarah used 'Ashie', Roman was reminded of how Rachel had started giving Caleb nicknames about how good he was at things, even though Roman knew he could have done them ten times better. Roman beared what he had brought with him and the duffel bag that Jill had chosen, while Sarah took hers and the one that Mary Beth had kept with her. It had been agreed that the two strongest there should take the extra packages. Richie kept his in the pilot's compartment while flying. Roman wondered if Richie would be able to fly the aircraft the entire trip to the island. He would need to be on his guard. It was still an unnerving thought that they were planning on conducting a plane crash. Roman hoped that Jace had Tyler hadn't been lying to him when they said that, because of the type of electric power they used, there wouldn't be an explosion. Just in case, there were already lifejackets and parachutes, but no air masks. Roman wondered vaguely how the earlier Genedeaues had managed to sail to the break-point and then simply been washed ashore.

The walls to their compartments looked too frighteningly thin. Roman easily found a dozen scratches and areas where the paint was peeling. There were no chairs in the compartment or any overhead storage, which they wouldn't have used anyway. The area did, however, include overhead lights, which could be adjusted to all different brightness. Roman kept his off, since it was still daylight. Because the plane was meant to be scrapped, the Talismen made sure that only the necessities were there. They needed the lights to find their belongings, and were not to waste

[249]

their flashlights or matches. The compartment, however, did have carpet. Roman guessed that it would've caused too much effort and money to remove it. Roman knew that the plane had been bought by the Talismen, and then modified by a sector near Roswell. They weren't flying very high, only a few hundred feet, but Roman didn't like their chances if there was a hole somewhere in the body of the shuttle. Whether it was previously a mail carrier or one designed for sky-diving, it had still been enough to sell either at an auction or online. Aside from them and their luggage, the compartment was stark. The piercing rumble of the engines and the speed they were moving was enough for Roman to wish for his Ipod.

"So that Chad guy was the best Talisman in all of Sugarland?" he asked over the howling of which origin he didn't want to know.

"The only one available, more like," Renaldo said. Roman internally agreed.

"Hey, we're past the point of no-return, so try to think positively." Roman hoped that he sounded more confident than he felt.

"Yeah. Hey, maybe we'll find a nice dragon that'll fly us across to the gems." Renaldo rolled his eyes.

"Please don't mention dragons," Ashley begged. She looked like she was going to be sick. Roman had never seen Ashley be the least bit scared, especially since they had to account for Renaldo's jinxing power. He understood completely why she was afraid, but it didn't reassure him.

"Come on, there's at least, what? Seven…" Sarah counted on her fingers, "Talismen that survived this at the mansion right now." Roman thought that the number would've been higher than that. "And before the incident with Mr. Kyle's brother there were dozens more. And there's more all over the world."

Renaldo and Ashley looked thoughtful.

"All right," Ashley agreed finally.

They tried to make small talk as best they could, but failed miserably. No one honestly cared about each other's online classes or the latest television shows. The trip was taking too long. There were no windows in their compartment, which made Roman feel trapped. It also meant that he couldn't tell how much time had passed from the sun's position. But they would be crossing a time-zone, so it didn't matter much. They hadn't bothered to bring watches, since the kind of time that those told didn't apply inside the vortex they were currently moving towards. It could be light for ten minutes and then dark for twenty hours and then light again for three days, for all they knew about where they were going. Roman tried to blame Tyler for not properly describing what they were about to encounter, but simultaneously knew that he couldn't bring himself to; he knew that if he had an apprentice, then he would probably tell the same. The other mentors always described their trip as one long blur, like they were moving through a dream, or more likely a nightmare. But their journeys were judged by what condition they came back in, and whatever came to them later on. Some went through the most dangerous and frightening days or weeks of their entire lives, and others traveled through with ease. All who went through seemed to come out with some sort of inexplicable bond. They couldn't remember very clearly why they felt so close, but the connection was just there.

Sarah always compared the trip to the Island as a right of passage, as a test or initiation. Once you went through, you had the greatest amount of freedom that a Genedeaue could have, and the most efficient form of self-defense, or offense, or something that fell into neither category. Once you had your gem, you could live a normal life, become an official Talisman, be more valuable to the Strayers, or play superhero for kicks. Roman had heard stories from some of the more experienced Talismen about some who went to the Island and then became Rouges or ended up on the news for some heroic act. Roman tried to picture Ashley, Renaldo, Sarah, or Richie as Rouges or heroes. They would be heroes if they stayed with the Talismen, but some thought that it was more useful to help in every-day affairs. Roman thought that Ashley and Renaldo would fit the role as Rouges, though Renaldo might be too reckless. Sarah would've been perfect at anything, he thought. Richie wouldn't abuse his powers even if it

[251]

would win him the lottery, not even if he used the money to recompense for however he cheated. He would make a good superhero, Roman considered, if he was slightly more subtle.

It was strange, how his thoughts wandered, across the vibrating floor of the plane, phased through the walls, flew like birds across the Gulf, and back home. Not to the Talismen mansion, and not to St. Jefferson's. No, home. Back to his home in Houston, so tiny compared to the mansion. Back to the *Heights*, down to *Beverly Street*. He had pushed the thoughts of where he was raised out of his mind for the past two years. The scent of the carpeting he used to roll his *Hot Wheels* around on, the comforting hum of the near-collapsing washing machine, the distinct smell of spaghetti cooking on the stove. Roman was surprised that he could remember in such detail the one area of the wall that the paint always seemed to chip off of and how the neighbor's dog would always bark at exactly three minutes past four every day. Roman remembered exactly where he would normally do his homework. He had gone to an elementary in a different district then; he had only spent his fifth and sixth grade year in Caleb's district.

Funny, that I'm remembering this when I'm about to be put into mortal danger.

He felt lonely as he remembered his old school friends. He recalled the time that he and Jasper had tried to convince his mom that Roman had been stabbed to death by smearing him with lip gloss and ruffling his shirt. This had been in the first grade, sometime around his birthday. It of course hadn't worked, but his mom had gotten a laugh out of it. He remembered Stella, a girl in his kindergarden class he was sure he had been in love with. She ended up dripping blueberry juice on his lips during nap time, using the blueberries she'd stolen from Austin's lunch pack. Roman had decided, afterwards, that Stella was not the girl for him. Roman remembered the more recent years, when he and his friends spent their time either going to each other's houses, watching tourists get mugged, playing pranks on the idiotic gang that had once attempted to drown Harold's pet catfish, and looking in the newspaper and trying to win all sorts of different

[252]

contests and sweepstakes. Normally they didn't find anything that they could even enter. Other times, they would enter and never win. Sometimes they would win smaller sweepstakes along the lines of a *Walmart* gift card or tickets to see a new movie.

But one time they won a big sweepstake from a large furniture company that Roman had never heard of. But his mom, though not in favor of him entering all of those contests, was a fan of their 'carefully carven coffee-table designs'. Those kinds of contests normally asked for an address or an e-mail account, which was why Roman's mother wanted him to be cautious when giving out personal information. But it was worth it, eventually. Or it had seemed like it. The prize had been an all-expenses paid trip for a week to an average hotel in Phoenix, Arizona. His mom was thrilled, since they never traveled. It was perfect, during their winter vacation, when school wasn't in session. And the trip was scheduled to be on the week of Roman's birthday. Roman managed to translate that from 'good news' into 'this means we don't have to buy you another birthday present since we'll be taking you to Phoenix (even though you're the one who won us this vacation)'. But it didn't matter; Roman couldn't have asked for a better winter break than getting his own room attached to his parent's, a pool, an all-day buffet, and not having to pay for cable.

His friends, who had also entered the contest, didn't win. They all pretended to be resentful, but couldn't stop from congratulating him before he left. Plus, Roman got all of the presents that everyone else had been planning to give him to play with on the trip, since they would miss his real birthday. But they hadn't expected that he would never come back from the trip. The last time he had seen the particular group he would fool around with on the weekends, they were all gathered in one place when he gave them the good news. The last one of them he remembered talking to was technically over the phone at the hotel because they didn't have to pay long distance. But as for in person, it had been four days earlier in the park, with his friend Michael. They had ended their conversation with the words 'see ya later'. Roman felt obliged to laugh at the irony that they never did see each other again, but his lips were glued shut.

Later, he could find absolutely no explanation as to how he had managed it; he had lost himself in memories and fallen asleep.

18. Turmoil After Tedious

Φ   Φ   Φ

His sleep was dreamless, and not enduring. This was most likely because Roman had spent the majority of the ride to the airport asleep. They were still awhile away from the Island when he awoke. Typically, he had been drooling. According to Sarah, he had rested his head on his arm, on top of his suitcase, and closed his eyes. According to Renaldo, he'd had a seizure. According to Ashley, she had tried a spell from a magic-kit she had bought and used it to hypnotize him. Roman decided to trust Sarah.

"How long was I out?"

"An hour or so. We honestly have no clue," Sarah replied.

"I'm jealous," Ashley complained. "I don't think I'll be able to sleep to save my life, which I very well might need to at some point.

"I'm going to go check in on Richie," Roman escaped from the cramped compartment, not enjoying the attention that he was getting.

Roman knocked before entering, but he didn't wait for Richie to invite him in. Richie didn't look up from his well-worn, leather seat. A tilt of his head was the only sign that he was aware of Roman's presence. The walls appeared slightly more compact in here compared with the ones in the chamber where they others were.

Roman closed the metal door behind him with a daunting creak in its hinges. Roman had had to be careful to step over a threshold that was at least five inches above the floor level.

"How ya holdin' up?" Roman asked once he was sure he was free from the gripping gazes of the others.

"I am having no trouble with fatigue, if that is to be the case of what you are referring to." Roman almost smiled to hear the familiar, yet still alien way that Richie organized his sentences without a single touch of dialect.

"Are you sure? Because we can't afford for you to be tired once we crash. The sooner you wake up, the better."

"Are you or Sarah readily prepared to fly this aircraft for the next few hours?"

"If you're fine with flying, then by all means, keep flying. Because it's been decided that I'm too incompetent, remember?"

"You are perfectly competent, if you are accompanying us *and* being our leader."

"Whatever." Roman wasn't sure how to get out the question that had been nagging at him every time he had seen Richie since he became the leader. If he wasn't about to ask something important, then he either would have already asked it or left the room. He was sure that Richie would sense his hesitancy at any moment.

"So…are you excited to finally get your gemstone?" he inquired.

"There are many obstacles to conquer before we reach the area with the gemstones."

"Maybe not."

"And afterwards, we would have to find how to work ours and then leave the island."

"Yeah. But that should be the easy part, right?"

"Not necessarily. There could be many complications. You must have the picture of where you wish to be transferred to. If you are teleported to the wrong area, then you can no longer transport, which could be disastrous."

"Do you think we'll even make it that far?"

"The favorable possibilities outweigh the option of us dying."

"Well, I figure you've actually calculated it with a calculator, so I believe you."

"I did not need a calculator."

"Right." Roman hesitated, then scolded himself for being such a coward for no reason. He was nervous about asking his own teammate a simple question. His year-younger friend that, at this point, he was supposed to have complete faith in.

"All right, enough beating around the bush," Roman sighed. "Why were you acting all funny earlier?"

"To what actions are you referring?"

"The way you were looking at me when we were given the news! Why you voted for me and how you looked at Renaldo and, I don't know, convinced him to vote for me, too!" His voice was exasperated, but he kept his volume low so that the others wouldn't hear.

It was finally Richie's turn to sigh. "Mr. Garretson has informed me that you know a suitable amount, so I assume that it does not matter whether I tell you or not."

"What? What do I know?"

Richie shook his head gently, which added to Roman's growing anxiety.

"That would be Mr. Garretson's dream that you somehow witnessed."

It took a moment for Roman to realize what he was talking about.

"You mean the one about his brother? What does that have to do with you," he searched for a word, "*hypnotizing* Renaldo?"

"I am aware that Mr. Garretson has informed you that you are destined to do something that is currently unimaginable. He will not tell me what this might be, though. I simply think that you would make a good leader, and this might also fabricate your skills. Renaldo and I have…an interesting past. He knows when I am being serious about something."

It crossed Roman's mind that Richie was always serious, but decided not to mention it. It also occurred to him that Mr. Kyle had included Richie in their tiny secret.

"How long have you known about all of this?"

"I have known for longer than you have, ever since Mr. Garretson had the dream for the very first time."

"Does everyone else know?"

"No, only me and Mr. Garretson."

"Why did he tell you?"

[257]

"I had the dream before he knew that I had. I went to see Mr. Garretson, to ask him about why I might have had such an odd dream, and he explained that he'd had the same dream. But he had had a different dream, as well, the one where you are included. And he also had a third that you do not yet know about, but he has asked me not to mention that to anyone, including you."

"But I had a third dream, too! About Mr. Kyle's brother when he was older." Roman made sure to refer to Trent Garretson as Mr. Kyle's brother.

"Mr. Garretson's third dream had nothing to do with his younger sibling. And you informed him about your third dream, so he would not have asked me to keep that from you. We are not sure how you were to have that particular dream."

"But you *are* sure how I dreamt the same dreams as Mr. Kyle?"

"Yes, we do know."

Roman sighed, trying to keep himself from yelling at Richie or running out of the cockpit or both.

"But what was it that you did with your eyes with Renaldo? How is it that you made that fire illusion?"

"That is a simpler question. I am sure that you are aware that riddle solving is my first-rate power, so that could not have been the reason. The answer to your question is more along the lines of how some people with blue eyes can appear with the illusion of their eyes being water."

"But that normally happens when they're crying, right?"

"Not necessarily. But, as I'm sure you know, it is very rare for someone to have one eye that is the color of both of mine, let alone having both eyes that are orange."

"I thought that it was impossible."

"If it was not possible, then why are my eyes like that?"

"I figured it was because you were a Genedeaue."

"Not everyone with blue eyes is a Genedeaue, like you."

"Yeah but..." Roman stopped himself, since this was pointless. He was frustrated that he had learned nothing from talking to Richie except that there was nothing special to how he

[258]

convinced Renaldo to elect Roman as their leader.

"What about what you said about having a past with Renaldo?" Roman wondered suddenly.

"It is not very much, and Renaldo has asked me not to tell of what happened to his parents. He currently would be living with his aunt and uncle if it had not been for what happened to Jacob. But we have been friends for a very long period of time."

Roman thought at first that Richie was kidding, since Roman couldn't see his face. But Richie did not explain that it was a joke when Roman did not laugh, like he always would. Renaldo never seemed like the friendly type, especially with someone like Richie, who Roman actually respected. Renaldo was the kind of person that would do nothing but make fun of Richie's odd way of speaking, and Roman expected that Richie would have gotten tired of listening to Renaldo's outrageous comments that never turned out to be real and label his pranks and such as childish. They were complete opposites.

"I believe that Renaldo never talks about what happened to his parents either because it is very painful or because of his jinxing powers. No one ever seems to notice, but when the subject is of something that is very poignant or reflects his past then he has much effort in controlling his jinxing abilities. It may be that he is afraid that it might even happen again if he is to relive it in his mind."

Richie paused, as if expecting Roman to make a comment.

"When Renaldo first moved to America, we became great friends with each other. Ironically, and I do not pretend to know why it is ironic, when my parents decided to move into North Lake village three years ago, his aunt and uncle suddenly decided that the petroleum business near Katy was better than in Ohio. When Mr. Garretson came to collect us, we both did not live at the mansion. Not too long ago, my parents died of the swine flu, and I moved into the mansion."

Roman knew that when Richie said that he knew why Renaldo's parents decided to move to Katy, he meant that Renaldo had accidentally, or perhaps even purposely, jinxed his parents into finding some sort of business opportunity in Texas. He noted that Richie's voice dropped an octave when he spoke of his parent's death. The swine flu had not been very long ago, and was still considered a threat. Roman had never seen Richie show the slightest amount of frailty. Roman knew that Caleb would have been saying, to correct Roman, that Richie never showed anything except arrogance, though he would've said it in a more humorous way, Roman guessed.

"That's all?" Roman asked.

"Yes. The rest of our story together would be what you have witnessed of us at the mansion."

Roman, like he had wanted to do so many times before in this conversation, had to keep from bursting out. He had wanted to say that he had never seen him and Renaldo together, or together with anyone else except Chris. Renaldo tended to mull around with Elliyo and Gabriel, who, although they were close to his age, were still older than him. Roman normally saw Richie with Treaver, Millo, previously Jacob, and even Ashley. Roman always thought that it was odd that Richie would be able to stand being in the same room as Ashley for more than a few minutes.

"How long do you think that it'll be 'til we're at the Island?"

"I have no method of being able to tell how long it has been or how long it will be, but we are coming up on a stretch of land that I assume is Florida. It will not be long in reality, but you may as well settle in because it will be more than a few hours. But depending on the weather, which is supposed to be clear, there is no way of telling how long it may be."

"Lucky we didn't start this trip during hurricane season, right?"

"Yes."

Roman rolled his eyes at Richie's dry sense of humor.

He retreated to the main area of the plane, forgetting to step over the threshold and tripping in the process. Roman took his previous seat in the corner of the room with Sarah across from him, Ashley closest to him, and Renaldo in between Sarah and Ashley.

[260]

"So, what did he say?" Ashley asked Roman.

"Hmm? Oh, he said he was fine, unless Sarah wants to fly the plane for the next few hours."

"No, thank you," Sarah responded immediately.

"Well, that answers that. So...what was the last movie you guys saw before the curfew ban?" Renaldo said, slightly more polite-sounding than usual, and too obviously nervous.

Roman's mind flashed back to when he, Caleb, and Mrs. Haldrige had seen *Exploding Cows: The Next Generation* at the *Cinemark* on the same day that Sarah and Danny had come to take Roman to the Talismen mansion. Sarah seemed to be thinking the same thing.

"That *Exploding Cows* sequel." Roman shrugged.

"I can't quite remember the last time I went to the movie theater," Sarah said.

"Same," agreed Ashley. "Besides, we've—"

Roman was suddenly thrown forward, along with the others, as something he could only guess was turbulence hit. The duffel bag slung over his shoulder fell forward and the zipper burst open, spilling out all sorts of medicine (which he couldn't name but knew what they did) over his head and across the floor. Roman struggled to keep the suitcase he had picked from doing the same, both from annoyance and fear that he would be skewered with his own sword. The luggage collapsed on top of him, and Roman threw it off just as the plane was steadying itself again. The others were either clawing at the carpet to stay in place or piled against the far wall. Roman helped Sarah get to her feet.

"What was that you were saying about Richie being fine?" Renaldo growled.

"Well, he *was*." Roman glanced anxiously at the door leading into the pilot's compartment. "I'd better check on him."

Before he could move an inch, Richie's voice was on the intercom.

"Are any of you all injured?"

"No," Roman called in the direction of the cockpit. "Just maybe a bruise or two." He looked forlornly at the debris of the duffel bag spread around the cabin. "Ugh, I guess I'll have to clean that."

"I am not sure what has just occurred," Richie's voice came again in its static counterpart. "The plane did not encounter a wind variable, and we have not hit anything that I can see."

Roman paused before picking up something that was good for both burns and sore stomachs.

"Then what's the problem?" Ashley demanded.

"He just said that he didn't know." Renaldo rolled his eyes.

"You are *so* lucky that you're smaller than me."

"Is there any damage?" Sarah implored, helping guide Ashley away from Renaldo.

"Not that is indicated by the sensors. It only can pick up a parallel frequency," Richie told them.

"In English, please?" Roman snapped.

"It is picking up a signal directly below us on radar."

"This hunk of junk has a radar?" Renaldo blinked.

"Yes."

"Well, what's it picking up?" Ashley sounded more nervous than before.

"I am not sure, and there is no way to check without landing."

The others looked at Roman expectantly, reminding him that he was still leader.

"Umm..." he was on the brink of making up his mind when Richie made another announcement.

"The object has disappeared."

"What?"

"The strange object that the radar had been sensing is gone completely."

"Well, that settles that."

Roman gathered the remnants that he could scavenge, which was not too difficult in the desolate compartment. They all tried to return to their previous comforts, but this attempt was fruitless. Roman kept shifting in his seat and glancing at the door they had boarded through. No one tried to fake a decent conversation, but instead were left to their own private thoughts.

The rest of the trip was dreary, dull, and antagonizing. It seemed to last for at least a day before they hit the invisible barrier that they had been warned of by their mentors, shortly after a screeching *bang*, and were all immediately plunged into unconsciousness.

All, except for Roman.

19. No Sticks, No Stones

Φ   Φ   Φ

The others collapsed before Roman's eyes. He immediately panicked at both that the plane jerked downward, and the realization that he was alone in the aircraft. The others were slumped over their luggage, still clutching it, as they had been informed to do for the end of the flight. They had all attached and activated their parachutes and lifejackets beforehand when Richie noted that they were past Florida. Roman was lifted off his feet. The lights above Roman flickered, then ceased to work, plunging him into total darkness. He didn't remember screaming, but someone did, and he was the only one that had been awake. He considered for a moment that he might have simply fainted like the others before him and was dreaming, before something sharp dug its way into his right arm. He yelped.

Not knowing what else to do, he clawed his way, upside-down along the ceiling, toward the pilot's station, knowing at the same time that at any moment they might hit the ground or water or foliage or, the idea almost made him lose his lunch, lava. Tyler had told him that the island would not still be exposed to lava, since it would be warped after the explosion. But, then again, Tyler had also told him that he would have been in a deep sleep by now.

Something hit Roman's head. A rail. A rail that ran along the edge of the door. He considered opening the door for a moment, but through all the panic that he was enduring, he at least had the sense to dismiss the idea.

Someone's parachute burst open, smothering Roman while yanking the duffel bag off his shoulder with a string. It vaguely crossed Roman's mind that there wasn't supposed to be wind inside the airplane before he felt the air pressure of falling at who-knows-how-fast snatch the air from his lungs.

[264]

Then, he lost unconsciousness.

The first thing he noted when he awoke was a stinging feeling in his right arm, and aching all over. He rolled over, wanting to pull the covers back over his head and fall asleep again. But he rolled onto something wet. He opened his eyes to find a dirt mound in front of him. He sat up, and would have jumped all the way to his feet at the recalling of what had happened, if not for the fact that his right arm screamed in protest. Roman tried to pull his leg out of the mud that was now engulfing it, but when he tried to move his arm, it wouldn't obey him. While rubbing his eyes with his left hand, he tried to move the fingers on his right hand. Nothing.

He dared to look at his arm, which he had to prop with his foot to see. Then he noticed the pain. It was like a streak of lightning shooting through his entire body. He felt like retching at the sight of the angle that it was bent. He knew that it was broken. It was swollen and turned a sickly purple color. He felt like curling in a ball and shivering. It took much effort to stop the spasms that now coursed through his body when he tried to move. He also noticed that his arm was covered in mud, like most of the right side of his body. His eyes weren't processing from the fogginess that he was experiencing. In truth, he was trying not to cry from sheer pain. He had never broken anything before, and he knew perfectly well that it wasn't just a crack, it was a full break. He forgot the name of the bone, and he didn't have x-ray vision, but he could see the bone very clearly in his mind. Out of the two that circled each other to make his arm, the one that connected to his thumb was broken with one end smashed into the second bone, tearing through the muscle.

He was aware of a warm body next to his, someone's hand on his shoulder.

"Roman, are you all right?" Sarah's voice barely pierced the ringing in his ears.

"He's awake? Final-Oh my god, what happened to his arm?" Ashley shrieked.

"Whoa, at least we brought bandages," Renaldo

commented squeamishly.

"It is a good thing that we completed our medical-use classes." Richie sounded awed instead of sickened. "It will be good practice for bandages, and Roman can inform us if we are doing something wrong."

"If he can keep from fainting, first," Sarah said worriedly. "He's not answering. Roman, talk to us."

Roman moaned in reply, and even that threatened to tip the scale he was using to block the vomit from reaching his mouth.

"Well, he can hear us; that means he must be fine," Ashley snorted.

"We can deal without the sarcasm, Ashie."

"Well, we can't leave without him. As a matter of principal, we can't leave until he says we should. I say someone replaces him."

"Ashie, I'm not going to be the leader."

"Might as well be," Ashley chimed.

Ignoring her, Sarah gently touched Roman's swollen forearm. He nearly screamed, except for the threat of either fainting or losing the contents of his stomach. But another spasm escaped his control, and Sarah quickly let go.

"Why's his arm broken, anyhow?" Renaldo asked.

"I don't know. He probably broke it from falling a bazillion feet. Ever consider that?" Sarah sighed.

"None of us broke anything, which is a miracle. I mean, not too many people can say that they survived a plane crash."

"Not too many people can say that they can do flips off the sides of apartment buildings and live, but you choose to brag about the *plane crash*?" Roman felt Sarah's hand touch his forehead.

"I get cocky *one time…*"

"I'm not insulting you. I honestly think that it's amazing to be able to survive a hundred-and-seventy foot drop by bouncing off the outer walls. Not the way I'd spend my Sunday afternoon, but still impressive."

"When did Ashley jump off a seventeen-story apartment

[266]

building?"

"Last summer."

"Why?" Renaldo inquired.

"Can you people please focus?" Sarah begged.

"We're Genedeaues, remember? That's our excuse for not concentrating."

"We need to get him some water, I think he has a fever."

"I'm not sure if the fever is the worst of our problems."

"She's right," Renaldo said, "we should at least get him out of the mud bank. Who's bag has the tent and mats?"

"The one that Mary Beth brought. Ashie, could you get it?"

Roman heard the rustling of leaves. It was good that he could at least focus on sounds and that the ringing in his ears was lessening, though it was being replaced by a burning sensation. It was warm outside, far too warm.

Sarah held a rag to his forehead. It was wet. Roman was aware that it was warm, too. Roman then processed that someone was crouching next to him. One thought at a time, Roman also knew that he was lying on a patch of very damp earth. It was like mud, but mud that wasn't deep enough to be much of a problem. His leg was still stuck in something cool. He remembered that his shoe was still on, with double socks.

"It is best to get his leg out of the bog. We do not know what is in it." Richie was the one crouching next to him. Sarah shifted the rag slightly while Richie pulled his leg out of the mud. Roman tried opening his eyes, but the world was spinning. He closed his eyes again.

"Should we be wasting the cleanser on that?" Renaldo asked.

"Would you rather waste the water bottles?"

"Sarah, you are supposed to let it set in for half an hour."

"What?" Roman felt the cool towel pull away from his forehead, which instantly re-inflamed. Roman moaned in response. It felt like it kept getting more and more intense.

"Uh, got any tranquilizers?"

"For what reason would we have tranquilizers?"

[267]

"For this!"

"Well, we didn't exactly plan this," Ashley grunted. Roman recognized a scraping sound.

"Good, let's get this camp going. Who's on first watch?"

"I will be on watch first," Richie volunteered.

Roman felt himself lying down. The ground was so comfortable, now. His arm had gone strangely numb, and the aching in his body became gradually less as he let himself drop. It felt like hours before his head reached the dirt and mud, and when Renaldo warned that he was fainting.

Roman dreamed that he was having a HHC training session with Treaver back at the mansion in the basketball court. Roman had his copper sword with the dragon designs, Treaver had a simple knife. But Treaver wasn't going on the offensive, so Roman tried to flip the knife out of his hand, but Treaver kept dodging his blows. There weren't any obstacles up this time, but Treaver didn't seem to need any.

"Gotta be quicker than that," Treaver laughed as Roman clumsily missed him by a whole foot. It was as if he'd never held a sword before. There were other weapons scattered around the floor that Treaver seemed to ignore completely. Roman dropped his sword and tried one of the mechanical spiders. He aimed very carefully at Treaver, who stood completely in the open, waiting for Roman's assault to come. Roman knew that, with Treaver being as quick as he was today, he would easily miss. But the only other weapon that Roman had to choose from was another knife, since arrows would have the same effect as the mechanical spider.

So Roman picked out a dagger next to his left foot, but kept the mechanical spider in his left hand, and poised the knife for combat.

"Haha! Two can play at that game, newbie." Treaver grabbed an identical mechanical spider, but instead of just aiming, he threw it at Roman. It wrapped every one of its arms around Roman's torso, and pinned him to the ground. The electricity was turned off, but how could Roman have been so slow?

[268]

Treaver made a tut-tut-tut sound from behind him. "Why did Tyler let you test against me? Everyone knows that you can't beat a year-long student with a three-monther."

"Three-monther? I got sent to the Island before you." Then it occurred to Roman that if he had been sent to the Island, then he wouldn't be there, having a training session.

"Ha, who would be stupid enough to send a three-monther to the Island?" Treaver's voice became different, a familiarly mocking, deeper, more sinister voice. Roman flipped over, gaining balance on the ground, to see not Treaver, but Danny beaming manically at him.

The words were out of Roman's mouth before he could stop them. "Danny, you traitor! It's your fault that Jacob's dead! How could you?"

"My fault? Oh, no, that's not my fault," Danny said, crouching next to Roman, grinning as he struggled to stand, or at least sit up, without any luck. "It's *your* fault Jacob's six feet under, remember? I'm not the one that led a few incompetent students into an obvious trap."

"Pond scum!" Roman blurted out the first thing that came to his mind. That was the insult that Ashley used to describe Elliyo and Gabriel.

"Says the one who crashed a plane into a pond."

"That wasn't my fault!"

"Oh, right. You're just a slow-as-snail newbie. You couldn't have stopped that plane if you tried. Even the Island doesn't want you there, otherwise your powers would have saved that broken arm of yours." Danny tilted his head and pouted, seeing that Roman's arm was completely fine. "Well, that's not right. Let me show you how the Strayers always put things in the right order."

Danny lifted the knife and shifted the coils that now kept his arms at bay, exposing the same place where Roman had sensed the break before. Roman flopped his body into Danny like a fish out of water. But Danny just laughed, disappeared, reappeared, and sent the knife deep into Roman's arm. Roman tried not to scream as he felt the excruciating pain sweep through his arm and a spasm wracked his body.

He gasped as his eyes flew open to reveal a green-colored fabric wall. Roman felt his nose being tickled by the tarp before him. Roman sneezed, and the motion caused his body to erupt in another spasm of pain. He groaned and flipped over. There was a ceiling made of the same fabric a few feet above his head, glowing with weak light. A blanket was wrapped around Roman's feet. He kicked it off; he was already too warm, and terribly thirsty. His head was resting on nothing but the same sort of green tarp around him. He was too dazed to realize right away that it was a tent.

"He's awake!" someone yelled very loudly from nearby.

Roman moaned. They were being too loud. The voice was echoing in his head. The ringing in his ears was completely gone now. Roman vaguely knew that it was Ashley's voice. Roman turned his head to see her sitting next to him, leaning against the edge of the tent. She had changed clothes from the last time he had seen her. Her blond hair was put in a tight bun, even though she normally wore it down. She didn't have any makeup on, which Roman hadn't known that she'd worn until now.

There was a shuffling as Richie climbed into the now cramped tent and sat next to Ashley. Richie's jet-black hair was ruffled and he had also changed clothes. His orange eyes were alert and wouldn't stay still, while Ashley's looked dull and strangely bored.

"He's awake?" Renaldo called from somewhere outside.

"Yes, he is conscious."

"You boys really need to start trusting me more often," Ashley snorted, crossing her arms.

"Roman, can you speak?"

"Yes." Roman's own voice sounded alien. It was rigid as if he hadn't spoken in days, which was most likely the same reason why he felt so desperately thirsty.

"Whoa, someone swallowed a toad," Ashley laughed nervously.

"Can you sit up, as well?" Richie had done the impossible; a Genedeaue had stayed on topic in a time of crisis.

[270]

Roman tried to sit up, and found it difficult with his broken arm and his whole body feeling like it had gone through a ringer. Eventually, panting, he did sit up, leaving slightly more room in the tent. Roman coughed, and instinctively tried to cover his mouth with his elbow, but found that his arm wouldn't raise to his mouth. Instead, Ashley called him disgusting.

"Roman, we have spoken of your condition, and have decided that there is no reason that you shouldn't have been protected from injury as the rest of us were. Are you considering any ideas of why this might be?"

Roman shook his head, which made him slightly dizzy. Then he recalled how he had not fallen unconscious like the others.

"I wasn't knocked out like the rest of you." His voice still didn't sound proper, and his throat itched to talk.

"What?" Ashley asked perplexedly.

"I wasn't knocked out when the plane started to crash. When we entered the Island's field."

"That's ridiculous. You were probably dreaming."

"Did you have any dreams?"

"No, but what about you, Richie?"

Richie shook his head.

"Well, Renaldo or Sarah probably did, then. And maybe you just now dreamed about it."

"You were unconscious when we all awoke. But you were injured and it was hours before you finally arose. We are not sure how long it had been exactly, but we had all started stirring around the same point."

"And that's more freaky than you being hurt and us being unscratched," Ashley added.

"Well, I've got nothing." Roman tried to turn around and crawl out of the tent, but ended up on his back.

"Do not try to move, Roman."

"You're not going anywhere without that arm healing, and you're gonna have to tell us how to make that happen."

"Guys, Sarah's back!"

"Where was Sarah?" Roman asked.

"Scouting."

"By herself?"

"I had to watch you, Richie was trying to get some doohickey—"

"A device to purify the water without the cleanser to keep from wasting what precious supplies—"

"He had to get some doohickey of his running, and Renaldo's keeping guard all over the camp to keep everything else out."

"Roman's awake?" Roman heard Sarah's anxious voice outside. She slid in through the entrance, taking away the room that Roman had made by keeping to one side.

"Is he all right?"

"He can talk, at least. And he can sit up."

"Then why's he lying on his side?"

"He had attempted to move out of the tent."

"Hi, Sarah," Roman said.

"Did he say anything about why he was hurt?"

"He doesn't know."

"It doesn't matter. Let's get his arm in a splint, since a sling won't do us much good."

"We'll need three or four sticks around the length of my arm." Roman said instantly, even in his daze.

"Well, at least now he's making sense. Except we already covered that *and* the bandages *and* the string," Ashley stated before Roman could interrupt.

"Um, guys? Can we please focus on our other little problem?" Renaldo's voice came from outside of the tent.

"What other problem?" Ashley and Roman asked simultaneously.

"Sorry, I got distracted by Roman," Sarah apologized. "It's not much. I just saw footprints in the mud next to the plane. Or, shoeprints, I guess."

"Who's shoe?"

"None of ours. It's a bigger size than any of ours."

"I will get to work on Roman's injury while you three discuss the tracks," Richie volunteered.

[272]

There was chaos when they tried to squeeze out of the tent without touching Roman or knocking Richie into him. Then, the tent felt strangely empty to Roman.

"First, you should sit up," Richie instructed him.

It was easier than before, since he already had his left arm in a supportive position and there was only one other person in the tent. Roman hauled himself upright, suppressing quick, shallow breaths.

"We have all the materials necessary for repairing your radius, temporarily, but—"

"My what?"

"The bone that you have broken. But we have not taken a close look at it nor will a splint be very effective in either mending it or stopping the swelling. You will have to have it looked at once we arrive back at the mansion. Hold out your arm."

Roman could move the bone that connected his shoulder with his elbow, but simply lifting it would shift around the broken radius. So Roman gingerly held the lower portion of his right arm with his left. Even though he tried to be as gentle as possible, the swollen area stung the moment he touched it.

"It's only broken in half. There aren't any other fragments." Roman asked Richie, "So it's possible to keep it in place, right?" Roman didn't know why he was asking; he knew that no matter how tight the splint was, it would not stay in place until the tendons were healed in the areas around his forearm, and even then, he would need some professional help with it.

"Not currently," came Richie's expected answer. "But it's best to keep it from doing any further damage to your arm."

Roman nodded, causing his mind to feel slightly nauseous from the mix of sudden movement and the intensity of the stinging in his arm.

"We have medicine for the swelling." Richie disappeared momentarily, leaving Roman gazing outside of the tent. All he could see were what seemed much like plants that were swirls of brown and green. Before the tent entrance, there was regular dirt that appeared partially black and charred. There were no rocks,

[273]

not even the tiniest pebble scathed the surface of the ground. The dirt, in return, gave the appearance of sand that would sink if you stepped into it. Roman could see the footprints that Richie had left and the tracks that knees had made as all of the others were crawling into the tent. But aside from them, not even a bug stirred anything in sight, which wasn't much.

Richie came back in with a vial of something deep purple.

After drinking, Roman couldn't feel any immediate effect except that it quenched part of his thirst. Richie had also brought in fever medicine, which, instead of helping with his throat, nearly made him choke.

"Renaldo has gone with Sarah to investigate the tracks they have found," Richie informed Roman as he was laying the vials aside. "You will have to keep your bone as aligned as possible, since I will not be able to work with it due to all of the swelling and without x-rays. Without any treatment, this will be very painful."

"Gee, thanks for the encouragement."

"Your first-rate power will help you to adjust it properly, correct?"

"Yes." Roman sighed.

Richie waited patiently while Roman tried to work up the courage to start. He was saved by Sarah sliding back into the tent.

"Just as I thought, not any of our shoes made those tracks. Do you think the warp trapped someone else here?"

"Not unless they are Genedeaues, and even then, they would have had to enter at the precise moment we did to arrive in the same area, which is impossible unless they were in the airplane with us. Every part of the plane that was loose has disappeared completely. The warp would have destroyed any non-Genedeaue living cells."

"Then there's nothing else that could've made those tracks."

"Just another question left unanswered," Roman stalled.

"How are things going with Roman's arm?" Sarah asked, after a pause.

"Well, he is now concentrating, and he has taken his

[274]

inflammatory relief and was now about to adjust his radius so that I will be able to properly set the splint."

"Good, get on with it, then." Sarah shuffled to sit in the entrance, giving Roman some breathing-space.

Roman moaned and swallowed theatrically. Simply touching the area where his arm was swollen was more uncomfortable than he would have liked, moving it slightly made him want to scream, but moving the bone itself caused spots to form in his eyes. Sarah gave him a damp towel to bite on, which helped about as much as setting his hair on fire. As Roman's progress was too slow for him not to growl, his dream flashed back into his mind. Danny hacking at his arm probably had been the result of his arm stinging, but the dream had seemed too lifelike to simply ignore. Roman wondered if he was having a continuous dream and was simply fainting again. Roman had no idea how he managed to concentrate with the dream flashing through his mind and the excruciating pain.

Eventually, he knew that his arm was as good as it was going to get with their primitive methods of mending. Richie and Sarah took about a quarter of an hour (they couldn't know for sure), which would've taken longer without their training, to set Roman's arm. Roman's arm felt sore and had a stabbing pain simultaneously when the splint was finished. It was all he could do to keep from moaning or collapsing.

"Well, that's all we can do, for now," Sarah sighed.

"Can I go out of the tent, now?" Roman inquired.

"You're the one that gets to skip his watch *and* guarding the luggage *and* scouting. Why do you want to go out of the tent?"

"I *really* need some fresh air."

"Fine then. Richie?" Richie crawled out of the tent first, then stood aside to let Sarah, who was helping Roman by supporting his right side since he couldn't crawl. Roman expected to be nearly blinded by the light outside, but the sky looked the equivalent of before a hurricane.

The entire sky was shrouded in a foggy haze that glided smoothly off to Roman's right. He couldn't see the sun at all, but

[275]

a sort of glow that normally would have signaled its hiding place emitted from several different spots. The air was deadly still, like the Island was holding its breath. Roman listened for the sound of the wind whistling in his ears or the feel of it ruffling his hair, still watching the sky, but nothing came. He had been outside for not even a minute and it was already palpably different from Texas. It was evidently humid, which at least he was used to, but it did not help with his thirst. The clear dirt that he was crouching on did not give way underneath his feet, though it gave the impression that it would give way any second. The plants were an odd mixture of ones he knew and ones that were ferns stretching six feet high. As far as Roman's experience told, trees were the only plants that were supposed to be six feet high. The air gave no hint of upturned or stirred dirt or even the marsh that seemed to engulf anywhere beyond ten yards away. Roman only smelled things that reminded him of lettuce, spinach, and St. Patrick's fried carrots. The smells that he had never encountered outweighed the ones that he recognized. The assault of scents made his eyes water, but at least didn't make him vertiginous or cause him to sneeze. The air was undisturbed by the sounds of any birds or bugs, and there were no other animals in sight, which Roman was thankful for. Sarah helped him to stand. The unscathed dirt reached only until the bank of thick plants and, to his left, a lake that stirred with brown muck. There was no grass anywhere, and not a single leaf fell from the canopy of plants around them. Roman looked around the camp they had set up. Next to the tent, piled very neatly and guarded with both Ashley and a trapping net that had been delicately placed there so that the slightest touch would cause it to topple over, was all of the luggage. It was cleaver, considering that there was no wisp of wind or bugs or birds to land on it. Any animals wanting to go exploring would immediately tip over the luggage without breaking through the net and alert everyone in the camp. If they had to flee on a moment's notice, then all they needed to do is push the luggage over, collect it, and have someone retract the weights that held the net to the ground with precision. There was no need for a fire, since it was light out, warm, and all of their food was carefully sealed and none of it raw.

There wasn't too much to see. It was obvious that the others had no intention of staying in this particular area. Renaldo paced the circumference of the dirt area, steering a few feet clear of any woods or marshes. Ashley looked questionably at Sarah, Richie, and Roman as they appeared. Roman couldn't see anything unpacked but the tent (for which they had a spare in case they needed to escape quickly and leave it behind), the clothes everyone else had changed into (appropriate for the weather, with their previous outfits safely packaged), and their weapons at their disposal. Ashley had a knife strapped to her hip and the shape of a metallic spider printed in the side of the knapsack she had on. Sarah had a sword and knife hanging from a sort of belt and her quiver and arrows, which looked ridiculous on her, strapped to her back. Richie, the same. Renaldo had a knife and arrows, as well, but nothing else. No one had touched Roman's copper sword or knife. Renaldo and Ashley, being the youngest and the smallest, didn't have swords. That would only slow them down, and they'd be just as well off with a knife. The others had small backpacks like Ashley, which they had tucked into their luggage until they had reached the island. Their backpacks matched their clothes; all short-sleeved and luckily the color of the surrounding blackish dirt. Sarah, who just recently gotten back from scouting the plane crash, which Roman couldn't see, even though he thought it would be noticeable, had a sort of camouflage jacket that matched the plants and cover-pants that appeared the same slurry texture of the marsh. Roman liked the marsh, it reminded him of the bayou back in Katy, which was the only familiar thing here.

Renaldo and Ashley had gray caps on, which didn't stand out in the dull air around them unless they moved. Ashley had been writing cursive, bubbly, flowery letters in the smooth dirt that formed a list of the things that they needed. Roman knew it was a check list from the marks next to each of them. She was obviously jaded from sitting and guarding the luggage. Renaldo had started weaving a trench where he and the others had been circling the camp. They were dangerously distracted, and Richie

[277]

suggested that he could take Ashley's place as luggage guard while she helped Sarah with Roman. Renaldo decided to continue with his incessant pattern, starting to dig into the trench purposely. Roman wondered why they didn't simply carve their names into a tree and throw meat into the forest. It would've had the same effect as what they were doing right now.

"We shouldn't stay here much longer," Roman observed.

"Yeah, we're waiting on you," Ashley scolded him. "Can we leave now? The sooner we get going, the sooner we get to our gemstones."

"Which way should we go?" As soon as the words were out of Roman's mouth, they all instantly looked in the same direction. The opposite way of the lake, straight into the marsh.

Roman realized how odd it was that they all instantly knew which way the gemstones were located.

"Um, what just happened?" Renaldo called out.

"I believe that entering the area of origin for the inclined—" Richie started.

"Our instincts are kicking in," Sarah finished for him.

Richie didn't look happy about Sarah interrupting him, but nodded in accordance.

"I don't know, do you feel up to it, Roman?" Sarah wondered.

"Well, it's not going to help if something finds us here. I say I'll go as far as I can."

"What if we can't find a place to camp as good as this?" Ashley asked skeptically. "Because it's bad enough that we have to watch behind our backs every second, but I'm not going to carry you across the Island."

"Well, if we don't find a good place to stop, then that's not just Roman. That's all of us, eventually," Sarah pointed out. "It's not like Roman has any blood to attract anything to us."

"Roman should rest for a while longer," Richie suggested. "I can see that he is swaying on his feet." Roman had hoped that no one would have noticed that he was slightly dizzy from thirst and not having moved this much in a long time.

"I'm just anxious to get going."

[278]

"You're not fooling anyone, idiot." Ashley sneered, "Don't think for a freaking second that we're going to let you lead us when we have to drag you along."

Roman sneered back at her. Ashley got the look that she normally got when she was about to hit someone. "Don't make me break your other arm." She went over to say something to Renaldo, who was just finishing checking the lake side.

"She's going to get arrested someday, isn't she?"

"Who, Ashie? She's hitting people before she turns eleven so that she can't legally get in trouble. Why not take advantage while you can?"

"But the legal age is ten."

"The police always let ten-year-olds off the hook."

"Oookay, when's her birthday?"

Sarah thought for a moment, then frowned. "Oh, no. Her birthday's the twelfth. That only gives us less than a week to get home."

"Only in real time. We could spend years on the Island and come back in weeks," Roman encouraged her as she led him back into the tent.

"Yeah, but we could also spend a day here and have it be months. What if we miss her birthday?"

"Then we'll take her gem before she finds it and wrap it for her. And then you'd have the best present ever." Roman smiled. Sarah pouted at him.

"Get some sleep, or I'll haunt your dreams forever on," Sarah said, shaking her head. She sat in the corner of the tent. "And make sure to change out of those clothes when you wake up, or else let's hope that any predators here are blind."

Roman looked down and saw that he was wearing the same tattered clothes from the airport. Shorts, luckily, a gray t-shirt from *Aéropostale*, and a white undershirt, which explained why he was so warm and another reason why he was dehydrated. The place where they had landed was as humid as summer time back in Katy.

"Any chance you've got any water to spare?"

"I'll get a canister." Sarah slung her knapsack off her

[279]

back and zipped it open. She took out a fresh, see-through, plastic, bottle of water and the knife that Roman had packed. She handed him the knife and the water.

"Try not to roll onto the knife in your sleep," she told him indifferently.

"It's nice that you care so much," Roman commented, taking a huge swig of his drink.

Sarah laughed. "Nighty-night, funny boy. Err, day, I suppose. It's been daylight ever since we woke up."

"You're going to be staying in the tent while I sleep?"

"As long as you don't kick me in your sleep."

"No kicking or rolling. Got it. I'll also try my best not to breathe too loudly."

"Why so sarcastic?" Sarah mockingly tilted her head to one side.

"It's not like I can help whether or not I move in my sleep."

"Easy; don't have nightmares." Sarah shrugged.

"Yeah, that makes it much easier." Roman rolled his eyes.

"Dreams are suppressed memories. Think of something nice before you fall asleep. It'll help you fall asleep faster, too."

Roman realized that she was being completely serious. He gave her a quizzical look.

"Just don't waste all of your water," Sarah said.

Roman laid down, propped his head on the extra tarp and his arm against a bag that Richie had brought in to serve as a pillow while they were still talking. At least he wouldn't have to worry about his arm getting worse if he didn't move. He tried to think of St. Patrick's, but that backtracked as far as happiness went. He tried to relax his mind, but realized from the slight sting in the back of his mind that indicated that his eyes were focusing on something, that it wasn't working. He tried to think of something else that made him happy besides new video games, and thinking of something to think about caused his mind to become farther and farther away from sleep, even though he was secretly exhausted.

He remembered how he had gotten lost in memories on

the plane ride here. What had he thought about? He vaguely remembered thinking about St. Patrick's at one point, but that hadn't worked. He wanted to shove the answer aside once it came to him; he had been thinking about his old home back in Houston. That was too closely related to his parents. But once he had thought of it, his mind had already started getting into more detail. He was specifically remembering an old ice cream shop where his mom had taken him often. He wondered if it was still open, and if he could get his usual ice cream; only one scoop, but it had a cherry and chopped cashews on top. The flavor was caramel, even though it didn't taste like caramel. But Roman had never cared, even after he had tasted real caramel on his seventh Halloween. There was always one worker who knew his mom and they talked while he wolfed down his chocolate-coated cone.

Then he thought of how the newspaper that he had taken to reading while he was confined to mansion grounds told about an event that the mayor of Houston had decided officially to do for New Year's. Jace brought the mail in from outside the mansion gates every day. Roman had watched something on the central TV at St. Jefferson's which was taking place downtown called the "Glowarama", where they had these cool special effects that were probably ten times better in person. The newspaper had said that it was being made the official event for every year. That one time, watching the Glowarama, when no one was fighting over what to watch while Ms. Simpson turned a blind eye, when the channel was on the news, period, was one of the times he could relatively relax. There was a big New Year's party going on at a recreation center that they had taken the kids to the following day. Roman assumed that they wanted an excuse for letting their employees off for the day, but it was still enjoyable. Roman remembered scarfing down as much pizza as his stomach would allow, swimming around, and then managing to find a hole in the fence. When no one was looking he snuck out and had just begun thinking that the log he was poking with a stick was an alligator when one of the attendants found him and he had his *Captain Underpants* books taken away for a week. The idea made him smile.

[281]

Then Roman remembered a *BB gun* fight he'd had with Jasper, Carlos, and Austin in Memorial Park. Roman had a pistol, Carlos had a cool automatic gun that Roman didn't think even existed in the *BB* world, Jasper had an old one that had a hole so big that he had to cover it to keep the ammo inside, but Austin had a rifle-edition that had belonged to his grandfather back in the nineteen forties. Austin had been the first out with about fifty bullets having hit him somewhere that would count as a kill shot. Jasper had won even with the hole in his gun. Roman had come in second. Carlos complained afterwards that they should've picked the southern portion of the park, where the trees were low enough to climb. So the next time that they were to meet up they met at the south portion, but Roman, Jasper, and Austin arrived earlier than Carlos. So they climbed the tree that was nearest and had the most branches and ambushed Carlos when he came close enough. Roman wondered if he was smiling, but found that instead his lips were half open. He had been almost asleep. He would've noticed that Sarah had been right if it hadn't worked so well.

She was definitely right, because he felt a sweet dream about ambushing Caleb with a *BB* pistol coming on. His last thought before he reached it was remembering that Sarah's mom had been a psychiatrist.

20. Mice and Spice

Φ   Φ   Φ

Happy dreams had the same result as any other dream had on Roman; he awoke with drool dripping out onto the bag that Richie had brought him. No one had disturbed him, which was good, because he didn't want to be disturbed. He knew he had gotten the rest that he needed, because the soreness that had invaded every muscle in his body was now only in his arm. He kicked, just to annoy Sarah, but Renaldo had taken her place halfway through his nap.

"Hey!" Renaldo jumped, and then sat glaring hideously at him.

"Sorry, I thought that Sarah was still in here. You see, she told me—" he stopped when Renaldo seemed very unsatisfied by the response. Roman sighed, "Never mind. How long has it been?"

"Only one rotation," Renaldo said, crossing his arms.

"Which is..?"

"About as long as we can stand. Come on, time to leave."

"Hold up, *I'm* the one who's supposed to say that," Roman corrected.

"Then you can be the one that helps himself out of the tent with a broken arm."

"Mutiny on the ship!" Roman grinned.

"Come on, captain." Renaldo supported Roman's right side as they left the camp. The broken bone was by far worse than his eye being shot with a *BB* bullet. Roman knew that, metaphorically, his bone was being held in place by a thread, while literally, it was being held in place by almost nothing. He was thankful that there were no short hills as far as the dirt. The others had packed up most of the camp, but not much had been out, in the first place. They had packed the net, and instead of scouting, Ashley and Richie were both guarding the luggage in its place. Sarah circumvented the perimeter of the camp, not looking at where she was walking, since a clear path had by now been worn for her.

Some pieces of their luggage locked together to make one big pack to carry along with them. The duffle bag, Ashley's suitcase, and Sarah's suitcase all connected, as did Roman's and Richie's. The others kept their backpacks on in case one of them got separated from the group. Sarah noticed Roman and came to sit with the others, and grabbed Roman a pack. Roman took it graciously with his left hand. It had a strap that he could tie around his waist. To his astonishment, the color changed to conform with what they were wearing. The others had managed to pack a lot of things while he was upstairs getting his sword. Inside the backpack was Roman's marsh camouflage, water, snack portions, the medicine both for his arm and something that would heal both burns and cuts, and a fire-lighter.

"We adjusted these packs for what the terrain's like. The winter stuff is in one of the big suitcases with the rest of the currently useless stuff. Restroom's in the woods, so consider yourself lucky that we're rationing," Sarah told him. "And we tested the luggage and it's actually pretty easy to carry. There's only four. Renaldo gets his. Ashley and I get the largest load, and Richie will carry yours."

"Stupid arm." Roman hated not being able to carry some of the load.

"Yeah, stupid arm couldn't survive a plane crash. Roman, do you honestly not realize that if you weren't protected from crashing like the rest of us, then you're lucky to be alive?"

"Sorry, my head's too thick to realize the full extent of my arm's rebellion." Roman rolled his eyes. "Should I change in the tent?"

"Would you rather change in the woods?" Renaldo inquired.

"Yeah, tent sounds great."

Renaldo helped Roman back into the tent and left. It was dreadfully difficult to swap shirts with his broken arm, and very

[284]

painful, but Roman was too modest to call for assistance. After a long struggle and approximately eight minutes of thinking about ways to slip the shirt on, he finally managed. He kicked off his pants easily enough; it was much more difficult getting the other pair on.

Roman finally called for someone to help him out of the tent. When Richie helped him stand, Roman observed that the others were already packed and fully ready to go. A sole suitcase was left out to pack the tent in. Richie helped tuck the blanket Roman had been using into his backpack, and Roman then found that it was very hard to close *Velcro* straps with one hand. At the same point that Richie finished helping Roman, Ashley finished packing the tent. Roman carried nothing, but he tried to stay as close to the front of the group as possible.

Roman soon found that in the forest, which was exactly like the bayou back home after a rainstorm, it was impossible to keep his balance, not knock into trees, and pull his legs out of the wet spots that he occasionally got stuck in due to his broken arm. Normally, they would leap from dry spot to dry spot back home in the area of the bayou that surrounded the mansion. But here, there were no dry spots, the water was ankle deep at its shallowest, and over knee high at its deepest. This was more like a swamp, since it hadn't rained in the estimated two days that they had been there, and there wasn't a dry patch in sight. Roman knew that the murky lake that he lain eyes on earlier was an extension of the swamp without trees. After they had wandered a few inches into the water, they had all changed into boots to keep anything that might inhabit the water away. *Unless they have sharp teeth,* Roman thought.

The water was a solid brown, and stirred no silt when they trudged through its depths. The various plants had run out at the water's edge. A musty gutter smell took domain here, and tasted salty on Roman's tongue. The smell never changed, never wavered, but sometimes felt...cooler. It wasn't as humid in the swamp as it had been in the open. The water appeared empty apart from the trees and vines that surrounded them. Sarah and Ashley, carrying three bags between them, sometimes had to slip away from the group to fit the mixture through the larger gaps in the trees. Roman was irritated how, at one point, he tripped on what he hoped was a stone in a shallow area. He landed on his side, so his fingers barely brushed the water, but his pack came back up soaked through.

Since he couldn't navigate successfully on his own, Renaldo helped him by catching him any other time that he fell. Sarah had been alarmingly accurate when she had said that they might not be able to find a spot for camp. The tent wouldn't float with everyone huddled inside, and it wouldn't very well stay supported in the twisting trees. The trees reminded Roman of a scene from an old movie where the characters are in a jungle, and in one area there are thick trees with vines that were sometimes snakes. The vines hung from the trees like curtains and were a thick green color.

They must get plenty of water here.

The trunks of the trees were all a ruddy-brown pigment. It sometimes disturbed Roman when one tree showed up entirely red, but still had green leaves. Roman was both disturbed and irritated by the color of the trees, since he had just struggled to dress himself with a broken arm for camouflage that now didn't work. It also occurred to him that he could've just changed pants without any help and then asked for help with his shirt. They passed a floating log, which reminded Roman of the one back at the rec-center that he had thought was an alligator. The thought of an alligator being next to him in the water made him uneasy, but it was obviously a log. The bark had turned from reddish to yellow, and Roman witnessed the oddest kind of pink mushrooms growing from places where some of the bark had been stripped away.

Roman would've adored talking to distract himself, but whatever tactics they had for conversation starting had depleted extravagantly when they were secluded at the mansion, and destroyed completely when they tried and failed at comfort on the plane ride there.

"What do you think will be on the other side of this marsh?"

"If there *is* another side," Renaldo mumbled.

"I'm hoping for a nice mountain with a cozy cave," Ashley replied wistfully.

"Want to drop off the mountain top instead of an apartment?" Sarah said, barely sustaining the oncoming giggle. Everyone laughed.

"Someone picked up some tips from Treaver," Roman commented. "Now he just needs to teach you how to hold the laugh until *after* you tell the joke."

Sarah pretended to sneer at him, which made Roman smile.

"I believe that when the marsh is empty, it will be more of a dense forest, considering that the area preceding the marsh was so," Richie answered Roman's earlier question.

"Kill-joy, much?" Ashley said. Roman didn't know whether she was referring to how they had gone back to the uninteresting topic Roman had concocted, or that she had been hoping that "brain-boy", as she called him, would say that a mountain was the most probable possibility of terrain. But Ashley seemed to be right, because the water level dropped to ankle level at deepest; they were heading uphill.

Renaldo seemed to notice this, as well, "We weren't in an unlucky crash-site. We were probably just past the part of the swamp that we'd have to swim through."

"Or, from the amount of logic on this Island," Ashley responded, "we were probably just past the part where the invisible, pink unicorns would've skewered us with their horns, healed us, then killed us again."

"How can they be invisible and pink at the same time?" Sarah asked, helping her duck under a particularly thick tangle of vines from a few low-set branches. The redder the trees were, the more vines they had. Roman was learning a lot about plants that he'd never see again.

"That's the joke," Renaldo sighed. Roman could've guessed that he would've rolled his eyes, but found it hard to concentrate on any of that when his bad arm hit a tree when a sudden drop into the mud caught his foot. The pain caused his

[287]

eyes to go cross and he thought his head would explode. Richie had stopped him from falling completely, but hadn't spared his arm the pain. Renaldo quickly shuffled forward, back to his position supporting Roman. He had dropped back when the water had started to become shallower.

"Gee, thanks, Renaldo," Roman commented. He knew it was unfair, but he wanted something to keep himself from just gritting his teeth.

"Shut up, klutz." Only Richie and Roman heard him, so there were no reproachful replies from Sarah or Ashley.

In a matter of minutes the ground was dry enough for Roman to walk by himself. Their boots were soaked, but, being leather, would dry easily enough. They were covered with a sooty brown pigment wherever the water had touched them, which easily brushed off with a simple touch. When they stepped, even without the swamp water around them, they made a *slosh*.

Richie had been accurate enough when he said that they would end up in a forest, to Ashley's dismay, but the ground plants were thin, along with the trees. No leaves littered the ground, which gave them an advantage as far as making noise and, due to the soft dirt that would've caused the leaves to slip from underneath them, balancing. They were still continuing uphill, every bare patch exposing the smooth, dark dirt that had been at their previous camp. The trees were thin, but plentiful. They diverted from their other red color to their regular brown and green colors. Without worrying about the plants, Roman had plenty of time to worry about the animals. They hadn't seen any sign of wildlife, unless they had counted the tracks from the plane. It both relieved and bothered Roman in some ways. He was relieved that the only trouble they had run into was his arm. But what if they were being too detectable? For human standards, they learned to walk virtually silently and be as quick as vipers with weapons. But if the animals here had good enough hearing, or were close enough, they could effortlessly hear the sloshing of their soaking socks or Roman's clumsy trekking. Roman knew that wolves could smell whether something was injured or not from merely their tracks. Roman wasn't barefoot, but could something tell that his arm was broken from the smell of…what? The swelling? But with all of the noise he was making, a racket even for regulars, nothing would need to smell his arm to find them.

The others were being as inaudible as a coin dropping from two blocks away, but were they making enough sound to attract anything?

If they were, something would've found us by now, Roman calmed himself.

The dirt was not doing anything to relieve his anxiousness. With its smoothness, the slightest disturbance caused an obvious trail. They all left footprints, very obvious footprints. At least when they were in the water, if they passed through one area, there was no way to detect it.

The smell of musty water that Roman would've bet his left arm was not safe to drink, passed away with their footsteps. It was still the same shade of light it had been when Roman had woken, with no way to tell how long they had been wandering. Roman only knew that once he wasn't focusing on navigating through the swamp, even if his mind was still occupied with worries, he was very ready for a long nap. He was practically dragging his legs at this point of their journey. He told himself that it would be best if he wasn't sending out a beacon to every animal within a mile, and, like Ashley suggested earlier, it might be hard to find a better place to camp once they cross through this area. But Renaldo beat him to it.

"Maybe we should stop for the day; it must have been hours now," he complained openly.

"What do you guys think?" Roman said, "I know I'm worn out. And it'd be better if I weren't so tired that I can't help making as much noise as an elephant."

"More like a herd of elephants," Ashley corrected. She was always so considerate when helping him.

"Thank you for interrupting me." Roman continued, "and we might not be able to find a much better place to camp."

"Better?" Sarah raised her eyebrows. "What if it rains and there's a mudslide? Have you *seen* how loose the dirt is? And we're in the middle of a forest with trees covering anything dangerous. This isn't exactly a four-star hotel, Roman."

Roman paused to consider this for a second. The fog clouds that blew above them didn't help with the rain problem, but the trees would also help conceal them from predators that relied on sight. But then, that's what their camouflage's job was. Roman looked at each of the others for their reactions. Ashley didn't seem to like the idea of carrying the three luggage cases through the maze of trees before them. Richie looked tired, as well. Renaldo only appeared indifferent.

"Sarah, if you want to keep going, then you can keep watch while the rest of us take a break," he said irrevocably.

Sarah gave him a quizzical raise of her eyebrows, then sighed. "Fine. Except we can take *turns* on watch, thank you."

They spent the night at a spot twenty yards away. They had explored the surrounding terrain and failed to find a superior rest spot before they could go no further. Roman was on first watch with Sarah. They each ate some creamed corn from five over-sized cans. Roman had almost completely forgotten that he was starving, due to the pain in his arm. The camp had a similar design as before, but the now steep slope didn't permit the cleaver trick with the net and the baggage, so they squeezed them into the tent and managed to spread them over the bottom to form a sort of mattress. It wouldn't have been very comfortable. He and Sarah circled the camp, making a rut similar to the one from their previous camp. Roman was to watch the camp. Sarah, the forest.

Roman didn't trust his camouflage very thoroughly, but it was better than nothing.

"Why can't the clothes be like the backpacks and blend into what's around them?" Roman whispered as he heard the others' comforting talking die away as they fell asleep. Roman had no idea how they managed it.

"There's a problem with that. The backpacks turn the color of the thing that they're touching, and they were touching the clothes and the air, which they're not supposed to copy. Your clothes would copy your skin. Even the outer clothing would just mimic the inner clothing."

Roman imagined what it would be like if he had gotten his blend-in clothing. He no longer wanted it.

"Well, that sounds like a fail for whoever was testing it."

"Ha, yeah. Sounds like it." Sarah paused for a second. "Who or what do you think made those footprints?"

"I don't know, maybe there's some sort of shape-shifting animal here."

"And it just so happened to pick our shoes?"

"Maybe it was disguised as the ground, and can only transform into things it touches." Roman tried to keep himself from laughing. He needed Treaver to teach him that, as well.

Sarah tilted her head to one side, and gave Roman her least comical look possible. Roman laughed, and hoped that it didn't sound nervous. But, of course, she could read his eyes.

Sarah rolled her eyes and walked steadily ahead of Roman. He didn't know why she was taking the footprints so seriously when they had put miles between them and here. After a circle around the camp, Sarah turned around and walked backwards, letting their deep-set tracks guide her feet.

"What d'you want your power to be?" she asked.

"I want to be exactly like *Aqua Man*," Roman answered flippantly.

Sarah sighed.

"Err, what do *you* want your power to be?" Roman probed apologetically.

Sarah thought for a moment. "Not sure. I guess we're supposed to be happy with whatever power we get. The mentors always are, and I'm perfectly happy with my current power."

"Why? Got any secrets to hide?" Roman teased frivolously.

Sarah didn't smile. She studied Roman's face. Just when Roman was feeling extremely nervous, she smiled.

"Well, that time you definitely kept your poker face on."

"You totally fell for it," she breathed.

"Well, you fell for that DVD I gave you being actually store bought instead of pirated."

"What a shame, now I'll have to call the police on you when we get home." Sarah didn't fall for it.

Roman smiled. Sarah pulled back into a normal walking position and walked beside him.

"Should we be farther apart?" she wondered. "Because then nothing that's too fast for us won't get as far." Roman considered the thought, but he knew that they couldn't talk above a whisper for other animals and not waking the others, which meant that they wouldn't be able to talk if they split up.

"Um, no. We'll get bored too easily, and that means the same result as our last camp. If we're off guard we're even worse off than being too close together," he concluded.

"Hmm, good point. It's nice to talk, though."

"Yeah."

"So what's the name of that kid you used to always hang out with before you joined us?"

Roman was startled by the question. There were a few kids that sat with them at lunch, but Caleb was the only one that Roman hung out with every day after school.

"You mean Caleb?"

"Yes, that's it. One of you must have mentioned his name to me before, but we saw you with him a lot before everything. You know, Talisman business, and all."

"Hmm. I wonder what Caleb thinks happened to me." Roman knew that he meant it. They had collected his things from his locker after hours, and *they* meant Tyler, not Roman himself. Only the mentors were allowed outside the mansion grounds, and even then were to be cautious, keep tabs on where they were, and stay in public places.

"Probably thinks that you moved. It's even more convincing since Treaver, Chris, Jasmine, Cole, and I are supposedly your step-siblings, and we disappeared without a trace, too." Roman noticed that she pointedly left out Danny, who the other students wouldn't know was no longer living with them.

"Danny, had better stay away from there, too."

"Let's talk more about Caleb, huh? So you guys must've been friends a long time, right?" Sarah quickly evaded the subject

[292]

of Danny. Roman glanced at her, her eyes were fixed on the woods she was supposed to be watching.

"Yeah, ever since I arrived at St. Patrick's," Roman agreed, momentarily forgetting to keep his voice down.

"Think he's getting along without you?" Sarah wondered frankly.

"Ha, oh he'll be fine. Maybe he's too preoccupied with Rachel to remember me. I'm sure Allan will tease him enough for the both of us."

"I think he'll remember you. Do you remember the other kids that went to St. Jefferson's with you?" Roman ran her words over and over again in his mind, scanning for any insincerity. He found none, even though he was still offended by the question.

Sarah detected this. "Sorry if it's a bit of a sensitive subject. But eventually you're going to have to—" Roman didn't let her finish. She had been trying to talk about Roman's past for at least a week now at every opportunity, and he was sick of it. He was not going to let her do this on their trip to the Island.

"Look, I don't want to talk about my past," he said a little too harshly. But he thought that Sarah deserved it from how obtuse she was being. "You said before that I'll get over it eventually, but now isn't the time! If I'm not ready, then I'm not ready, all right? Not everyone is so quick to forget about their family."

Sarah had been orphaned years ago, and then joined the Talismen. She hadn't talked to Roman about it, though it seemed like most of the other kids knew. She never seemed depressed or worried about anything, and especially not about her family.

But Sarah hadn't completely gotten over her loss. She rounded on him. They were standing glaring at each other instead of making their rounds about camp. But this, Roman was practically oblivious to.

Sarah's eyes shone like Richie's had. "You think I've forgotten about them?" she demanded. "You think that not wasting away my life by keeping everything bottled up like a *brandy* is a *crime*? You think that I don't get offended when people talk about how they hate their cousins and I don't have

[293]

one? I was trying to help you!"

Roman had never once since he'd met her heard her sound so enraged, not even with Danny. No, this was directed at Roman. Deep inside, Roman was shaken, but the rest of him felt like it was being challenged. He went through all of that, too, which was basically what she was saying. But *helping* him? This was not helping him, this was making his eyes steam.

"*Help me? HELP ME?* You're helping me by saying that I'm such a crybaby and can't be as heartless as you?" Roman knew that more than half of that was an exaggeration, but he wasn't good with words, and couldn't find any better way of describing this on the spot. In the back of his mind, he knew that they were fighting over nothing and that neither of them even knew what had happened to each other's families.

"I'm not! And I can't believe that you would even think that—" Sarah was interrupted a second time by a shuffling sound coming from the tent. She had heard it just before Roman.

Sarah's head whipped around, searching the campsite. She froze, a horrified frown crossing her face. Roman was still staring daggers at Sarah, panting with his fist clenched. His head hurt with every heartbeat as a horrendous headache took over his rational thinking. Shakily, he followed her gaze. At first, he saw nothing. Then his eyes detected the slightest motion near the entrance of the tent. Something was moving, and it wasn't one of the others.

With an unspoken command, both Roman and Sarah took out their weapons; Roman his dagger, Sarah chose the mechanical spider from her pack. Roman didn't see any obvious organisms, or any tracks in the dirt besides their own. Then, something flew at the tent, only to bounce off its surface, sending out the smallest of ripples at the entrance. Roman saw another flash of mouse-brown against the dry greenery.

Roman and Sarah stood completely still, ten feet away from the tent, where the others still slept. Roman thought that maybe they had been awakened by their fighting, but wouldn't linger on it, since he needed all of the concentration he could

[294]

muster right now, which wasn't something that he could normally supply. He heard nothing and smelled nothing that differed from the mustiness of the humidity, so he waited for another of the flashes.

There, a flash of the same color! A ripple in the fabric. A shadow across the ground. Several shadows...

Those weren't shadows, they were lighter than the ground beneath them. More mouse-brown against the blackish, muddy dirt. One of the spots flung itself at the tent once again like a flea. The others soon followed until there were five bouncing off of the entryway at a time. The zipper kept the entrance closed, so whatever the assault was, it didn't have much effect.

"We need to wake the others," Sarah came to the conclusion a split second before Roman had.

"How? Any noise we make could affect those things."

"If they didn't hear us yelling then I'm pretty sure it's a safe bet that they aren't noticing us no matter how loud we are."

Roman was contemplating, forming a strategy in his head while he watched the fruitless attack by whatever those were, when he noticed a motion outlined against the side of the tent. The zipper was unfurling when Roman and Sarah called out to stop.

But the zipper was halfway down. Roman saw the tiny specks disappear inside the tent. Roman and Sarah rushed forward, toward the tent. There was now screaming. Ashley screamed the loudest, Renaldo cursed, and Richie gasped. There was thrashing so forced that, if had not been for the luggage inside, the tent would've tumbled down the hillside. Roman and Sarah froze outside of the tent, wondering if they could even fit inside, since they couldn't blindly throw or shoot or hack with the others there. But that problem was fixed when Ashley and Renaldo half-fell, half-scrambled outside, bringing the other half of the zipper down.

All of this had occurred in under a minute. Richie was still inside, but no longer yelping. Sarah called out his name worriedly. He poked his head outside, looking as irritated as if someone had awakened him from a good nap.

"You were guarding the camp, so how is it that you managed to let these past?" He held up something that squirmed in his grasp. It froze as Roman had imagined a possum might when playing dead. It was mouse-brown, which happened to be a very well-placed analogy, since the tiny creature looked like a deformed mouse. Light-brown fur with the same visible density, a stout tail, and fuzzy ears that were as evident as its whiskers and tiny muzzle. Small hands and feet that were equipped for climbing. It wasn't similar to a common wild mouse, it was slightly larger, around the size of the ones at *Petco*, about two inches from nose to tail-tip. Except its hind legs were less squat than Roman was comfortable with. They hung limply, as long as a kangaroo's were relative to its body. Roman looked at the ground around them, and there were no tiny footprints made by these mice.

"Richie, you shouldn't be holding that," Roman ordered. "What if it's poisonous?"

"If this creature was poisonous, then I would already be able to feel its poison, as well would Renaldo and Ashley."

"It's *vermin*! You shouldn't touch vermin, it's not clean!" Ashley squeaked.

Sarah smiled. "Afraid of mice, Ashie?"

"Those things caused the plague to spread in the thirteen hundreds! Who knows what kinds of things it could be carrying?"

"Paranoia?" Renaldo suggested.

"Shut up. Just get those things out of the tent!" she directed Roman.

"It's like you're only referring to me," Roman said, raising his eyebrows.

"I am! If you two hadn't been arguing with each other then those things wouldn't have made it into our tent at all!"

So they had overheard. That must have been exactly why someone was awake to open the entrance to the tent. Roman wanted to argue with Ashley, but knew that he had absolutely no words. He felt his cheeks growing warm as Ashley glared at him. He felt resentful toward Sarah because she had started it. Even if she had meant well, she was smart enough to know that Roman wouldn't enjoy talking about his past. Feeling forced, he climbed into the tent with Sarah's help, which he didn't appreciate, and saw all of the strange mice hopping on top of the suitcase that held some of the cans of food.

"Well, we know what they were after," Roman commented in a sardonic tone.

"Any ideas on how to get them out?" Sarah asked him.

"Either kill 'em or throw them something far away from the camp."

"They'll come back if we toss them something. And we don't know how dangerous they are or if we can kill them."

"The one Richie picked up didn't seem too dangerous," Roman sighed.

"But do we really have to kill them? We could just get them out and then move camp."

"Or they could follow us. If we just kill a few then they'll be afraid of us and leave."

"If that's the best option, then *you* can kill them," Sarah said stubbornly.

Roman swallowed. "Fine, we'll think of something else. How about we catch them in something?"

"And then what? Abandon them in the woods to dehydrate? We could just leave them enough food to hold them until our scent wears off."

"That would be a week."

Sarah moaned in exasperation. "Guys? Any ideas?" she called out to the others, "Cause we're stumped."

"If we had an idea, don't you think we would've told by now?" Ashley answered. "The longer this takes you, the longer until we can sleep again. But then again, maybe someone else should be on watch. So there's me—"

"I will be on the subsequent guard," Richie volunteered immediately.

"And brain boy," Ashley finished.

"First thing's first," Roman resolved. "Let's get that suitcase out of this tent."

"I'll get it." Sarah sighed after a glance at Roman's arm.

[297]

She grabbed the handle, being careful to avoid the bouncing, hyperactive mice that were searching for an opening in the bag. It wasn't difficult; they were startled by the shadow hovering over them and scattered onto the nearby luggage. She hauled it on top of the other bags and dragged it out of the tent; the mice following in her wake. Ashley moaned at the sight of their numbers. There must have been three dozen brown, furry rodents.

"Well, they can obviously smell pretty well," Sarah commented, putting her fists on her hips.

"Anyone got the pepper-spray?" Roman meant it as a joke, but then knew that that was a solution.

"Someone's been holding back on us." Sarah half-smiled. But there was some sort of edge to her voice. Maybe she was referring to more than just Roman's idea. Roman could tell from the look in her eye that she was still upset about their argument.

"It's in my pack," Roman responded, deciding to ignore her tone.

Sarah disappeared back inside the tent and the jumping mice swarmed onto the bag she had left behind.

"I wonder how much those things can eat at once," Renaldo remarked. "Hopefully they'll like nice and spicy."

"If they don't, they're dead," Ashley sneered at the small hoppers.

"I do not believe that we should pose ourselves as threats to them," Richie argued matter-of-factly.

"What are they gonna do about it?" Ashley demanded.

"Spread paranoia," Sarah replied as she climbed out of the shelter.

Ashley narrowed her eyes at Sarah, which she returned with a mocking pout. Roman figured that Sarah was in a very bad mood to mock Ashley. And, once again, it all led back to him.

"We should begin to move the marquee," Richie suggested to Roman.

"The what?"

"Marquee means a big tent," Ashley said, still looking uncertain from the look that Sarah had given her.

"Yeah, you guys get on that while Sarah and I lead the

mice away." Roman turned, not very anxiously, to Sarah. "What do you think? Should we just lead a trail, or won't they fall for that?"

"Only one way to find out." Sarah shrugged. She sprayed the footprint that she had made with the spray. At first, nothing happened. Then Roman noticed that there was still no wind at all on the Island.

"They can't smell it. They need to be closer to it. They must've just followed our trail from before to find the luggage."

"That issue can be solved without difficulty," Richie spoke up. He lifted the mouse that he had been holding. Ashley made a gagging noise. The mouse was still paralyzed. Richie walked over and dropped the mouse inside Sarah's footprint.

At first, it just laid there, motionless.

"Do you think it's dead?" No sooner had Renaldo suggested this than the rodent started sniffing around. It scurried to the edge of the footprint and then searched the perimeter. It strayed slightly outside at one area, and seemed to decide that it liked it inside, near the pepper. It paused, and Roman saw a flash of pink as its tongue lapped at one piece of pepper. It jumped three feet high on its powerful hind legs, leaving a small shift in the dirt where it had launched. Ashley yelped and dove quickly behind Richie, as if the mouse was going to attack her. Ashley seemed to realize that everyone was watching her and slipped back to her original position, glaring at Richie as if it were his fault.

The mouse landed and hit the ground running over to the mice on top of the suitcase. It nuzzled one mouse that seemed larger than the rest and they both paused for a moment. None of them made any sound aside from the thumping from their jumps on the bag, but they all followed the mouse that Richie had put in the footprint. Renaldo grabbed the suitcase before the creatures could have a second thought while Richie, Sarah, and Ashley started packing camp. They pushed away Roman's offers to help, saying that he was useless with his arm. Roman watched the mice go insane with their leaping as they each tasted the pepper, and wondered vaguely if they could eat the pepper without having

[299]

any side effects. But that wasn't his problem, and it was too late, in either case.

Sarah sprayed the trail twenty yards away from the camp, ending at a small puddle that the mice might find some seeds in. The mice gratefully cleared the area of pepper and continued to sniff the minuscule dirt particles for whatever remained. They started on the same path that Sarah had just made.

The path still continued uphill, leaving fewer and fewer puddles and vegetation. Roman was worried that they might be coming upon a desert, but the humidity in the air begged to differ. The normal colored trees turned a golden-yellow. Not like the sickness-yellow that had overtaken the decomposing tree, but a nicer, richer color that reminded Roman of wheat. The golden trees grew thinner, until they were like the flagpoles at St. Patrick's. Roman momentarily ignored the thrashing pain in his arm as he felt a pang of resentment toward himself; everything he saw reminded him of his old life. It was as if the Island itself was taunting him. The dirt reminded him of the track. The sky reminded him of science class when they were watching a documentary on the *Galapagos Islands*. Roman had never been to any other island, and wondered if they all had clouds that seemed to patrol the area between the sun and the ground. The ground, bare of leaves or grass, strikingly resembled the parks in Houston during winter.

Roman gritted his teeth and turned to the shock in his arm to distract him from his thoughts. It worked, but wasn't much of a compensation. Roman noticed that Richie's breathing was coming in short gasps. Ashley had her eyes closed, and Sarah looked strangely uncomfortable. He stole a glance over his shoulder to see Renaldo staring at the ground like it was going to fall out from underneath his feet, but Roman could relate to that suspicion. Were they all having the same connections as he was? He knew that Sarah had quite a haunted past, and that Richie might be experiencing the same thoughts as Renaldo. But both of Ashley's parents were alive; they had even been relocated to the mansion after the incident with Jacob. What could she possibly be thinking of? Roman suddenly felt certain that they were all having troubling thoughts.

"Why don't we take a water break?" Roman said, pretending to be exhausted.

He noted how all their eyes lit up at his suggestion. They each sat on one of the suitcases, opening the water bottles in their packs. Roman knew that they should be careful with how much water they drank, since the water was steadily disappearing as they went uphill; but he gratefully drank a pint from his own bottle. When everyone was done sipping, they still looked reluctant to continue. But Roman, after letting them get a grip on reality, told them that they should cover more ground.

"Should we make a log of all this stuff?" he wondered out loud as they were trekking, "since we're not going to remember any of this stuff?"

"Nothing except us, our gems, our weapons, and the clothes on our back ever make it back from the Island." Sarah rolled her eyes, reminding Roman that they were still mad at each other.

"That reminds me, we're going to get our own students, aren't we?" Renaldo sighed, as if it were a dream come true to tutor someone that would probably be older than him.

"Or we could sign up for one of the other bases," Sarah reminded them. "The one in Oregon is having some trouble with underwater investigations."

"Yeah, but that's a bit advanced for freshies," Ashley commented. "We'd need some experience with the lower-level missions that are here. Or back home, that is."

"That's right," Roman took up her response, "we're *all* going to be newbies once this is over. Who's going to take my place?"

"I'm sure no one's going to have any trouble replacing you," Sarah said, with another edge to her voice. It stung Roman, even though he couldn't tell exactly what she was referring to. That he was a bad student? That she would find a new friend? Or that she could do something dark to him? She wouldn't go that far, would she? She was smart enough to know that Roman had barely any idea of what he was saying.

She was also smart enough to avoid offending you, a nagging voice started in the back of Roman's mind. Roman took this as another effect of the Island and ignored it as best he could, which, in truth, wasn't too successful.

"Do you presume that Mr. Garretson would assign us any of the current students at the mansion?" Richie wondered.

"What, like Treaver?" Roman asked, grateful for the change of subject. "I don't think so. It'd be more complicated to know what Tyler's taught him, and that goes for everyone. And we'd have different teaching strategies too, right?"

"But we're in middle and elementary," Renaldo sniffed, "and we already have more time than Mary Beth and Rebecca, et cetera. We'd have to have something to do."

"I wonder if they'll get any new students while we're gone," Ashley said, surprising everyone.

"I guess it's possible, but even then, they'd have to give him or her to someone else," Sarah responded.

"But then it'd be easier for them to transfer teachers," Roman went with Ashley's idea, "unless we're gone for a really long while."

"I hope that we are not on our journey for too long," Richie replied.

"Why not?" Renaldo asked.

Richie had a look of surprise on his face for a moment, then relaxed it, continuing his usual cool expression. "It would simply be more difficult for us."

Ashley narrowed her eyes at him. Roman had absolutely no clue what was going on behind the scenes. But he noticed that Sarah was dragging her feet and making noise, while everyone else that didn't have a broken arm kept silent. Roman remembered that she had had the least amount of rest of all of them, since Roman had been the one on watch that had gotten enough rest. He considered persisting just to punish her, but knew that it wasn't a good quality in a leader to use his opportunities as revenge.

"We should stop for a while; I think the mice are far enough behind." He pretended that the mice were the only reason that they were headed onward in the first place.

Sarah glanced at him with a curious expression, then turned away and helped Ashley set down their luggage.

"Are we just going to set up camp here?" Renaldo asked.

"Why not? I doubt that we'll find a better place. But we can send someone out to explore, anyway. Especially someone who got a lot of sleep. Sarah and I will be resting along with whoever doesn't want to keep watch or scout. It's probably best that no one scouts alone and there are only three people who want to stay up, unless Sarah changes her mind."

"I never told you what I wanted in the first place," Sarah sneered, "but I'll be happy to take a little nap. So that leaves out scouting."

"We already agreed that I'd be on the next watch," Ashley volunteered.

"And we also have decided that I will watch, as well," Richie said.

The side of Ashley's mouth twitched. "Sure, why not?"

Roman looked at Renaldo. "Well, I might as well get some shut-eye if I'm expected to be on the watch after this."

"You will be."

21. Predators, Problems, and Pets

Φ   Φ   Φ

The camp's design was the same as the last, in order to match the steep terrain. Richie and Ashley were left on watch while Renaldo, Sarah, and Roman were allowed to rest. Roman was thankful for Renaldo being in the tent, for he was sure that Sarah would give him grief if they were in there alone. It wasn't cold and he didn't need a blanket, even with his fever gone, but he felt he needed something to cling to. Roman purposely avoided Sarah's suitcase, and ended up using the royal-blue briefcase as a mattress along with Renaldo's leather case. The ones he had chosen would normally have been cool, but instead sucked the coldness from his body. Roman wished that there was a cool breeze to make up for the humidity, but no such luck.

Roman's arm slid into a crack between two suitcases, not large enough for it to fall through, but somehow comfortable. Roman closed his eyes for what seemed like only a minute before Ashley's scream woke him up.

Roman lay still for a moment while he comprehended what he was hearing. It took a moment for Ashley to scream again, confirming that she was in trouble. It wasn't the same scream as when Richie held out the mouse, it was filled with less disgust and more terror. Roman jumped out of his blanket, forgetting once again that his arm was broken and wincing as a spasm of pain broke out. Sarah and Renaldo were already out of the tent. Roman struggled through his confusion to get into a sitting position. Then something slammed into the side of the tent, unhinging one of the poles supporting it, leaving the tarp to encase Roman entirely.

Roman had found his pack and his knife by the time the tarp was stripped away from him. It was, typically, still daylight outside, with the same foggy clouds. But the smells were different. A sort of sweaty smell mixed in with something that reminded him of dogs after it rains was the first scent he picked up. But it was not dogs that greeted him. Flashes came down from the trees, colors from black to white to blue and anywhere in-between, to join some that were already fighting with Roman's friends. He caught glints of lights, reflected off of the Talisman weapons and something that came off of the strange creatures flailing limbs. They were only around three feet high when on all four of their limbs. Roman could see one that was holding still. It looked much like a lioness, same in color as well. It had unnaturally pointed ears, and a tail that was as bushy as a common house cat's. The glints that Roman had been seeing were the claws, which it swiped more than once trying to get past Richie's concentrated sword blockade. It had brown eyes that looked strangely like human eyes with whites, an iris, and a round pupil. Its front legs had a sort of transparent layer of skin that hung out loosely, like a bat's folded wings, except these were an extension of much more powerful limbs. As Richie managed to get a blow into one of the flaps, it let out a sort of wolfish snarl, baring long fangs. Roman was slightly relieved that only the front teeth were sharp, and that the mouth design was more like a human's, with molars in the back. The teeth of an omnivore. But Roman didn't have much time to feel relieved, as one that had white fur and bluish stripes along the upper part of its body started to prowl toward Roman. Roman held out his knife, which seemed feeble against the predator approaching him. Roman looked around to see if more were creeping in on him. There were slightly less than a dozen surrounding them. The trees where the latter ones had leapt from were slightly backed up against the camp. This had been an ambush, until one had disturbed the tent and broken the ranks that looked now so perfectly organized.

The one advancing on Roman seemed so easily associated with a tiger that Roman's hand trembled. The eyes of this one were green. It had a short snout, much different from the long, skinny one that had belonged to the first. But Roman didn't dwindle on its muzzle. The eyes were so intelligent that Roman cold see how they focused on the knife, and grew angry. Its lips curled back with more of a hiss than a growl. Its eyes flicked from Roman to the knife. It slowly skirted to Roman's left, hunched over like a wolf with its head slightly lower than its shoulder blades. Roman moved to the left with it.

The creature, sensing this change, tried going right. Roman followed once again, wondering how he might be able to reach his mechanical spider and turn the shock on with his good arm broken and his other arm holding the knife. Roman swallowed, knowing that the animal glaring at him was looking for an opportunity to strike, and that if he took the time to even reach for his pack, then he would have those yellow fangs sunk into his neck.

The creature quickly jumped high in the air, about ten feet, Roman guessed, and reached forward with its claws. Roman ducked to one side, slashing at the animal as it landed, forcing it back. The animal looked even more frustrated than before. Roman guessed that force normally worked for it. Roman heard a thud behind him. He stole the quickest of glances over his shoulder to see one of the beasts, green-furred, had a bloody gash over its chest. It was dead, Roman was sure of that. He looked up to see Renaldo with a sword that was so stained with scarlet blood that Roman didn't know what its original color had been. Roman forced himself to concentrate back on his animal, since his glimpse back had been only a second, but far too long. Roman had the confidence that Renaldo had his back. But the creature in front of him, upon seeing its dead partner, roared with ferocity much stronger than a lion's. Roman felt himself become dizzy for a moment, then forced himself to hold onto the adrenaline flowing through his veins. The tiger-creature tried to walk around Roman, over to Renaldo, who it had a murderous look in its eyes for. But Roman stepped over its path, blocking it from reaching Renaldo.

It was a standoff. The tiger-animal sniffed at the air after a moment, and its eyes glowed in anticipation. Roman felt the beads of sweat running down the back of his neck become searing hot. Roman heard Sarah scream somewhere behind him.

[306]

Sarah? Roman was confused for a moment. He was supposed to be fighting with her, right? It was so bad that he had considered that she might do something for revenge. But…why? Her scream had the opposite effect of his on him, currently. If his life didn't depend on it, he would have turned around right then and attacked whatever was scaring her. He would've charged the biggest of the creatures.

That was it! They had lured Ashley and Richie toward the trees so that their larger numbers could spring on them. That was a tactic often used by wolves, more or less. It had the same design. Whatever he was remembering from his biology section of third grade, it was at work in his head. The one in front of him recognized that its comrade was dead, killed by Renaldo. Wolves always avoided the least amount of damage they could. That was why the tiger-like one wasn't attacking him right then. It knew that Roman's knife would've done some damage if it got the chance, even though it could've easily stripped Roman of his face within seconds.

Without thinking, letting the Genedeaue side of him take over, it was as if all of the fears in the world were gone. It was a movie, and he was simply watching it. This was the Island where generations of Talismen had come before him. It was *his* movie, he and the others were the main-characters, and they were *not* going to die until they could resolve the story. Roman felt his arm at work. The pack was in his hand, a knife in the neck of the tiger-cat. He dropped the pack to the ground and had a mechanical spider out before his brain could register what he was seeing. Then, the mechanical spider was electrocuting the blood-red animal that had left Sarah's leg with a bloody gash. Purple lightning danced across the animal's body. All heads were turned, animal and human, to the red-furred cat.

It wailed what sounded like something between a yelp and a cat when someone stepped on its tail. One of the creatures rushed forward, a brown and green camouflage-furred one, with yellow eyes. Once it had gotten its share of electrocutions, it decided to back away. The others soon followed. They disappeared into the trees without a trace.

[307]

Roman felt a pang of dizziness as he snapped back to reality. The knife...how had he managed to kill his adversary? Roman had blamed himself for Jacob's death, and had felt as much guilt as he had thought possible over it. But this was much worse. There was no question who had killed the cat-creature. And worst of all, Roman felt strangely pleased that he had been able to do it. Those eyes, they had been so human, so intelligent, but now would be desolate and lifeless. He had blood splattered on his boot. It wasn't his blood, it was tainted with yellow specks. Roman retched, and fell to the ground grasping his head with his good arm. He wished for nothing more than to faint again, no matter what the side effects or consequences. He couldn't think about anything else but to drop unconscious on the spot. He felt his head and heart trying to break out of his body. He wondered faintly, his only other thought, if he was having a heart attack. He should've been able to answer that question, but the last thing he wanted was to give back into the Genedeaue side of his brain.

Warm arms were around him. He shoved them away. There were strange vibrations. He moaned. And then there was something sharp in the back of his neck.

He knew that his wish of being unconscious had been granted when he awoke inside of the tent. He desperately wanted to crawl back into his dreamless sleep. Had it been dreamless? Or was the stolen, computer-sized camera and time traveling real? He told himself no, but found it hard to believe. Had the attack been a dream? That felt more likely. Maybe they had never even gone to the Island. Maybe they had been trying to get the stolen camera back the whole time. Maybe the cat had brought her kits in for the photo-shoot. After a moment, he wasn't asleep enough to know what he was remembering.

He tried to shift his arm to see if it was still in the spot between luggage bags where he had left it. If it wasn't there, then they were at the studio trying to figure out the culprit. Not only was his arm there, it was broken.

Roman moaned, since this was a sign that the fight had

been real and that his older counterpart would never go to baseball practice with him after the investigation.

"Hey, he's awake," Sarah's voice rang out loud and clearly.

"Finally. There's nothing to do out here but make straw people," Renaldo complained.

Straw people?

"I believe that it is a larger concern that we are leisure prey for anything seeking us," Richie's voice approached.

Roman tried to open his eyes, but once he had, they stung as if there was toxic miasma floating liberally in the air. Roman grabbed his face with his one good hand.

"What happened?" Roman asked, recalling the sharp pain in the back of his neck.

"The label came off," Sarah explained in a coaxing voice, "but it's some sort of knock-out liquid."

"*Sedative* is a common term," Richie told them.

"I thought that we didn't have tranquilizers," Roman said.

"Well, it turns out we did. So there."

Roman sat up, and immediately felt a wave of nausea come over him, and lay back down. "So you guys gave me medicine to make me unconscious?"

"Yup. Feel lucky, Ashley didn't get that luxury. We wasted it all on you."

"What's wrong with Ashley?" Roman tried opening his eyes again. He had to continuously blink, as if he hadn't seen daylight in years. That's when Roman saw bandages on various areas of his friends bodies, mainly arms and legs, but Richie had a nasty cut across his nose, where skin was dangling off. And Renaldo had a nasty scar down near his left eye. Roman had to keep himself from staring at their worst injuries, and turned his head to notice a lump next to him in the tent.

He flipped over entirely, his muscles screaming in protest. Light-blond hair came out of a blanket next to him. Ashley. Her breathing was rigid, even in sleep. Her head was buried under her thin, green blanket.

"She was nearest to the creatures when they attacked,"

[309]

Richie said dejectedly. Roman wondered if he was in pain from his nose injury, even though he had sounded fine the last time he had spoken, because Richie's voice sounded forced and cracked.

Roman knew what was wrong a second before Richie explained. Luckily, there was no internal bleeding or broken bones, and he knew how much trouble a broken bone could be. Her leg had obviously been poorly protected when she had been attacked because, even though Roman's power wasn't x-ray vision, he could clearly see that she had four clear slashes down her thigh. Her arm had a deep bite, with a couple dozen blisters and other various openings.

"Have you bandaged the wounds?" Roman asked.

"No," Renaldo said sarcastically, rolling his eyes, "we wanted to save them so we left her to bleed."

Roman ignored him. After all, whether her wounds were bandaged or not wasn't their main concern. Both her injuries already had small infections. Additionally, her gashes were all on the left side of her body, and that was nearest her heart. Roman remembered something that he had picked up back on the plane when the medical supplies had spilled. There were two different medicines that would help, since she had a minor blood poisoning and a minor infection. They had less than a day until the ointments wouldn't be enough to help her. They would need to use a needle for the blood-poisoning serum and stitch the other wound before they could apply the ointment.

Roman explained the urgency of the situation to the others, whose faces grew darker with every word. Roman tried not to focus on the fact that Sarah didn't seem to be angry with him anymore, and neither was he with her. Roman risked sitting up straight. Richie immediately disappeared out of the tent to get the medicines once Roman suggested that they should be brought in soon.

Richie returned along with two extra bottles, which were Roman's medicine for treating his own arm. The others were determined that Roman should at least take half of his dose before he continued.

Roman obeyed, and then they set to work instantly. Even

[310]

though Roman's power was being able to tell what would heal people, that didn't make him any more immune to the repugnance of freshly infected blood and flesh. Renaldo handed him an empty bottle as he automatically retched. Renaldo and Sarah's main concern at that moment was the odor, but Roman's main concern was that one canteen of water was already empty enough to retch in.

Renaldo left the tent at one point, but Richie helped apply the blood-poisoning medicine, since Roman couldn't hold his left arm steady enough without his other arm to balance it out. Roman decided that, to slow down both infections from spreading quickly, they would wait until the blood poisoning antidote had been drained from Ashley's system, then apply the other infection medicine.

Afterwards, out of tradition, Roman requested a wet cloth. Sarah and Richie departed, but Richie returned with a slight look of confusion across his face. Once Roman took the cloth, he noticed that the water wasn't warm. It was comfortably cool. Roman looked up at the peak of the marquee, expecting to see the familiar several spots of sun just barely perforating the fabric. Instead, he saw utter darkness. It was as sunless as the sky during a rainstorm.

"Richie, why isn't it warm outside? What happened to the humidity?"

"You may wish to investigate for yourself." Richie helped Roman out of the tent, though Roman was reluctant to leave a patient alone. As a matter of fact, he was still injured, bile rising in his throat from movement.

Roman expected the same line of trees, slant in the hill, and slight clusters of brush here and there, that were the camp that they had left. The loose dirt that he had spotted when the others left the tent he thought confirmed this. But Roman wasn't sure if what was surrounding them could be considered trees. Long, golden strands sprouted in every direction. The steep incline had disappeared entirely, along with the bushes and stout foliage. The long strands were like tall grass. Ten foot high tall grass. The golden flagpoles had turned to spaghetti. Before, at least some of the trees were still brown and green, or at least had bark. But now, in every direction was the soft, tilted grass. Roman expected them to start waving in the breeze at any moment, until he remembered that there was no breeze here. The sun was blotted out by the towering grass. The trees before, however, had walking space between them. They would be lucky to have an inch between these stalks. The tent was on top of some of the springy grass that had been plucked out of the ground, forming a sort of hay-bed. Roman could see a path where they had come from, and separate paths off in side directions of where they were headed, most likely where Sarah and Renaldo had vanished to.

"Renaldo had been regurgitating, and Sarah was attempting to help him," Richie explained.

"Help him throw up?"

"No, he was continuing to *throw up*, and Sarah was attempting to stop him. He had already lost all of his food and had been clearing out the remaining bile by the time we found him. It was when you requested a cloth that Sarah and I had found him missing and she followed his trail."

"And they aren't back?" Roman figured he had been taking in the scene for at least a minute.

Richie shrugged; once again Roman couldn't help but notice how odd it was for Richie to do so. Roman couldn't blame Renaldo for feeling sick after seeing Ashley, since he had retched himself.

"How'd you guys get Ashley and me here?"

Richie pointed to a spare, three-person blanket that was lying next to the tent, blood-stained and with cleanser slowly trickling off to form a stream that steadily flowed right in comparison to where they had come through.

"We have applied the cleanser to remove the overall scent of blood," Richie explained.

"What about the smell from the cleanser?"

"That scent is repelling, whereas blood, to most predators, would mean an easy meal." Roman considered this for a moment, his only argument being that these weren't like most predators.

But was that really true? The ones that had attacked them had traits from other predators, and the jumping-mice looked exactly like a slightly mutated version of the mice that kids kept as pets.

"You guys just dragged us here?"

"We decided that staying in one area was not a highly recommended option."

Roman muttered his accord. All they had to do before starting off again was wait, both for Renaldo and Sarah to return, and for Ashley to wake up. Richie was going to watch over Ashley, even though Roman had volunteered.

At least there are more distractions out here, Roman considered.

He tried to stop his mind from wandering to the visions from yesterday. They were coming back more clearly than they had been when occurring. The astonishment on everyone's faces, the dying cry of the animal he had killed, the momentary taste of blood as a drop strayed to his mouth, open and panting. He had charged the creature with the tiger stripes and ducked under it, barely avoiding being bitten straight in the neck, but taking a blow from the cough of blood that followed.

He didn't succeed very well at keeping them away. He tried to turn his mind back to the coma-induced dream with the stolen camera and time traveling. That made things even worse, because his dream had hints of everything that had happened preceding it. One of the poodle's puppies had the face of the creature that Renaldo had killed, but very much alive, staring blood-thirstily at Roman from across the room. The shadow of the thief had been sparkling electricity like his mechanical spider. Roman tried to ignore the fact that all of his qualities were antagonistic in his dream and the creatures that had attacked them were seemingly innocent. This, of course, was false, he told himself. They had attacked *him* in reality.

After five minutes, he couldn't stand it anymore. He had to get away from the looming stalks of gold, the blood trickling out of the tarp, Richie's occasional shuffle in the tent that gave him a thumping in his temple. He couldn't blame Ashley for being unconscious, but Sarah and Renadlo should've been back

[313]

by now. Where were they? It never took Roman more than a few seconds to finish vomiting.

"Richie, do you think that Sarah and Renaldo got into some sort of trouble?" Roman wondered, trying to sound concerned instead of distressed.

"Do you suppose we should leave the camp unguarded while searching for them?" Richie asked, his head appearing at the entrance to the tent. His orange eyes were glowing again, not fiercely, they were simply shinier than usual. They looked forlorn. It was like he was fighting back tears, but nothing else gave any hint of that.

"I think—" Roman started, then jumped as something made a crunching sound off to his right.

Sarah and Renaldo came back through the trail that they had made. Sarah gave Roman a weak smile and nodded, as if a problem had been taken care of. But Roman knew that there was a whole new problem immediately. Renaldo would've looked fine to Sarah, Richie, and Ashely, but not to Roman. His power didn't allow that. Even though Renaldo only seemed slightly depressed, Roman immediately knew that the swamp water in Renaldo's pack wasn't just a nuisance to wipe off of their canteens.

"Renaldo, have you eaten or drank anything lately? Since we got out of the swamp?" Roman asked anxiously.

Renaldo nodded, frowning at Roman's expression. "Right after we dragged you guys here. I needed some water and had about a pint."

Roman's stomach flipped. "Sarah, get the medical kit."

"Why? What's wrong?" Sarah wondered, "Is it Ashley?"

"No, apparently the swamp water got into Renaldo's water canteen. There's a reason that he was throwing up so much."

Catching on, Sarah rushed over to Richie, who had overheard and plunged back into the tent to get the kit out of Roman's duffle bag. Renaldo's face became slightly less dark as he gasped and his stomach convulsed.

Renaldo had drunk tainted swamp water, and Roman only

hoped that they could get it out of his system quickly.

Roman had to take shifts along with Richie and Sarah to make up for the loss of able-bodied people. One guarding the camp, one resting, and one person looking after Renaldo and Ashley. This continued for several hours. Roman had been on the rotation of looking after them when Ashley woke up screaming. Roman called Sarah in whenever Ashley needed a bed-pan, while Roman was, unfortunately, in charge of Renaldo's. At least Renaldo didn't have very much to pass, while Ashley would've had extra. Aside from the small talk that every once in a while occupied their attention, it was tedious, as Ashley and Renaldo constantly pointed out. Renaldo couldn't keep anything down, so they didn't use their limited supply of food on him. Roman feared that the poisonous water had already made it into his bloodstream. Ashley was occupied for a minute with canned peas. But when it was clear that Ashley and Renaldo, who both either couldn't or refused to sleep, were wasting their energy complaining, they set off.

Ashley could not walk on her own, so she was dragged on the blood-soaked mat. Renaldo managed to keep on his feet for around two miles before the sickness started to take effect. Then he was dragged along with Ashley. Roman, with his broken arm, couldn't carry anything more than his pack and, needing his left arm for carrying instead of holding a weapon or balancing, his duffle bag. That left Richie and Sarah to carry six pieces of luggage. Sarah took the three-piece one while Richie had the two-piece. They each tied ropes around their legs, the other end connected to knife-hacked holes in the mat, so that they could drag the others along. It was slow progress, about a mile and a half for an hour, because Sarah kept having to stop to rest, or Richie would drop something, or Roman would lose his balance on the rope. There was no room on the tarp for the luggage, even though Ashley and Renaldo offered to hold them while they were dragged. But their offers were brushed away, since Ashley couldn't risk tearing any muscle on her arm and Renaldo couldn't sit up without effort.

[315]

At least we aren't still headed uphill, Roman told himself, trying to overcome the fact that their sturggles were accomplishing next to nothing. His arm banged, once again, against a particular stalk of grass that was still mostly tree, and he cursed. He took a long look at everyone. Sarah sweating away their water, Richie doing an odd dance due to his foot rope and the separate luggage items, Renaldo passed out, and Ashley lamely trying to use her good arm to scoot the tarp along.

"This is ridiculous," Roman stated, stopping.

"The understatment of the century," Sarah panted, letting go of the huge package that she had been dragging.

"Yeah, we need to think of something else."

"If we could think of something better, then don't you think that we'd be doing that?" Ashley demanded.

"Well, we're a long way away from our gemstones, and we can't rest for too long. We only have so many supplies." They could all tell from the same sense as before that they were still a while away from their destination.

"Maybe we could make a raft or something out of this hay," Ashley suggested.

"Anybody know how to do that?" Roman asked.

Sarah shook her head along with Ashley. This was not one of the many creative things that they were taught at the mansion. But Richie started plucking some of the stalks from their places, along with gathering some that they had crushed along the way.

"Where did you learn this kind of thing?" Roman couldn't help but wonder.

"I was a member of a *Cub Scouts* troop when I was seven and eight years old," Richie said absently.

Roman exchanged at look with Sarah, shrugged, and bent down to untie the rope around his ankle.

Many of the strands had to be cut with their knives, but luckily, they were long and bendable enough to work. Roman suspected it took a good part of two hours to make something large enough, similar to a raft, to hold more than one suitcase. Roman couldn't keep a grip on the strands and tie them at the

[316]

same time with one arm, and once they no longer needed to collect any more stalks, he could do next to nothing to help. Even Ashley knew how to tie the most intricate knots when the stalks had reached their bendable limits. Roman guessed that her coordination power helped considerably.

Sarah had trouble not breaking the stands too short and couldn't tie knots as well as Ashley or Richie, but she easily accomplished more than Roman did three times over. They used the last of their rope to arrange a way to drag their things along with Ashley and Renaldo. Roman still carried his duffle bag over his shoulder, but used his arm to grab hold of one end of rope. Sarah still dragged her three-piece, but Richie was able to assist with one of his hands, while the other tugged at the second rope. It was still slow going, but they didn't have to stop as often. Roman didn't see much difference as his arm continued to throw him off balance or kept bumping into the endless stalks.

They set up camp with the same arrangement as before. They made sure to check if the food cans had any dents, even the ones that weren't in Renaldo's pack. They used the special cleanser they had brought to clean the rest of their water. Renaldo woke the instant that they had opened the first can of beef, and instantly fell back into his dream-world when stomach convustions reminded him that he couldn't eat anything.

"It appears that his sickness may be affecting his powers," Richie observed, his brow creasing.

"What do you mean?" Sarah inquired after a sip of purified water.

"He woke up right when Sarah opened that can of beef," Ashley said. "And then he got dizzy when he realized that he couldn't have any. Richie's saying that he's accidentally jinxing himself."

Roman would've marveled at how Ashley had interpreted Richie's words before he had when the luggage, carefully set with the net outside the tent, collapsed. Roman knew that Richie had been correct as he held the net in place while Sarah adjusted the gear. Renaldo must have just jinxed that as well.

"That could either come in handy or be a disaster,"

[317]

Roman commented.

"You mean another disaster," Sarah corrected. "Aha," she held up the first leaf that Roman had seen on the Island, "this is what set it off."

"How'd it get here, though?" Roman asked.

"There still remains no trace of wind or any plants with leaves in this area," Richie agreed, perplexed.

"I don't know. That only adds to your theory, Richie." Sarah shook her head and tossed the leaf aside. Instead of flitting back like anything that light Roman would've expected to, it continued to fly over to land on top of Renaldo, still snoring on the tarp.

They had stopped attempting to figure out whether it counted as night or day a long time ago, since the dots of sun only shifted slightly, but never disappeared. The long stalks of grass had gotten steadily thinner, now revealing a choice bit of light. On the second camp watch, Roman tried to count how many suns were in the sky, but even though his eyes didn't hurt as they normally would have while staring up to the sky, his vision shook when he concentrated on one dot of yellow for too long. It was like trying to see something already moving behind a waterfall of gray fog clouds.

His shift with Sarah went smoothly. Roman was glad that they were out of the area that seemed to push everyone's tempers to their fullest. Although they could never take back what they said or thought, he was sure that the argument was behind them. No apologies were necessary, which they seemed to agree on without more than a look. Richie kept insisting on taking the medical shifts, even though Sarah thought that it would be more efficient if Roman ran them. Ashley's face was normally pale, and despite the heat, her skin was cool to the touch. Roman saw that she was healing at a very slow rate, but Renaldo was getting steadily worse. He began coughing in his waking time, and kicking in his sleep. He never snored anymore, which worried Roman even more.

Roman didn't enjoy contemplating it, but he wasn't sure

whether he would pull through or not. Every drop in Renaldo's health was a surprise to Roman. Sometimes he had heart burn and while other times he began scratching at his skin like there were millions of ant bites there. His health sometimes improved, but barely. Most of the time, an aberration meant that he was getting worse. But Roman could see no regular pattern, as he normally did with flus or colds. Sometimes Renaldo's eyes rolled almost entirely inside of his eyelids, and would stay that way for twenty seconds before he came to, seemingly not remembering any events of the past few minutes.

They continued on their march, which seemed endless. Roman had the idea of making straw supports on the tarp and curving the ends of their raft so that they could push them instead of pulling. It would also make a clear walkway for the present company with broken arms. Richie noted that if there was something like a sudden drop in terrain or more predators, then their baggage, along with Ashley and the regularly unconscious Renaldo, would be helpless.

So their pace stayed the same, Roman cursing as each stalk hit his arm and worsened its condition. They often didn't journey very far in between camps. This increased Roman's worry about them reaching their gems soon enough for Renaldo. After they set off from their fifth camp, Roman could've sworn that their luggage was considerably heavier. He found his theory confirmed by the deeper trenches that their cargo left behind in the clear dirt. During their next camp, Roman suggested that they check their inventory and dispose of their empty food cans and other useless tools. Ashley seemed to strongly disagree and insisted that they keep going and that they were wasting time.

"A strong request for the one who's being dragged along," Roman sneered. Ashley looked furious at the suggestion that she was slacking off, but Roman waved his hand and started to unzip the royal blue suitcase resting on the ground.

"Let's just *move on*," Ashley moaned. Everyone conscious turned to stare at her. Instead of making a comeback to an insult, she had resorted to begging. Richie and Sarah joined in on unpacking. As Richie was inspecting a compartment on the inside of the main section of Renaldo's leather case, he suddenly jumped back and yelped, a noise somewhere in between a regular sound of surprise and a mouse's squeal.

Roman had his knife out in an instant and Sarah had what was left of her arrows pointed at the bag, since she had lost more than the good majority of them in the fight with the predators. But Ashley made a squeal noise of her own and was trying to move her good leg to stand up.

Richie scrambled away from the case, and stopped at the edge of the clearing they had made. Ashley shouted something unexpected.

"Pongo!"

Something beige leapt out of the suitcase and was on the tarp next to her within two seconds. She wrapped her arm around it and shielded whatever it was from Sarah's arrows. Sarah's bow slowly made its way to point at the ground as she stared in confusion at what Roman could not see.

"Ashley, what is *that*?" she demanded heatedly.

Ashley looked like she was going to cry. Her cheeks flushed red, and her grip tightened around whatever she was holding.

"He wasn't doing any damage," she said lamely. "I was going to tell you guys about him, but I never got around to it."

"What were you intending to do with it?" Richie questioned as he stumbled to his feet, his brow furrowing, looking half confused and half angry.

"I just thought that he might be able to help us…when I saw the leaf I knew that it couldn't have just shown up, powers or no powers, unless something else shifted it." Ashley tried to sound innocent, but couldn't keep her voice from cracking. "I've checked his teeth, and he's a herbivore. Besides, it couldn't do any harm to keep him until the end of our trip—"

"We should not be interacting with any wildlife. We could interrupt its natural cycle or disrupt any number of natural traits or habits or—" Richie started, fuming and almost stumbling over his words.

"And how have you been feeding it?" Sarah demanded,

[320]

"We only have so much food. And that thing slowed our progress by making our stuff a lot heavier." Sarah put her hand on her hips, her bow now slung over her shoulder. "Where did you find it, anyways?"

"Whoa, wait," Roman interrupted, "what is it?"

Ashley unwrapped her arms to reveal at first glance what was tufts of multi-colored fur. Looking closer, most of its fur was beige, with spots of red around its back and legs. It had black, leathery wings on its front legs like the predators from before. Its left wing was torn down the middle, reaching up all the way to its arm. It had brown patches of fur around its eyes that made it look like a raccoon. It was larger than the average cat, and looked like a mixture of lemur, bat, and raccoon. Its body in the shape of a lemur, the stance of a bat, when standing, but had small claws on the end of its seven-digited hands and opposable thumbs like a racoon. Roman immediately saw it as a threat, knowing raccoons to be considered vermin locally. Its eyes were entirely round as that of a rodent. They were pure yellow, apart from wide pupils that looked slightly dilated to Roman. Its tail flicked back and forth like a cat's, brushing against Ashley's arms, which were still clean from not touching any dirt recently.

"Does camouflage even exist here?" was all that Roman could get out, not dropping his knife.

"Roman, we can study the wildlife in our nightmares," Sarah scolded. "Ashley, are you telling us you've been keeping it as a *pet*?"

"Not permanently. But Pongo gets his own food—"

"You *named it*?" Sarah and Richie both gasped, except Richie's was more formal and had the word 'have' in the middle.

"You named it *Pongo*?" Roman said stupidly.

"He reminded me of an orangutan, and their scientific name is pongo-something. And his spots reminded me of *a Hundred and One Dalmatians*. He wandered into the camp when Richie and Sarah were stuck debating who would look after us on the other side of the camp. He just sort of walked over and sniffed me."

"And you didn't call us?" Sarah demanded.

[321]

"I thought it might make him scared. He was injured," she pointed to the torn wing, "and I saw some of these in the trees flying away really fast before we were attacked by those things." Ashley seemed to think that this improved her case. "Besides, he was kinda...cute."

This set Sarah, Richie, and Roman off immediately. Renadlo woke up during the middle of the shouting bout. Renaldo didn't seem to mind the fuzzy monkey that was crouched down in front of his face. On the contrary, he reached over and pet it. Pongo licked his fingers, and he dosed off again.

"Well, it's in the past," Sarah dismissed, "but we should drop him while we can."

"What?" Ashley cried in exasperation. She turned to Roman. "Please, Roman! He isn't doing any harm! Besides, he can't fly."

Roman was astounded and skeptical all at once. Ashley hardly ever used his name, and she never had begged him before.

"Do you think it's being cute on purpose?" Roman asked Richie and Sarah, not knowing what to do.

"Do you believe that it may be somehow affecting her senses?" Richie inquired.

"Erm, yeah. I think. Maybe."

"But cuteness isn't a natural sense," Sarah objected, not helping her point, but stating the facts. "The only animals we know that are affected by a sense of cuteness are humans, and there aren't any other humans on the Island, right now."

"The only animal that *we* know. This isn't exactly a science fieldtrip." Roman said, biting his lip. "It might just follow us if we try to leave it behind."

"His name is Pongo," Ashley said, sounding much younger than ten or eleven.

"Oh, yeah?" Roman inquired, wanting to snap the stupidity out of her, "Come here, Pongo."

Pongo obeyed, to everyone's astonishment. Pongo walked across the ground like a baboon and on its knuckles. He stopped and sat at Roman's feet, looking up at his face. Roman couldn't help but see the same intelligence he had seen in the predators in

[322]

Pongo's yellow eyes. Pongo looked much like a child, sitting on his bottom with his hands hanging into his lap, in between his outstretched legs. Roman felt his eyebrow twitching.

"We could tie it to a sturdy stalk and just leave him," Roman suggested. Ashley squeaked and bit her lip.

"But we used the last of the rope pulling together the carrier and pulling Ashley and Renaldo," Sarah pointed out.

"I believe that Ashley may have a more effective treatment if she had a companion." Richie stated blankly. Roman remembered how bad Ashley had been after the attack, and how she had been healing at a steady pace since a while ago.

So this is why she's been getting better...

Renaldo hadn't seen Pongo until just now, when he'd awoken. Roman concentrated hard. Renaldo's health currently was improved just a little bit. He wasn't kicking in his sleep, as he had been for the past several hours. Was he dreaming about Pongo? If Pongo walked along beside them, he wouldn't slow them down. In fact, considering that he learned his new name in less than a day, they might be able to train him to help pull along their burden. And if they couldn't get to their gems and the promise of healing...

"If he starts making the slightest bit of trouble..." Roman warned, shifting a glare between Ashley and Pongo.

Sarah's reaction was: "You're not honestly thinking about *keeping* it?"

Ashley's reaction was: "You mean he can stay? Yes! Come 'ere Pongo!"

Pongo pranced over to Ashley, sensing her excitement. Ashley hugged him, picked him up, and sat him back down on top of Renaldo, laying face up. Renaldo sleepily wrung his arm around Pongo, who lay down, comfortable to be out in the open instead of hidden inside an oversized suitcase.

Sarah sighed. "A slight bit of trouble? What if he kills us in our sleep?" she muttered to no one.

"Who's being paranoid now?" Ashley smirked.

[323]

22. Unexpected and Unwelcome

Φ   Φ   Φ

Since they couldn't spend much more time resting, they left the camp behind within about five minutes. Pongo did as Roman suggested, and walked along beside the tarp, just within reach of Ashley's gentle strokes of his fur. Renaldo woke up not too long afterwards and, without questioning anything, began following Ashley's example of petting Pongo.

Roman knew that they were well over half way to their gems, all of which seemed to be in the same area. He vaguely wondered how big the Island was, and if it necessarily had to fit inside the boundaries of where it originally was. They must have traveled at least fifty miles, and still had quite a few more to go. He wished that he could keep his knife in his hand, in case Pongo wasn't all lovable monkey. Sarah looked just as agitated, if not more so. Richie seemed fine, keeping his attention on dragging. Roman was trying to concentrate on the condition of Renaldo, who *was* improving, and Ashley, who had been healing at the same pace as early yesterday, or that very day, or maybe three days ago. Roman felt that his hair would turn gray before he was twenty if he tried to figure out time and distance on the Island. For all he knew, he might already be twenty.

It didn't concern Roman that the only part of his arm that had gotten better was where the swelling had gone down. He didn't know whether or not he had gotten used to the constant burning, or if he just knew how to handle it better. He doubted the latter, since he kept banging his broken arm against the giant grass stalks. Roman still wanted to teach Pongo to help pull. He managed to convince Ashley that he could help pull along the unevenly-tied parts of the tarp, while still in petting reach. She didn't want Pongo to hurt his wing any further, but Roman told her that it was a clear cut. That meant that it was a perfect tear,

[324]

not having punctured any veins, if it had any in its wings. The bad part was that it would heal at a miniscule pace, if it healed at all. Upon hearing this, Ashley blamed the predators from before, calling them evil for the damage. Roman knew that if flying was the main defense of whatever Pongo was, then once they had left the Island, it was very likely that, unless he had good friends, Pongo was done for. He didn't tell Ashley this, and either way he didn't believe it. With opposable thumbs, the rest of his body perfectly healthy, and flexible tail, Roman had a hard time convincing himself that flying was his *only* defense.

Then again, those weren't average coyotes that had attacked them before.

It was Roman's turn to sleep at their next campsite. Renaldo and Ashley were both awake and, judging from how long Renaldo had slept before, he would be for a while. Richie kept an eye on Ashley and Renaldo outside, Sarah on the camp boundaries, and Roman was to stay in the tent. He thought that his aching arm and the rope burn from where it had been attached to his heel would keep him awake for hours, if they would even stay in the campsite that long. But he was very wrong. He didn't know if he had laid down before or after he had fallen asleep, just that he didn't have enough sleep by the time Richie was shaking him awake.

Pongo sometimes did an odd little dance when he tripped on something while helping to drag the tarp. He would fall back, jump high in the air, land somewhere three feet away, and bounce in place, howling, until Ashley coaxed him into pulling again. Renaldo, with his eyes closed most of the time, would simply groan about 'where his kitty went' and grab at the air where Pongo had been hauling his share. Pongo did get his own food, striding the impossibly thin grass stalks like they were stairs and coming back down with a paw full of seeds.

Roman drank his last drop of water from his canteen at their next campsite. He rummaged through their extra supplies for a new canteen, just for emergencies, since he had already had enough water to keep himself going. But the pocket with the extra bottles was empty. He asked the others if they had moved anything around in the luggage after they had ridden themselves of their trash. Everyone's canteens were over halfway empty, and they all knew that the waters were supposed to be in the one specific bag. Roman woke Sarah and explained the situation. She started rummaging through the different suitcases, sometimes looking in the hidden compartments that Roman had been absent when they were filling. There was no extra water. They checked the now-asleep Ashley's pack, and Renaldo's. All Renaldo could keep down was water, so he had been drinking more than he would've usually had. Even though they had been carefully monitoring his drinking, along with everyone else's, they would run out of water within a day.

Roman felt a pang of panic. They were in an endless maze of tall grass, with no sign of water anywhere. It was all probably underground, since the grass had to live off something. The soil didn't look like it could hold very much, anyway. But they couldn't spent their time digging. And the stalks likely took up the majority of the water before it sinks very deep. Roman felt very thirsty all of the sudden. They were taught that a healthy person could survive for four day tops without water. And they were in a very humid place, with two people fighting off possibly-fatal injuries or sickness, with the rest working extra hard to haul them along, working up a sweat.

Then a thought occurred to him. Pongo disappeared every once in a while to find his own food and do his business. Where has he gotten his water? They keep all of the empty canisters in the 'useless-bag', the suitcase that held the winter supplies and previously their empty food cans. Roman didn't suspect that Pongo had taken any water. They had done an inventory check when they were cleaning the water, right after Renaldo's poisnoning, and they each claimed their share of water, adjusting to different amounts of work and treatment. Even if they didn't keep a constant watch on Pongo, they would've each kept track of their own water, and after they found Pongo, they had continued with their inventory check at the next campsite, with all in order, according to Richie.

What Roman was contemplating was that Pongo knew

where to get more water. He had known the Island better than they did when he was a baby, and Roman trusted his instincts. Roman was all of the sudden thankful for Ashley's naivetés.

He immediately set the idea in everyone's minds. Roman, being the best rested, would follow Pongo, on Ashley's instructions, to whatever water source he had been using. It was their best option, if you counted digging, dying, or searching aimlessly as options. Ashley, before he had explained the water situation, looked as if she suspected that he would take Pongo away and never come back. She relaxed a bit when Roman told her about their dilemma. She had been trying to seem more mature ever since her behavior earlier towards Pongo.

Without any spare rope for a leash, Roman had to try his best to keep up with Pongo when Ashley had told him to find water. Pongo had started at a dogtrot immediately, leaving the others to call out good luck. Roman had no idea how Pongo could navigate through this thick tangle of grass, which was now his least favorite plant, since there were no paw prints left behind from before and no wind to carry a scent. Roman had a flash of the predator sniffing him from a distance of less than a yard, but that was much closer than how far they had already traveled. Pongo wasn't, however, leaving tracks behind this time. Roman was just wishing that the Island could go back to having no grass and more swamp water when they immediately entered a clearing.

Roman was so caught off guard that he almost stopped in his tracks. Roman guessed that it would've been another camp site or two until they found this. Since the only grass on the island was in the enormous maze they had just come from, in its place were wildflowers. Thousands and thousands of wildflowers as far as he could see, starting five feet from the grass that ended abruptly behind him, over to a trench with a gushing river flowing through and beyond. They had amazing colors and shapes, and most looked like they belonged in a rainforest. Not only were there the beautiful colors of bluebonnets, there were also some that glowed an eerie yellow-green, while others were pure red, maroon, gray, orange, green, even the color of the

[327]

ground, and some looked like fog clouds with odd light patterns like swirls all over them, and every other color that Roman had never expected a flower to be. There were some in a patch nearby that were shaped suspiciously like kangaroos, with the petals twisting and turning. Others had small discs on top, while others looked like potato skins, barely holding on to the curly shape they had adopted. Roman thought he caught one that reminded him of chalk, looking like it was painted in sky-blue powdered sugar. Each different set of flowers practically had a line separating them, without two different kinds of flowers mixing together in any area outside their own. Each patch had about a square yard of space. Roman was never one to collect flowers, and it was looked down upon to pick wildflowers in Texas, plus he didn't trust anything strange on the Island, from the plants to the animals, but he felt compelled to pick one and sniff it. That was the oddest part. Pongo didn't seem to even notice the flowers, but Roman wanted to examine one because he could smell nothing. Once, when he and his mom had been driving along the *I-10*, they had pulled over to look at the glorious bunches of wildflowers at a rest-stop. Roman remembered something like perfume. He also remembered his school play, the one before winter break, where they could buy the actors roses. They had an intoxicating aroma. Roman wondered why these had no scent and no openings for pollen that he could see, added to the fact that there were no bugs on the Island. Then he noticed the sprouts growing just off one flower about a foot away from him. These flowers could obviously reproduce for themselves.

The river was about six feet wide, small compared to rivers he had seen, but much clearer. He could see the clay at the bottom, since there was no proper silt to make any mud. It shimmered in the oddest places, since the sun wasn't in correct alignment. It was cleaner than most swimming pools he had seen, with only the occasional petal from the collection of blossoms nearby. Pongo charged straight at the stream, coursing through a group of flowers that were scarlet with yellow spots and shaped like the chicken tenders at *Burger King*. The banks of the river were slanted, with blood-colored clay, free of dirt, and dropped

[328]

about two feet before reaching the actual water. The river itself seemed to be at low tide, since there was no rainfall that Roman had seen to raise the water level.

He, timidly at first, followed exactly where Pongo had stepped, which was difficult because Roman's shoes were much bigger than Pongo's paws. Then, Roman started to get excited. He pulled out the canteen that he had brought with him and set off at a jog across the few yards of wildflowers that separated him from Pongo and the stream. Roman clutched his cleanser tight, hoping that he wouldn't forget about it and gulp down a few liters of non-sanitized river water. Pongo was waiting for him at the bank, sitting and watching him like a child. Roman stopped next to Pongo at the edge of the sandbar, covered in dirt and flowers instead of sand. The drop wasn't very far to the water, but the stream was deep, and flowed relatively quickly. He just had to make sure not to slip. Here, there was slick clay, and Roman didn't like the blood color, and there wasn't a rock in sight. Roman could see the bottom, but, judging by how obscured it was, it was at least ten feet deep. This was odd because it wasn't that wide by far.

Roman wondered how he would get the water. He couldn't bend down and reach two feet, with only one good arm and no place to grip aside from the loose dirt.

So close, yet so far away, Roman sneered and growled in frustration at the old saying that he never seemed to understand until now. He didn't know who had invented the saying, but currently, he wished that they never had existed.

Roman sized the canister. Could he use it to reach the length that his arm couldn't? No, it wouldn't do them any good for him to fall in the river. He'd have to hold the canister with his good arm and balance by crouching, which most likely wouldn't even work. Could Pongo help?

"Pongo..." Roman hesitated.

It's just a monkey, what's he gonna do? Put my stupid questions down in his biography?

Roman sighed. "Pongo, is there any way to get to the water? How have you been getting it?"

[329]

Pongo headed upstream. As it turned out, the edge of Roman's vision wasn't the horizon, as he had thought. They were standing on the crest of a short hill before he knew it. At least, the part they were at was short. The magnificent flowers, one kind a color he had never seen before, still stretched onward. Their part of the hill was about eight feet above the flat plain before them, consisting of nothing but wildflowers and, at the edge, a crumbled mountain. The area below them was where the stream was ground level, the clay still shimmering a few feet deeper. But farther on, towards the mountain, was what caught Roman's attention. He immediately knew what it was, without being told, or seeing what was beyond the sharp drop a hundred yards straight ahead. There was the first solid rock Roman had seen since arriving. But it was covered with soot, not too different from the black-brown dirt, and the bare areas showed pure black. Was it stone? Beyond the edge, Roman could see the edge of a gigantic crater. Storm clouds swirled in a circle above head, like a hurricane, except without the eye. All of the wispy clouds that had followed them since their arrival seemed to accumulate here. Several lightning bolts struck one single area, which Roman gaped at. They only hit in one place, and never anywhere else. His senses were screaming at him. He was no longer tired, thirsty, or in agonizing pain from his arm. He couldn't remember the last time he had felt so estatic. His vision shimmered. Not like it was a heat wave, or that he was dizzy, but everything beautiful seemed to sparkle. The lightning, not the flowers, the rock underneath the soot, not the soot itself, the clay in the river, not the water or the distant promises of sun.

Pongo still was waiting by the stream, looking confused by what had stopped Roman on the hill's crest. Roman was hardly aware of Pongo and the stream. Everything else was the crater and the ruins and the clouds and the lightning. He couldn't concentrate on anything to his left or to his right. It might've been the end of the world and he wouldn't have known it. All he could truly concentrate on was the crater.

Their journey was finally over, he realized. What did it matter whether they had water or not? They could be home

[330]

within two hours. Pongo let out a sort of screeching sound. Roman was aware of a tugging on his pants. Roman was about to tell Pongo to stop, but he had trouble remembering what he was going to say. It was hard to shift his gaze from the beautiful sight before him. He didn't know how long he stood there, jaw dropped, transfixed, with Pongo pulling at his pant leg, but eventually he felt his senses coming back, the feeling waning. He glanced at Pongo to see that he was urgently pestering him about the water. Roman looked to the right of the stream, seeing that beyond it was a cliff. On top was another forest, except the trees were sooty black instead of red or green or brown. There was a good amount of area between the ravine and the cliffside, covering all in the sooty dirt instead of flowers. The river was narrower here, only about four feet wide, but flowed even faster. Roman knelt down with his canister open, knowing that they should still have water for Renaldo and Ashley, but Pongo wasn't concentrating on the water. Pongo continued poking and jumping on Roman.

"What do you want?" Roman demanded irritably, nearly losing his balance after one particularly rough shove from Pongo. "What is it?"

Pongo seemed to want to lead him somewhere else. He kept running a few feet away and swinging his arm.

"You've already found the water, Pongo. This is what we asked for. We don't need anything else."

But Pongo would not concede. He started pulling at Roman's good arm, and Roman knew that it he wanted that arm for getting the water, he would first have to follow Pongo. They had only walked three feet upstream when Pongo had reached what he had been trying to show Roman. Roman glanced at what Pongo was indicating towards with his winged hand.

It was a footprint. Implanted in the loose dirt that covered the area just before the river, with some scraped off the side, as if someone had stumbled, was a footprint. Roman recalled the others finding tracks back at the crash site. Roman hadn't seen it, but they had said that it had been too large for any of their feet. There was a number nine stamped into the center of the print.

Roman knew that no one on their expedition had a shoe size even close to nine. He was the oldest, and he had a size six and a half.

Roman nealy fell back in astonishment. He glanced around for more footprints. There was a crushed flower in front of him, and the clay at the bottom of the stream was slightly less smooth than anywhere else, but that was hardly anything.

Pongo suddenly tried to pull Roman away. Roman knew better than to argue after what Pongo had just found. Roman didn't like the fact that there was someone else on the Island. It wasn't supposed to be possible.

Neither was being conscious on the plane ride, the nagging worm in the back of Roman's head whispered. Roman told himself that technically he had just been late collapsing, but it was difficult to believe his voice of reason when Pongo was insisting that he jump over the stream after doing so himself.

"No fair, you've got wings!"

Pongo held out his torn wing.

"Ugh," Roman moaned. There weren't any tree branches for the clovus-jump here, and his broken arm wouldn't help him balance. He was thirsty and tired, and he should've been heading back to the others at the very least. At least four feet wasn't very far.

Roman backed up, annoying Pongo immensely, and just as Roman heard the shouting, he was launched across the river, with another sickening crunching sound as he crashed ontop of his arm.

Roman would've screeched in pain if it hadn't been for the sudden wad of fur blocking him from drawing a big enough breath. The wind had been knocked out of him during the lading, and Pongo managed to cover Roman's mouth with his arm. Roman would be thankful later, but now he was upset that some of Pongo's fur had shed, and he wasn't sure if he had spit it all out.

There was no chance of turning back on Pongo's urgency. Roman's splint was entirely crushed, and as Roman tore it off, he saw the angle that his arm was bent. Roman thought it was a miracle that the second bone in his arm hadn't been more than fractured. The inflamed swelling cumulated immensely in the twenty seconds it took for Roman and Pongo to crash, splattering dirt everywhere, over to a fissure in the cliff side. Like everything else, besides the flowers, it was engulfed in soot. After Roman had gotten deeper into the crevice, stone underfoot, he saw that it could've easily fit a person holding their arms out to their sides, and also that it was really made of a yellowish sort of stone. Mist curled out of one of four basketball-sized holes above their heads. The fissure was hidden by a boulder in front, not unlike the one inside the Talismen ground, except the inside was of the same yellow-beige pigment. Roman didn't want to know why the steam was coming out of the holes, but he didn't have any choice but to accept it descending upon him as Pongo insisted on not only staying, but crawling under the boulder. Roman wanted to draw the line at this, until he once again heard shouting, this time more powerful and increasing in volume with every second. Roman had to drag his arm underneath with him, barely containing a scream of agony. When he grunted, Pongo tried to cover his mouth again, but Roman smacked his paw aside.

It was surprisingly spacious under the rock. There was even enough space for Ashley to join them. It was almost completely dark, their only sight being through the crack in which they had just rolled under. Roman was breathing heavily, but his breath was stolen from him when the pair of shoes came into view.

They were definitely from the twenty-first century. Roman had seen some kids in his own gym class wearing those shoes. A pair of *Sketchers,* probably the same kind he had seen by the stream. They had a red streak across the side, a small spot of the same color on the toes, and black laces. The sole of the shoe that Roman could see was white. They made a stomping sound on the stone, and left wet footprints wherever they stepped. Whoever they belonged to, they seemed to be in a hurry. They clomped in every direction in sight. A second pair came into view, much smaller, a size four maybe, and quieter. They weren't *Sketchers* like the other pair. Roman had never seen this type

[333]

before. They had a slightly springy quality to them when they walked, with a large area of space between the sole and the ground. It seemed to be mainly supported by the heel and toe areas. They were like miniature *Moon Shoes*, except purple with silver stripes around the front. There were no laces, just straps. Roman couldn't see much above the ankles of the owners of the shoes, but he caught sight of white socks on the first person, along with slightly tanned skin. The ones on the second person had no socks and slightly darker skin. Roman's breathing came back, but barely. It was certainly silent and shallow enough so that the strange characters before him couldn't hear. He was considering giving himself up, as the people seemed to be searching for him.

But then Roman recognized one voice that spoke.

It was the traitor himself. The one who Roman blamed for Jacob's death. The reason that they couldn't stray beyond the boundary that protected the mansion. Roman felt that he should've known from the start, not just from the footprint at the plane crash, or his dream, but from the day they met at school. It was all that Roman could do to keep from leaping out of the hole he and Pongo hid in and start to strangle the Strayer, Danny. The fact that he couldn't move his right arm helped somewhat with staying put.

"They might've scaled the cliff side," Danny said, his voice sounding deeper than the last time they had seen each other, "or maybe ran off somewhere else."

"How could they have climbed the entire hundred-foot cliff in, what, eight minutes?"

Roman thought he would gag from the gasp he had to hold back. The second voice was none other than Victoria Chuffinch.

"Don't underestimate 'em. Especially with that idiot Rowland on their team."

"If he's an idiot, then why shouldn't we? They're in over their heads. They don't know when they're beat," Victoria scoffed.

"It's only the training center. We should've focused on

the one underneath the *Smithsonian*. I say that we should just ambush them."

"But if there's one beast on this stupid chunk of rock that'd do it for us, then I'll be selling my soul to Emote. He's going to find out sooner or later, so there's less than no point. Like you said before, it's just a school for those little brats. And it's not like they could've come up with too much useful stuff in the past few years." Victoria's shoes disappeared, but her voice remained, "Either way, we've got more than one out there, and that's excluding you. And they've just now gotten the main computer up and running. Check inside the holes," she added, "there might be something."

"I doubt it." Danny's shoes disappeared. Just when Roman thought they were gone, they started speaking again.

"We should never have gone ahead...You know, it might've been easier just to have stayed put," Victoria commented. "You got lucky, threw it away, and now look at where you are."

"If I got lucky the first time, then I got lucky twice. Three times, even. You two coming along, and then that plaster-bomb idea. I can't say the same for Chaze or you-know-who."

"I think that she was nice. But Emote won't do that until she'd gotten that kid from St. Patrick's onboard. You know, he wants to call her Manny."

"Why Manny?"

"You know," Victoria explained as the voice started fading away, "like on that *Nickelodeon* show, Manny's got the same last name." Roman heard no more. He didn't try to crawl out of his hole, even after Pongo climbed out into the light, squinting, waiting for Roman.

Roman wished that he knew what they had been talking about. How had they followed them to the Island? They knew that they were there, so why haven't they killed them, yet? They also said that there weren't any animals there, which Roman knew too well wasn't true. Danny had apparently fallen into the river.

The gems! Roman felt like he wanted to hit himself with a

charged mechanical spider for not realizing it before. If they were still there, and haven't killed any of them yet, then they hadn't gotten their gemstones! It would be much easier to dispose of them with second-rate powers. They couldn't just leave after finding them, if they didn't think that the Talismen could be destroyed by anything besides fatigue. Roman jumped out, unsuccessfully, and so suddenly that Pongo covered Roman's mouth as he almost let out a cry of pain. Roman accidentally bit Pongo, who didn't look at all happy about it.

Pongo had obviously sensed Roman's anxiety enough to retrieve the others for Roman. Roman didn't have time to run all of the way back, if he could even cross the stream without snapping his neck. Danny had carelessly left footprints in the dirt, Roman saw as Pongo hurried off. Victoria had two prints where she had jumped off of the boulder, but after that, there was nothing. Roman suspected the shoes that she had been wearing contributed to that.

Roman vaguely wondered where the stream ended if the crater was as big as he'd seen. He wondered if he could still get to the crushed volcano without crossing the stream.

Only one way to find out. Nothing to lose.

Roman ran as well as he could upstream without crying out in pain, which was roughly four miles per hour. He felt a slight pinching in his ankle, but that was easy enough to ignore with the inflammatory agony from his arm. At least there weren't any stones to stumble over. Roman tried to focus on the task at hand, but between the nausea from his arm and the reality that he was a Genedeaue, it was exceedingly difficult. He noticed how there was a slight pattern in the swirling clouds. The suns shifted in unison with the middle of the swirling. The center always had a small thundercloud, without any rain, hanging just below it. Roman was almost to the edge of the rocks now. The flowers on the other side of the stream looked so interesting that Roman was almost tempted to jump back across the stream to get to them. He found more focus in the realization that the crater was wide enough to not only fit the whole of the stream, it seemed to be *producing* the stream.

Roman decided warily to turn his thoughts, in a dreamlike state, over to the oddity of the stream's source. By not concentrating, he found that it was easier to concentrate. He wasn't concentrating, so he didn't process that this made no logical sense to him.

The rocks jutted in waves. Roman stepped on the rocks, leaving the last of his footprints behind. He realized that he should follow the areas of parted soot. They weren't tracks, but they told him which way Danny and Victoria had gone. Not even Victoria's specialized shoes couldn't help but part the grains of dirt that had never known wind. Roman climbed over the slight incline at the edge of the crater. Roman's unconcentrated concentration suddenly snapped. With his Genedeaue instincts gone, he realized the amount of power that he could feel swirling around him. His heart felt like it would leap out of his chest, and his neck, and his head, and his stomach. It was a good sort of pain that he felt.

Roman found that his attentiveness had increased considerably. Then he could sense the slight changes in heat as he walked forward. It wasn't the wind. He could feel...something....coming from the ground. It wasn't heat, or vibrations. It wasn't any other sense that he had ever known before. It seemed much like how they had known in which direction their gems were. He heard a distant crunching sound, and instinctively knew that it was very far away. But best of all, he couldn't take his mind off of the alarming and wonderful sight that now beheld him.

Colors he had never seen before, neons, primary, secondary, tertiary and beyond. Some that looked like animals, some like liquid, some that seemed so sharp that they would cut his eyes if he looked at them closely enough. Some blended into the rocks, others seemed more and more blatant then the last. He knew that there would be one that stood out among all of these. He knew exactly where his Bermuda gem would be.

Roman didn't think, he simply gave into his own Genedeaue instinct. He knew that if he thought about everything

[337]

surrounding him, then he would either faint from lack of energy or his head would simply combust. He walked, as if in a trance, the pain in his arm gone, feeling better than ever, off to his right. Roman knew not how fast he was going, nor how long he wandered. The only thing that he remembered, after seeing and sensing everything preceding it, was plucking what had seemed like the only thing in the world at the time; something royal-blue. It was made of shimmering octagons, inside of each was a heptagon, then a hexagon, then a pentagon, until Roman couldn't see any farther into it. It made a perfect cube, somehow, out of the octagons. He realized that his face was less than an inch from it, with his nose almost grazing it. His Bermuda gem. He knew it was his, and his only. He could feel the sense of the earth and the center of location instinct he had felt for the gem coming from inside. Roman felt like he could stare at it for over a hundred years and not learn everything about it. He couldn't picture any other gem around him. He was afraid that it was some sort of an invasion of privacy if he so much as looked at another gem.

He ran to the edge of the still rock, pointedly ignoring the thousands, maybe millions, maybe billions of other gems around him, the crystalline stone clutched tightly in his right hand. Roman stopped at the foot of the crested current.

My right *hand?* Roman lifted his right hand. He could lift his right arm! Roman examined the rest of his body. It was as if nothing had happened since he'd left the airport, not a knot or bruise as proof of their difficult journey, let alone his broken arm and torn muscle. He was still thirsty, but it didn't feel fatal in the slightest bit.

Then he remembered the stream and that he should've found out where it came from. He also remembered Danny and Victoria, but only when he turned around to find them aiming two knives straight at his chest.

23. Now Sticks, Now Stones

Φ   Φ   Φ

He'd blown it. Now, it was him against two other Genedeaues, both with their powers and weapons. He didn't know what his power was, and his only weapons were in his pack. If he reached for his pack, he would be dead in an instant.

Both Danny and Victoria looked unruly and muddled. Their hair was sticking out in clumps and was blatantly unwashed. Their shirts and pants had cuts and slashes in what seemed like random places. Victoria's outfit looked well prepared for the Island, just as Roman's group's was; brown, except her pack was pitch black. Her pants went almost down to her knees. The sleeves of her top were ripped so that Roman couldn't tell how long they had originally been. Danny looked several inches taller than the last time Roman had seen him. His face bones were palpable and his hair, also longer than it had been before, fell almost to his shoulders. His outfit was a gray undershirt with a laceration straight down the middle. He had jeans, though the bottoms had been torn off to about his knees. They were both panting heavily, as if they had just run a long while, and Roman noticed that Danny was missing a front tooth. They looked like they had been through the same as the Talismen, though they claimed not to have met any animals.

Roman knew that his only option was to run. But while Danny had a malicious glaze in his eyes, Victoria lowered her knife and sighed dejectedly. Danny glanced at her, swallowing, and he momentarily appeared confused. Roman felt the same gleam of confusion fall across his face. Victoria threw her knife to the ground, the last thing Roman expected her to throw it at, and shrugged. She looked at Danny to do the same. Danny, catching onto this, adopted a furious expression. A silent conversation seemed to cross between them through their expressions, and ended with Danny lowering his knife, though not throwing it to the dirt like Victoria.

Victoria crossed her arms, straightening her back. "Well, what now?"

Roman probably looked much more baffled than before. Nothing in his hands, he stood with his hands half way up to fists, around waist level, his gem feeling like extra weight momentarily. He lowered them and shot an inquiring look at them both. Danny answered with a sneer, but Victoria spoke.

"Where's the other Talismen?"

"It's *where are*," Danny muttered.

Roman narrowed his eyes, still not speaking.

Victoria sighed again and rolled her eyes theatrically. "If we wanted to kill you all, you'd have been dead the day you arrived from your little mansion."

"How'd you get in the same time lapse as us?" Roman demanded.

Danny remained outraged. Victoria looked slightly cautious, but, seeing that Roman wanted answers first, replied, "We snuck onto that cargo-plane. Smelly thing, isn't it? To keep us from being flung from the plane with ya'll, we set off a plaster bomb, as if you know what that is, and that kept you from seeing us if ya woke up before us. It set off one of your parachutes. Why the hell did ya'll bring parachutes when you knew you'd all be unconscious?"

Roman knew that he had asked the same thing, and remembered the parachute rope around his arm. His *right* arm.

"That's what broke it, wasn't it?" Roman was astounded.

Now Victoria looked confused, Danny looked like he was going to make a rude remark. "What broke?" Victoria asked.

"A parachute string wrapped around my arm before I fell unconscious. I bet that's why my arm was broken when I woke up."

Danny chuckled, shaking his head with his eyes closed mockingly. Victoria still looked confused. "The parachute went off *after* we were unconscious. We only know about it because it was the only one activate when you all left the site, and that was one question about the plaster in the first place."

Roman took this in. Once again, the subject of not being unconscious with the other Talismen and waking up after them was evident.

"The others went out like lights at least a minute before I did," Roman confessed, relaxing his shoulders slightly. Both Victoria and Danny looked confused at this.

"Let's focus, can we?" Danny demanded finally. Victoria shook her head vigorously, as if clearing it.

"Why haven't you killed us?" Roman demanded.

"You're not complaining, are you?" Danny sneered.

Victoria elbowed him in the ribs, which were showing through the tear in his shirt, along with dried blood.

"It's a long story," Victoria dismissed.

Roman clutched his gem even tighter. "I've got time."

Victoria pouted and frowned. Danny stared at the ground.

"Fine," he said suddenly.

Victoria glanced at him, looking momentarily worried, but Danny neither looked up nor said any more.

"After Danny left the mansion, he didn't report back to Emote," Victoria confided cautiously.

"Who's Emote?" Roman interrupted eagerly.

At this Victoria rolled her eyes. "Our *leader. Duh.*"

Roman's mouth fell dry. "What about Trent Garretson?"

"Emote was his assistant. Once the leader dies, the assistant takes over. All Emote ever tells us is that 'you should be careful who you trust', and we all figured out the rest."

Roman's head spun for the tenth time that day. Trent Garretson was *dead*? Had Jacob died for *nothing*?

"You okay?" Danny questioned half-heartedly, raising one eyebrow. "Is it honestly *that* surprising to you that he would murder Garretson?"

"No, it's—nothing." That didn't seem to satisfy either of them, but they held their tongues as Roman asked his next question.

"So what happened after Danny left?" he focused on what Victoria had been about to say.

[341]

"He couldn't report to Emote, because his spying was the only thing he had going for 'im. He was there for the execution, realized what would happen, and then left. Danny was good at other things, sure, but to Emote, everyone only has *one* job, and when you're useless, once you're trash, he throws you out. We've got other spies, and Danny's the most useless."

Roman had no objection to Danny being referred to as *useless*, but something else bothered him. He interrupted Victoria's story again. "Why are you telling me about your spies and your leaders?"

"*I'm getting to that,*" she hissed, obviously annoyed. "Going to interrupt again?"

"No," Roman said coolly.

"Well, he tried to hide out at this old warehouse. Me, Mark, and Chaze, other agents, found him easily. Our jobs were search and destroy. When we found him, Chaze and I started worrying about what'd happen to us if someday we couldn't do our jobs. So we decided to help Danny here.

"Since Chaze and I were friends with Luigi, this guy in technical-whatever stuff, we got him to switch jobs for an hour. He showed us how to do everything, even though this could cost him an awful lot. Not his life," she added, "but a lot. Chaze shut down part of the airport, knowing that you guys were going to have your flight soon. And when you came along, Danny and I just snuck through. Your security needs to account for closed-off air vents, ya know. Anyway, we figured that once we'd gotten our gems we could be loners, or *Rouges* as you'd say. We didn't dare go farther than you did, since we didn't know what to expect. And we wanted to wait until ya'll got your gems before we snuck in."

"You don't have your gems?" Roman inquired.

Victoria and Danny held out their empty hands.

"And we left footprints behind the only time that we *did* go ahead of you."

"So *that's* why you were looking for me in the rocks."

They looked surprised that he'd known that for a moment, then nodded in unison.

[342]

"How did you know when we were having our trip?" Roman asked.

"You guys were scheduled for April seconds before you arrived," Danny spoke. This struck Roman as odd, but he couldn't stop to consider it now.

"What happened to that guy, Mark? You said that he found Danny with you."

"Oh, he had an accident," Victoria dismissed, with a glinting stare straight into Roman's eyes. Roman knew she was telling him that it hadn't been an accident.

"Now what?" Roman said after a silence.

"That's exactly what I asked you!" Victoria said exasperatedly. She comically threw her arms about, then winced in pain.

"What happened to you guys?" Roman asked.

"A small run-in with the trees."

"The trees?" Roman looked at the forest on top of the cliff, but it was gone entirely, including the ash that had covered everything from the roots to the highest leaves.

"What are you lookin' at?" Danny growled.

"There was a forest up there," Roman whimpered, not knowing what horrors still awaited them.

Victoria and Danny looked like they had just found four Romans holding out knives at them.

"There's more," Victoria urgently warned Danny. "They've got to be coming for us."

"Who's—or what's coming for you?" Roman insisted.

"No time for explaining. Just run," Danny ordered, not taking his eyes off the cliff top. Victoria quickly grabbed her knife, and Roman felt the doubt of a trick cross his mind. The other two were quickly off in the opposite direction of the gems, the same way that Roman would've been headed if he was to meet up with the others, who should be there any moment. Roman had less than a second to decide whether or not to follow them. Any more time wasted could mean disaster.

To buy himself some more time, he started after them, since he'd have been going in that direction anyways. He should convene with Ashley, Sarah, Renaldo, and Richie, at least to let them know that he wasn't in much danger from Danny and Victoria. They would only know that he was in danger, since Pongo would simply get their attention without explanation. If he followed Danny and Victoria, they could either ambush him or give him more information. If they were going to give him information, then he could come back with Ashley, Richie, Renaldo, and Sarah as reinforcements, figuring that their gems would heal them like his hand. He ignored the fact that others before them had come back with injuries, deciding that this time was different. And could he really be much assistance against 'the trees' with no idea how to work his power? He had been hoping that his gem would tell him at least what it did by some means of his newly acquired sixth sense.

Danny and Victoria started drifting to their left. Roman was closest to Danny, since Victoria was faster and lighter than him, and he was slowly gaining. But Roman would not catch up, because he continued straight across the field of flowers they were now crossing toward the tall grass. He thought that Danny saw him as they steadily went in opposite directions. Danny waved, maybe calling out something. He hadn't known, because he had already been enveloped by the stark grass.

He found it considerably easier to navigate through the limited space with both arms available. It wasn't long before he heard a few familiar voices arguing. Not bothering to make out what he heard, he leaped through the dense forest toward his teammates.

Sarah almost screamed from surprise. Richie fell backwards. Pongo jumped up and down excitedly, and Ashley's eyes were wide until she saw that it was Roman. Renaldo was again unconscious and only slightly better than when Roman had left. He was snoring, which was a good sign. They had been hauling their luggage in their usual fashion, which Roman had forgotten to account for when he expected them to be quick. Of course Pongo couldn't tell them to travel light, or at least not give them a reason to.

"Roman! Pongo came back to get us. He was insisting for

us to hurry and bring Renaldo and Ashley at the same-" Sarah started at his arm, which was no longer so pointedly twisted and limp.

"How is it possible that your arm seems to have healed from your absence?" Richie beat her to the question.

"Got my gem," Roman held up the royal blue square. "I think that they have some sort of healing property on this Island."

Sarah looked shocked, Ashley seemed excited, Richie narrowed his eyes and seemed to mouth the word *healing properties*, and Renaldo continued with his snoring.

"We really need to hurry," Roman said. "You guys can leave whatever you don't bring in your packs, it's less than a mile," he indicated to the grass stalks, "and we need to help—"

"Sorry for not being so fast with one less person to pull." Sarah rolled her eyes. "Are we just going to carry Renaldo and Ashley?"

"You don't have to carry me!" Ashley protested. "I only need to lean against your shoulders or something."

"We'll have to settle. Now there's a reason for this. You see, Danny and Vic—" he started out.

"No time, judging from your tone this is a long story," Sarah interrupted. "Just start hauling that eight-year-old."

"You should not exert yourself in pulling Renaldo while speaking," Richie commented, helping Ashley to her feet.

"What does *exert* mean?" Roman demanded. Richie didn't answer him, so he simply obeyed.

Roman and Sarah pulled Renaldo while Richie supported Ashley. Roman suggested that Sarah and Richie both carry Renaldo while he supported Ashley while they unhooked their baggage, since he was their sort of doctor and then it would be equal effort. But Richie, without giving his usual droning clarification, wanted to carry Ashley, and Ashley did not protest.

They made good time, compared to how they had been traveling before with their bags, but certainly less than four miles per hour. Roman had subconsciously decided that they would all get their gems first, since they would then all be fully healed and have extra weapons. Before leaving, Roman had quickly found

[345]

his copper sword. But he couldn't find its sheathed belt, so he had to balance Renaldo's left side with one arm, which wasn't too hard with Sarah also supporting him with both arms. Roman didn't like the fact that he could only help Renaldo with one arm; it made him feel like his arm was still broken. They took the path he had worn, which, even though it was narrow, was faster going than having to make their own way. When Roman's pack, still around his waist, started banging against Renaldo's head, he switched it to his shoulders. Pongo was helping by running on ahead and getting rid of tricky stalks by bending them far enough sideways so that the others could get through. Roman was very much warming up to Pongo.

Roman did not *exert* himself too much by talking. He wondered how the others would react to seeing Danny and Victoria. He felt like he had far too much time to wonder. He had already said Danny's name and half of Victoria's. Roman caught Sarah glancing at him from time to time, knowing that Danny had something to do with their hurrying. He wouldn't have mentioned Danny's name otherwise.

Renaldo had stopped snoring and Roman thought he would be waking any moment. Ashley was favoring well. It was almost as if she'd been practicing. She was, however, sweating hard and occasionally grunting. Most of the time she looked at Richie, but sometimes she closed her eyes to take in a particularly painful blow. The stalks were hardly ever thin enough for them to break easily. Roman had had enough trouble with the ones that weren't bent, but Ashley was dealing with worse hardships from those. Roman thought that Richie was inconsiderate for not letting Roman help her, since he was healthier and stronger in the first place. But Richie had a worried looked across his face every time Ashley so much as winced.

Roman nearly fell over with relief when they emerged out onto the field of flowers. Ashley actually did. The others all stopped or had to regain their balance when they beheld the stunning sight. Richie didn't look away when he was helping Ashley up, and Ashley had to grope for his hand when her eyes remained paralyzed. Renaldo's eyes opened, along with his mouth. His normally large eyes became twice their normal size. Roman was ready to stop any one of them from picking or smelling any of the flowers, but they simply stood rigid until a crunching sound overtook them.

"Come on, we need to get going," he urged.

Sarah and Ashley shook their heads to clear them of their trance, Renaldo started to drool onto Roman's arm, and Richie simply blinked and started to follow Roman, Renaldo, and Sarah across the field with Ashley as fast as his feet could carry him. The stream looked different from before. Before it had had exact patterns of currents, clearer than crystal. But now, it was like regular rivers, surging in areas where it had been disturbed. Roman could almost see the waves where something had touched the water as if they were tangible footprints being carried downstream. As he was helping Renaldo, Roman noticed for the first time that Renaldo's hair was starting to drop from his head, and waved when his body was shifted. He could see the black hair almost curling. Sarah had barely managed to keep her hair straight, let alone the usual curly and knot-free. Richie's hair looked almost the same, but longer like Renaldo's. Roman looked past Richie, toward the stream, suddenly remembering how thirsty he was.

Roman sighed. They would at least all forget their thirst when they felt the power of their gems. They trekked on and Renaldo started to moan. Roman knew that he was missing Pongo. Roman was considering whether or not he should call back Pongo or not, since there were no more stalks to remove, when the others froze. Roman stopped walking, too, half because of Sarah pausing, and half because he was almost as mesmerized as the others.

They had walked over the crest of the hill, and instinctively knew that their Bermuda gems were close. Roman followed the others as they walked, zombie like, over the field and into the crater. This time, with his own gem, Roman had most of his senses back. Some of the gems were simply disappearing out of thin air, but none were appearing or reappearing. Roman wondered, if they were the only ones on the

[347]

Island, who did all of these thousands of other gems belong to? Were there going to be others who travel to this Island after them? How long have these gems been here, and how long will they be here? Roman spotted the river circling through one sector of the crater, with some gems sparkling beneath its surface. It was formed in a deep pool beneath a ridge where the water sprouted through a crack. Roman could still see the bottom, though it was a darker blue, being farther away from the sun's rays. Roman also saw what had been making the ridges of water back in the other part of the river.

Renaldo had dropped from his arms, eyes wider, if possible, than before, and was crawling toward the gem piles, forgetting entirely his pain. Richie had let Ashley drop and crawl while he, in his own mind, did the same as Sarah in their search for their gems. While the others, either walking or crawling, in a complete daze, mouths open, went very slowly, Roman watched the last of the giants crashing across the river.

Trees, ten feet tall or more. They were ash-black. None of the sooty grains had been washed away in the river. They had no leaves or foliage, only more branches, bare and sharp. Roman couldn't see their eyes if they had them, because they were headed in the other direction, toward the very end of the cliff. There must have been eight of the tree monsters, all black or gray, all with razor pointed branches, all with feet made of roots and arms made of bark, all marching after what seemed like two ants from this distance. It didn't take Roman very long to realize that those ants were Victoria and Danny. They were running up a steep hill that led to the top of the cliff from the side.

Panicked, Roman threw his head in the direction of the others. They were making their way slowly into the crater. That wasn't good enough. Victoria, Danny, and probably the trees would be out of sight by the time they all gave chase. Pongo was all that Roman had right then. He was sitting next to him, watching the others crawling intently towards their gems. He didn't seem to notice the trees, or the distant crunching noise. It all seemed completely normal to him. The only abnormal thing going on were the four humans picking up shiny rocks.

[348]

"Pongo, come," Roman said, getting the attention of Pongo's round, yellow eyes. He set off as fast as he could run without tripping over any of the gems, which was a pretty fast pace compared to how fast most eleven-year-olds could've gone. He splashed across the river, apparently not gaining the attention of the trees, and heard Pongo's splash a few moments later. Normally Roman would have been faster than Pongo, but Pongo's padded feet were made for the stone and ash. Pongo ran ahead for a moment when Roman had to slide around a few stalagmites, but Roman ended up pulling ahead of Pongo when they climbed out of the crater. Before, they had been keeping at the same pace as the trees, but now Roman was gaining. He ordered Pongo from over his shoulder to keep the others company and lead them to the cliff when they had their gems.

Just me now... Roman didn't like the way the thought made his stomach turn. He pushed it out of his mind so that it wouldn't slow him down.

He had tried breathing through his nose, but his lungs felt constricted as he reached the rock of the hill. He knew that it wouldn't do any good for conserving energy, but he started panting through his mouth. He paused at the bottom, his hands on his knees. The trees were a hundred yards away, and Roman had to decide whether to follow up behind them, which would mean them turning on him as soon as they realized that he was following, or he could run along the edge of the cliff and wait for an opportunity to arise.

You can't always wait for an opportunity, Tyler's words rang in his ears, *Sometimes you've got to* make *an opportunity.*

But how could he make one? He couldn't throw his sword up a hundred foot cliff and mange to hit one of those trees. And if he could, what good would his sword do?

Nice choice of mentors, now I'm doing things as reckless as Tyler.

Then an idea hit Roman. He set off along the cliff side, ignoring the stitch that was about to overtake his side. He pulled his pack from over his shoulder, slowing him down because he had to take caution of the footprints that the tree monsters,

[349]

Danny, and Victoria had left behind when coming in the opposite direction. The footprints looked like several trucks had driven ten times over each individual spot. Roman couldn't make out Danny and Victoria's prints if he had been trying, but he needed his gem for what he was about to do. It was definitely more reckless than his idea of following the trees. His pack had gotten soaked in the stream as Roman had crossed it, and his gem was slick with water.

But as Roman held the gem in his hand, a strange rush came over him, of the same power that he had experienced before. And with that surge of power, he suddenly knew what his gem would allow him to do, and why he was dangerously wrong about the others being healed by their own gems.

His gem gave him much more hope for his idiotic plan. He stopped ignoring the stitch in his side and let the pain reach his senses, knowing deep down that what he was attempting should be impossible. But his theory was proven to be true when he felt nothing. He ran faster when he wasn't concentrating on avoiding pain. He looked up, remembering that he needn't squint to see on the Island when his eyes were toward the sky. He was now along the side of the last tree. The other trees were not far ahead of the last, but neither were Danny or Victoria. They had a fifty foot lead on the trees, which was less than Roman had seen before. Roman started to pant again when he realized that the trees, though they couldn't outrun him, were gaining on them. Danny and Victoria still had their injuries, and they didn't have Roman's power. Roman concentrated on his first power. They were fatiguing rapidly. Roman prayed that he would have the right timing for his plan, no matter how reckless it was.

Roman passed the place where Danny and Victoria had found him before, heading into areas where he hadn't been before. Just as he had hoped, the grass stalks ran along the cliff at a good distance. The cliff began to curve, and Roman was thankful that Danny and Victoria were running along the side of the cliff, probably so that they could jump if they needed to, or so to avoid the trees further back along the cliff, now hidden from Roman's view. They were no longer ants; they were now flies.

The cliff edge looked too smooth to climb, and Roman hoped that that would change as he ran along.

He was now far from the others, and out of sight of the stream by a long shot. He felt that he had run a mile at least, which he just about had. But he wouldn't let the complaint cross his mind when he knew that Danny and Victoria had already passed this way twice.

The only problem that faced him going at this pace was shortage of breath, whether it was through pain or though the empty feeling in his lungs, he could feel the dearth of oxygen reaching his muscles. With his first power, he was able to detect his exact conditions, knowing that voluntarily or involuntarily, his muscles would soon slow down.

He needed what he was looking for, and he needed it fast. He glanced at the glimmering stone above his head, and past it at Danny and Victoria, almost in reaching distance of the trees, now. Danny, without the specialized shoes, was behind Victoria by at least a yard. Victoria seemingly didn't want to leave him Danny behind.

But then, Danny tripped. Roman's plan for saving both of them, or maybe neither, was now impossible. But he had to try. So he prayed his plan would work; otherwise, Danny was dead.

Roman was level with the trees. The first paused to reach down for Danny. Danny couldn't seem to stand, and Victoria couldn't seem to move. She stood frozen, watching Danny, face down in the dirt. Roman stood level with the trees, which now gathered in a half circle before Danny. Time seemed to slow down again as the tallest tree reached out its hand of branches to pick up or crush Danny or both. Roman had plenty of time to take a deep breath, letting all of the coldest parts reach his lungs. Being out of breath, he needed every second, which seemed like hours, to take away the thousands of coughs fighting to replace the inhale. Roman, still ignoring every aspect of pain, yelled at the top of his lungs, hoping for quick results.

He cursed the Island and every aspect it had ever held, taking more breaths while the trees stopped to look at where the sounds came from. He cursed the plants of the Island, since he

[351]

had grown fond of some of its animals, and he cursed the very soil, the multiple suns, and all native aspects except Pongo.

A stunned silence followed. Without any wind, there was absolutely nothing. The brook so far behind, there was no sloshing of water. No bugs to buzz, no animals to stop and listen. Everything stood still for what seemed like longer than when the tree had reached for Danny. The only movement, Roman saw as if it were happening right in front of him, was Danny lifting his head to stare at him.

Then the shaking started. It was like someone was rocking his bed while he was sitting on it, but times a thousand. It wasn't a sound, until the yellow rock began to crack and rumble. The part of the cliff in front of Roman started to slide off its base. It was either an earthquake or a land-slide. The trees went down with the ground towards Roman, two sections near the edges, each with a yard's worth of a berth being spared. These berths spared Danny and one tree in the back, but caught Victoria off of her feet. She slid down with the trees, down with the rock, down towards Roman. Roman knew, regrettably, that his plan had worked. He had insulted the Island, and was now to be punished, taking the trees down with him. But an extra factor had been added. It would take a miracle to save Victoria.

Then the familiar words with their familiar voice rang in his head as he watched the marble-like rock fall and slide towards him; *"If there's one beast on this stupid chunk of rock that'd do it for us, then I'll be selling my soul to Emote…"*

Anyone who insults the Island will be lucky to live the year, no matter how miniscule the insult. Victoria had been lucky just to live this long after saying that. It was as if it had all been rehearsed. What would Danny have tripped on? There weren't any common stones on the Island. His nose was dangling over the edge of the part that had fallen away. Roman had been thinking about his plan before. Danny tripping wasn't unlucky, it was the exact opposite. Roman's first plan was to provoke the Island once he had found an area of the cliff where the yellowish stone was loose, but had to stop early because Danny had tripped. It all seemed to come together when the rock came crashing down.

[352]

Roman learned better than to mess with the Island as he was buried alive.

24. Death and Distortion

Φ   Φ   Φ

There's just no taking advantage of this Island, Roman thought as he clutched his gemstone, using his healing power. He had known that he could regenerate his health quicker than a flashlight turns on as soon as he clutched the gem in his hand at the foot of the hill, watching the trees tromp on their chase. That was his plan, to have destroyed the trees in a landslide while he himself would have been healed.

The rock was surprisingly easy to move off of himself. Roman knew that Victoria was dead. She might've lived if she hadn't insulted the Island, but he knew that in this case, there was no chance. Even though moving the rock was simple, it must've been ten minutes before he saw light. That was when he realized that most of the dirt at the foot of the cliff had shot up like water and landed on top of the pebbly grave. Not a sign of the trees was left as he clambered out of his hole, cutting himself on the sharp edges of the rock and healing instantly, instead tearing most of his shirt and splitting his pack into pieces. The cliffside looked as smooth as ever, simply curving in at the areas that had just been stripped of its contents. It was almost as if something had used a cookie cutter on it. His sword lay ten feet away, untouched by dirt, lying as if on a trophy pedestal. Roman looked up. The sky was the same as before, but there was no sign of Danny or the last tree at the top of the cliffside. Roman gently tiptoed over to his sword. It felt exactly the same as before, except it was slightly colder. A drop of condensation made its way down to the hilt, making a point of sliding over the designs of dragons. The crystal clear water reminded Roman of the stream. Slowly, so that Danny could follow him if he saw, and so the silence would warn him of the remaining tree, Roman walked back toward the others.

He had probably run close to two miles, and had to walk the distance back to the crater filled to the brim with the dazzling Bermuda gems. Sarah and Richie stood next to the stream as Roman climbed over the hill. Renaldo lay face down with his hands in the beginnings of the river, while Ashley soaked her injured leg and arm in the cool, clean water. Roman normally would've been skeptical, but seeing as her wounds were only getting cleaned instead of infected, Roman was willing to let it slide. Pongo was swimming in the pool, the one in which the trees had stopped on their rampage. There had been no sign of Danny the entire way back, though Roman had searched. When Pongo paused to glance at Roman moving at the crest of the hill, his black, leathery wings floated like tin foil at the seam of the water along with his drenched fur. His fur stayed the same color, unlike most hair when wet.

Sarah and Richie met Roman at the end of the crater, wondering where he had been. They hadn't felt the earthquake or heard the landslide, and had no clue besides Pongo as to where Roman had gone.

"We just couldn't follow you because Renaldo and Ashley were still in bad shape," Sarah explained as they walked back down to the pool. "Why did your arm get mended and the others stayed the same? We all found our gems." Sarah held out a silvery-blue gem that seemed to reflect light. It was made up of tiny triangles that formed a sort of imperfect sphere. Richie held his, fiery orange like his eyes, but perfectly round. It was almost like a pearl.

"We have also made a discovery," Richie explained as they reached the pool. Ashley seemed to pick up on this.

"Yeah, your gem only works when you put it in the water of *this* pool. Isn't that cool?" She held out hers. Without any surprise, it was a fluffy shade of pink. Made of isosceles triangles, scalene on the sides, that formed rectangles and other triangles, it made altogether a sort of triangular hour-glass shape. Ashley laughed, gathered her hair, and put her gem there like it was a bow. Hers didn't reflect the light like Sarah's. Neither did Richie's. Both of their gems never had light reach the inside, while Roman's trapped it and seemed to glow.

"Did Renaldo find his?" Roman wondered.

"We couldn't have pulled him away if he hadn't." Ashley rolled her eyes, looking happier than she had since Roman had agreed to keep Pongo. "Renaldo, show him your gem." When she asked this, she said it as if she were talking to a very small toddler. Renaldo acted like one too. He always had his mouth open, and his eyes didn't seem to concentrate on anything. But he pulled his gem out of his pack.

It was a darkish brown color, with red spots in random places. It took the shape of an octagon and had triangles on the sides. The center that made it a 3D shape were squares that reached up to the edges of the triangles. His was like Sarah's, reflecting the little light from the multiple suns behind the clouds and fog.

Roman thought that the swirling clouds and lightning were very appropriate as he told his story. Renaldo acted again like a young child as he sat, mesmerized by his story. Sarah, Ashley, and Richie all looked horrified by every detail, which Roman couldn't blame them for. Roman couldn't remember what Danny and Victoria had said exactly when they were convincing him that they came in peace, but thought that he did a good job of getting their point across. He hardly remembered half of the exact wording of what he had heard when hiding with Pongo underneath the boulder. He told them his original plan along with his SRP to help explain how his plan would work. They didn't look as horrified when he told them about the rockslide burying him as they had when he explained that Danny and Victoria had snuck onto the Island in their plane.

"Why didn't you tell us they were on the Island before?" Ashley demanded.

"You said not to talk," Roman defended himself.

"*Richie and Sarah* said that you shouldn't talk," Ashley corrected.

"Very grateful that we carried you here, aren't you?"

"I told you that you didn't have to carry me," Ashley said, crossing her arms.

[356]

"Uh, yeah. We kinda did," Sarah grunted.

"*Either way*," Roman cut in, "what are we going to do about Danny? If he's still alive, where'd he go?"

"Does it matter?" Sarah asked, narrowing her eyes.

"Come on, he could be useful. Somehow."

"Isn't that what we thought the last time?" Ashley hissed. "And look how well *that* turned out."

"In the consideration that we *do* trust him enough to take him to the mansion, then we would have to keep a careful watch on him." Richie's argument was fair, but that didn't help the voting. Renaldo was half loopy, Richie and Roman both were saying maybe, while Sarah and Ashley said a firm no.

Roman was about to run the thoughts over in his mind, sighing, when Pongo suddenly leapt from the pool. A shadow passed over their heads. Before they had all looked up, it had happened. Just in a single instant, what was left was Pongo's decapitated head, purple blood streaming from it and his body, and Danny charging with a sword that was stained with the same purple blood. Roman had his sword up in an instant, colliding with a satisfying *clank*. With Danny's momentum, Roman had been knocked onto his back. Roman kicked Danny off, sending him only a few feet, since he had missed the solar plexus.

He was aware of Ashley screaming helplessly, of Renaldo sitting up, mouth open, watching as if Roman had been telling another story, and of Sarah and Richie standing up. But Danny had been kicked back into Sarah, who dropped the mechanical spider she had been holding. It fell into the river and sent sparks flying everywhere. Luckily, Renaldo had pulled his legs put of the water to sit Indian-style and watch the show, and Ashley had jumped back in surprise and clambered over to Pongo. The gems that had been hidden beneath the surface of the water shot out of the water and through the air. As Roman jumped to his feet, the gems came back down in a shower, hitting them each on the head several times.

Danny came back for another strike. Roman wasn't expecting Danny to make a straightforward assault, simply slashing sideways. That was far too easy to block. Either Danny was mad, or he was about to change directions once their swords clashed and relieve Roman of his leg. In case he attempted the latter, Roman flipped his sword to his left hand and blocked down as Danny's blade switched courses. Silver and copper flashed, Roman and Danny each tried to rob each other of their swords with a trick at the same exact moment.

"We learned that one in the same class," Roman yelled at Danny. "Why are you attacking us?" Everyone paused when Roman asked the question; Danny was panting. The glare in his eyes wasn't mad; it was vengeful.

"You betrayed us. I knew once you ran off. And then you killed her," he whispered.

Roman took on its meaning in an instant. "I thought you'd need backup," Roman reasoned, "and I didn't mean for her to die."

"Then why did you risk it? You should have let them take me so that she could've gotten away instead of trying your little stunt."

Roman snapped. "I saved your life! And she would've died anyway for calling the Island stupid! It's not my fault that she died!"

Danny looked as if he hadn't heard the last two lines. "YOU SHOULD'VE LET ME DIE! IT WOULD'VE BEEN BETTER FOR EVERYONE!"

With that, Danny charged one last time. Only when their blades were about to meet, during one of his breaths, instead of breathing out, he coughed up blood. The blood-stained sword appeared through Danny's heart, straight out of his gray undershirt. The fresh blood flashed against the dried blood from the earlier attack of the trees. The blade-end disappeared as he dropped to the ground, eyes wide open, with all light from them gone.

Richie wasn't panting, and Roman couldn't read his expression. His eyes were closed as he slid the blood-stained sword back into the sheath slung at his side. His hand held some of Danny's blood that had flown past the hilt. Roman had his share of blood on his shirt as he stood staring at the quiet eleven-year-old, mouth open. Even Renaldo seemed to have understood what had happened, as he no longer looked amused by the sword battle.

The scarlet pool of blood seemed to reflect in Danny's brown eyes as he lay motionless. The blood was flowing faster than Roman thought possible, covering all of his clothes, none of it stirred by any breath as it passed his open mouth. The blood never reached the crystal clear water of the pool or the stream, as most of it eventually sank through the dirt, staining the blackish-brown grains red as it went.

Roman hardly caught the words as they were uttered, but after a few moments comprehended the whisper. It was like in Spanish class when he was reading new material, and he had to concentrate to grasp each word's meaning. As if it were an alien language to him, Roman slowly heard Richie repeat Danny's last words, without any change to fit his odd dialect.

"Better for everyone."

Richie picked up his gem before anyone else could move, and disappeared.

Roman didn't know how long they all simply stood motionless, for he only moved when Danny's blood started licking at his shoes. He was horrified by the sight of Danny's blood and almost yelped when it touched him. Danny's sword was wrapped in it. Roman tensely picked up his silver blade. He couldn't avoid getting his hands smeared in the blood, but with his memory of the color, and the weight and feel of the metal, it was real silver. The blood dripped easily off of its point. When Roman moved, Sarah started breathing again, and Ashley started to cry. Renaldo looked confused, and started tossing his head in every direction, as if Richie had teleported somewhere. Roman knew Richie had teleported, and would be back at the mansion, without any memory of what he had done besides what he would witness in his nightmares. At least with the nightmares he could tell himself that it wasn't real.

Maybe that's why he left. Maybe he didn't want to feel so awful from killing Danny. Roman completely understood the

[359]

thought. He had blamed himself for Jacob's death, and now for Victoria's, but both were indirect. Richie had murdered Danny, whether he had just then wished for it or not. Richie would've been feeling worse than Roman by far. He remembered how he'd felt after killing the catlike creatures that had attacked them.

Roman had to step over Pongo to get to the stream, and felt queasy when his shoes grazed the purple blood. Pongo's fur wasn't tainted by the blood, like how it had seemed untouched by the water. Roman couldn't help but feel a deep pang of grief when looking into Pongo's now empty eyes. It was almost as if his pupils, already small, had completely gone from view. Pongo had saved his life several times in the past few days, and his last act was doing so. What had Roman ever done for him? There was nothing he could do to repay him now.

Roman forced himself to look away as he reached the start of the river. He gently dipped Danny's sword in the water to wash away the blood, only it slipped out of his grasp from the slickness. Roman gasped and tried to take it out from the depths with his own sword, but it too slipped from his hand.

Roman cursed, then watched as his sword seemed to melt. The bindings at the hilt were still left, but every part that had contained copper simply melted away. He could see the liquid metal start to flow down the stream, but when they reached Danny's blade, the particles wrapped around every part that was silver, until the whole blade had a copper-coating and there was nothing left of Roman's old sword but the bindings that proceeded down in the current, out of sight. An unexpected slosh of water brought the sword within reaching distance.

Roman carefully lifted it from the water. It seemed completely copper, with the same weight and feel to it. Roman looked at the hilt of the sword. It now had the designs of what looked like a mixture between a monkey, a raccoon, and a bat. Proudly marching across the sword, glazed in copper, with both wings at full health, was the frozen image of Pongo. There was even some sort of shading, down to the last detail, for his fur. Roman touched the pictures of Pongo, who was dead behind him, and thought that he could hear his monkey-like screech.

Roman wiped a tear that had escaped his right eye away from his cheek. Whether he would forget Pongo or not, the sword would still keep his memory, and that was how he decided to repay Pongo.

"It's time for us to go," Roman sighed. Sarah and Ashley nodded. Roman wondered if they could possibly get Renaldo to concentrate enough to get him back home safely. They couldn't wait for his senses to come back to him, because he would only get worse now that Pongo was gone.

Sarah caught on, and as soon as she started coaxing in vain for Renaldo to concentrate, Ashley caught on and had much more progress. Renaldo had disappeared only a moment before the crunching noise came.

Roman's head whipped around to see the newly made army led by the remaining tree charging from the edge of the crater. Ashley yelped and disappeared, and Sarah followed. Roman got a clear look at the trees for the first time. They had gleaming eyes the color of burning coals and firewood, with splits in their trunks that resembled mouths. Giant twigs four inches thick were their fangs. Roman felt like he would be struck paralyzed, but then the leading tree spoke.

"ANGELIKA SMASH WERELR! WERELR KILL WITH ABENT! ANGELIKA KILL!"

The strangeness of the words that erupted with a rough, throaty growl seemed to shake the fear out of him with sheer confusion. All Roman knew was that in a few seconds the trees would be on him. He didn't have time to ponder what some of the trees words were, or why some of them were in English. Roman concentrated hard on his gem.

Get me home!

He was no longer on the Island, with the trees crashing towards him, the lightning crackling above his head and devoid of wind and all other noise except the babbling brook. But he didn't hear the hum of the mansion's air conditioning, the usual talk of either late-night or daytime, or the television from the lounge, or the commotion of the kitchen, either.

It was almost completely dark except for the lights of a busy city through one window, spilling an orange type of illumination onto one section of a beige carpet. The small areas of wall that he could see were painted white, and were different from the indigo that he was used to, but still, in an instant he knew exactly where he was. He was so curious, he tempted to turn on the light switch that he knew was only a room-crossing away. He was headed in that direction before he could stop himself. But where he had failed in stopping himself, the jingling of keys in a lock succeeded. An alarm went off, but was silenced by someone putting in the right combination. He was back at the window the instant he heard footsteps and the kitchen light turned on, and he was out the open window and halfway across the garden by the time the light was on in his old living room.

Roman had to stop his resentment, anger, grief, and jealousy from spilling over into tears as he raced along Beverly Street in the direction of the Studewood shopping center. His gem had obviously considered home as back in his old house in Houston. That was his resentment. His grief came from the reminder of his parents, the anger at himself for considering his old life home instead of letting go and looking ahead, and jealousy for the person, a woman from the sound of the high heels, and whoever lived with her for taking his home as their own. He still had his sword, and felt strongly that he would be arrested if anyone saw him with it. But no one went out for a stroll this late at night, Roman could still tell. He finally stopped at an old coffee shop that he had never paid attention to before, cars speeding down the second largest street in the *Heights*. He looked up to see the old clouds of smog aiding the city lights in blocking out the moon and stars and most of the night sky. The coffee shop was closed. It had a name that he figured he would be laughed at for trying to pronounce, cream-colored brick walls, and windows where you could look outside while drinking coffee and eating doughnuts. There were also a few previously black patio tables and chairs, all broken, rusty, and or vandalized. A payphone was across the street, but Roman would have to take the cross walk at the end of the block to reach it accounting for both jaywalking and not getting hit by cars.

In Katy, the street lights were almost always on, the stores were mostly open at night, there was close to no graffiti or illegal advertisements along the walls of buildings, and you could easily go for a midnight walk without getting robbed or into trouble. Even the *Heights* had its downsides. Roman walked over to pick up the front cover of a half-burnt newspaper caught underneath one of the patio chairs. He read the date.

April 11, 2010

He didn't know what time it was or how long the paper had been there, but he assumed that it was still summer time of the same year they had left for the Island. Through all of his mixed feelings, he thought for the first time of how well the others faired in getting home. Sarah and Ashley had been frightened like he by the army of advancing trees, Richie had just killed Danny, and Renaldo was trapped in his own world. He did not rule out the possibilities of them arriving at the mansion, but neither for getting themselves lost in places farther away than downtown.

He proceeded across the crosswalk to the payphone, constantly looking over his shoulder for police officers concerned with twelve-year-olds wandering the streets alone at night and people that might recognize him. He doubted that many would without getting up close, since he had changed hairstyles, so as not to remind himself of his past, and had grown several inches, maybe even over a foot. But he reached the phone unchallenged. It was then that he realized that he had no money, and the other option was the operator. He didn't enjoy the prospect of explaining to suspicious cops why he was this far away from where he lived, late at night, most likely looking like he had just rolled in a dumpster.

Roman knew that if he asked any residents if he could use their phones, they would shut their doors, lock them five times over, and possibly alert the police. In Katy, some strangers might give him the opportunity, but Houston was much different.

But another thing that was different in Houston was that in the Heights there was plenty of loose change lying around, if you knew where to find it. A trick that Carlos had taught him when they were only in third grade was how to pry open the broken-down water fountain's latch to reach through the hole in the other end, and get to the quarters that many dropped from the vending machine next to it. They had been surprised at the time by how many people managed to miss the slot by about three quarters of a foot, but they didn't complain. Roman hoped that Carlos hadn't emptied their small money-maker any time recently, and that the vending was still up and running. But to get to the *7-11* with the fountain, he would have to go back the way he had come, past his old house. Roman decided to take the longer route, which involved several more cross-walks and almost twenty extra minutes.

Roman barely felt any joy when he used his sword to pry open the fountain to find eighty-nine cents. He was exhausted. Time was different on the Island from the world that Roman was used to, but he suspected that he had been awake for at least a day, along with plenty of drama and exertion. Roman tried his best to keep his sword from dragging on the pavement as he slowly made his way back to the payphone. He realized that some things indeed had changed when he passed another payphone only a block down from the *7-11*. He was grateful for the convenience, and tapped the mansion's number carefully so that he would not waste what little money he had. The mansion's line wasn't detectable by tracking, nor could they hotlink it to do so, but Roman carefully reminded himself to whisper into it, since there were more ways to spy than with technology.

"Hello?" Rebecca's familiar voice came from the other end. "Who is this?"

"Rebecca! It's me, Roman. I'm in Houston, around Studewood Street. I need you guys to come and pick me up."

"Roman! Everyone's been so worried! Sarah, Renaldo, Richie, and Ashley all got here over an hour ago and you've been nowhere! BRB, I need to go get Mr. Kyle."

"Gotcha."

[364]

It seemed far too long for Rebecca to get Mr. Kyle. Roman was still trying to ignore the familiar sights while struggling to stay awake, and the night pressed in on him. After spending so much time thousands of miles and a time vortex away from civilization, he jumped at every passing truck, coughed from the smoke, and the lights of the city stung his eyes with such ferocity that he blinked over fifty times a minute. Roman wondered if the time on the payphone was limited, which seemed likely. When Rebecca finally returned, it was with Jace instead of Mr. Kyle.

"Roman, where are you *exactly?*" Jace demanded immediately.

"Umm, I'm still on Studewood Street, which runs through the east part of the Houston *Heights*. I'm a block…um…north east of a *7-11*. It's got neon lights on, so you shouldn't have trouble finding the *7-11* if you drive straight down the street. How are you going to get here?"

"We'll take Mary Beth's *Bug*. We can't bring the helicopter, but luckily you won't freeze, since it's spring. It's a school night, so you shouldn't get any trouble from students."

None that care about school…

"Just hang tight. We'll park outside the first *7-11* we see. What color are the lights, though?"

"Red."

"A'ight. We'll be there in anytime from an hour to two, depending on traffic. Try not to draw attention to yourself."

Before Roman could respond, he heard the buzz of the call ending. He sat down next to the pole and kept his eyes on the street, not daring to look at anything. He watched the passing cars, and jumped at every bird and cat. He stared at the headlights of the cars until he couldn't hide from their light even with his eyes closed. The tail-lights from the lane closer were softer on his eyes, so he instead played a game with it. He stared at the pairs until the lights were stamped into his pupils. He started turning his head at different angles to stare at the beaming illuminations. He was trying to make a picture, but the earliest lights faded away before he was halfway done.

[365]

When he gave up his game, he sat still, thinking that the others would get there any moment. After what was at least twenty minutes of yawning, the only things keeping him awake were the cars that he thought he saw spots on and the occasional fluttering paper that startled him. Then he took to pacing. He was certain that he'd been awake for more than a day at the very least. His clothes were for the humid climate on the Island, and Houston at spring's prime was not too different, except at night, with a breeze coming in from the south.

Then it occurred to him that the first thought that had come to him when he'd found his gem was that he could stare at it all day. He settled back down, cringing from the cold metal of the payphone and concrete. His gem, trapping the light of the city, didn't quite glow, but Roman could see it clearly enough. He kept on straining his eyes to see if he could see the level of his gem with squares, but his eyes, already too exhausted to be anything more than dry, quailed and shook under the effort. So he ran it over and over again in his hands.

But if he had been focusing, he wouldn't have fallen asleep.

25. A Real Happy Birthday

Φ   Φ   Φ

"Try it again."

Roman felt a numb pinching feeling in his chest. He moaned.

"It lives!" Roman recognized Treaver's voice. "Great idea, Cole."

"It *was* being rhetorical," Cole growled.

Roman opened his eyes, confused. He last remembered being in the parking lot of the isle with a *7-11*, and now he was in the infirmary. The only major difference in here from when they had left was an extra table, plastic and turquoise, next to the door entering the bathroom. Roman was on the bed next to that table. An orange blanket covered his feet. Cole, Elliyo, Treaver, and Gabriel, holding a stick, were next to him.

"Rise and shine," Treaver chimed, wheeling his chair slightly closer. "You know, the beauty sleep's really working well for you. Your eyelashes are *so chic*." Treaver did a hand flick along with his Paris Hilton impression on the last two words.

Elliyo laughed, and Gabriel put the stick on the table. "Cole suggested that we poke you with a stick to wake you up."

"I still think that we should've stuck with my water bucket idea." Treaver shrugged exasperatedly.

"What we really should've done was play yodeling music," Cole said, his arms crossed, his face expressionless. A small crease of a smile appeared when the others laughed.

"It'd wake him up or give him nightmares, one or the other," Treaver added, getting a chuckle out of Cole. Roman hadn't seen Cole do anything nearly as exciting as laugh since Danny left.

"How long have we been gone?" Roman asked, sitting up.

"A week an' a day. Perfect timing on your part." Treaver said, "Mr. Kyle's setting up for Ashley's eleventh."

"Yeah, her birthday presents are nightmares," Cole commented, back to his depressed mood.

"Where's my gem? And my sword?"

"Dude, we couldn't pry the gem outta your hands," Treaver laughed.

Roman realized that his fist clutched his royal blue gem. He held it up, getting lots of interested looks from the others.

After a silence, Treaver spoke up. "It's kinna weird. The sword's different from when you left. It's in your room, 'cause I guess it's yours now. Did you have any dreams about that? If so, please share because I would *very* much like to know how that happened."

"No..." Something very odd occurred to Roman. He knew that it hadn't been a dream, but he could remember everything that had happened on the Island. He had remembered last night in Houston, but had been too tired to realize it. He was still in his beat-down clothes, and he could remember how each tear and stain had gotten there.

"Where's Sarah, Ashley, Richie, and...Where's Renaldo? Is he alright?"

"Renaldo's fine, but Ashley's in the back room," Treaver indicated to the entrance behind Roman's bed. Roman climbed to the other side of his bed. The light in the room was turned off, and Ashley was there with a few monitors hooked up to her arm, fast asleep.

"Millo says that you've got healing as your second power," Treaver continued. "Any chance you could test it out on her?"

"A big chance." Roman climbed out of bed with his gem. Ashley's leg had gotten worse, but healed completely as soon as Roman touched her, concentrating.

"Did it work?" Gabriel asked.

There was a blanket covering her leg. Roman pulled it back to reveal his well-done work. The leg of her pants were still torn and bloody, but all that remained of her injury was a white scar. There was the same result with her arm. Roman felt slightly nauseous after doing that, as if he had been up all day instead of five minutes.

"Renaldo was easy, according to Jace. He was bragging about how well he did for at least an hour," Cole explained. "Some sort of remedy, I don't know. Mr. Kyle had all of you examined as soon as each of you arrived."

"Richie popped up in the middle of our basketball game," Gabriel complained.

"He almost fainted when he did, though," Elliyo put in, "and Chris nearly hit him with the ball after stealing it from Jay."

"Sarah showed up in the lounge," Treaver said, "but she blocked the screen. The nerve of some people. And Ashley arrived in the kitchen. Renaldo was up in his room moaning when we found him."

"*You*, however," Jace came through the door, "we had ourselves a lot o' fun trying to find you. There are at least three or four *7-11*'s in Houston, and we were lucky enough to find you on the second one. We drove around the building until we saw you by the payphone. You were asleep, but you looked dead."

"Did I miss anything?" Roman wondered.

"You missed our money budget coming back. The day after you all left, the bank gave us a very nice little call. Apparently someone had been having fun with our cache, but we sure didn't give anyone here our numbers. We figured that it was that weasel, Dan*ielle*."

Roman almost wanted to defend on Danny's behalf, but he wanted to discuss it with the others who had gone with him about their memories of the Island before telling anyone else.

"And we built a deck on the mansion roof," Jace said. "It's nice up there when the weather's fine. We made a rail around the edge and everything. Jay thought that he'd try out his engineering skills, so we all set to work. He begged me to classify it as TUC, so on one day, everyone was working on it, along with the free sessions that Jay had with Chris and Millo. Plus there were some people who honestly wanted to help…Well, it's nice up there."

"Okay, um...am I allowed to leave the hospital? Ashley's fine, too, by the way."

"She is? Oh, right, healing power. That'll come in very handy. Yeah, you can go," Jace agreed.

Jace stayed behind with Ashley while Roman, Treaver, Cole, Elliyo, and Gabriel left the room. When Elliyo let Gabriel out of the room first, Roman was reminded how dependant Elliyo was on others.

"So, where's my welcome home presents?"

"How about I let you touch my arm?" Cole suggested.

"That's a very high-ranked gift on Cole's behalf," Gabriel said.

"Well, since I'm Treaver's only friend, I bet he's ecstatic about this."

"Oh, yes, Mighty One. I am humbled in your presence," Treaver rolled his eyes as they headed into the lounge.

"He must've been desperate to come hang out with Cole," Gabriel snorted.

"Desperate to hang out with *me*? I'm not wearing a mirror am I?"

"Well, the past is in the past," Roman dismissed. "Now you may *all* worship me."

Roman had been punched several times by the time they walked into the lounge.

Sarah was talking happily with Jasmine, Stacy, Chris, and Millo. She was sitting on the couch, wearing her usual t-shirt and Capris, her hair freshly washed, half-curly and half-wavy, her skin clean for the first time in a week, looking perfectly content. Stacy had gotten a hair-cut, and Chris' hair was longer than Roman was used to. They all turned their heads when Roman and the others walked in. Chris waved them over, while Sarah stood up to hug Roman. Chris shook his head mockingly. When Sarah was done, Millo hugged Roman. Roman ruffled his hair, making Millo laugh. It was good to know that Millo had managed without him. Jasmine smiled politely, since she hardly knew his name, and Stacy gave him the benefit of a fist-pound.

"Richie and Renaldo aren't here?" Roman inquired,

sitting in an armchair to the left of the couch.

"Well, nice to see you, too." Sarah rolled her eyes, sitting down on the couch just before Stacy could take her spot. Stacy pretended to sneer, and Sarah stuck out her tongue. "Renaldo's either moaning about his stomach to Jace or sleeping upstairs in his room."

"We just left Jace," Treaver said, sitting down next to Stacy, who suddenly looked uncomfortable.

"Then it's the latter."

"So what about Richie?"

"Wasn't he with Ashley? He's hardly left the hospital." The others looked surprised.

"He wasn't there," Cole concluded. "Probably helping Kyle with Ashley's party. Don't worry," he added to Roman and Sarah, "I'm sure it's slightly for you guys, too."

"I'm not a guy," Sarah said. "But thanks for the reassurance."

"Are Mary Beth, Jay, Ringo, or Rebecca here?"

"Why wouldn't they be? You've only been gone a week, we still need the force field," Chris said.

It occurred to Roman that they didn't know that Danny hadn't told Emote about their identities, and now he was dead. This reminded Roman why he had to get the others alone, and ask them if they remembered anything. If they did, then they weren't telling anyone. Roman tried his best not to show an expression.

"I just wish that we could go back to school," Treaver said. "Can you imagine? When you're *in* school, all you want is to get out. But now that we've had a four-month va-ca we want to go *back*."

"It must be really depressing for Jay," Jasmine sympathized. "He wanted to go to *Northwood*, and he worked *really* hard to get in."

"Yeah, college, parties, foreign girls…You can't beat that with a mansion full of the nineteen people you see every day." Chris said. "Everything we've got here you can get at college. Well, except other Genedeaues, training sessions…I'm gonna

[371]

stop now," he added at the looks everyone else gave him.

"Well, I'm going to go find Richie," Roman told them.

"Yep, Roman's got amnesia," Chris shook his head. "He doesn't remember us. Sad, really."

"Oh, shut up. Keep that up and I'm never using my healing on you."

Millo laughed. "Mr. Kyle would make you."

"Let 'im try." Roman chuckled, "Nice to hear your voice again."

"No accent?"

"Hardly any," he confirmed. "That reminds me. Sarah, what's your power?"

"Geez, I thought you'd never ask," Sarah rolled her eyes. "It's not really something I can show you. It's just that, according to Millo and my gem, confirmed by Gabriel, I am immune to other peoples powers."

"Indirectly," Millo corrected.

"Yeah, so if I was made of metal, Jace couldn't rust me, but he could rust a support beam above my head and make it fall on me. Comforting thought, but now I know what to avoid if I ever get turned to metal."

"And I can't tell if she's clean or not," Gabriel looked frustrated, "though, considering the two hours she spent showering, I'd say she's clean."

"I'll take that as a compliment," Sarah thanked him.

"Yeah, and Roman," Treaver started out, a strained look on his face. Roman wondered if he had missed anything horrible that he hadn't heard about. But he had obviously forgotten most of Treaver's personality. "No one wants to tell you this, so I guess it's my job. You really *should* take a shower, too."

This gave Roman an excuse to leave the room and gather everyone. But he decided that he *would* take a shower, excuse or not. Afterwards, though, they celebrated Ashley's birthday in the ballroom. It was around four in the afternoon when Mr. Kyle announced that the party would be starting. Ashley, of course, was the last addition and had delayed the celebration for about an hour. She woke up an hour and a half after Roman, and then they gave her half an hour of mental rest, since she, Roman checked, had forgotten most things about the Island. She remembered a 'fuzzy monkey' fighting off a 'demon stick', but only from a nightmare. She said that at the end, the monkey was killed with a knife that the stick had, and it's blood was made of blueberries. Roman was saddened by this, as it didn't honor Pongo's memory as well as he would've liked.

Renaldo came down for the party, looking sick to his stomach, but better both physically and mentally. The ballroom was decorated more than it usually was. Roman had never been to any meeting in the ballroom, and had figured that it was symbolic. But this took that away. No one else had wanted a birthday party, either out of the extra work everyone had to do before their budget had resumed its customary course, or from embarrassment and modesty. Roman hadn't wanted to celebrate his birthday for a much different reason than Sarah and Ringo, whose birthdays had both passed. Tyler's was upcoming on the twentieth. But whether or not Ashley wanted a birthday party, it wasn't every day that someone returned from the Island, and returned alive. Returning on someone's birthday called for a celebration.

The microphone stand was in its usual place, but the tables were all straightened out in rows with a vertical isle down the center. The chandeliers had multi-colored bows on them, each with silver sparkles decorating the cloth and occasionally (whenever Chris or Cole succeeded in hitting one with a wad of paper) showering the tables with glitter. Roman reminded himself to ask where the others got these sorts of things when leaving the mansion grounds was restricted. The tablecloth was the same, but each table had buttercups, which would be blooming right then. There were ribbons that ran between the portraits of past Talismen leaders, colored green. Roman noticed Rico Martinez, whose name Roman had read on the fifth floor office door during his first odd dream. The memory of the dreams made Roman shiver, even though he had just been through a much worse reality. At the end of the isle, slightly off to the side of the steps leading onto the stage, was a magnificent cake. Ashley would approve. Pink icing with white frills, flower-shaped sprinkles, areas of chocolate, vanilla, strawberry, rocky road, and others were marked by colored, miniature umbrellas protruding to form borders on specific sections of the cake. There were six sections, but several different edges. The cake formed the shape of either a misshapen buffalo or pachyderm. It seemed odd to have an unruly shape when whoever had made the cake had gone to all of the trouble of flavoring and decorating. Roman went up to see the cake, along with Treaver, who leaned on the edge of his wheelchair to see over the edge of the table the dessert sat on, and Mary Beth seemed to be looking for flaws, and Rebecca, stared admiringly.

"Did Tyler, Jay, and Jace *ever* consider putting a chair rise anywhere in this mansion?" Treaver muttered heatedly.

"If you'd rather, we could lift you up," Roman suggested.

"Oh, hey Roman. Yeah, very funny. But you've got no idea! I'm the only one who hasn't been allowed up on the roof! And I can't remember the last time that I rode in the helicopter."

"I figured you'd be used to it by now," Roman inquired.

"Yeah, you'd think. Anyways, I can see the umbrellas, but what's it shaped like? I can't tell from looking at the sides."

"I honestly have no logical idea."

"It's Belgium. The shape of the country," Mary Beth answered, flustered.

"Why would they do Belgium?" Treaver wondered.

"That's where she was born, and it's where her dad's from. How does the *A* on the location of her town look, Roman? It's not crooked or anything?"

There was a pink *A* near the northern tip of the Belgium-shaped cake. It looked fine to Roman, but he couldn't take his mind off of the prospect of tasting every different flavor.

"I think it looks very straight, unless you turn the cake around. But honestly, I don't think that anyone will care."

"Then I'm obviously not anyone. Ashley's probably having trouble staying conscious, and if she's disappointed by this cake I don't know how—"

Treaver laughed halfway through, saying, "I'm pretty sure that little Ashley will approve of this. But, just to make sure, mind if I do a taste-test?"

"Yes, I *do* mind. Feel lucky that I'm not your teacher, *Serapher*," she added with a sort of venom.

"Yes m'am, I do feel lucky," Treaver whispered to Roman as they headed towards a table that wasn't near the stage or the exit, to the same seat that Cole used to sit at with Danny. Cole and Chris had knocked down one of the bows and were trying in vain to replace it before Mary Beth turned around.

"Here comes Sarah and Jasmine," Treaver pointed out as Roman sat down and he positioned himself at the edge of the table.

Sarah was pulling Jasmine in by the arm. Jasmine was obliviously embarrassed for anyone to see her. Sarah was dressed lavishly, wearing a gold necklace with a tiny ruby on the end, a dress-like shirt without sleeves and with frills of purple along the edges and diagonally down the center, a long, black skirt that fluttered when she moved, and black dinner shoes with the heels cut off. The top layer of her hair was done in a ponytail behind her head and hanging down, while the under part had been groomed vigorously. The curls shinned and waved at leisure. Jasmine had red *Toms* with sparkles as her dinner shoes, a red, full-body dress, a necklace with different gems, (Roman could tell that they were fake) and her hair, which was normally straight, was curlier than Sarah's. Jasmine's glasses were gone and she wore eye shadow. She looked very shy, but with Sarah pulling her arm and Stacy pushing her from behind, they got her into the room. Stacy's hair was curly on one side and waved only slightly on the other, and she was wearing a red tee with a red skirt that billowed like Sarah's. Stacy easily had more makeup on than Jasmine and Sarah combined, having eye-shadow, cover-up, blush, and her nails were painted the same sparkly red as her dress.

"Gee, you'd think that it was one of *their* birthdays," Roman commented.

"What happened to the tomboys we knew and loved?"

Chris demanded of them as they came towards them.

"How did you guys get ready so fast?" Cole wondered, blinking frequently.

Jasmine managed a real blush without makeup. Sarah laughed.

"Well, either you guys are jealous or impressed. Probably the latter, but either one works for us," Sarah taunted.

"Well, I'm not sure about impressed," Chris said sardonically. "You can come back in two years if you want to impress a teenager. But definitely not jealous."

"Roman and Treaver sure look impressed," Stacy giggled.

Roman felt himself blushing and saw Treaver react the same way.

"I'd agree," Chris nodded. Cole chuckled.

As Sarah, Jasmine, and Stacy made their way to the table closest to the stage, Roman caught Tyler watching them, half leaning, half floating against the doorway. Roman's mentor had lifted weights as long as he'd known him, and it never had seemed to have made a difference. But after a week away, Roman could see how well everything had been working. Tyler, of course, was turning sixteen soon, so he seemed big to Roman anyways, but Tyler's shirt, a mock camouflage design, had short sleeves, revealing his muscles, which seemed much larger than Roman remembered.

Roman glanced at Treaver, who had indeed noticed Tyler staring at the girls. Treaver did not look happy in the slightest bit. Treaver had always quarreled with his mentor for a reason that normally wouldn't have been detectable. Roman had thought at first that it was no big deal, and had almost forgotten about it. But recalling how Stacy looked uncomfortable with Treaver sitting next to her and everything that had happened before Jacob's death, Roman remembered that Tyler liked Stacy, and so did Treaver.

Roman had stopped thinking about this when Jill, Jace, Elliyo, Gabriel, Ringo, Millo, Mr. Kyle, and lastly, Richie all entered within five minutes. Treaver, Roman, Chris, and Cole put their table together with the one behind, even though they were

[376]

circular, and invited Millo, Elliyo, Gabriel, Renaldo, and Richie to sit with them. Jace sat near the front of the isle while Mr. Kyle made his way to the microphone stand. Ashley at last came in, looking fresh compared to how she had been two hours before, and sat with the rest of the girls on the other side of the isle near the stage. Tyler, Ringo, and Jill sat near the back of the room on the boys' side, and Mary Beth and Rebecca joined the other girls. No one had organized it this way, but the girls were all on the right of the isle and the boys on the left.

This was the first joke that Mr. Kyle made a reference to, and joshed them about their lack of creativity. Mr. Kyle seemed older, as he had seemed since Jacob died. But this pattern didn't seem to have had an end yet. Once again, his small beard seemed straggly and his skin seemed wrinkled. He was as thin as usual, but his clothes dangled off as if they were too short. A few gray streaks showed from his black head of hair. His voice cracked from time to time. First, he congratulated Roman, Renaldo, Ashley, Richie, and Sarah for all coming back alive and receiving their gemstones. Then he announced each of their powers: Roman, healing, and Sarah, being resistant to others' powers. Roman was on the end of his seat for the other powers, which he had not learned yet. Richie had *'magnetism'*, Ashley had *'unlimited flexibility'*, and Renaldo, *'refreshment'*. Apparently, once Renaldo had regained sanity, Jace's solution had nothing to do with Renaldo's recovery. Jace did not look happy at this, but apparently, Renaldo could go longer than anyone else without eating, drinking, or rest. Renaldo showed this off by dancing up onto the stage. He had apparently been faking being sick. This also did not do anything to please Jace.

During each announcement, loud applause rang out. Even louder applause came with the wishing of a Happy Birthday to Ashley. Ashley blushed and dropped her head as the cheers rang out. She looked even more nervous than Jasmine had been from showing up in an extravagant dress. Ashley was wearing a pink tee and jeans, but she didn't need any makeup to blush.

Afterwards, which got many a *woot* from the boys, was the cutting of the cake. Jace left to get silverware and plates while

[377]

Mr. Kyle cut the cake. No one had put candles on the cake, but Ashley pretended to blow at the umbrellas, laughing the whole time. Altogether, Roman was happy to be back home, and happy for Ashley and the others on their accomplishments, and was looking forward to being a mentor during what was expected to be the best period for the Talismen in a long time.

Epilogue

Roman heard footsteps walk by the entrance to the laundry room. He peered through the keyhole, and was thankful to see that it was one of the others that had gone to the Island. He'd caught a glimpse of Sarah's ginger hair as she walked past. Roman opened the door, about to call her name, when he saw that she had disappeared. He quickly put the towel that he had been folding on top of the nearest washer and slipped out into the hall.

A door closed. It was the new one that led to the rooftop. Roman hadn't been up on the roof, yet. He had been presented with laundry duty, since he was now a full-fledged Talisman. The door was in between the stairs down to the fourth floor and the room Roman had been in. Roman followed silently, except the door creaked as he opened it. A short climb of stairs was between him and the new patio deck. He held onto the support rail, though Jill and everyone else had done a professional job. It was made of plain wood, but it didn't so much as creak like the door, let alone rock like a seesaw.

The first thing that met Roman's eyes was the blinding moonlight. The moon seemed brighter than ever, even though it was almost a new moon. Only a small waning crescent was left, but after more than a week of seeing nothing but sun, the illumination stung Roman's eyes. In the suburbs of Katy, you could usually see the moon, and most of the time the stars, if not many lights were on. But in the outskirts, where there weren't any places with harsh artificial light, the stars were dazzling. Roman could see a few constellations, but he had never been good at astronomy. Some light coming from the mansion blocked out the more amazing things that he had seen in pictures, but his eyes still ached from staring at the sky for too long.

A warm spring breeze tingled Roman's skin, cast ripples across the lake, and rattled the leaves in the trees. The patio was made of wood panels propped against and nailed into the roof of the mansion. There was a rail along the perimeter, with gaps that you could stick an arm through, and it was around three and a half feet high. The patio deck itself took up a good portion of the side of the mansion. To his left, Roman could get a clear view of the mansion gates and the road beyond, to his right he could see one edge of the courtyard garden, now blossoming with different varieties of flowers in the spring weather. Behind was the side of the roof, ahead was the lake, followed by endless trees. Sarah was leaning against the rail, looking at the lake. She had changed back into her regular clothes, which meant, unfortunately, that Roman would probably be washing her dress. She turned her head when Roman appeared, and then smiled.

"Isn't it beautiful out here?"

"Yeah," Roman agreed, "but the moon kind of hurts my eyes."

"Might as well get used to it."

"How come you didn't get stuck with any chores? I had to do the laundry. At least I got in enough cake and TV beforehand."

"Oh, I did my chores before you woke up. I wanted to be relaxed during Ashie's party, and it's worth it to come up here. I love the breeze, and the lake looks so cool."

"Yup," Roman steadied himself next to her, watching the lake, half to shield his eyes from the moonlight. "Hey, there's something I need to ask you."

"What?"

"Do you remember anything from the trip to the Island?"

"Of course not. I had a nightmare last night about giant mice made of wood. But it wasn't all that bad, once you realize that it's just a dream."

"Well, something really weird happened. Both on the Island and now."

"Roman, you can't know if the nightmares are real."

"No, it's not a nightmare. I can remember everything that

[380]

happened on the Island." He was going to wait for that to sink in but it wasn't long before Sarah reacted.

"What? What do you mean?"

"I just...remember everything. That monkey Ashley dreamed of? That was some sort of animal that she sort of...liked. He was a kind of pet. And that's the design that's now on my sword. But that's not the same sword that I left the mansion with..." Roman found himself blurting out every detail from the time that the others fell unconscious to when the trees were rushing towards them. Sarah said nothing, but gasped in the appropriate places, like when they met Danny and Victoria, when Roman was buried alive, and when the swords merged together. Roman told her about how he had remained conscious when the others collapsed, about how they had activated their gems, and even about every minor conversation and the long days of dragging their luggage. There was a silence afterwards. Then Sarah put her hand on his arm.

"You're sure that this wasn't just a dream?" she asked when he looked up at her.

"Positive."

Sarah had been staring at his eyes, probably to see if he was telling the truth. She sighed and leaned back against the rail. It reminded Roman of, what seemed like years instead of months ago, when he was outside of the Cinemark, leaning against the rail, watching the duck swimming below. That was when he had met Sarah, but now it seemed like Sarah had always been there, like a sister.

"I don't get it. But you *should* talk to Mr. Kyle about this. He at least has the right to know that it's safe to leave the mansion."

"Right, I know."

They both stood still for another minute, listening to the trees blowing in the wind and watching the ripples on the lake.

"Roman, you said that we had a bad fight at one point when we were all strung up," Sarah finally broke the pause.

"Yes."

"What was it about?"

[381]

Roman searched for the right words. This was one thing that he hadn't considered important when telling the long story.

"Well, we were both on lookout. And we started talking. Then...you asked me about my family," he waited for her to react, but she didn't say anything, "And I got mad. Really, really mad. Then we just sort of...started arguing. And I said that...well, I'm really sorry about it but...I said that you didn't care about your family. Which was a total lie," Roman added as quickly as he could, his heart beating faster until he was sure that she wouldn't say anything. "And you said that I should get over it eventually. Well, not that *exactly*, but that's what got me started. And then the jumping mice came, which sort of ended the fight."

Roman thought that there would be another pause, and was getting ready to break it with a sigh. But Sarah cut him off. "Roman, what *did* happen to your family?"

There wasn't any accusation in her voice. Roman normally would've detected pity, but this time it was an honest question. Sarah really wanted to know. It was as if it had been bothering her for a while. Roman, for once, wasn't upset. His memories had come back to haunt him on the trip to the Island, and he was almost completely alone in knowing what had happened to them.

"Me and my friends back in Houston used to search through the papers for adds that could win us prizes. And this one time, I won a trip, all expenses paid, over a school break, to Phoenix. My mom was so excited...it was a perfect trip. And everything was taken care of, and it was perfect timing. A once in a lifetime opportunity. And it was over my birthday, which was something to celebrate. The trip would've actually saved us money because then we would've cancelled my party. But, on my birthday," Roman felt his voice beginning to crack, and cleared his throat.

"On my birthday, at exactly midnight, right when it started, the fire alarm woke us up. You can tell what happened next." This would've been a good conclusion to Roman's story, but he didn't feel like stopping. He felt like if he stopped, then he would cry or faint, or run back downstairs. "If I hadn't gotten that stupid paper and then it never would've happened! If I had stayed up like I normally did to count down to my birthday then I might've woken my mom in time! Maybe if my dad had never left then he would've been able to help us! If—"

He felt like chocking. His adrenaline rush had been stopped dead when Sarah put her arm around his shoulders. He was panting. It felt like his heart hadn't gotten enough oxygen, he had to pant to get it started again.

"Too many *ifs*. It happened. The same with Pongo, Danny, and Victoria, right? You're honoring Pongo's memory by remembering him, and letting us remember him. And what did Danny say?"

"He said that it should've been him instead of Victoria, that he should've died."

"He obviously liked Victoria."

"What?"

"Don't you get it? Even if he felt no purpose, then he still mentioned that he should've taken her place. He wanted her to have lived while he died. And what happened to him?"

"Richie…"

"Yes. And if Victoria was a ghost or an angel or whatever, do you think that, if she liked him, too, that she would want him to have died, or even wished that he was dead?"

"Well, then they could be together."

"Roman. Come on, even *you* can't be that thick. Then he could've honored her memory. It's like an unspoken death wish. If someone cares about you, then they want you to be happy. Victoria, if Danny liked her, and she liked him back, would've wanted him to be happy. Happiness prolongs your life, you know. The more stress, the less happy you are, then the shorter your life. If you're the only one who knows about what happened to your family, besides whoever witnessed the fire, of course, then that puts more stress on you. If you get bitter whenever someone brings up a topic as common as that, and you snap at them, that wouldn't make your mom proud, do you think?"

"I *know* that she wouldn't like it."

"Well, you don't *have* to tell everyone, but it's better to

[383]

share these kinds of things. One reason to keep a diary."

"How did we get from emotional to diaries?"

"You know that we have trouble with these kind of things, beings Genedeaues." Sarah took back her arm and continued to lean against the rail. Roman realized that, apart from his outburst, they had been whispering.

"Well, you couldn't have concentrated for a few more minutes..?"

"How about you concentrate for a minute," Sarah sighed, not meeting his eyes. Roman knew, though it wasn't spoken, that she was about to repay him for sharing his past with her. "That fire sounds a lot like the storm."

"Storm?"

"We were on vacation two years ago," she started, "me, my two little sisters, and my parents were going to a family reunion in Scotland. We were almost there, when lightning hit the plane." He thought he heard Sarah's voice shake a little. She took a deep breath, "It hit one of the engines; luckily we managed a water landing. I kept hold of my little sisters, Lilly and Luna. The plane hit the water before we had our air masks on. I was put on a little safety-boat with Lilly and Luna, it was children first. But the storm was even worse outside. It was raining hard, and when we were close to the shore a huge wave hit us and took the boat under. I couldn't see under water and my glasses fell off, but I managed to grab Lilly's hand. Luna was only six, and didn't know how to swim, and I couldn't see where she went. Lilly was eight and she could swim a little." Now Roman was sure he heard her voice become unsteady. "I kept her head above water until a helicopter found us, but she'd fainted a couple minutes earlier. When they pulled us up, they pulled her into a back room and said that I couldn't see her." She took another deep breath and straightened her shoulders.

"After a few hours we reached a hospital. I stayed up all night, waiting for my family. The next day some people in white suits came into the waiting room and pulled me aside. They said that Lilly had gotten hypothermia, and was very weak. Also, a side storm had broken off of the original one, and formed a tornado. They said that it struck the reunion building, and did a lot of damage. At first I didn't believe them, because I'd never heard of a tornado in Scotland, but they showed me a TV broadcast about it. It was *horrible*. Lilly died the next day, and there hadn't been enough lifeboats for everyone on the plane. My parents were good people. Some of the rescued said that they'd let the others get on. They found everyone's bodies from the reunion, except my cousin. So no parents, no family, and no siblings. I never went to an orphanage, like you, Mr. Kyle found me right away."

"Your whole family was at the reunion?"

"Yes. My mom didn't have any siblings, and my dad had one sister. My cousin had the idea that the whole family should get together and celebrate what we had left, because his mom, my dad's sister, died recently. No one knows what happened to her."

"I-I'm sorry." Roman was shocked by how she seemed to know exactly what happened to him: a freak accident.

"All Talismen and students, may I please have the gratifying prospect of you all paying attention for a moment." Came Mr. Kyle's normal announcement on the speakers. Jill hadn't left those out of the patio deck, but they were quieter than usual. It seemed like they were stepping out of a dream after what Sarah had just told Roman.

"This must be important, if he's trying to entertain us with a joke," Sarah remarked, recovering herself quickly.

"What joke?"

"Well, we have trouble paying attention…"

"Oh, I thought that jokes had to be funny." Roman cleared his throat, which seemed to have lost all moisture.

"To one of our recent arrivals, we have a special position that we would like to discuss with you in my office…" Roman and Sarah straightened up, knowing that it would apply to one of them.

"Roman Rolfe Rowland, please come and see me for discussion of being re-stationed to another Talisman base. You have received this honor under my recommendation, and approval from William K. Allgemein, the stationed leader for that

base. Further details will be disclosed to you in my office. Out." Mr. Kyle's announcement ended.

"Re-stationed? What about becoming a mentor?"

"Roman, do you have *any idea* how lucky you are?" Sarah's eyes shone. "The day after you get back from the Island getting to go and get real missions? On the frontline? *Any idea?*"

"But what about you guys? What about Millo?" Roman was surprised that Sarah wanted him to accept.

"Roman, this is the training center. Think about how hard it will be to get another opportunity like this? Millo can join you when he's ready, and he needs to be independent. And if he's not ready, then we'll take care of him. He's our responsibility, too."

"But why so suddenly?"

"I don't know. Why get sent to the Island so suddenly? Roman, everyone comes and goes eventually. You need to at least go and tell Mr. Kyle about the Island. This would be so good for you. This isn't about all of us. What if they need you?"

Roman thought this over in his head, which now felt as tired as it had been last night. "I'll see what the details are and tell Mr. Kyle about the Island. Then we'll see what happens."

When Roman was halfway to the stairs, Sarah called something.

"Roman, if you do go...write or talk to us whenever possible, all right?"

"I don't know if I'm going—"

"Roman."

He sighed, turning around. Sarah had walked up to him. "Yes?"

"If you do go, you should keep this." She bent to pull down her sock. She revealed an anklet with a ruby similar to the one on the necklace she had been wearing earlier, with a gold chain like the last. She took it off and held it out to him.

"An anklet?"

"*My* anklet, idiot. I know that you have an unusually short attention span, so this'll keep you from forgetting us."

"I won't—"

"Don't ruin the moment. Just keep it, will you?"

[386]

Roman looked at her pleading eyes. This obviously, for some reason, meant a lot to her.

"Thanks." He sighed and put in his pocket.

"Just keep *most* of your head out of the past, all right?"

"All right."

Roman climbed the steps that led inside, without the nice breeze or rustling of the trees. His eyes had adjusted to the moonlight, and he didn't want to leave the terrace. It was like getting out of bed for the first day of school, and he didn't want to leave. But he had a lot to talk to Mr. Kyle about on his last night at the mansion.

About the author

Elizabeth Robinson is a freshman at Cinco Ranch High School in Katy, Texas. She spends her time outside of school practicing sports and playing piano. She began work on Talismen: Birthstones late in the 6th grade and finished the first draft about a year later. She is proud of having had the self-discipline to write this book, as well as the courage to publish it. And, most of all, she is thrilled to finally see it in print.

www.ingramcontent.com/pod-product-compliance
Lightning Source LLC
Chambersburg PA
CBHW020322180626
46812CB00001B/5